'He leaned forward so swiftly to kiss her that Elizabeth did not see his eyes. When their lips parted, the Tudor's expression was merely tender. "I will come every night that it is humanly possible, there will be times when we are parted by necessity." He leaned forward again and touched her face gently. "At such times I will write you a letter every night – or a little every night if I have not time for a whole letter . . ."

'Elizabeth lay back when the door closed behind her husband. She was both spent and content. Henry was certainly kind, as Margaret said, when he was well used . . .'

Roberta Gellis

The Dragon and the Rose

MAYFLOWER
GRANADA PUBLISHING
London Toronto Sydney New York

First published in Great Britain
by Granada Publishing Limited
in Mayflower Books 1979

ISBN 0 583 12876 9

Copyright © Roberta Gellis 1977

Granada Publishing Limited
Frogmore, St Albans, Herts AL2 2NF
and
3 Upper James Street, London W1R 4BP
1221 Avenue of the Americas, New York, NY 10020, USA
117 York Street, Sydney, NSW 2000, Australia
100 Skyway Avenue, Toronto, Ontario, Canada M9W 3A6
110 Northpark Centre, 2193 Johannesburg, South Africa
CML Centre, Queen & Wyndham, Auckland 1, New Zealand

Made and printed in Great Britain by
Cox & Wyman Ltd,
London, Reading and Fakenham
Set in Intertype Plantin

To Charles because . . .

'. . . to prevent or heal full many a strife
How oft, how long must man have patience with his wife.'

ROBERT DODSLEY
To Patience (1745)

Chapter One

A thin, high shriek, like that of a small animal being torn apart, pierced the heavy walls and thick oak doors of Pembroke Castle. Jasper Tudor, earl of Pembroke, winced almost imperceptibly. He had heard and seen many small animals, both wild and human, torn apart, but this was no Welsh poacher nor marauding weasel. The shriek was repeated, higher, thinner, more desperate. Pembroke clasped his hands together in a brief, nervous gesture, then let them drop. It was a shame that his sister-in-law, the young countess of Richmond, should die this way. He shook his head at the impenetrability of life and the inexplicable quirks of fate.

That his brother Edmund should have married little Margaret Beaufort at twelve – as soon as she reached the legal age of consent – was reasonable. Margaret was the only daughter and the sole heiress of John, duke of Somerset, and her dowry and immense inheritance were reason enough. Personally, however, he had been much surprised when Edmund consummated the marriage. True, twelve *was* the legal age of consent, and it was true, too, that Margaret's male children would have a close, if irregular claim to the throne, but still Jasper himself would have waited until the child had become a girl of at least fourteen or fifteen.

Who would have thought that the seed would take root in so raw a field? Yet it had. Who would have expected that Edmund, so young, so strong, would be dead seven months later? Yet he was. And now little Margaret would die, also.

Jasper became aware that the cries had stopped. Growing impatient of waiting for news, he pushed open the door into the room in which his sister-in-law lay. His ears perceived the thinner, fainter wail of a newborn babe, but he did not look in that direction. He turned his head towards the bed. Jasper was fond of little Margaret, little indomitable Margaret, who, when her husband died, had simply patted her swollen belly and said that there would soon be another earl of Richmond. Now

7.

her face had that transparent pallor associated with finality, but her eyes were glowingly alive.

'I told you,' she whispered. 'It is a man-child. I told you Richmond would live again. He shall have Somerset, too. He shall have everything.'

'He will have everything that is his by right.' Jasper bent over her. 'I swear it upon my life and my honour.'

'Henry – I want him to be named Henry.' Margaret's whisper was becoming fainter. 'For the king—'

For a moment Jasper was surprised. He had expected to name the child Edmund if it lived and was a male – Edmund John – but he would not argue with Margaret, whose limit of endurance had been reached. He murmured assurance and took her hand, watching her eyes close. If that was what she wanted, the child would be named Henry – but for the king? Jasper thought for a moment despairingly of his half brother the king, feeble, weak-willed Henry, who could only obey the last order given to him. Then he realized that Margaret meant Henry V, whose wife had been Jasper's own mother, the babe's grandmother. Pembroke went to look at the infant, glanced back at the bed and shook his head. Great Henry! Poor little thing. He could not remember ever having seen so puny a child. Richmond lived again, but, he feared, not for long.

The days crawled past. Margaret ceased to bleed, and her lips regained a faint rosiness. Henry Tudor, earl of Richmond, breathed; not much more could be said for him. Sometimes he had strength enough to suck, but usually his wet nurse squeezed her milk drop by drop into his little mouth while his mother watched with anxious eyes.

Days grouped together and became weeks. Margaret could sit up, and her cheeks began to bloom. Henry Tudor, first coddled into life, now signalled his desires with a lusty wail and an increasingly greedy mouth. As weeks grew into months, Margaret, gowned and kerchiefed in the highest fashion, smiled over her red-faced, screaming son, unswaddled so that his napkin could be changed. He was thin; he would always be thin, but he struck out powerfully with his little arms and legs.

Margaret's anxieties calmed with the passage of years, but to Jasper young Henry always appeared frail. It was true that he seemed to contract sickness readily, but he fought off the

8

ills with his mother's stubbornness, recovered and clung tenaciously to life.

Mother and child grew and were content. Yet Jasper could not keep Margaret under his protection always. Pressure was being exerted upon the weak king and, through him, upon Jasper. So great a dower must not go unattached. Perhaps Jasper would have resisted the king, cajoling and uttering veiled threats until Henry VI's feeble mind shifted again, but the country was buzzing with a discontent directed against Henry's advisers. The leader of the discontents was Richard, duke of York, and his supporters traded unhealthy tales regarding Margaret's relationship with her husband's brother.

Those tales were not far from wrong, Jasper admitted secretly as he came into the chamber where Margaret was teaching the three-year-old Henry to count. When Edmund married her, Jasper had not cared, but now that she was grown into a woman— It was incest to take a brother's wife; Margaret had better marry. He stood, uncertain of how to introduce a topic distasteful to them both, while Henry, seeing the bestower of many honeyed tidbits and marvellous toys, leaped up to embrace his legs.

'Come and play, Uncle Jasper.'

'No, today I am the wicked uncle.' Jasper delighted in telling Henry the most blood-curdling tales of wicked uncles to see the little boy shudder in delicious terror while he begged for more. 'I have come to steal your mother away.'

'No, no! Mama will never leave me.'

'Oh, yes. That is how it must be, but you know how wise the Lady Margaret is. She will trick the wicked uncle, run away and come back to you.'

Henry gurgled with laughter. It was a game they often played, and since Margaret had always returned, it was one he loved. Jasper swept him off his feet to throw him in the air. As ever, when he rough-housed with his nephew, he was startled by the fragility of the little body under the clothes. He caught Henry in a tight embrace and kissed him tenderly, then set the child on his feet and patted him as he told him to run away and play.

'You should not tease him, Jasper. What if an accident befell me? He might in truth blame you.'

'Aye, but it was in my mind. Today I am the wicked uncle

9

and I have come, indeed, to separate mother and child. You must marry again, Margaret.'

It was not the first time he had said this, but Margaret sensed a difference in his manner. 'I suppose I must,' she said slowly, 'but I cannot see why Henry and I should part.'

'I cannot let him out of my hands. You know that. His blood is close in line to the throne. Besides that, unless you have other children, Henry is heir to your estate, in which your husband would have an interest only while you lived.'

'And you are his heir to your brother's estate.'

'Margaret! You cannot believe that I would harm a hair on Henry's head even for the assurance of heaven. You would not lose him if you married Buckingham's younger brother. He has agreed for you to stay here at Pembroke – as I told you before.'

'I refused the elder and now must take the younger?' she flashed.

'Margaret, my Margaret, you do not know how ill things sit. That French she-wolf the king married has turned the whole country against him. There will be open war soon – not one small battle here and there, but war. This marriage will give you Buckingham's ear, and Buckingham's ear will be of value if I am killed in battle. I tell you, I cannot let Henry out of Wales, and in Wales there is not one of blood or station fit to wed with you.'

Margaret's flush of anger faded from her face. 'Killed? Not you, Jasper!'

'Others die so. I would be assured of the boy's safety – and of yours.'

'I— I will think of it.'

It did not take long for Margaret to admit that Jasper was right. Stafford would be a gentle and considerate husband, and union with Buckingham would certainly be of value in the present state of the nation. The marriage was simple and quiet; in a few days the bridegroom departed and life went on as before in Pembroke.

In the nation at large, however, matters went from bad to worse. All too soon there was civil war. Jasper dutifully went out to support his brother the king and his hated queen, yet Buckingham was able to remain neutral. He favoured the king but saw his deficiencies. As long as Henry VI ruled, even nominally, there would be trouble. The king was growing more

10

imbecilic and more dependent upon his wife every day, and the queen was hated by the people and nobility alike with a ferocity seldom exhibited against a royal consort.

York prevailed at last. Edward, the heir of Henry's old enemy, Richard, proclaimed himself king in 1461, and, after the disaster of the battle of Townton, there could be no doubt that he was king indeed. Margaret held her breath. For weeks she kept herself and Henry in readiness to flee to Jasper, who had taken refuge overseas. Buckingham, however, made peace with the new king, and under his sheltering wing Margaret and Henry lived quietly at Pembroke. Henry was now technically penniless, since Edward IV had confiscated the estates and titles of Richmond for his younger brother, but Margaret never let him forget that he was the true earl of Richmond.

She taught him the dignity of manner and the distance she felt necessary to a great position. Yet she laughed to see the six-year-old draw that dignity about him like a cloak with guests or formal introductions, for Henry was a merry-minded and affectionate child. He had learned that unnatural manner quickly – he learned everything quickly – and he did not forget.

Nor did Henry forget people. Hardly a day passed without his asking for Jasper. Finally, growing impatient with his mother's lame answers, Henry's grey eyes flashed a danger signal.

'Then, tell him to return. He has been on his business long enough. I want him.'

'The business is very important,' Margaret hedged, too frightened and tired to deal with one of Henry's tantrums. She knew that no one else could manage him in a temper. He would scream himself sick, and then she would have the burden of nursing him – to add to all her other burdens.

'It is not true. He has gone away because he does not love us any longer.'

'No, my son. Uncle Jasper will always love you.'

'Then, tell him to come back. Tell him I am sick.'

The grey eyes shone shrewd in the little face. He remembered well how even his slightest indisposition had brought a worried Jasper to his side, how he could win any concession from his uncle when he was ill. Margaret had a strong suspicion that Henry had often made himself ill, crying himself into a fever to play Jasper against her and to win some coveted trifle

11

from his soft-hearted uncle. It was too much. Her iron control broke.

'He cannot come,' Margaret wept. 'There has been a war, and the new king has taken away your estates and says you are no longer Richmond. He has taken away Uncle Jasper's estates, too, and would kill him if he returned home.'

She did not know how much this would mean to the child, but if it prevented him from plaguing her and making himself ill, it would mean enough. The dangerous sparkle died out of Henry's eyes; they resumed a more normal, speculative glow.

'Uncle Henry is no longer the king?'

'He is the true king, just as you are the true earl of Richmond. But evil men can deprive kings, and earls, of their birthright.'

'Then, the new king is an evil man?'

This was dangerous talk, even for a seven-year-old. 'No, no,' she hastened to amend. 'It is hard for a little boy to understand. You see, Uncle Henry was not really a good king. A good king must be clever, and Uncle Henry, alas, is not clever at all. He did things which were unwise, which hurt all the people in this country. Perhaps King Edward did a bad thing when he took Uncle Henry's crown away, but he did it for a good reason – to make the country safer. Sometimes it is necessary to do a bad thing so that good may come of it. Now, Henry, we must not talk of this any more, and you must never speak of it to anyone. To no one, ever.' She looked into the child's puzzled face. 'You know there are things that children must not do that grown-up people may. To speak of kings is one of these things.'

As Edward IV's grip on the kingdom grew more secure, he grew less fearful of Buckingham and of the rebelliousness of the Welsh. He wanted Henry as a weapon to bring Jasper to heel. Then again, with his claim to the throne, Henry might even become a danger to himself. With this in mind, the king sent letters to Margaret offering her a place at court among his queen's ladies-in-waiting and a place for Henry among his henchmen. Margaret replied that she was grateful but that she did not love the life at court. Moreover, Henry was a frail child of delicate health and could not bear the heavy air of the city. Then, secretly one night, they fled Pembroke to the remote vastness of Harlech.

This move kept them free for some years more, but in the end Edward's man took Harlech and Henry became Lord Herbert's prisoner. But Lord Herbert was no fool. He knew the value of the pawn he held and allowed the boy every freedom he could, seeing to it that little Henry had the finest instructors in every branch of learning, in archery, swordsmanship and jousting. He gave him rich gifts of arms and books. Margaret's fears ebbed under Herbert's mild wardenship, only to rise up with renewed strength when he was killed in one of the innumerable skirmishes that plagued the unsettled times.

Who would come to take his place? No one came. Margaret was not greatly surprised. She had heard that Edward's strongest ally, the earl of Warwick, had turned against him. His throne was again in danger, and he had neither time nor men to spare. But the winds of rumour blew into a gale, reaching even to Harlech. Margaret rejoiced when Warwick, now a sworn upholder of the Lancastrian cause, landed in Devonshire.

Wales welcomed Jasper as England welcomed Warwick. Now it was Edward's turn to flee, and Jasper returned to his beloved Margaret and Henry, bearing news of the restoration of Henry VI. Would the nephew he had not seen for almost ten years remember him? His fears fell away as the young man embraced him with a child's abandon.

'Uncle Jasper! Uncle Jasper!'

'Harry! Let me go. Let me look at you.' Jasper laughed, returning the embrace as warmly as it was given. How could he be formal with this impetuous boy?

They stood with clasped hands, gazing at each other, only to embrace again.

'Am I to have no share in this welcoming?'

'Margaret. How beautiful you've grown!'

'Listen to your uncle, Henry. See how he knows just the balm to apply to a wounded woman?'

Henry flushed slightly. Margaret had been teaching him courtly speeches, but for once he did not learn readily. He was graceful and could bow and kiss a hand with the best, but to offer flowery compliments to his mother seemed unnatural, and he had little opportunity to talk to other women. Margaret kept gentlewomen in her service, but none of sufficient rank to marry her son. She was truly pious, and her sense of duty kept Henry's contact with these women to a minimum. Had her son

13

turned his eyes to the serving maids, she might have looked aside – or she might not. The question never arose; they were too coarse, too unclean, too stupid or uneducated for Henry's taste.

'You are not betrothed, are you, Henry?' Jasper had remarked the flush.

'No.'

Was there a shade of regret in eyes and voice? Margaret's trill of laughter caught Jasper's attention before he could decide.

'Indeed he is not. Lord Herbert raised the question twice before he died, but each time Henry took to his bed with a fever, so the trip was put off.'

That raised a new anxiety. 'Are you often sick, my boy?'

Margaret laughed even more heartily, and Henry flushed again. 'When it pleases him,' she said.

'You have never taken his frailty seriously enough, Margaret!' Jasper retorted unfairly. 'When we go to London, I will have the king's physicians attend him. We will find the seat of these troubles and drive them out.'

'To London?' Henry asked. But a troubled Jasper was studying his flushed face. He smiled. 'I do not need a physician, uncle. I am very well now – most of the time. It is true that I pretended to be sick to avoid the betrothal. When will we go to London?'

'As soon as I am sure Wales is quiet. It will not be long. My people's hearts were never Edward's.'

Margaret smoothed her gown. 'It will be pleasant to see the new fashions and have a reason to dress my hair. Jasper, Henry is almost a man. Let him travel through Wales with you to see more of the people.'

Jasper's hesitant nod could not cover his anxiety. 'Will not so much riding tire Henry?'

Mother and son laughed in chorus. Riding was Henry's strongest point; he was a remarkably fine horseman. 'Oh, uncle! I have ridden in the hunt from dawn to dusk and come home only hungry enough to eat a good dinner and weary enough to sleep sound.'

Chapter Two

Henry VI's restoration had lasted only a few months and already there were grumblings of dissatisfaction. Warwick's present policy had been rejected by Edward IV because he knew it would be unpopular. But Edward, York or no, had been a wise king. Jasper said as much to Margaret and Henry in a fit of temper. They must go to London at once.

It was necessary that Henry meet the king. Still, he was not prepared for feeble Henry's shambling figure, the loose lips, the dazed eyes. Years of captivity had done nothing to improve Henry VI, who was able to pay attention for only a few minutes when sternly addressed. Yet he did so when Henry Tudor was presented to him, gazing into the fourteen-year-old's face and seeing there something that pleased him.

A trembling hand came to rest on the kneeling boy's head. 'A likely young man. See how calm his eye, how well-shaped his head. A regal manner for one so young. Rise up, Henry Tudor.'

Henry looked at his namesake with despair. Was not a king special, even if he were not clever? What was here to reverence? Here were fine garments, but even they hung all awry. No, not even the shell of appearance.

'You know,' the king continued in his wandering way, 'my grandfather was earl of Richmond, also.' He had forgotten that Henry no longer held the title. 'He was attainted once, even exiled, but he came back and won the throne from that bad king, Richard II.' The king's eyes widened with fear. He giggled. 'You would not do that, boy, would you?'

Henry did not hear his mother's intake of breath nor see Jasper take a half step forward. 'You are my uncle,' he said clearly, 'and I must love you. It is not my right, as it was Henry IV's of blessed memory, and Richard II is long dead.'

When they were alone, Margaret complimented her son. 'You pleased me well, Henry. You gave a right good answer. What made you think of it?'

'The king sounded suspicious of me, so I reminded him of

15

our blood bond. For the other matter – that is history known to all. It could not hurt to repeat it.' But Henry did not smile with pleasure as he usually did when his mother praised him. 'Mother, I am a child no longer. It is time that we talk of kings.' He turned away from her, walked to a window and stared unseeing out at the formal garden. 'I cannot love or respect this king,' he murmured.

Who could? Margaret wondered, but she said only, 'Your uncle the king is a good man. He is kind and gentle and wishes much to do right.' Henry remained at the window. His mother went to him and placed her hands upon his shoulders. 'Henry, the best king is one who rules by himself after listening to all his advisers. But there are other ways a realm may be guided aright. In any case, it is wrong to break the line of descent. Think how much blood has been spilled because of this shifting from the true line.'

'And is bloodshed always bad? Why, then, are men taught to fight?'

Margaret turned her son round and kissed his brow. 'Such questions! Yes, it is bad, but it may be done for a good cause. The Devil inspires some men to evil. Mustn't we put this evil down? Henry, if some man forced his way in here and wished to beat me or dishonour me before your eyes—' Her son's hand shot to his smallsword's hilt. 'Aye,' she laughed, laying a finger on the hand that clutched the sword, 'to shed blood protecting your mother – would that be bad?'

'But, mother, your body gave me life! You nursed me and fed me.'

'Has not your country done the same? Does not this land give you all things? Is it not also a mother to you?'

Henry jerked free of her hand. 'Yes, and I love that mother, also. Is it right to give her such a husband as – as this king?'

But Henry VI was not to be king for long. The young Tudor saw the Lancastrian party with its ineffectual leader split into factions in the face of rumours that Edward was gathering forces to return. Jasper's frantic efforts to steady the king and smooth over differences among the Lancastrian nobles merely carved the worry lines deeper between his brows and hardened his grim mouth. Rumour proved true. In March, Edward landed in Yorkshire.

Jasper fled to Wales to raise an army, taking Henry and

16

Margaret with him. They did not ride fast enough. Just before Chepstow, Henry turned to the thunder of hooves, becoming alarmed when he saw an unfamiliar look of indecision on his uncle's face. The party following them were enemies! Henry's eyes flew to his mother, but Margaret's face had blanched and her hands held tight to the reins. Their horses were tired and there was no safe haven.

Henry shook with mingled fear and rage. That anyone should seek to harm him was incredible. In the fourteen years of his life, he had known only kindness. Even Lord Herbert, who had scared him at first, proved to be kind and protective. Over the pounding of his heart he could hear Jasper calling orders. The men-at-arms formed ranks, and he pulled into line with them. After that, all was confusion – a pounding of hooves, shouts mingled with screams and groans, the bright flash of steel, and spurts and streaks of red.

Later, three men lay still in the road. A riderless horse careened wildly with one shoulder dyed an unnatural colour, but, in the distance, the horses' rumps waddled as the attackers fled. Henry laughed aloud at the sight. It was the final ignominy of defeat, that one should appear comical. Yet a hasty glance backward showed those three still forms. Death was not comical. The three looked lonely and unprotected on the open road.

At Chepstow they were admitted only after Jasper swore they would purchase horses and pass on. Events became vignettes set into periods of numbness for Henry. He was wakened once by his mother's fervent embrace. He heard Jasper snarl at her in an unnaturally gruff voice.

'But, Jasper, he is hurt.' Margaret was weeping as he had never seen her.

Henry looked down at himself and saw his right hand and arm coloured an ugly red-brown. The ease of his own laugh, the naturalness of his voice, surprised him. 'Nay, the blood is not mine.'

'Harry, Harry, I am proud of you.' Jasper's voice was too loud. He clapped him on the shoulder so hard that Henry staggered. 'You are a man blooded this day.'

Later, his mother's cry broke into his half sleep once again. 'No, Jasper, not that – you had it from the king!' His uncle was seated at a table counting coins with a worried frown, stripping the rings from his fingers. He raised his hands to unhook the heavy gold collar of S's, when Margaret cried out. Now she pulled off her own rings and whispered breathlessly, 'Take them, take them. What need will I have for jewels now?'

When there were fresh horses, they rode on. Henry prided himself on being a horseman. He could ride the longest, hardest hunt with the best, but this was different. When the horses were tired, they dismounted, changed their saddles to other mounts and rode again. Henry reeled, looped the reins about his left wrist and clung to the pommel with his free hand. Through eyes almost blind with fatigue, he preserved one clear picture: his mother cradled in Jasper's arms, her cheek marked by the cruel mail shirt, weeping; and above her bent head, his uncle's face twisted with fear.

The weight of that fear lightened when they were willingly received at Pembroke. Margaret and Henry passed some quiet days there while Jasper rode out to rally his countrymen. Henry now slept in the great bed that had been his father's when in Jasper's castle, but he did not sleep peacefully. There was an airless, waiting quality to the quiet which boded ill. Henry lay in the great bed and trembled. Evil was coming, and he was afraid.

After the battle at Barnet on April 14th, where Henry VI was again made captive, the days passed like the wains of the peasants, slowly and with creaks and groans as accompaniment. The news of the battle of Tewkesbury reached them through a messenger from Margaret's husband. The queen had been taken; the prince, Henry VI's heir, was dead. The Lancastrian cause lay dead, too, murdered along with sixteen of its noblest and most powerful adherents. Buckingham had not taken sides; if Margaret came into her husband's protection at once, his older brother's influence with Edward would keep her safe.

Henry knew that Jasper had not been at Tewkesbury and felt nothing but relief. He could not understand why his mother should become almost hysterical with crying, clutching at him, kissing him and holding on to him as if she would never let him go. But a few days later he saw his uncle enter Pembroke a sleepwalker, and he fled from the awful knowledge that Buckingham's influence could not save Jasper. The boy avoided his beloved uncle to wrestle alone with the love and fears that tore at him. Must he follow Jasper or his mother? The loneliness only increased his torment, and he sought wise counsel where he had always found it – in his mother's chamber.

When he entered, his mother was kneeling on the floor, embracing Jasper's knees and wailing. Henry stood rooted at the door.

'I will not do it. They would hunt us down to the ends of the earth.' Jasper's voice sounded dead. 'I will run no more. I will fight and die here where I belong. God knows' – his sudden anguish rose over Margaret's moan – 'I tried to reach them in time. We fought our way half across England. We could have turned the tide of that battle, but we came too late. I will not be called a traitor by those few of us who still live!'

Jasper tore himself loose from Margaret's grasp, but Henry fled before they saw him. He knew nothing of what happened between them on the following two days, but midmorning of the third day shouts of alarm filled Pembroke. The drawbridge was lifted, and men-at-arms ran to take up defensive positions. Whatever his mother had planned to do, she had waited too long. The time had come to fight and die. Henry shook, whether from fear or fever, and his shame drove him forth. Dressing quickly, he seized his sword and ran out.

'What has happened, uncle?'

Jasper turned, and Henry became light with relief. Whatever the evil, it had some good mixed with it. Jasper no longer looked dead or afraid; he was very simply angry.

'Our own people have turned on us,' he growled. 'That is Morgan ap Thomas out there who demands our surrender.'

Henry knew perfectly well what the defensive power of Pembroke was. The tactics of war were as much a part of his everyday lessons as Latin, French, swordsmanship, and horsemanship. 'They will have a long wait,' he said quietly.

'May the souls of that clan writhe everlastingly in hell! Morgan's brother David is on his way with another force – Morgan says a larger one.'

'Then, we will have to fight' – Henry laughed – 'if he does not lie. The Welsh fight well, but they lie better.'

The anger died out of Jasper's face, and an expression Henry could not judge replaced it. 'My God,' he said softly, 'you are a man indeed, though you have little enough growth to tell of it.'

A few months past Henry would have been flooded with pleasure at such praise from his idolized uncle. Now he knew that Jasper was a man as he was a man – though a man he loved,

19

and loved to please. Still, he remembered how, as a child, he had often fooled Jasper by pretending illness.

He put the fond memory aside. 'Uncle, can we parley with them for a safe-conduct for my mother? Buckingham has promised her free pardon if she yields. She told you?'

'Aye. I thought of it, but I dare not. I cannot trust Morgan's promise. I am a fool – ten times a fool. She begged me to fly with you the day I arrived, but I would not listen.'

'With me?' Henry's eyes widened. It had never occurred to him that he might not be included in the pardon.

'I thought running and hiding would kill so frail a child,' Jasper sighed, more to himself than to Henry. 'And what is life as a hunted exile? Better to be dead after a short terror than to live constantly with fear.'

Outrage blocked out all other emotions in Henry. 'Why, if my mother is pardoned, am I excepted?'

'Because you are a man, and she is but a woman.'

'Surely Edward cannot plan to destroy every male who favoured King Henry?'

Jasper studied his eager face. This was no helpless child, however frail. Margaret might well be right when she insisted Henry was exceptional and that there was still hope for the Lancastrian cause. But whether another chance for freedom would come or not, or if Henry was captured to die on the block, it was high time for him to know why he must run or die.

'No, Henry. Edward, may he be damned, is not senseless. He will pardon those he can pardon safely. You, my boy, he cannot pardon – ever. Your mother is the grand-daughter of John Beaufort, the grandson of Edward III. Royal blood runs in your veins. No, this damnable Edward will not soon forget. How can he, when your great-grandfather was brother to Henry IV?'

'Half brother,' Henry responded mechanically. He knew his ancestry, but he had never known, never been told, how it might threaten him. 'But he was a bastard.'

'Has a bastard never sat upon a throne?' Even in the midst of their danger Jasper had to laugh at the boy's fresh ignorance in such matters. 'The William who conquered England, another of those relatives of yours, was a bastard.'

The juxtaposition of bastard and conquest clarified matters indeed. Edward himself had his throne by conquest and would be only too aware that divine right was but a feeble weapon. Here was Henry, the last male descendant of John of Gaunt. Even a bastard line barred from succession might serve as a rallying point for rebellion.

'Harry' – Jasper was no longer laughing – 'you were *not* excluded from the pardon offered your mother. She believes, and I think she is right, that it was offered her in order to lay hands on you. You understand that whatever fine words Edward says or sweet promises he makes, you are too dangerous to him to be safe.'

Henry merely raised his brows. In this moment he had lost all the serenity of his boyhood, and he was numb.

Jasper saw only his calm. 'To think that I needed to learn from a boy more than twenty-five years my junior how to face misfortune! But now, Harry, go tell your mother that I will come to her soon. I must make sure they are settling down to a siege and will not attack. God preserve me from being the means of removing one of Edward's worries! I will have you safe out of here to plague him yet.'

In the event, their escape did not prove difficult. Because the taking of Pembroke castle would have cost many lives, and because old loyalty to Jasper still bound them, the brothers ap Morgan agreed to compromise. They would let Henry, Jasper, and Margaret go if the castle were yielded without a fight.

'But where will we go, uncle?' Henry asked.

'To France,' Margaret replied. 'Henry, your grandmother was Catherine of France; for very shame Louis cannot deliver you up to Edward.'

'Of course.' Henry forced a smile, but he felt only distaste.

'Will you come with us, Margaret? I can—' Jasper stopped, caught up by something in the young woman's face. She was shaking her proud, high head, those determined lips almost invisible as she pressed them together and held back her tears.

'I cannot come with you, Jasper.'

'Mama, no! Why?' Henry's new man's voice cracked alarmingly, but his composure held. Margaret, after all, had taught him control. Who knew it better?

'My son.' Jasper felt an intruder when he heard the tenderness of that voice. 'My beloved son. What would happen, the good Lord preserve us, if you should be taken? I cannot take the risk. Perhaps if I were at court, my influence with Buckingham could save you from – from—'

'From death.' Henry's composure verged on cruelty.

Jasper looked from one to the other. He had under-estimated both. In this bitter moment, the steel spirit of each showed. Margaret trembled all over, but her straight back never betrayed her royal breeding. Wrong side of the sheets indeed! Here was a queen, a lady of blood. No upstart like Edward's wife, the new 'queen' of England. Henry stood in frigid silence. The down on his cheeks belied the manliness of his bearing. That child whose temper tantrums had rocked the old fortress was gone forever. In its place was a young man whose icy stillness and control were almost frightening. Jasper had a single flash of regret for the laughing child he had lost. It was swallowed up in his enormous pride in these two dearest of all loved ones. He knew Margaret's courage of old; he would never doubt Henry's again.

'We will get away safe, mama.' It was a promise.

'Yes,' and that was all.

Margaret turned to Jasper. 'There is another, a most important reason for me to remain in England. You must have someone you can trust at court. Who better than I?'

'But, Margaret, will you be safe?'

'My good, my dear Jasper. I will be safe. Do you forget who my husband is? Buckingham is fond of me, you know. I am such a complacent wife and so rich. How could Edward dare offend his brother by punishing me, when I come weeping to tell how the wicked uncle wrested my child from me and carried him away, I know not where?'

'They will never believe the tale.'

'Why not? Have I not given up the joys of marriage, the delights of court life, for fourteen years only to be with my frail son?' She smiled. Were those blue eyes still more liquid? 'What do Buckingham and Edward really know of me except that I am a stupid, doting woman with one sickly child. Would a doting mother – a young woman with no experience of the intrigues of court – send her son away and into dangerous exile when offered a free pardon for him?'

'Well, they will suspect, but Edward dare not offend Buckingham.' Could Margaret make him laugh even now? 'I would

22

like to know, Margaret, how you intend to support the notion that you are stupid.'

'I think that I will be pious and – and devoted to learning.'

'Mmm, that is good.' Something silent passed between them. 'Priests and scholars travel a great deal. They will make fine messengers.'

It was settled. Henry hardly heard the final exchanges. He was to leave the country of his birth, where, even as an outlaw or a prisoner, he would be known and loved. He was to beg sanctuary, even bread, among the French! He felt shame in every kindness or unkindness the French might offer him – Henry, descended from Edward III, the Hammer of France.

Chapter Three

The ship shuddered and groaned, heaved up, slid down, and the wind screamed through the rigging. The darkness was made absolute by sheets of rain which blinded the eye. There was nothing to see – black waves flowed into black sky. Pitch, roll, heave, roll. Henry lay facedown on a coil of rope lashed so that he would not go overboard, washed away by the waves cascading over the deck. He was not conscious of how the ropes bruised his body. He was not afraid. During his brief intervals of lucidity, he prayed only to drown, to die.

Another spasm of dry retching tore his body. There was nothing left in him to vomit. He was dried out by six days of unremitting nausea. Jasper hung over him, clinging to the ropes which bound him, alternately praying and cursing. If the storm did not soon abate, the boy would die. He huddled closer as the captain shouted some incomprehensible gibberish and seamen ran about the deck. Lifting the sodden cloaks which covered Henry, he pressed his body against his nephew's. Perhaps a little of his warmth would pass through the wet clothes. He wished that he had stripped them both naked when the ship was less lively. Now he dared not loosen Henry's bonds. Before he had been afraid to remove clothing in which money and jewels were hidden, but what did money and jewels matter? Henry was dying.

Some hours later a new motion knocked Jasper's head against the rail. He jerked upright and saw a sullen sky, mud-green waves flecked with white, and – straight ahead – land! They were safe. Henry! The boy was still. Dead? No, he was warm and breathing. The rain had stopped. Jasper covered Henry with the topmost cloak, which was almost dry, and staggered to the captain.

'Where are we?'

'Not sure. Brittany, mayhap.'

'You promised to take us to France.'

Exasperation showed on the captain's weary face. 'God

24

makes the weather and the wind. I only try to keep them from sinking my ship. I told you before we left that a storm was coming.'

'But the weather is better now. Can you not go on to France?'

'I could. It would not take much above a week to get there – if we got there at all with this battered rig. And what of the boy? Do you think he'd last another week?'

Jasper forgot the man's impertinence when he glanced toward Henry. Was he asleep or in that coma which precedes death? 'Land, then! Make land as soon as you can.'

He dared not touch the boy. If Henry were asleep, it would be cruelty to wake him. They docked at last, and Jasper released the boy's bonds, gathering him in his arms to carry him ashore.

'Uncle, I want to walk.'

Relief swept over Jasper, and admiration for his tough little nephew. Henry seemed to need no more than steadying on his feet, though shudder after shudder shook him. His eyes took in the miserable town, the grey clouds, the sea.

'Is this France, uncle?'

'No, Brittany. I will buy horses so that we can ride to France'.

'Must we?' Henry's voice betrayed his faintness.

'Not now, boy,' Jasper replied, tightening his grip. 'Rest and get warm. You must regain your strength.'

'I did not mean now, uncle. I meant— Can we not seek a haven here? The Breton people are like our Welsh. I – I do not love France.'

'Nor I, but you have some claim upon the French king and none upon Francis of Brittany. What is to stop him from selling you back to Edward?'

But the choice was not theirs. The innkeeper, sensing that this was no merchant family, sent for the local nobleman and delayed them with one excuse after another until his patron arrived. The gentleman recognized his own kind at once. He was kind, he was courteous, but he was also daft. In a very few days, Henry and Jasper found themselves being presented to the duke of Brittany.

Francis II was a big man, no longer young, with a kindly, shrewd face. Henry felt more secure the moment he looked

25

at him. He welcomed the two strangers in a deep, pleasant voice, and asked for news of England. Jasper told the truth. They were penniless exiles fleeing for their lives.

'Aye, Lord Pembroke, I can understand why you would not be welcome to Edward, but you, young man' – Francis turned to Henry – 'what crime have you committed?'

'I was born.' Henry's careful schoolboy French concealed the quick calculations going on in his mind. He could pretend ignorance or try to conceal his importance to Edward. Still, the longer Francis had to consider his value, the higher the price for him would rise. And the higher the price, the longer the haggling. Every day out of Edward's hands was a day gained, a day in which something might happen to their benefit.

'I am now the closest living male relative of Henry VI.'

'*Pauvre petit*,' sighed the duchess, sitting beside Francis. Henry's clear eyes rested on Francis's wife. He smiled, permitting his lips to tremble. One could not have too many allies, and Duke Francis seemed fond of his wife.

'And what do you want from me, gentlemen?' Francis was still smiling at his duchess's remark.

Jasper hesitated. France seemed safest, but, though Francis and Louis were now at peace, they had been enemies a long time.

'I would like to stay here.' Henry's eyes remained on the duchess, 'but, of course, my uncle knows best and must decide.'

'Francis, you cannot turn the child away,' the duchess pleaded, her hand on her husband's arm.

The duke's eyes met Jasper's, and he smiled broadly. 'I have no intention of doing so, my dear. You are perfectly safe here now, Lord Pembroke,' he added. 'I hope you also will wish to stay.'

'Most certainly, my lord.' Jasper's voice sounded as sincere and hearty as he could make it, but he did not fail to notice Francis's use of the present tense in his assurance.

Margaret sat with folded hands and downcast eyes. Though her complexion was marred with weeping, she was remarkably beautiful. Henry Stafford wondered briefly how he had come to take so little advantage of his position as her husband in the past. He put the thought aside to concentrate on the more immediate problem.

'You must have some idea where he has gone. You must. You have long known Jasper Tudor. I know you received letters from him when he went into exile before. Think! Where are his common hidey-holes?'

Two slow tears made shining tracks down Margaret's cheeks, but her voice, although scarcely above a whisper, did not waver. 'I have told you,' she said wearily. 'He was in Ireland when he wrote to me. More than that I do not know. He never wrote where he was or who his friends were lest his message fall into those hands he feared.' Margaret raised her eyes. 'Jasper desired news of me. He did not write to give me news.'

It was logical enough, but Stafford was uneasy. He took a few hasty steps away from Margaret and then returned. Low-voiced, meek, denying him nothing, never refusing to answer, Margaret nonetheless made him uncomfortable.

'You gave him your son. Can you tell me you did not ask where he would take him? I tell you, Henry is in far greater danger from the mad notions Jasper will instil in him than from our just and gracious king.'

Margaret's lips moved silently for a moment, and Stafford hissed with impatience. She was praying again.

'I did not give him my son,' she said. 'I have sworn it on my soul. Do you think I court damnation?'

Stafford shook his head impatiently. On any other subject that remark would have closed the discussion. Margaret believed in God and in damnation as few priests or prelates did, but her husband was not in the least sure she would try to avoid damnation if she thought her eternal sojourn in hell would benefit her son. He regretted bitterly that he had not demanded his marital rights more frequently, not only because the woman was desirable but also because, if she had conceived again and borne another child, her devotion would be divided. As it was, he had no weapon to use against her.

He dared not try physical mistreatment. She was so frail she would die if she were not gently used. And if she died, her estates would go to the crown, since her son was alive but disinherited. Stafford did not pretend to himself that the king would make over those rich territories to him. He might receive some small part, but those ravening beasts, the queen's Woodville kin, would batten on the lion's share – whatever they could snatch from the claws of that other beast, the king's brother,

27

George of Clarence. The most annoying part of the whole thing was that he was tormenting Margaret though he believed she was telling the truth. She probably did not know where Jasper had taken the boy and, equally probably, she had not agreed to let him go. She was neither a clever nor a strong woman, and she doted on the child excessively.

That thought brought Stafford's eyes back to his wife. His brother kept insisting that he question her. Buckingham did not agree with him about Margaret's brains or will; he believed that she was both strong and infernally clever. Nonsense! Margaret never resisted him. The smallest pressure made her yield at once. And she never thought about anything beyond her boy, her God, and her clothes. When he spoke to her about the court, she seemed to listen, but when he asked for her opinion, she said such things as, 'That is ungodly.' Or, 'Did the queen's headdress bear a veil?'

It was unfortunate she did not know where Jasper had taken Henry. Had she known, the king's agents might have been there waiting for them. Of course, the boy's whereabouts would not long be secret. Whoever had him would soon open negotiations. In any case, it would be best to take Margaret to court now. There had already been unfavourable comment about the fact that she had not paid homage to the queen. Stafford ground his teeth. The Woodvilles were hinting that Margaret had refused to come to court. They hoped to build a strong enough case of lies against her to make her seem guilty of treason so that the king could confiscate her properties.

'Very well,' Stafford said, 'if you do not know, you do not. I will tell you once more that Henry would be safer here than taking a death chill while he hides in hedges and ditches. When you have word from him, tell me. Now, there is something else. The queen desires that you come to court.'

For a few moments Margaret kept her eyes lowered. She did not wish Stafford to see the blaze of satisfaction in them. Then she looked up. 'Does this displease you, my lord?' she asked meekly.

'Displease me? No, no. Of course it does not displease me.' All he needed, Stafford thought, was to have this fool of a wife say that in public. He would be the one with confiscated estates. 'Why should your going to court displease me? I was

28

a trifle concerned because your manner may cause you trouble. It is necessary to hold oneself very lowly before the queen, very lowly indeed.'

Consternation flooded Margaret's face. 'Am I so stained by the sin of pride?' she asked anxiously. 'Do I seem to hold myself too high?'

'No, Margaret, for God's sake, do not undertake a whole series of penances to humble your soul. I did not say you were too proud. To me, your manner could not be bettered. The fault – and do not repeat this – lies in the fact that the queen was not born of high enough estate. Her pride needs constantly to be upheld. Do you know that she demanded that her own mother and the king's sister, the king's own sister, serve her upon their knees? Once her mother fainted before she was permitted to rise.'

'Thou shalt honour thy father and thy mother,' Margaret murmured.

'Now, that,' Stafford exclaimed with intense irritation, 'is exactly what I meant to warn you against. You must not say things like that to the queen.'

'I did not make up those words, my lord. They are God's commands to mankind.'

'Do not be so stupid!' Stafford shouted. 'What has God's word to do with the queen? Leave her soul to her chaplain.'

'Yes, my lord.'

Margaret shrank back a little as if alarmed by his violence, and Stafford came forward and patted her shoulder kindly. With an effort, Margaret kept herself from shrinking further. It would have been unkind and, as to her general feeling, untrue. It was only when his weak character was openly displayed, as it was in this fear of the queen, that Margaret felt she despised Stafford. And she had no right to complain. She had chosen him deliberately for just the characteristics that repelled her now. Jasper, Margaret thought, oh, Jasper.

Some weeks later it was as if Margaret were hearing an echo of the cry in her heart, for the queen was saying sharply, 'Jasper! Jasper! You do not seem to have any other answer to any question we ask. Have you never thought or planned for yourself?'

Margaret looked into the haughty, still-beautiful face. The large, slightly protuberant almond-shaped eyes stared back

29

from either side of the fine straight nose above the exquisite mouth. The petulant droop of Queen Elizabeth's lips alone marred the loveliness of that perfect oval face framed in a glory of golden hair.

'What had I to plan, Your Grace?' Margaret murmured. 'When my husband died, I was given into Pem— I beg pardon, Jasper Tudor's care. He left my son to me. Why should I care for anything else, except, of course, my salvation?'

'You are a silly woman, but not so silly as that. We think Jasper Tudor spent overmuch time in your company, and you were ready enough to receive him.'

Suddenly the queen's meaning penetrated to Margaret's mind. Elizabeth was not probing for political news about Henry and Jasper, who were now known to be in the court of Francis of Brittany. A wave of colour washed over Margaret's throat and face. Her eyes grew wide with horror.

'Incest!' she gasped. 'You would accuse me of incest? He was my husband's brother. For such a sin there is no penance, only hell.'

Queen Elizabeth made an irritable sound. She thought there must be something between them. What else could keep Margaret in Pembroke Castle all those years, when she had a perfectly good husband and an open invitation to court? Perhaps the blush was of guilt. But now even the queen's lewd mind found it hard to believe.

'There is no sin that cannot be cleansed with penance – especially rich, gold penance,' she said cynically and with contempt.

She stared down at Margaret, who had been kneeling before her for half an hour. A silly woman, but harmless, and in a way an asset to the court. Her piety would lend an air of propriety to the ladies and, who knew, might even wake some conscience in them or in the king so that his lechery would be less open. Moreover, Margaret was very beautiful. If Edward tried her and she refused him, it might be possible to inflame him to confiscate her property. And if she did not refuse him, Elizabeth thought, her eyes and mouth hard, she will be humbled – she and her holier-than-thou soul.

'You have lived too little in the world,' the queen said. 'We believe it would be to your benefit to serve as one of our ladies. How does this offer sit with you, Lady Margaret?'

30

'It is my pleasure always to obey Your Grace,' Margaret murmured submissively.

The queen held out her hand, and Margaret inched forward on her knees to kiss it. It was odd, she thought, Henry VI's wife had been hated for her pride, yet she had never demanded that her ladies crawl about on the floor or hold conversations on their knees. And whatever her faults of character, Margaret of Anjou was of high birth and noble blood. Only an upstart like Elizabeth Woodville would need to humble her subjects. Another thought came to Margaret that made her smile. The very devotion to God that the queen scorned was what made the queen's service light to her. Unlike the other ladies of the court, who often wept with pain from kneeling, Margaret's knees were so calloused with praying that it bothered her not a whit to kneel to the queen by the hour.

If Francis's original intention had been to barter Pembroke and Henry for Edward's assistance in a war against France, that intention soon altered. His childless duchess took to Henry unreservedly. Francis, too, developed a deep affection for the clever boy and, as weeks passed into months and months into years, affection deepened into admiration.

In England Edward was too busy consolidating his grip on his kingdom to bother about Henry. When he did make an attempt to buy him, it was too late. Francis's regard for the refugee had grown paternal, and Jasper had proved extremely useful in fighting for his adopted country. Still, Francis was too cautious to refuse Edward outright. He set an astronomical price on Henry's head and took great pleasure in the shock of Edward's envoys and their attempts to bargain.

When Henry was eighteen, another group of envoys arrived from the English king. Henry's strongest supporter, the duchess, had died a few months previously, and Edward was now offering something more attractive than money to Francis. The king of England proposed war against France as Henry's price, coupled with the promise that the young Tudor would be treated honourably. Had the decision rested with Francis alone, there would have been little question of Henry's safety; but the duke displayed his affection for Henry too openly, and now many among his nobles wished to be rid of him. Francis could not afford to alienate his nobles with Edward amassing an army

31

across the Channel. Should the English king invade Brittany instead of France, claiming that he had done so because of Henry, the disaffected nobles might well refuse to support their duke.

Francis accepted Edward's offer, but he insisted that he bring Henry to Edward personally – as soon as the war against France was launched. Fortunately for the Tudor, Edward was sinking deeper and deeper into a slough of dissipation which was wrecking his constitution. Only a tiny part of the army he promised assembled, and Francis was able to ignore the agreement. Meanwhile, Henry worked hard to better his position at the Breton court. He used all his persuasive powers to urge Francis to take another wife. The move was a shrewd one, and when the new duchess bore a healthy child in 1477, the Bretons were appeased. Their fears about Henry began to fade, for, though the child was but a girl, the next might be a healthy son.

Henry absented himself from court a good deal in the next two years. He did not wish to incur the hatred of the new duchess by vying with her and her daughter for Francis's affections. Out with Jasper, he learned military science in the field, and Jasper learned that his nephew had an uncanny ability to judge men. Surely that was good; yet what had happened to Henry? Even the most casual conversation became significant. If a man commented on the weather before a skirmish, Henry would judge him by the comment. He urged his men to drink with him, while he himself drank little, but only sat by watching, watching. To Jasper he might say, 'This man is trustworthy,' but Henry Tudor trusted no one.

The years had been bitterly hard, more so for Henry than for Jasper. Jasper had long been accustomed to the life of a soldier and enjoyed it. He need not walk a tight-rope between the duke's affection and the jealousy of the nobles, nor maintain appearances at court without an income. No agent of Edward's ever tried to slip a knife between his ribs. Jasper's soldiers saw his worth and loved him, while Henry's court companions regarded him with emotions ranging from mild distaste to violent, jealous hatred. Henry was being driven in upon himself. He was not less genial – he loved a joke, a stirring tale, music or a lively dance as well as ever – but a watcher stood behind his eyes, and that watcher did not join in the merrymaking.

Because he saw clearly, Henry could not ignore how even those men who loved him also feared him. Jasper himself, who treasured the boy as his own child, feared when the watcher gazed out from behind the love in Henry's eyes, for that watcher in Henry which saw into the naked soul, once called into being, could not be dismissed.

Henry grew in upon himself, but he also came to understand his power over men. If Jasper's men fought because they loved him, Henry's would die for him because they feared him more than death. Yet he was gentle and did not like to fight. Indeed, he showed a most unmanly distaste for bloodshed.

At the birth of Francis's second child, Henry and Jasper travelled to court to celebrate the event. The feasting was lavish, the ceremonies magnificent, but enthusiasm was lacking. The second child, too, was a girl, and the duchess was unlikely to bear another. Henry noticed the cold glances when he approached to kiss his protector's hand. Francis embraced him with the warmth of a father, and the duchess offered her hand and then her cheek. She was no enemy, but she did not look as if she would live to help him long.

'You will not leave Francis again, Henry, will you?' Her voice was faint.

'Not if he desires me to stay, madam, but I am of little use.'

'You give him comfort,' the duchess sighed, 'and he may have need of comfort soon.'

Her prediction came too close to Henry's own fears, and he steered the conversation into merrier channels, soon bringing a smile to her wan lips.

'You see,' she said as he bowed in parting, 'you do us both good.'

Little good he did himself by endearing himself to Francis, Henry thought, shunning the black looks of the Breton nobles.

When envoys came again from England, Francis agreed to permit them to take Henry back with them. Perhaps he would have resisted had Edward's offer been less fair. The king of England said the realm was quiet and content and that he no longer feared rebellion. It was time to seal the breach between York and Lancaster. He would give his eldest daughter, Elizabeth, to Henry as his bride.

Only chance brought Francis news of negotiations for the betrothal of Elizabeth to the dauphin of France. Fearing

33

treachery and an alliance fatal to Brittany, he sent men thundering after the envoys to bring Henry back.

Francis's men found Henry still in Brittany. He had taken to the tricks of his childhood and made himself sick. The English envoys dared not cross Henry while still in Francis's duchy and had agreed to let him seek a physician. It was all the leeway he needed to escape into a church and claim sanctuary. This was not the first time, nor would it be the last, that Henry's quick wit saved him from death.

When they were reunited, Francis told Henry what had caused his change of heart. 'Of course, Edward has two other daughters, but I will wager that neither of them was meant for you.'

Henry shrugged. 'Even if one were, my every word and move would have been watched. I would have been a prisoner in a gilded cell. You must know he would never trust me in arms, nor in government.'

'No, I suppose not. Henry, do you seek such duty?'

'I am no idle popinjay.'

'True. My son, do you long for England?'

'My lord, do you never look back on your childhood and it seems an enchanted time of joy with no pain? Yet you know the happiest child suffers much. When I look back, it seems that England was a land of milk and honey, and I dream. But my waking mind knows better. I love my dream as a dream. I do not believe it to be a real thing. In truth, I can say to you that I do not long for England.' God forgive me, thought Henry.

'It is well, for I believe there is no place for you there – nor ever will be. That will be England's loss and my great gain, for you were born to rule, Henry.'

Henry stepped back nervously. If Francis should suspect him of unhealthy ambition, his state would be desperate.

'Yes. My first wife, may the good Lord protect her soul, saw it when you were but a child, and I have seen it grow in you. Did you know my first duchess urged me to find a means to make you my heir?'

'My lord!' Henry's even manner never betrayed surprise, but so wild a plan shocked him out of his cultivated sangfroid.

Francis chuckled. 'Well, she was a good woman and followed her heart. I knew it was impossible then to force you, who had no slightest kinship with me, upon the barons. Now, however,

34

there is a means to bring us into the closest kinship. What say you to being my son by marriage, Henry?'

For a moment Henry stood stunned, then dropped heavily to his knees. 'Whatever I could say would be an insult by expressing too little gratitude. That you should give even a single thought to such a union gives me greater joy than—'

'Save your fine speeches, my son. You will need that golden tongue of yours to move others than me. Mind, I love you, but I did not think of this plan to benefit you alone.' Francis allowed Henry to kiss his hand and then raised him. 'Any other man of high enough birth would scarcely wish to leave his own land, and, even were he willing, Brittany would not be first in his heart.'

Henry was bold. 'My lord, I do not hate England, but you may be sure I will never further Edward's interests over Brittany's.'

'That had passed through my mind,' Francis said with a laugh. 'You love me, Henry, and, living here, you might win Anne's love and make her happy while you cared for the land.'

'I would try – but I am twenty-two, my lord, and she is but a baby. Also, I understand men – women are another matter.'

'You should apply yourself more to their study,' Francis gibed, for he had heard that Henry was a pious prude with regard to women.

'I will certainly set myself to study Anne.' He flushed faintly. 'If anything that I can give her will make her happy, she will have it.'

Francis shook his head and smiled. 'I believe she will be content with my choice, but now it is more to the point to seek a way to make my vassals content with it. Fortunately, there will be time. Anne is only two years old and need not be affianced for a while. This plan must remain our secret until we can teach my lords that it is better to have a noble ruler who loves Brittany than one who, a Breton himself, would raise his kin higher than is meet and rule his country ill.'

While Henry studied one child with interest, Margaret studied another. During her first few years at court, she had hoped the struggle between the queen's kin and the king's would disrupt the country again and give Henry a chance. That had not happened, although Gloucester, Clarence, and the Woodvilles

35

seemed to live in a constant state of enmity. Margaret now believed the balance would hold and that Henry's chances for a return to England and his release from penniless obscurity rested in the offer of one of the king's daughters as a wife. Edward was growing more and more secure as he realized there was no diminution of the people's love for him. They forgave him his dissipation, his drunkenness and lechery, the greed of his courtiers, everything, for the sake of his kindliness to the commons and his interest in the monetary prosperity of the land.

In fact, Margaret was not sure that Edward had been insincere in his proposals to Henry. She knew of the negotiations with France, but there had been little hope of agreement there at the beginning, and another princess, only a year younger than Elizabeth, was available. Of course, Elizabeth would be best. Margaret looked across the queen's reception chamber to where the fourteen-year-old princess was playing the virginal and singing softly. If the marriage could be achieved, it would be no bad thing. The girl bid fair to be as beautiful as the mother – more beautiful, in fact, because she lacked the sharpness of feature that betrayed the queen's meanness. Perhaps the oval of the face was not so perfect and the nose a trifle too short, but the mouth was far lovelier, full and generous with a tilt to the lips that betrayed the princess's readiness to laugh. The eyes, too, were a softer blue and held a twinkle of mirth in their depths.

The queen, who did not care for music and cared even less for a daughter who was beginning to rival her attractions, made an impatient exclamation, rose and withdrew. The room waited in perfect stillness, Elizabeth's hands frozen on the keyboard. Five minutes passed, ten. A page scurried across the room, one ear bright red where it had been cruelly tweaked. Another ten minutes and the door opened to admit the queen's brothers, Rivers and Grey. A soft sigh ran through the chamber. Elizabeth's uncles kissed her hand and passed on into the queen's inner chamber. The tableau of ladies waiting stiffly against the walls hung with fine cloth of Arras broke up as soon as Rivers and Grey disappeared. The queen would be busy with them for some time. There was a trifle of uneasiness, of wondering whom they were planning to destroy now, but the queen's absence generated a feeling of relief.

Margaret trod across the red carpet, aware of the contrast it made with the brocade skirt of the princess's blue gown. 'Your playing is wonderfully improved, my lady,' she remarked.

Elizabeth smiled. She liked Lady Margaret in spite of the fact that many of the other ladies made fun of her piety and prim ways. At least Lady Margaret did not mouth proprieties and then sleep with Elizabeth's father like half the other ladies at court. It was interesting that in spite of her beauty, which seemed to the princess completely unchanged from the first time she had seen her, the king never looked at Lady Margaret with other than respect.

'Thank you,' Elizabeth replied. 'I dearly love music.' Then a shadow darkened her eyes. 'But it is wrong of me to forget that others do not care for it so well.'

That was not a remark to which Margaret could reply, since the person who disliked music – or at least disliked the attention paid her daughter when she played – was the queen. Margaret made a soothing remark about books also being a great comfort. The sooner Elizabeth was married and out from under her mother's thumb, the better off the girl would be, Margaret thought. She did not like that shadow of fear in Elizabeth's eyes. Yet Elizabeth was no coward. Margaret had seen her whipped for some misdemeanour – more shame to her mother for so humiliating the child in public – and she neither cried out nor pleaded. This was a different kind of fear, of disapproval more than of pain. There was a sensitivity in Elizabeth that did not come from her father or her mother. Perhaps from the old duke or duchess of York – yes, it could come from there, for Richard of Gloucester also had it.

'My son loves music, too,' Margaret said. 'He writes to me that it is his chiefest pleasure.'

Something flickered in Elizabeth's eyes. Margaret suddenly wondered whether the girl was aware that her name had been used to tempt Henry back to England. If so, did she approve? Could she be induced to press her father to marry her to Henry? Edward was very fond of his eldest daughter, very fond of her – fond enough, perhaps, to marry her to a man who would not take her away. But if Elizabeth knew anything, she also knew enough not to betray herself.

'You must miss him,' the princess said softly. 'It is sad that he will not come home.'

37

'He will not come without his uncle.' Margaret gave the excuse she had been using recently to explain Henry's refusal of even the most flattering offers. 'I have written that he would be safe, and I think he believes this, but Henry loves very hard when he loves. He does not change his love for his advantage.'

Elizabeth looked aside, her fair complexion stained faintly with rose. 'That is most admirable,' she murmured.

'I suppose so,' Margaret agreed with a light laugh, 'but at this time, so that I might see him again, I almost wish it were otherwise.' To say more would be dangerous and obvious. Though Elizabeth was young, she was no fool. Margaret had said enough to give the girl something pleasant to think about.

Chapter Four

The elaborate game of convincing the Breton nobles that Henry was a suitable husband for Anne stretched out through weary years. Henry's part was to use his golden tongue with effect, drawing upon what the watcher behind his eyes sensed to flatter and cajole. Francis's part was to ram Henry's virtues down his barons' throats, and one way to do so was to raise up a more offensive favourite. Pierre Landois, an upstart rascal with a clever mind, insinuating manners, and a rapacity startling even in a rapacious age, was advanced to power. In comparison to Landois, Henry was a paragon.

A few weeks before Henry's twenty-fifth birthday, news came from England disturbing enough to distract him from his purpose. Margaret's husband was dead. The messenger who brought the news was sent back at once offering asylum in Brittany if Margaret thought herself to be in any danger. Before that messenger could have returned to his source, another scholar with a parcel of books for Henry appeared. Edward IV did not want to see the great-granddaughter of John of Gaunt lonely and uncomforted. He thought it would be well for her to marry again. Lord Thomas Stanley, steward of Edward's household and closer to the king than all but a few others, had been proposed. Henry sent another frantic invitation, daring, in his fear for his mother, to outline his high hopes in Brittany.

Margaret read Henry's urgent missive with a tender smile. She was now nearly forty years old, but the beauty that came from the fine bones under the flesh was unchanged. True, there were dark hollows beneath her eyes, her cheeks were thinner, and her translucent skin showed tiny wrinkles where laughter and tears had stretched and washed it. The changes only enhanced the quality of fragile purity that drew men's eyes and yet held them back from grossness.

Dear Henry, how constant he was and how foolish to worry about her as if, after all these long years, she could not take care of herself. She rose as gracefully as a girl and moved

39

toward her writing desk. A scratch at the door made her quicken her step, thrust Henry's letter inside and step away as she called, 'Enter.'

The page announced Lord Stanley, and he trod in virtually on the heels of the child.

'You will think me quite mad for returning so soon, Lady Margaret,' he said.

Margaret's lips quirked; she struggled for composure, then gave in and chuckled softly. 'My dear Lord Stanley, no woman has ever thought a man who flattered her was mad. Since the only business between us is that of our proposed union and since you are urging it, I can only assume you have discovered more cogent arguments to that purpose. That is most flattering and not, to my mind, at all mad.'

Lord Stanley had stopped abruptly and started to draw himself up, when Margaret laughed, but there was only kindness in her eyes. He came forward again, his thin face intent. He was not a large man, rather of middle size but well made, and he carried himself with the easy grace of the courtier-soldier that he was. The high, broad forehead betokened intelligence, which was also apparent in his dark eyes; the full, well-shaped lips told of passion, but the chin – Lord Stanley would be a frail reed to lean upon. That was all to the good, Margaret thought. She had strength enough for both.

'Then, I must depend upon that little feminine weakness,' Thomas Stanley said, 'although I do not flatter. My regard for you is – is most sincere, most sincere indeed. Lady Margaret, I have returned not with cogent reasons but – but to make a confession. You have protested at the unseemly haste with which the king is pressing you into a new marriage. It – that is my fault.'

'Yours, my lord?'

Lord Stanley drew a deep breath and looked away. 'I have long loved you, Lady Margaret, longer, in truth, than is honest, for my heart had turned to you before my wife's death. You shine like a pure wax light among the stinking, smoking torches that most of the court ladies have become.'

Margaret made a half gesture of distress, and Stanley's voice checked. It was rumoured that his wife had been touched by the king. If so, he had been too weak to protest, but there

40

was honour enough in him to feel the shame was not worth the profit.

'As soon as I had word of Stafford's death,' he went on after he had unclenched his jaw, 'I went to the king and – and demanded you.'

'My lord!'

The shock in her voice reacted upon him like a blow in the face. He winced and stepped back a little. 'If this is – is disgusting to you, Margaret, if you think you cannot bear to have me as a husband, I – I will withdraw my suit.'

'Thomas' – it was now Margaret who stepped forward and took his hand – 'do you mean that?'

'Yes,' he exclaimed bitterly. 'When I came to you earlier, you were so uneasy and so glad when I took my departure. It galled me. I was angry. First I told myself that I would force you to love me. But whatever the fools at court think, I know you are not the kind to yield to force. Then I bethought me what my wife would be— I could not endure to live with your hatred. It is better to lose you entirely. I am sorry, Margaret – sorry. I would have made you a – a good husband. Better than others the king, or the queen, might choose.'

He pulled his hand from hers and started to turn away. Margaret gripped his arm. 'Wait, Thomas. I was only surprised by what you said. I do not hate you. Before, it is true I was eager for you to go, but it had nothing to do with you as a person.' It had to do with Henry's letter, but Margaret could not admit that. 'I only felt I was being hurried and harried. I could not understand why. It is not decent. My husband is dead not two months.'

Lord Stanley clenched and unclenched his free hand. 'I am sorry. I knew you would be offended, but I dared not wait. There are hungry mouths gaping for you, Margaret, and some of them have teeth that would grind your frail bones.' He felt her stiffen and continued quickly, 'I am not threatening you, my dear. I am only trying to explain why I have acted seemingly without consideration for your grief.'

Margaret shook her head. 'Since you say you love me, Thomas, I cannot lie to you. I do not grieve for Henry Stafford in spite of the more than ten years we were man and wife. He was kind and I was fond of him, but I never loved him. I have loved only once in my life – as a woman loves a man – and that man I still love.'

'I will win you,' Thomas Stanley exclaimed enthusiastically. He thought she meant her first husband, twenty-five years in his grave, and he did not care about that shadowy devotion to a dead man.

'I can give you no assurance of your success,' Margaret said gently, 'but I can promise that I will not try to resist you, Thomas. If I become your wife, I will try to love you.'

'You will accept me, then?'

Margaret smiled. 'I never meant to refuse – only to gain a little time.'

That was the exact truth. Lord Stanley was very close to the king and one of the most powerful magnates of England. For Margaret's political purposes, the match was most advantageous. She would have accepted a far less pleasant husband to further those purposes.

Lord Stanley's face clouded. 'I would give you the time if I could, but I do not dare. Margaret, the king is not so well as I would like. He finds it harder and harder to resist the harpies that tear at him. We must be married as soon as possible. I – I promise I will make no demand upon you if – if you—'

'How kind you are, but it is not necessary. I am willing to perform all my wifely duties as best I can. Just do not expect more than I can give, Thomas. I will withhold nothing by my will. What you do not find is not there for any man to find.'

He did not reply to that but drew her closer, watching her face. Margaret looked up at him submissively. 'My lady, my lady,' he murmured and lifted her hand and kissed it, 'I will enshrine you in gold and pearls.'

'Oh, Thomas,' Margaret protested, 'I beg you not to say things like that. I do not mean to offend you, but it makes me think of the queen, and—'

Worry and indecision replaced the possessive happiness in Lord Stanley's expression. 'Margaret—' he began.

'Come and sit down,' Margaret urged, 'and tell me – if you wish, of course – what is troubling you. What did you mean when you said the king was not so well? I have not been at court for many months because of Stafford's illness, but Edward is still a young man, and he is very strong.'

'Not so young or so strong as he once was. It is his way of

42

life. He will not amend it, and Hastings encourages him, matching him bottle for bottle of wine and acting as his pander. Then, too, his spirit has no rest. He bemoans the death of Clarence, looking with hatred at those who pressed him to it, but so much power has he given into their hands that he dare not move against them. Moreover, there is also justice. The king knows they urged the act for the good of the realm as well as for their own greed. Clarence was a danger to the king.'

'He loves you well, Thomas. Could you not urge him gently to abate his indulgences? And surely it could do no harm to offer soothing words—' She stopped as Thomas shook his head.

'He is changed, greatly changed, since you saw him last. We must marry at once, Margaret. I fear— I fear greatly—' He dropped his voice nearly to a whisper, although they were alone in the room. 'If you wish to be rid of me, Margaret, I will give you the means. You need only repeat what I tell you now and the king's headsman will see that I do not trouble you any longer. I fear the king will not live out this next year.'

After Lord Stanley left, Margaret re-read her son's letter with great care. She had already refused his first invitation to seek sanctuary in Brittany, saying she thought Lord Stanley would make an excellent husband. Her supposition had now been abundantly confirmed. What was more, it was clearly apparent that she would be able to exert a powerful influence on him. Margaret bit her lip. If Edward died and the realm passed quietly into the hands of his son, Henry would do well to marry Anne of Brittany. Probably he could come home safely after Edward's death, but to what? His estates belonged to others. He would always be suspect.

However, Margaret did not believe that Prince Edward would inherit peacefully from his father. Gloucester and the Woodvilles would never be willing to work together, and the prince would not be strong enough to keep the peace between them. If civil war came, Henry might have a chance if – and only if – he was unmarried and free to wed Edward's daughter. Margaret took down a book she knew well and began to turn the pages. She went back to her writing desk, examined the quills there, chose a fine one and began to mark certain passages.

The reply Henry received to his announcement that a betrothal had been proposed between him and Anne of Brittany was so cryptic that he could scarcely understand it. He begged a leave of absence from court to bring Jasper back for the Christmas festivities, and he took the priest who had carried Margaret's message with him. Jasper read the short innocent letter he carried, listened twice to the equally innocent verbal message, and carefully scanned the marked passages in the religious text he brought. Gold coins chinked, and the priest was dismissed to be set on his way towards France in the morning.

'Well, uncle?' Henry asked impatiently.

'It may be that the Lady Margaret did not send that message. She is not usually addle-pated,' Jasper said slowly.

'I thought of that, but who else would be so clever as to divide it so that it appears three innocent admonitions to a son? No, if someone else sent it to prevent my betrothal to Anne, would they not have been more anxious for a clearer message?'

'I suppose so. Also there is the matter of the time limit. That does not sound like an enemy.'

'Then my mother expects something to happen in England within the next six months – something perhaps of more importance to me than marriage to the heiress of Brittany. What, in the name of God, uncle? What could be that important?'

Their eyes met and Jasper nodded his agreement. 'Edward's death – only that.' Then he frowned. 'I still do not see why that should prevent you from marrying Anne of Brittany. If your mother thinks your estates and title will be restored by Edward's son, that would merely enhance your chances in Brittany. What is more, the betrothal here, which would assure Edward's heir that you would stay safe abroad, would increase your chances for restoration.'

Henry stood up and began to pace the room restlessly. Brittany was only a duchy, it was true, but its duke ruled as independently as any king. As the husband of a bride nearly twenty years younger than himself, it could be presumed that he, not she, would rule in spite of the fact that the right was hers. If his mother wished him to delay his commitment to become Anne's husband, it was only because she envisioned for him a position of even greater importance.

'Your mother has butterflies in her head,' Jasper growled, proving that his mind was running along the same track as Henry's. 'It is true that Gloucester, Buckingham, Hastings,

44

and the Woodvilles are bitter enemies who will pull England apart when Edward dies, but Edward has two healthy sons for them to struggle over. Not one of those factions would even glance at you.'

'I would agree, except that my mother does *not* have butter-flies in her head – ever. She knows something we do not know. Perhaps something too dangerous to trust to any messenger.' Henry sat down, aware that his pacing was a sign of his inde-cision, and he made it a rule never, on any account, to exhibit the fact that he had doubts and fears like any other man.

'Well, wild dreams are not Margaret's way,' Jasper admitted grudgingly. Now it was his turn to rise and pace the floor. In his opinion, England's throne was as far out of Henry's grasp as the moon, and he should not throw Brittany away for a lunatic dream. Jasper stopped in front of his nephew and looked at his quiet face and relaxed body with a mixture of irritation and pride. 'You have made up your mind already, eh? I never saw anyone like you, Harry. What to do in this case might drive a man mad, yet you think, decide, and, more wonderful yet, dismiss the matter from your mind so that it does not fret you.'

Henry smiled, then burst out laughing in the manner that was so infectious if you did not look deep into his eyes. Noth-ing could be further from the truth, yet the impression Jasper had was exactly the one Henry wished to give. 'But in this case, uncle, it is such an easy decision to make. I need only do nothing. If I do not prod the barons, they will not ask Francis to make the betrothal. Landois is not likely to become more sensible. I can lose nothing by patience – and patience is one thing of which I have great stock.'

'Do not be so sure you can lose nothing. Francis is not well. Remember the fit he had when he was insensible for an hour and then mixed in his mind for the rest of the day. What if a worse fit take him?'

It was something Henry had already considered, and although the possibility made him cold with apprehension no sign of that disturbed his smile. 'Such matters are truly in God's hands, uncle. What good would it do me to worry? Even if I had decided to press for the betrothal, it could not happen tomorrow – and tomorrow Francis might have another fit.'

'It never does any good to worry,' Jasper growled in

45

exasperation, 'but I have never come across anyone else on whom that knowledge had any effect – except a fool.'

'Sometimes it is of great value to appear a fool.'

Jasper sighed. 'That safety you will never have, Harry. When other men are thought fools, you are suspected of devious plans.'

Henry laughed again. 'That, too, may be of great value.'

Suddenly Jasper joined his laughter. 'It is the maddest thing, Harry. I know that I should be worrying for both of us, but your certainty that all will be well is like aqua vitae. Do you bewitch men into your faith?'

No, Henry thought, as he embraced his uncle fondly without replying, but I feed men on it as if I opened my body to let them chew my liver and suck my heart's blood. And so much as doing that is the pain it costs me.

The next news from England was all personal. Margaret was married and found Stanley much to her liking – even more than her previous husband. Jasper, reading between the lines, chuckled. 'She means, I suppose, that Stanley is a strong man of his hands with a wavering mind which she believes she can make up for him.'

'Also,' Henry replied, tossing a packet of coins and jewels from one hand to another, 'that he is richer than Stafford and allows her more of her own income to play with. I hope she does not send me too much and make him suspicious.'

For two months, they heard nothing more. Jasper grew restless and wanted to beg leave to return to the border, but Henry opposed this move. The last week in March, however, brought the information that Edward IV was very ill. A messenger a week later confirmed this, adding that his death was expected. Jasper bit his nails with tension, but Henry laughed and rode out hunting. It was very important to show the Breton lords how little the news from England affected him.

By April 9th, 1483, Edward was dead. Now even Henry found the strain of seeming disinterested too great. If the government passed smoothly to Edward's heir, he wanted to take Anne to wife. He did not wish Francis or the nobles of Brittany to suspect that his eyes had ever turned towards England. As a cover, he asked and received permission to ride the borders with Jasper. If events began to move swiftly in England, the number of couriers would betray Henry's deep

46

interest in events basically unconnected with Breton affairs.

The precaution was a wise one. By the end of May, Margaret's messengers were almost treading on each other's heels. The queen's brothers had tried to keep Edward's heirs in their own power, but Gloucester had been warned by Hastings and had seized the princes himself with Buckingham's support. The lines were drawn; Gloucester, Buckingham, and Hastings against the queen and her Woodville relatives, and the first round was Gloucester's. The queen with her eldest son by her first husband, the marquis of Dorset, and one brother were in sanctuary; her other brothers, Rivers and Grey, had been taken prisoner. Day by day the news became more dramatic and more significant. The members of the council that Richard of Gloucester had summoned did not trust each other. Hastings was being won over to the queen's side by the influence of Dorset's ex-mistress with whom he had formed a connection.

Then came Margaret's own chaplain, tumbling down on his knees at Henry's feet in exhaustion as he gasped out the news. Hastings was dead – seized at a meeting of the council and beheaded in the Tower courtyard without a trial. Morton and Rotherham were prisoners in the Tower and Stanley himself was being detained, although only in his own quarters.

'My mother?' Henry asked softly, but Jasper saw his nephew's hands clench into fists, those hands which were usually so relaxed in times of extremity.

'Safe,' the chaplain murmured, almost sobbing with weariness. 'She bides near to sanctuary, and there is a secret way for her to flee there if need be.'

'I thank you for that surety.' Henry's hands opened, lay quiet on the arms of his chair. 'Go now to rest and refresh yourself.'

'He will seize the throne for himself!' Jasper exclaimed.

'Nay, he could not! The prince is his nephew.' Henry was so shocked that the words were wrenched out of him before he thought. 'Richard of Gloucester, much as I dislike all the house of York, has been an able and faithful supporter of his brother,' Henry added defensively. 'I will not believe that he would turn on his brother's children.'

Jasper's face softened and he moved across the room to place a comforting hand on Henry's shoulder. He understood that his nephew was not defending Richard of Gloucester but

47

Jasper of Pembroke. 'Harry, there is not one drop of blood in me on either side that could give me a claim to the crown. Therefore – therefore, I say – you may believe I will never strive for it.' He could feel the muscles in Henry's shoulder tense and see his brief, unguarded expression of pain. Jasper bent and kissed his nephew's temple. 'In my heart I believe that nothing can come between us, that no hope of gain or power could make me lift a finger that was not lifted for your good. But I have lived for fifty-two years in a hard world. Who knows what a man will do, even an honourable man, when such temptation is put in his way?'

Henry twisted his head to smile at his uncle, and Jasper received a shock of pleasure. For once, both Henrys were smiling – the beloved nephew and that other who watched apart.

'On the day I must doubt you, I will have lived long enough. On that day, uncle, I will know there is no God, that this world and all else is the creation of some great Evil, and that Good does not exist.'

'Hush, Harry, you blaspheme.'

But for a while the events in England seemed to give substance to what Henry said. Richard of Gloucester first declared his nephews illegitimate and then usurped the crown. The wave of blood that was to engulf England gathered volume. Rivers and Grey, the queen's brothers, were beheaded at Pontefract without even the mockery of a trial. This information was brought to Henry by another of the queen's brothers, who arrived in Brittany in July begging for Henry's protection.

When he was gone, Jasper snarled, 'He as well as his brothers urged Edward to hunt you. All the Woodvilles are snakes. Why did you promise him your protection? You will have them all on your hands.'

Henry sat a moment staring ahead. 'I do not think,' he replied at last, with an odd mixture of regret and calculation, 'that there will be many left by the time Gloucester is done.'

The prediction seemed to be correct; the depths of horror had not yet been plumbed. Margaret's next messenger arrived only a day after Edward Woodville. First he confirmed Sir Edward's news, then he told Henry that all was well concerning Margaret's position. Stanley was again in favour and he and Margaret would take prominent parts in Richard's coronation on July 6th. Then he stood irresolute, licking dry lips. He could

48

not bring himself to say aloud what he had been told. At last he whispered into Henry's ear that Edward's sons, the young princes, had not been seen for many weeks and it was rumoured that they, too, were dead. Henry pulled his head away from the hissing sound and jerked to his feet.

'Wicked uncle,' he breathed.

The games of his childhood, which had given him so much pleasure, had taken on a nauseous reality. Henry had no love for Edward or his brood, but he shrank from this insane blood-letting. It was not until hours later, when he was tossing restlessly in his bed, cold despite the summer warmth and the robe he had pulled over him, that he could bring himself to admit that Richard's actions were not insane. If Gloucester wished to keep the crown he had assumed, Edward's blood must not survive to divide the country. Alone, Henry had no need to set a guard on his expression or emotion, and he trembled, reliving the terrors he himself had felt, finding himself, to his own surprise, weeping for those children who had faced a greater terror without support and had died in fear.

He drew a hand over his face, annoyed with himself for emotion wasted on enemies who, likely enough, would have wasted none on him. If I must weep, Henry thought, let it be for myself. Richard will not forget me, more especially if his enemies flee here to my protection. He will have excuse enough to threaten Brittany and, even if he has not strength enough for war, he can set the nobles against me again. And, what will I do with these people? How will I support them? How long can Francis bear their expense without resentment?

Chapter Five

While Henry struggled with practical problems in Brittany, Margaret struggled with emotional ones in England. From the time Henry was a quick-witted baby, she had dreamed dreams of power and glory for him. These were rooted in her very soul, but above them lay a heavy debris of fear. The years she had lived at Edward's court had displayed to her the horrors that grew around power and the smirching of glory that those horrors brought. Richard's bloody seizure of the crown brought all the evils of power into sharp focus, for Richard had been an honourable man and had been turned into a monster.

Could she desire such a burden for Henry? Even if he could support it and did not become a bloody tyrant, would what happened to Edward happen to him? Would Henry be swallowed by dissipation, grow fat and soft, rotted by his own lusts? She could not imagine such weakness in her son, yet what did she really know of Henry? For twelve years she had not looked into his face. What could be judged from a whispered message, from a few formal lines giving news of his health and welfare?

Margaret touched her coif to be sure the folds were straight and graceful, ran her finger around its edge to be sure that no hair had escaped to make her look unkempt. Her surcoat was of the richest emerald silk, her cotte of the purest white, its hem sewn with pearls that glowed softly when the surcoat was lifted and they caught the light. The clothes suited her, but that was not why she had chosen them. Green and white were the Tudor colours. A necklet of emeralds and diamonds, rings on her fingers; Margaret rose at last and looked into her mirror. Yes, she was grand enough. Her appearance would undoubtedly turn the knife in the wounded pride of Elizabeth Woodville, dowager queen of England and now no better than a prisoner in sanctuary at Westminster.

Shown into Elizabeth's presence, Margaret curtsied deeply but did not kneel, for in these circumstances that gesture would be considered mocking.

50

'Why have you come here?'

The question did not surprise Margaret. She had been the queen's lady for many years, but they had never been friends. Even aside from political differences, their natures and interests were totally opposed. Over the years, Margaret had found the queen to be vain, shallow, sensual, and pleasure-loving, unstable in her loyalties, selfish to a degree that excluded even her children. Although Queen Elizabeth was shrewd enough to see and grasp for what she thought was her good, she often spoiled everything by being unable to wait or plan for the future.

'Because we both desire the same thing and together, albeit we are only two women, we can achieve that thing.'

'What can I achieve – a prisoner in danger of my very life? I am helpless, succourless. I have lost my hope and my joy. My sons, my brothers, all are lost – lost.'

'I cannot give you back your sons or your brothers' – Margaret's voice trembled with deep and genuine sympathy. She might dislike and distrust this woman, but she could feel for her grief – 'but all else I can make sure you have again. And I can give you your revenge on him who has bereft you. More than that, you and I may bind and heal the wounds that have torn this land for thirty years. You have a daughter – I have a son. My son is heir to Lancaster; your daughter is heir to York. Let them join hands and there will be no stronger right than theirs in this land.'

Elizabeth was silent and tears trickled down her face. She was almost sure her sons were dead, and this visit of Margaret's made her more sure. Her tears, however, were less of grief than of fear. If her sons were dead, her own life was that much more in danger.

'What good are your promises? Will they bind your son? What force has he to achieve this thing?'

'If he does not achieve it, you will have lost nothing. Richard can hate you no more relentlessly even if he should hear that you have promised your daughter Elizabeth to Henry. And my promise that Henry will treat you with all honour – although you may have it in any way you desire including my oath upon the crucifix – will matter little. Your daughter will be Henry's wife. Elizabeth is as beautiful as you are, madam. What man will deny her anything she asks? Did you not mould Edward to your

51

will in far greater things than respect to a mother-in-law?'

That made sense to the dowager queen. A faint flush of colour came into her cheeks and her eyes brightened. Elizabeth was a good daughter. She would deny her mother nothing. Through her, power would be restored to her mother's hands.

'I desire nothing except to live in peace and to be revenged on that murderer.' Elizabeth lied. 'For that and for the good of the land which groans beneath a tyrant – I agree.'

'And your daughter, will she agree?'

'She will do as I say. Now, what would you have – a letter?'

'That would be best, for I must prove that this is not a dream of my own devising. I would like to speak to Elizabeth. If I could have some token of willingness from her to send to my son, it would be very helpful. He is gentle.' Margaret actually knew nothing about Henry's attitude towards women, but she wanted to be sure that the queen would tell Princess Elizabeth of the proposed betrothal. The girl should have time to accustom herself to the idea. 'Henry would not be willing to force your daughter against her will.'

'There is no need for you to speak to my daughter,' the dowager said sharply. 'I will see that a letter and token are made ready for you. When you send to your son to tell him to come to England, that messenger can carry my daughter's consent and' – the petulant lips curled into a sneer – 'her love token.'

It was done. Margaret returned home trembling, although she told herself no irrevocable move had yet been made. She knew that was false comfort. Having started on the path, she would tread it to the end; it was her nature. A week passed whilst Margaret's servants made tactful inquiries. Then she wrote to Lord Stanley that the heat of London oppressed her. If it was not disagreeable to him, she would ride into the country to refresh herself. His reply came as quickly as the messenger could travel. She was to do as she pleased. On no account should she trifle with her health but go where she would be most comfortable – and be sure to take her physician with her. Thomas Stanley was, if possible, more deeply in love with his wife than when he married her. She was perfect. Her virtue, her prudence, and her wisdom had been of more use to him in these troubled times than any other person's. He trusted her implicitly.

Margaret rode slowly north-west, heading for the cool hills of Gilbert Talbot's lands. He was her husband's brother-in-law. She could hardly pay a more respectable or less suspicious visit. Occasionally a man rode away from her entourage, made inquiries and rode back. She rested the night at Stratford-on-Avon, but in the morning they rode at great speed for Kidderminster. The horses were rested and baited and they rode forth again, but very slowly. Soon the sound of a large troop swelled behind them. Margaret bit her lips. This was the decisive step and, once taken, Henry would be committed.

Buckingham, who had supported Richard against the Woodvilles and even agreed to the execution of Hastings, was growing dissatisfied with his royal master. Some said he was nauseated and horrified by the rumoured deaths of Edward's children. Others believed that it was his hands which were stained with the princes' blood, and that he considered himself ill-used by Richard and ill-paid for his deeds. Margaret knew for a certainty that John Morton, bishop of Ely, who had been taken prisoner when Hastings was killed, was Buckingham's ward, and that he had been carefully feeding and nurturing Buckingham's dissatisfaction. She had been in steady communication with John Morton, a brilliant, devious man, through her network of scholars and priests, but she did not know whether Buckingham wanted to seize the throne himself or whether he would throw his weight behind Henry. She had ridden to the cool hills to find out.

Buckingham had a claim to the throne, but it was through Edward III's youngest son, Thomas of Woodstock, and broken by much female descent. Nonetheless, it was nowhere smirched by bastardy, legitimized or not. If Buckingham wished to contest Henry's right to the throne, he would have a most excellent case. Margaret heard his hail and pulled her horse to a halt. Her heart beat so hard that she could feel the pulsations in her throat, but she could not decide, even in those last few moments, whether she hoped or feared that Buckingham would agree to her plan.

'Well, Margaret, a good greeting to you. What do you here?'

'I fly from the heat – and other things – in London.'

Buckingham's face grew guarded. 'Is the king back in London?' he asked with an assumption of casualness.

53

He is afraid, Margaret thought. 'I know not,' she replied. 'I have ridden very slowly, being troubled in my mind.'

They had pulled well ahead of their escorts and no one could overhear. 'Troubled?'

'Nay, I will speak the truth to you, my lord, for you were my brother when my second husband still lived. I am afraid – afraid for myself and for my son. I fear that Richard will not rest until no man – nor woman – who carries the blood of Henry III lives. He has already sent envoys to Brittany demanding Henry's surrender.'

'Francis will not yield him. You need not fear for that, and Richard loves your husband too well to harm you.'

'Loves him so well that he imprisoned him when Hastings was taken. You know Lord Stanley had no part in Hastings's doings. Whom does Richard love or trust?'

'He has ventured much and has gained much. When he is sure of his gain, he will grow more trusting.'

'And others have ventured much and gained little – not even trust, perhaps?'

Buckingham did not answer but sat his horse studying Margaret. Finally he said, 'How old is Henry?'

'Twenty-six, and so prudent and discreet that Francis seeks to make him heir to Brittany through marriage with his eldest daughter Anne.'

'Is he betrothed already?' Buckingham asked sharply.

'No. I thought perhaps he would do better with an English bride – if one of high enough lineage could be found for him. He is the last of John of Gaunt's line.'

'Aye. So he is. Perhaps such a girl might be found. But Margaret,' Buckingham said with a complete change of expression from thoughtfulness to gallantry, 'no one would believe you have a son of such years. Why, you appear scarce older yourself – hardly less fresh than a young maid.'

'My lord, my lord, you flatter an old woman shamelessly,' Margaret jested in reply.

She had made her point and Buckingham had indicated his interest in it by agreeing that Henry might do better with an English bride. The rest could be left to Morton, and Margaret cheerfully helped support the light conversation which occupied the rest of the time she and Buckingham shared the same road. Mostly they spoke of the past – the only conversation

54

which was safe in these times, and Margaret applied a smooth coating of flattery herself when she touched lightly upon the peculiarity of fate which made Henry VI give her to Edmund Tudor rather than to Buckingham himself as bride. It had been her choice, not the king's, but Margaret submerged that memory in a good cause.

'Henry might have been your son,' she smiled, 'had matters fallen otherwise.'

'So he could, and likely we would all have been dead. Still, I may yet stand as father to him in some ways.'

With that they came to Bridgnorth where Buckingham had business. Margaret remained as his guest that night, planning to ride on to Shrewsbury the next day, but they spoke no more of serious matters. There were too many ears in a town to make such discussions comfortable.

Margaret and the duke of Buckingham were sensible enough to confine their conversation to small talk that would not betray what really filled their minds and spirits. The dowager queen had no such self-control. She was incapable of holding her tongue and, bereft of her brothers, she was greatly in need of a safe audience. Thus, even though she understood that it was not wise to wake her daughter Elizabeth's easily aroused emotions, she could not put off involving her at once in order to have someone to discuss the matter with. She brusquely ordered Elizabeth to write a letter of acceptance of a proposal of marriage from Henry of Richmond. Elizabeth looked at her mother with wide, frightened eyes.

'But, mama, I have not received any such proposal, and I do not think—'

'I have received the proposal, as is right and proper. What have you to do with such a matter? And you are not required to think. Do as you are told.'

'Mama, I am very ready to be obedient to you, you know I am, but—'

'But? But what?' The dowager's voice was shrill and furious.

Elizabeth quelled her internal trembling with an effort. She knew her mother could not and would not harm her. She would rather, in fact, be slapped than screamed at. The high, irrational shrieking made her nauseous and dizzy so that she could not think, and she needed to think. Over the years Elizabeth had learned that her mother was not very wise. Leaping

55

this way and that, like a fish after first one and then another, larger fly, the queen often ended with nothing. What Elizabeth needed to sort out in her mind was whether they were truly in dire danger as her mother said. There were also two other possibilities: her mother might simply be exaggerating her own fear grossly, or she might be acting a part deliberately to make trouble for Uncle Richard. Elizabeth had been told that Richard of Gloucester wanted them all dead and that they were alive only because the church gave them sanctuary. Elizabeth found it almost impossible to believe this. No, she could not – not Uncle Richard. He was so kind and so gentle. He never shrieked. He always explained softly what he wanted and made everything easy.

Nonetheless, her brothers were gone. Elizabeth's eyes filled with tears. Her darling little brothers. When first they were taken away, she had written to them every day, and once in a while she had received their replies. The tears spilled over. She had not had a letter for so long. Uncle Richard? If it were so, that he had harmed her brothers, was it not madness to do this thing? It would be open treason to accept a proposal from the head of the House of Lancaster.

'But Uncle Richard would not like it,' Elizabeth said. 'Mama, if he should find out—'

'Who will tell him? You? You little traitor! You think if you yield yourself, he will make you queen?'

'Mother!'

'So that is why you do not wish to write to Henry. You incestuous little bitch! What proposal has Richard made to you?'

Nearly choking with horror, Elizabeth gasped, 'Uncle Richard loves his wife. I am a little girl to him. He has never—'

'Little girl, eh?' the dowager sneered, running her eyes over her daughter's voluptuous figure.

At eighteen Elizabeth was rich and ripe, in the first flush of a beauty that would grow richer over many years. Elizabeth felt herself shrink. It was not modesty. She had more than once been examined by envoys like a Flanders mare, all but being told to open her mouth so that her teeth could be counted. She did not mind having her body appraised for political purposes. It was a fine body, and she was proud of it. Her mother's lewd

56

suggestion was something else entirely. Unwisely, Elizabeth burst into tears.

'So that is what Richard has in mind,' the dowager said thoughtfully. 'He needs to dispose of Anne first, of course, but that will not be difficult. She was ever a puling, sickly thing. She will die soon. Then—' She ran her eyes over her daughter, who was trembling and swallowing convulsively, fighting her disgust. 'Yes, he will have a fine exchange – a real piece of woman flesh *and* the rightful heir to the throne.'

'Mother, stop!' Elizabeth cried, her hands shielding her face. 'Uncle Richard would never harm Anne. He loves her. I am not heir to the throne. I have two brothers. Stop!'

Totally deaf to her daughter's pleading, the dowager stood biting her lip. Then she nodded decisively. 'There can be no harm in accepting Richmond's offer. Even if Richard found out, it would make no difference. If there is no successful rebellion, Richard will marry you and you will be queen. If there is a rebellion and Henry conquers, he *must* marry you and you will be queen. In either case our troubles will be over. Oh, stop that snivelling! Think over what I have said and bring me a letter soon – soon, I say.'

When her mother had gone, Elizabeth sank into the vacated chair and wept bitterly. Her brothers were dead; they must be dead. At first it was all she could think of. Then it dawned upon her that if her brothers were dead, it must be Uncle Richard's doing. And if he had become a monster that would destroy two innocent little boys to be sure of a throne, he might indeed also destroy the wife he once loved and marry his niece incestuously for the same purpose.

Not me, Elizabeth thought, not me. I am not afraid to die. I will die first. But she did not wish to die, and her mind scurried around seeking a defence. Then suddenly her sobbing ceased. Henry of Richmond would be her salvation. Uncle Richard had declared her mother's marriage to her father invalid on the grounds that her father had been previously betrothed to Lady Eleanor Butler. If she were betrothed to Henry of Richmond, she would be safe. She went to the table that held her writing desk and drew forth paper, quill and ink.

Margaret spent a tense and unhappy period in Gilbert

57

Talbot's home wondering whether Morton's judgment of Buckingham's disgust and dissatisfaction was accurate, wondering whether Buckingham would use her plan as a ruse to get Henry into his power so that he could remove another claimant to the throne either for Richard or ultimately from his own path. Before the second week of August was over, however, Reginald Bray, steward of Lord Stanley's household, arrived unheralded at Shrewsbury.

'Has something befallen my husband?' Margaret asked anxiously. If Margaret did not love Thomas Stanley with the deep passion she could have felt for Jasper if that had not been forbidden by the laws of her church, she came closer to it with him than with any other man. His warmth was contagious; she could not help but respond to it. And the more she responded, the more eager Thomas was to fulfil her every desire.

'No, madam, nor does he know of my journey. I left a message that I was called away on business, that is all.'

'Out with it, then.' But Margaret's tone was gay, for Bray was smiling broadly and she knew he was devoted to her. What was more, she did not for a moment believe that Thomas was ignorant of his steward's business. He was blind because he wished to be, not because he was a fool. He had hinted as much to his wife, indicating that he wished to be clear of any involvement only so that he would be capable of protecting her if her plans should go awry.

'Buckingham sent for me to advise you to obtain Queen Elizabeth's consent to the marriage of Richmond and her eldest daughter. If your son will take oath to make that marriage and no other, Buckingham will raise England in Richmond's favour.'

Margaret almost held her breath. 'That I have already. You may make a copy of the letter I have from her. Did he speak of his plans?'

'Most fully, madam. We were in Brecon, where he is safe, and Morton sat beside him all the while. If the bishop of Ely is treated as a prisoner, so am I. It is no trap. Richmond is to come with as large a force as he can muster, and Buckingham will raise the south of England in rebellion as near the day Richmond arrives as may be arranged. What of Richmond's agreement? Do you have that?'

58

'Is it like that my son will refuse a crown? But an army must be shipped and paid. Has Buckingham considered that?'

'Oh, yes. When he is sure of the old queen's consent, he will dispatch a man to make the proposal in his own name and to bring Richmond gold and letters of credence. I know the man, Hugh Conway by name, and naught but God's will could stand in Conway's path.' Bray laughed. 'Hugh could outface and beat the Devil at his own games.'

'I will send Thomas Ramme by different ways bearing the same news. He must also go to the dowager and obtain the letter and token from Princess Elizabeth that were promised me. In addition, Conway must bear Buckingham's own letter saying he knows that the first act of legitimation of my grandfather Beaufort carried no reservation of royal succession and that Henry IV's act, which inserted that phrase, was not valid. My Henry does not know this. I did not wish him to be burdened with the knowledge nor to be burnt up with hopeless ambition.'

Bray nodded and set himself to copy the letter Margaret gave him. He had been in the saddle almost constantly for a week and a half, yet he was ready to ride out again that day. Margaret, however, said that a few hours could not make or mar and that Bray should have at least one good meal and one night's rest before he left for Brecon again.

Henry Tudor was not happy. Of course, he was used to pressures, but those had alternated before – one time it would be lack of money that troubled him, another time the hostility of the nobles, or yet again he would worry over Francis's health, upon which, to some extent, his own depended. Now everything seemed to be adding together. His debts had grown really frightening, since he could not let his refugees starve or become so ragged that they were offensive or a cause for mirth. The sudden influx of Englishmen, especially those of higher rank, had wakened the fears of the Breton nobles who dreaded their own replacement by Henry's countrymen if he should marry Anne. And both of these problems were made dangerously acute by Francis's failing health. Most of the time the duke was rational and keen-witted as ever, but from time to time he had a spell where his mind wandered.

Everything at once was too much. Henry rested his aching

59

head against the frame of an unshuttered window hoping the breeze would freshen enough to cool him through the armholes and the small chinks between the metal plates of his brigandine. This armoured vest was covered with green silk rather than velvet, but it was still ten times hotter than a doublet – and Henry dared not take it off. So far two of the gentlemen craving protection had turned out to be Richard's agents. Henry's never-ceasing caution had kept him from real danger, but the necessity of the brigandine was attested to by a half-healed cut on his upper arm where a turned blade had marked him.

Henry slipped a hand into the neck of his garments and pulled them a little free of his sweat-soaked body. Then the hand dropped unobtrusively to his dagger, for footsteps padded softly down the room. His eyes slid towards the noise, although he did not turn his head, and his face now bore only an expression of good-humoured boredom. The dagger, hidden by his body as it leaned against the window frame, was half-drawn; there were two men.

'My lord?'

One of the men was in sight. Henry resheathed his knife, turned, and smiled. It was Ramme, a trusty man of his mother's. 'Greetings,' he said heartily, and then, as he took in the tired faces and dust smears, 'Is my mother safe? Well?'

'Excellently well and as safe as anyone in England can be in these days,' Ramme replied. 'My lord, this is Hugh Conway. We came different ways from England but met on the road.'

The pulse in Henry's throat was hidden by the high collar of his shirt, but its fierce leaping would have belied the calm of his expression could the messengers have seen it. 'And what brings you gentlemen to me in such haste and by separate routes? Is it of such note that you could not stay to refresh yourselves?'

'I am from the duke of Buckingham, my lord, and I bear—'

'Who?' Henry asked, his face freezing.

'Henry Stafford, second duke of Buckingham,' Conway repeated, 'and I bear letters and papers I would fain be rid of before they hang me.'

Henry held out his hand. 'Give them here, then. When a neck has been as long in danger as mine, hanging grows a common

60

thing scarce to be feared.' His smile was merry, his eyes turned down towards the pouch Conway proffered so that the messenger could not probe them.

A lord of high, cheerful spirit, Conway thought approvingly, even if his stature was no more than Richard's. It was to be seen, however, if he had the shrewdness that would be needed.

'And these letters, also, my lord,' Ramme offered as Henry was about to open the pouch. 'They are of the same import, I believe.'

Thomas Ramme's eyes were the ones that avoided contact. He knew Henry of old and had no desire to meet that piercing gaze. Although he had nothing to hide, Henry made him uncomfortable because he suspected that if he were ordered to jump out the window or murder his mother, he would obey. Henry, however, had not looked up. He scanned his mother's letters first, knowing that he could read her writing quickly and pick the important points out at once. The expression of bored good humour had been deliberately replaced with one of interest, which Henry felt would be more suitable, but even that expression congealed on his face until he wore an unmeaning mask. And when he saw the seal on another enclosed letter, he passed his hand across his eyes as if he did not trust them.

'Ramme,' he said very softly, 'you know where I lodge. Be so kind as to bid one of my Welsh servants to come here to me, and do you return, also. I am sorry to put you gentlemen to so much trouble when you are doubtless weary, but I must ask you to attend me until I have studied these proposals more finely. You know what is herein?'

'It is not hard to guess,' Conway replied. Henry's eyes flicked to him, and Conway swallowed and added, 'My lord.'

When Ramme returned with the servant, Henry looked up from his reading. 'Go find the duke,' he ordered, 'and beg him to grant me a time with him alone in his chamber. Bid my groom to saddle a horse for you, and when you have brought me word from the duke, ride post-haste to my lord of Pembroke. I will have a letter for you to carry. Oh, and send me a clerk with materials for writing.'

Francis sent word that Henry could attend him at once. By then the few lines Henry wrote to summon Jasper to him had been dispatched, and the messengers followed him to the duke's apartment. He left them just outside the door.

'What now?' Francis asked somewhat irritably. 'I have told you I will not give you up to Richard's envoys. Do you doubt me at this late date that you must speak to me each time they do?'

'I did not know they had audience with you today, my lord. I have received a proposal that touches on a plan dear to both of us. I have been offered the hand of Princess Elizabeth by her mother, the dowager queen. I have the Lady Elizabeth's very gracious consent to this proposal. And I have been offered the throne of England by the duke of Buckingham, who set Richard of Gloucester thereon.'

'What?' Francis gasped, and then, 'It is a trap.'

'It is well baited, then.' Henry shrugged and passed him the contents of the messengers' pouches. His face and voice were calm, his hand steady, but Francis did not miss the pale lips and cheeks. 'The messengers are outside. One has been my mother's trusted servant for many years. The other I do not know, but my mother's man vouches for him.'

Francis read the two letters written in French and obviously meant for him although they were addressed to Henry. He asked Henry to translate the dowager queen's letter and Elizabeth's note and then sat in silence looking from Margaret's seal to the dowager's to Buckingham's. Finally, he asked for the messengers, questioned them minutely as to their instructions and voyage and dismissed them. Then he handed all the papers back to Henry except Buckingham's letter of credit on a house of Florentine bankers.

'Write me an order for a bearer of mine to collect this sum.'

'What name for the bearer?' Henry asked, walking towards the table with writing materials which were always kept in the duke's chamber.

'Landois.'

Henry picked up the pen without an instant's hesitation or a single glance in Francis's direction.

'Stop!' Francis said. The pen suspended, Henry looked up inquiringly. 'Come here,' the duke ordered.

Obediently Henry laid down the pen and came back. Halfway across the room he could see the tears on Francis's cheeks. 'What is wrong, my lord?' he asked, hurrying to kneel at Francis's feet.

'Should I not grieve at the loss of such a son?' Francis asked.

62

'Landois is your enemy, yet you would put your chance for a throne into his hands at my word. There are many men who have sons of their flesh who would not do as much.'

Henry kept his eyes lowered. It had been such an obvious test that he was ashamed of giving the correct response. He was even more ashamed of springing the trap Francis had unknowingly set for himself. With a further welling of shame, Henry knew he would even use the trembling lips and voice his emotion had given him to lock the trap in place so that Francis could not escape it.

'Order me to say my word had been given to your daughter, my lord, and you will not lose me.'

'Do you have the right to the throne which Buckingham claims for you?' Francis asked, as if he had not heard what Henry said.

Henry shrugged again. 'If I do, I did not know of it, but I have sent for my uncle. He will know. I do not care about my right, my lord.' His voice choked and he forced the words, miserable but conscious of the fine effect he was making, unhappy but determined that Francis should not be diverted and escape committing himself. 'I would rather care for Brittany than rule England.'

'You would do this for me, Henry?'

Francis had been obvious, but Henry never permitted himself to be. 'And for myself. Can you foresee the life I will have if this venture succeeds? Will I have more peace in the land than Edward or Richard? Will I have peace at my own bed and board, married to the daughter of my bitterest enemy? Perhaps if I wed Anne, Richard will believe I have no desire for his prize and let me live in peace.'

The duke shook his head. 'More like he will come here to ravage this land as soon as he has broken England to his will. A man who has taken what is not his by right endlessly fears it will be snatched away. Marriage to Anne would only suggest to him that you desire to take England by conquest alone and that you have married Brittany's strength to do it. No, Henry,' Francis said, pausing to kiss the young man, 'you must go and be king of England.'

Dropping his head to Francis's knees, Henry sighed, 'As you order, it shall be done.'

63

Chapter Six

Jasper of Pembroke arrived before the sun set on the next day, followed by a band of devoted retainers sworn to die for him if need be. He could only imagine that Henry had sent that hurried note because Richard's emissaries had somehow convinced Francis to yield him up or, even worse, that Francis was dead. Now, in sight of the castle, Jasper hesitated. If he merely craved admittance, he would be allowed in without question, but he and his men had ridden all night and were in no prime fighting condition. To get out, if they had to carry Henry away, would not be so easy. A man sent forward to the gates returned with fair news. At least the duke was alive. Jasper hesitated again, then sent his man once more to ask that Henry ride out to him. He offered the lame excuse that he did not wish to bring so large an armed troop into the duke's residence.

Whatever Jasper's fears that his message would infuriate Francis or warn Henry's enemies, he did not need to endure them long. Henry himself appeared, dressed magnificently for a state dinner and still apparently chewing his last bite of food. The sight irritated Jasper enormously. He had had nothing at all to eat in over twelve hours and had been tortured by imagining Henry in the power of his enemies. To see him as calm and as high in favour as ever seemed momentarily to be more a cause for rage than relief.

'What the devil do you mean by sending me a message like that?' Jasper bellowed.

Henry slid his eyes over the tired group. 'I am glad to see you, uncle,' he replied sweetly, 'although I scarcely expected that you would bring half Brittany's army with you.'

'If you were ten years younger, I would warm your— I would see that you could not sit your horse to hunt for a week. Is this a time – with Richard's envoys at court – to play at such japes?'

Seeing that Jasper was really discomposed, Henry said pacifically, 'It was no jape, but there is no danger that requires armed men. I told you so. Dismiss them to take their ease in

64

the town, uncle, and come within. Do you rest, also, and refresh yourself. I must go back lest there be wondering at my hasty departure.'

It was midnight before Henry returned to his own quarters, where Jasper had chosen to wait for him. Seeing that his uncle was scarcely better tempered, Henry decided to attack rather than explain to change Jasper's mood.

'Why did you not tell me I had a valid claim to the throne of England?' he asked in a soft voice that was singularly unpleasant. 'You put me in a curiously difficult situation.'

'It was your mother's wish,' Jasper said. As the words left his mouth, he realized he had placed the blame on Margaret to avoid his nephew's wrath. Shocked at his cowardice, Jasper continued defiantly, 'It was my feeling, also, at first because a child should not be burdened by so heavy a fear and later because I did not wish to see you engaged in any hare-brained schemes to gain that throne which might lose you Brittany.'

'Uncle,' Henry said reprovingly, 'when have I ever engaged in any hare-brained scheme? And who are you to cavil,' he laughed, 'who came with armed men to storm Duke Francis's stronghold to rescue me if need be.' He took two quick steps, flung his arms around Jasper and kissed him soundly. 'Could aught be more hare-brained than that?'

'Who told you?' Jasper asked, pushing Henry away and refusing to be diverted by his teasing or the realization of how neatly he had been tricked by the feint of anger. 'And what difficulty could come of your lack of knowledge?'

'Little but the loss of a chance at that throne. I nearly sent away someone who came to make me an offer of it, setting him down as a liar.'

'Who never engages in hare-brained schemes? What nonsense is this, Henry? Stop your jesting. It is not meet, and it is dangerous.'

'Then, it is true? There was an act in the time of Richard II and it did not forbid the Beauforts the throne?'

'There was an act, and it did not reserve the royal dignity. Harry, what foolishness are you planning? Who could make you an offer of the throne?'

'Buckingham.'

There was a silence; then Jasper asked doubtfully, 'A trap?'

'Accompanied by a large draft upon Florentine bankers?'

65

Henry countered. 'No, the offer is confirmed by my mother and reinforced by a letter from the queen dowager offering me her daughter's hand in marriage.'

Jasper stared wordlessly at his nephew, then right through him as if he strained to see the future. At last he released his breath in a long sigh. 'If I did not know her, I would say your mother is a witch. She told me this would come about twelve years since when she begged me to fly with you. Mayhap she is more than a witch – a saint with foreknowledge. I began to think the matter was ordained, for I have known for long that you are not as other men.' Suddenly Jasper knelt. 'I desire the honour of being the first to do homage to Henry, king of England, seventh of the name.'

Henry did not smile, nor did he raise Jasper. 'You are the first,' he replied gravely, 'and when the time comes, you will be first in the eyes of all men. Before then, however, there will be much to do. Rise, Jasper, earl of Pembroke.'

'Give me orders, sire, and I will obey.'

Now Henry grinned. 'The first is that unless there be a formal swearing or other occasion, you call me Harry. I am not likely to hear that name on any other lips from this time forth. As for other orders, I will need an army to take with me. Better a small force, each one of which is a good fighting man, than a large rabble. Muster me such a force.'

'That I can and will. Do I work without Francis's knowledge?'

'No, he is committed to this venture and has promised me men and arms.' A shadow passed over Henry's face to be replaced by a somewhat cynical smile. 'Indeed, he thinks he is urging me into this. It is easier to have men and money pressed upon one – and a more sure way of getting them – than to beg such aid. And let it be done as quickly as may be.'

'Where is the need for haste? The longer I must hold a force together, the higher the cost, and these men are restless. They do not like idleness.'

'If need be, they can fight for Francis while they wait, but I do not think there will be long to wait.'

Jasper expostulated that rebellions take time to raise, but it soon became clear that Henry's guess was right. On the last day of September Hugh Conway appeared again, and this time he delivered his messages on bended knee. Buckingham pro-

66

mised to raise the whole south of England on October 18th, and Henry was to land as near to that day as possible. Francis redoubled his efforts on Henry's behalf, and by October 12th fifteen ships had been collected and loaded with the five thousand mercenaries Jasper had engaged.

The entire effort had been carried out with an efficiency surprising to all the principals except Henry, to whom the efficiency was owing. His genius for organization ensured that the ships were readied as the men appeared, that supplies were stacked where the men could be given their share without confusion as they went aboard, that, most amazing of all, the leaders of the multilingual, multinational force, worked together without dissension. Somehow the impression had been given them that to cause disruption of the plans of this leader would result in such extreme discomfort that it was far better to submerge one's dignity if that was necessary to obey orders.

Yet Henry offered no threats and little encouragement. He spoke of the venture as a certainty, but not an easy one. Man strives, Henry told the assembled leaders, but God decides the moment of success. It was possible that this effort would take England, but it was also possible it would not. Then the next effort, or the effort after that, would achieve the goal. The mercenaries were to understand that, succeed or not, their pay would be uninterrupted; if they did not succeed, they were to remain ready for another attack. There would be no disbanding of forces until Henry was king of England.

It was as well that Henry offered his men this assurance, for the moment was wrong. By the night of October 12th a gale had risen and, strive as they would, ship after ship was torn from the convoy and cast back upon the coast of Brittany. To Henry it was later evident that the storm showed the mercy of God and His favour towards the cause. As if to give him proof, his ship and one other came safe to England's coast – and the coast wherever he tried it, at Poole or Plymouth or anywhere in Devon and Cornwall, was in arms against him. Plainly, Buckingham's rising had failed. Had there been no storm, had he and his men assayed a landing, they would have been cut to pieces. Had they exercised caution and turned tail, the spirit of the men would have been broken, for they would have misunderstood and put down as cowardice what was merely discretion in their leader. No man could blame Henry for a

67

storm. He knew he had been saved from certain failure by Divine intervention, and his spirits were higher, his purpose firmer when they turned away from England's coast than when they started.

More proof of God's favour came. The wind set hard against Brittany and Henry was forced to land in Normandy. Instead of taking him prisoner and selling him to Richard, Anne, sister and regent for Charles VIII, gave him a safe passport to Brittany. She did more: in her brother's name she sent Henry money to pay his men, and a warm message of friendship accompanied the gold. This was no effort to rid France of his dangerous presence, either. If Henry wished to go to Brittany, the letter said, he could, but he should remember that France was open to him at any time and France would aid him when and as he desired.

By October 30th Henry was back at Francis's court. The duke welcomed him with pleasure and was not in the least discouraged. They must wait to discover what had fallen amiss, Francis said, but Henry was not to concern himself. There would be more money and more men. And Henry had ten thousand golden crowns from Francis then and there to prove that these were not empty words.

One thing alone preyed on his spirit – his mother's safety. Even that fear was not meant to distract him from his purpose. Before he was free of the necessary labours of meeting the needs of the flood of refugees who escaped after the failure of the rebellion, a gentleman who was no refugee and refused to give his name asked private audience. The audience was not quite private. Jasper stood at Henry's shoulder, his hand on his sword hilt.

'I must speak alone with Henry, earl of Richmond.'

'You are speaking alone with him. This is Jasper, earl of Pembroke, flesh of my flesh and blood of my blood. His ears are as mine; his silence is as mine. Speak or be still as you desire, for we are one,' Henry rejoined.

The messenger was not pleased, but after a moment he shrugged. 'I come to tell you of the welfare of Lady Margaret Stanley. It is her safety, not mine, which is at stake.'

The blood drained from Henry's face and he closed his eyes for a moment. Richard had Margaret; he held her life in hostage for Henry's. The choice was to return to England with

68

the messenger or to doom Margaret. Henry decided as quickly as the idea clarified. To go could not save his mother. Richard would kill them both or imprison Margaret with the knowledge that her son had bought her life with his. What life could she have with that knowledge? She might even be dead already and this a mere trap.

'Speak.' Henry's voice was soft, but it boded ill. He could see Jasper's free hand clinging to his chair, and he did not need to see Jasper's face to judge its expression, because the messenger paled and stepped back.

'In God's name, my lords, I am the bearer of good tidings,' he cried. 'It is only that news of my coming must not get to King Richard's ears. The Lady Margaret is safe in her husband's keeping. I am come from Lord Stanley himself to assure you of his love for her and that, though she be not free to send you news or aid, neither will she suffer distress.'

There was a long pause while Henry stared into the messenger's eyes. The man thanked God that he had been telling the truth, because the concentration in those glinting eyes seemed to harrow his soul. In fact, few men could lie to Henry, because he expected all men to lie to him and was constantly aware of hesitations and inflections others would not have noticed. His concentrated glare in this case, however intimidating, was merely a cover for his struggle with his unruly brain and stomach. So great was his relief that he had a nearly unendurable urge to vomit and faint. To show his relief, he knew, would only give Stanley a hold over him; so he swallowed his gorge and smiled. The grimace, thinning his lips and exposing his teeth, made a neat addition to the messenger's terror.

'I am glad to hear that,' Henry murmured. 'I will remember it in your lord's favour. It would be most unfortunate for him and his should any harm come to the Lady Margaret.' A few more words of slightly less threatening aspect were added as a dismissal and, at last, Henry slid a large, handsome ring from his finger and held it out to the messenger. 'The bearer of glad tidings is gladly received and joyfully dismissed. Go in peace.'

'Why did you give him that ring, Harry?' Jasper asked. 'God knows we are short of money. If you wished to be rid of it, I could have brought it to the Lombards.'

69

'That is good news,' Henry muttered to himself, 'very good, the best.'

'Of course it is good news. I tell you, I feared for your mother in my very bowels, but is that a reason to part with such a ring?'

'My mother? Oh, yes, thank God she is safe, but I did not speak of that news. Stanley is hedging against the future. If we come in force, he will not defend Richard.'

Now Jasper followed the line of Henry's thoughts, and he was made uneasy by their coldness. 'Some men do love women,' he said drily.

'Yes,' Henry replied impatiently, 'and my mother is such a woman as can easily be loved. I do not say he kept her safe to find favour with me, but he sent that messenger for no other reason. Therefore, he fears, expects or even desires my success. And if Lord Stanley feels thus, Richard's grip on England must be frail.'

'The news is good, but I still do not see the reason for giving the messenger a ring which could feed a troop of men for a week.'

'So that he, and his master through him, will not think that I need care for the value of one paltry ring.'

Henry's voice was patient, but plainly his mind was elsewhere. From then on he turned his attention more closely to the English refugees. During the next few weeks a group among them was singled out to become an inner council. Some were chosen for their birth and connections, others because they had some special ability or skill, and still others because Henry liked them as men.

The man he kept closest to him, to Jasper's dismay, was Thomas Grey, marquis of Dorset, the dowager queen's son by her first husband. To Jasper's protests that, whatever his name, Dorset was a Woodville at heart, shallow and untrustworthy, Henry made no reply other than an inscrutable smile. He had long since realized that Jasper thought as he acted, honestly and directly. If Jasper mistrusted a man, he would banish him if he could not destroy him. That seemed the height of foolhardiness to Henry, whose mind worked along other paths, especially when the man in question was powerful himself or had powerful friends and relatives. Those one must keep under one's eye, cozening them with soft words and, by

70

depriving them of all service while – if necessary – heaping them with empty honours, drain them of ability to do harm.

With the others whom Henry selected, Jasper had no quarrel, although he really approved only of Sir Edward Courtenay. Sir Edward was like Jasper himself, soldierly, honest, and, as eldest male relative, he was heir to the earldom of Devonshire, which had been forfeited by his cousin Thomas Courtenay for dying in the Lancastrian cause at the battle of Tewkesbury. Soon messengers began to pass from Courtenay to his many relatives in England extolling Henry's virtues, detailing his real claim to the throne, describing his growing strength and the increasing hope of a Lancastrian restoration. Henry, who wrote the letters, made sure to add that no Yorkist who did not actively oppose him would suffer. They would be protected by his proposed marriage with Edward's daughter Elizabeth.

Richard Edgecombe also won qualified approval from Henry's uncle. He had a decent family, a sharp wit and a smooth conciliatory manner that was very useful in dealing with men whose tempers were exacerbated by misfortune. In addition, Edgecombe had a minor genius for money, which permitted Henry to pass to him some of the problems of stretching their slender resources.

Richard Guildford fell into the same category and also won his place by having been one of the first four men active in the rebellion against Gloucester. He, too, understood money, although he was better at collecting it than at juggling figures for niggling disbursements. Also, he had a hobby which might be of great value – the science of new weapons and the means to resist them. He had a positive passion for big guns. No one else in the group knew as much about artillery or the type of defences which could withstand it. Guildford discoursed at length and at the slightest excuse of trajectories, impact force, and rigid versus flexible barriers. Henry, at least, listened whenever he could, although he was frequently reduced to helpless laughter by terms which grew so technical and so mixed with mathematical equations that Guildford might have been speaking a foreign language for all he could understand.

The other two puzzled Jasper. There was William Brandon, strong as a bull, a deadly and enthusiastic fighter, but not the type of man Henry usually sought out. If Jasper had not been as sure that Henry did not love flattery as he was that his

71

nephew was shrewder than any other man he had ever come across, he would have thought that Brandon's adulation had gained him his place on the council. Not that Brandon said much, but the sheer worship that shone in his eyes was clear to all. Perhaps Brandon had been chosen because he lightened Henry's mood. They gambled together with straws or pebbles as stakes, because Brandon was really penniless and Henry had not a penny to waste on play. They played crude jokes on others, roaring so infectiously with laughter that the butt of the jest joined the fun rather than taking offence. Henry always seemed younger and more human in Brandon's company. When he and William appeared together, men relaxed and spoke more freely than when Henry was alone.

To the constraint which most men felt in Henry's presence, Edward Poynings was an exception. Jasper reasoned correctly that his fearlessness had recommended him to Henry's notice. Besides this, however, there was outwardly nothing to set him apart from the many other gentlemen refugees. True, he was a big man, almost as strong and almost as good with lance and sword as Brandon, but so were many others. He had no notable special talents, no family or friends of great influence, and nothing beyond respect marked his manner to Henry. Yet of all the group, he was the one most often sent for in the dark watches of the night, and Jasper had once or twice seen a fleeting expression of pity and pride on his face when Henry had spoken to him and passed on.

Except for warning Henry against Dorset, however, Jasper had not expressed his opinion about his nephew's choice of advisers. More and more Jasper followed Henry's orders without comment and was satisfied to do so, satisfied that what Henry decided was best. He felt no resentment. It seemed such a natural thing, because Henry's manner was as sure and authoritative as the best of reigning monarchs'. When Jasper thought of the situation at all, he felt only astonishment that the tiny infant he had not believed would live, the loving child he had played with, had grown into such a man. Yet both the frailty and the love were still present, Jasper was reminded as he came into Henry's chamber in response to a summons. Henry was too pale, and mauve rings of fatigue showed under his eyes, but he smiled gaily and took Jasper's warm hands into his cold ones.

72

'Uncle, I do not see enough of you.'

'I have been busy – on your affairs, Harry.'

'I know,' Henry sighed. For a fraction of a second he looked uncertain. 'Will we ever have time to talk and laugh as we used to?' Jasper made no reply, and Henry's troubled expression was replaced by a mischievous smile. 'It is time to sting Richard again. Are you willing to put your neck in a noose for me?'

'Why not? A man can lose but one head, and mine is forfeit on my own account. I have little to fear in serving you.'

Henry had not released Jasper's hands and now pulled him closer to kiss him. 'You make yourself always less than you are. Uncle, I would have you summon every Englishman of note who is committed to my cause to be at the cathedral at Rennes on Christmas Day.'

'Secretly?'

'No. If there are any spies of Richard's among us, give them every chance to be present. The more, the merrier. I will have all those present swear fealty and do me homage as if I were already crowned king.'

Jasper did not question the bold move but set about his task. When he arrived at Rennes, he realized that Henry and his council had also been busy. By and large the refugees were a ragged lot, but they would not appear so on the great day. Rich clothing and masses of jewels had been begged and borrowed from wherever available, and those too destitute to provide their own finery were apparelled in borrowed plumes. The richly clad, bejewelled mass would make a brave show of power and plenty.

They were fortunate in everything, for Christmas Day dawned bright and clear. The rich colours of the robes glowed, the jewels glittered, spirits were lifted by the frosty air, and the voices of the choir sounded like those of angels filling the heavens. The interior of the cathedral, so oppressive and gloomy on a bleak day, was transformed into glory by the sun, which patterned its interior with ruby, emerald, and sapphire linked with gold and obsidian from the stained-glass windows. When mass was over and Henry, most magnificently robed of all, stood before the altar to receive the homage of his men, he knew he had done right. He had invoked and received God's blessing for his cause, and the expressions of awe and

73

dedication on the faces of the men who swore to him bespoke their devotion.

That he had succeeded in pricking Richard was clear from the counter-measures the king took. Buckingham had been executed in November, and Richard now turned his attention to the dowager queen. By working upon her vain and unstable nature, he convinced her to leave sanctuary. Elizabeth had been terrified, but at first the move seemed to have done no harm. Although he ordered that the dowager and her daughters remain under supervision, he did not approach them or urge any particular act upon them. Gradually, over the months, Elizabeth almost forgot that she was really a prisoner.

Now she knew it again, knew it with a cold terror that numbed her soul and would not even let her weep. She tried to forget, to remember only the time she had spent in Lord Stanley's household. Lady Margaret was so kind, so different from her own mother. She had mentioned Henry once and, seeing Elizabeth blush, had begged pardon and changed the subject. Elizabeth had been annoyed with herself. She wanted to know everything about Henry of Richmond. It had taken a good deal of finesse to bring up the subject again.

Lady Margaret had admitted she no longer knew her son very well – they had been long parted – but she took out some of his letters and gave them to Elizabeth to read. Elizabeth tried to recall them word for word – so tender, so loving, so playful – and the memory kept the cold terror at bay for a few moments. Of course, his letters to her were nothing like that, but that was quite proper. There had been only three. Elizabeth understood that, also. It was out of consideration for her safety. If a messenger with a letter to her had been taken, she would have been in great danger. And Henry had been right. Look what had happened when he vowed he would marry her, without even proof that she had agreed.

Now she was sorry that her own letters to Henry had been so formal. When he sent her a ring and a graceful acknow-ledgment of her acceptance of him, she had replied, sending him one of her last pieces of jewellery, a brooch; but she knew the wording of her reply had been stiff and without heart. Perhaps if she had been warmer, he would have thought less of the princess and more of the woman. But it was hard to show warmth in a letter. If she could speak to him, the

74

formal words would not matter. He would see in her eyes and her smile that she wished— Her mother could not stop the look in her eyes, Elizabeth had thought resentfully as she was made to rewrite one letter only because she had expressed a hope that she would please Henry. Her mother had scolded her. It was not Elizabeth's business to please her husband. He should be honoured by the hand of Edward's daughter even if she were a squint-eyed leper with the temper of a dragon.

That was true enough, Elizabeth acknowledged, as far as Edward's daughter and the earl of Richmond went – but what of Elizabeth and Henry? Her mother had said she was a fool. For a queen and a king there were no Elizabeths and Henrys. The earl of Richmond wanted to be king and for that purpose desired Edward's daughter. If Elizabeth did not remember who she was every moment, he would use her and then cast her aside like a worn-out clout once he was firmly established.

Elizabeth passed a dry tongue across her lips in a vain attempt to bring moisture to them. That thought had brought the cold back upon her. She tried to think of Margaret and her warm, happy household. Lord Stanley worshipped the ground Lady Margaret walked upon. Although he was not often at home, being much occupied with the king's business, his joy in returning and his sorrow at parting from his wife could not be disguised. But it was no good – no memory of safety could protect her now. Richard had begun to suspect Lady Margaret, and he had taken Elizabeth away and sent her to this bleak manor far to the north, where she was guarded like a prisoner, spied upon and treated with insolence by the women who were supposed to serve her.

With Elizabeth in his power, Richard felt more secure. Henry had sworn at Rennes to marry Edward's eldest girl as soon as he should be crowned king, but Richard had feared he would try to spirit her out of England and marry her first, thereby securing to his cause all those faithful to Edward's memory. Next King Richard sent another embassy to Brittany and, with that, Henry's luck seemed to run out.

Francis fell unconscious in the middle of a state dinner. It was Pierre Landois who received the ambassadors. Landois dared not move too quickly, because Francis had recovered in a few days from similar, though milder, attacks, but he promised

75

the envoys that if Francis remained irrational or died, Henry would be delivered to them. There was no need to act immediately, because Henry was not at court and did not know what was going on. Secure in Francis's protection, he had absented himself so that the duke's prevarications to the English ambassadors would be less obvious. After a week had passed, in which Francis remained partially paralysed and wholly incoherent, Landois stated his terms. A few days later, Richard boasted to several of his intimates that, for the small cost of Richmond's revenues and support for Landois against the nobles of Brittany, Henry Tudor would be delivered into his hands. Before Richard's elaborate letter agreeing to Landois's terms was written, a rider was careening through the night towards Dover.

The early tide found the same rider on a ship bound for Flanders, and two days later he was gasping out his message to John Morton, who had fled into exile after Buckingham's rebellion failed. The original messenger was sent back to England – it would not be healthy for his master to be mixed into this business – and Christopher Urswick, a trusted aide of Morton's, rode post-haste for Brittany. He found Henry at Vannes, much troubled by the news of Francis's illness, which had only then reached him, but when Urswick spoke his piece, Henry merely nodded.

'One thing must have led to the other. Can you endure another long ride, Urswick?'

'Aye, my lord.'

'Then, off to France with you. When you have eaten, I will have letters ready requesting a passport from Charles.'

'My lord, would it not be better to chance Charles's favour and come with me now? The French have already invited you to their country. If Landois tries to take you here—'

'He will not.' Henry replied so calmly that it was clear to Urswick that the beads of perspiration on his forehead were owing to his being too close to the fire. Indeed, he moved away from it just then. 'Landois has not yet enough power to call up the Breton nobles against me, and my forces are concentrated here at Vannes. He would need an army to take me. Why should he expose himself to such danger? He has sent me word of Francis's illness, and I doubt that he believes I could yet have word of his intentions. He must think that I will come very

76

soon to visit the duke. Then he will have me trapped without effort.'

That night Jasper and Edward Poynings were summoned to Henry's chamber. They found him already in bed, his eyes too bright and his face pale in the candlelight. Henry's news was received with a bitter oath from Jasper, who began to pace the room angrily, and with a frown by Poynings, who asked stolidly, 'Do we fight or run, my lord?'

'Neither. I have sent a message to ask how Francis does and whether he would be able to receive me. The answer will be affirmative, of course, but my messenger will have trouble on the road and be very slow in returning. By the time he does come here, I hope we will have word from Urswick. Meantime, uncle, you will set out with Edgecombe, Dorset, Courtenay, Guildford, and a suitable armed troop to pay your respects separately and ask how Francis does. As soon as you are able, ride for the border, instead, and take refuge in France.'

'But what about you, Harry?'

'If I can avoid a clash with the Bretons, even those favouring Landois, I must. No armed troop of which I was a part will move anywhere in Brittany – especially towards the border or out of the country – without opposition. I will follow later.'

Henry bit his lips. He was frightened, and he did not wish to be separated from Jasper. The two parts of him warred briefly, the small boy who needed to hide in Jasper's arms and the reasoning man who had decided upon the least dangerous of several unsatisfactory moves. When he turned to Poynings, nothing was left of the small boy but a shadow in his eyes and a hollowness in his stomach. 'Ned, you are the sacrifice. Are you willing?'

'If a sacrifice is necessary and I am most suitable – I suppose I am willing.'

'You are the only all-round able military commander besides my uncle. You must remain here to control the bulk of the men. I will also leave Sir Edward Woodville – not that he will be of much help, but his ships might be useful. Stay here quietly if you can. If Landois moves against you, use your judgment as to withstanding him or crowding all the men you can aboard Woodville's ships and abandoning the others. Tell them to spread through the countryside and name Landois as their pursuer. I think – I pray – they will be sheltered. Ned' – Henry's

77

voice was pleading – 'I am leaving you a disagreeable task.'

'So you are,' Poynings replied unemotionally, 'but some-one must handle it, and I will do as well as I am able.'

'But what will you do, Harry?' Jasper insisted.

'I am not yet sure. I must seize the best opportunity which presents itself, and what that will be I cannot tell, being uncertain as a reader of crystals.' Nor could either of you tell, Henry thought, if you were taken and questioned.

The lie he had told did not trouble him; Henry was never troubled by lying, because he did so only after considerable thought and with a firm conviction that untruth was the best and safest device. The same reason made it virtually impossible to trap him in a lie, because he uttered it with the force and flow of truth, without doubt or hesitation. His manner, therefore, was perfectly natural when he woke William Brandon before dawn of the day following his receipt of a French passport.

'Slug! Will you sleep all this fair day or will you ride hunting with me?'

'Softly, my lord,' William groaned, 'I was making merry last night.'

Henry laughed. 'Then, you must come. The air will clear your head, and I will explain why it is better to work all night than drink all night.'

Brandon was already out of bed and dressing, although he moved gingerly. 'I know. I have heard it before. You say you look no better than I, but your head does not ache and—'

'Yes. I see you know the words but have not learned the lesson. Well, the horses are ready saddled. Come below as silently as may be. The game is hunted out hereabout, but I have heard of a boar. You and I and the huntsmen alone, William. I do not want to share this sport with the others.'

They walked their horses without haste through the courtyard and down the streets, which were barely beginning to stir for the day's activities. No one paid any attention to the party clad and weaponed for hunting; it was too common a sight. They were first out of the gates, but that, also, was too common a practice for hunting parties to merit notice. Once free of the town, they loosed their reins and the fresh mounts gladly quickened pace into a gentle canter. William Brandon was too taken up with his physical discomfort to have noticed

78

that the men accompanying them were not in truth huntsmen but Henry's personal servants. He did notice that they clung to the still-empty road and travelled east, but only because the lightening sky was tormenting his eyes.

When Henry turned off the road into a little knoll of woods, however, Brandon really woke up. 'Sire, you cannot think there is a boar in this wood. It is no more than a marker between fields.'

'I do not think there is a boar in any wood hereabouts, Will. You and I have killed them all.'

Henry slid down from his horse and, under Brandon's startled eyes, began to undress. He threw off his rich cloak, pulled the sleeves loose from his brigandine and cast away boots and hose. One servant was gathering up and packing these items; another offered replacements in coarse homespun with a servant's tunic to cover all. Then a fine chain-mail shirt was unrolled from a saddlebag.

'Stop gawking, Will,' Henry laughed. 'Do you want to be sent back to England and lose your head? Well, I do not. Nor is it to my taste that the traitor Landois should grow fat on Richmond's revenues. We fly for France. Now, off with that cloak and on with the mail. You are a gentleman travelling with five servants. You visited me, found my court too poor and are taking yourself to Landois – if anyone asks. Come now, do not look so aghast. You are the only weapon I brought. Can you see me safe into France, William?'

'While blood and breath are in my body, I will see you safe into and out of anywhere – hell included, my lord.'

Henry laughed aloud. 'Onward, then. Be you sword and shield to me.'

Actually, he expected no trouble. It was nothing uncommon for him to ride out hunting and return only late in the evening. They had probably a full day and possibly even a day and a night before Landois's spies would grow uneasy and report his absence. By then they should be safe in France. Henry, however, had counted a trifle too much on Landois's caution and too little on the eagerness of Richard's envoys. It was not difficult to extract a letter from Francis demanding Henry's presence to comfort him. His muddled mind had forgotten the envoys and the danger and longed for his fosterling's soothing voice and calm manner. Perhaps the duke even dimly

79

understood he was almost a prisoner and felt that Henry could save him.

Armed with this missive, which Henry would not dare disregard, Landois's men had entered Vannes just about the time Henry left by another gate. It did not take them long to discover that the quarry was gone. Had they been Francis's men, who half accepted Henry as their next master, they would have sat down to wait his return. Landois, however, was too clever for that. The troop were mercenaries in his own pay, their captain a clever, suspicious man whose swift inquiries established that neither dogs not huntsmen had accompanied Henry. Poynings's assurances that Henry's clothing and valuables were still in his chamber went for nothing. If Henry was hunting, no harm could be done by joining him to make sure he returned; and if he had tried to escape, they would certainly be able to capture him.

Chapter Seven

Henry Tudor raised his head from his arms. The accounts on the table seemed to be muddling his brain even with his eyes closed. He stared out through the narrow window. Did the sun never shine in France, even in the spring? Henry looked down at his hands, which had always been thin and beautiful; they looked like emaciated claws, and his normally brilliant eyes were dull as he stared at them. It was nearly a year since he had escaped Landois, and the horror of that ride, twisting and turning, backing and hiding, without food, without sleep, day after day, was nothing to the horror of this past year.

At first it had not been too bad. He had been welcomed so warmly that his distaste for asking help from France had almost been removed. It seemed that he would have little to do but get his men safely out of Brittany and that money, ships, and more men would be showered upon him, ensuring his success. But Henry, who thought he understood court factions and intrigue, found he had much to learn. Francis's court was small and the plotting of the Breton nobles a childish game compared with the war of words and policies in which he was now enmeshed.

The first lesson came when Francis recovered sufficiently to understand what had happened. His steady affection was displayed at once by releasing Poynings and Woodville from what nearly amounted to a state of siege, sending money to them and giving his permission for the small army to join Henry in France. Instead of stimulating French fervour, this piece of good fortune gave it a sharp check. Henry realized that the French cared little who sat on the throne of England so long as that country continued to be torn by civil war. They would help him, but not to an overwhelming victory.

Henry changed his attitude skilfully. He had been trying to convince the French council of Richard's weakness, his own strength, and his ability to win a swift, sure victory. Now he exhibited uncertainty; Richard was strong in the north, he confessed, and it might take a long time to bring the country to heel. He would need French help – perhaps for years. His pleas for that help and his protestations of gratitude stuck in his throat so that he could not eat and was constantly sick at his stomach.

The manoeuvring, however, brought a piece of good fortune – the best he had had in a very long time and one that lasted his entire life. Henry had bowed gravely and turned away from a conversation with the duke of Orleans, the leader of one of the political factions, when he was approached by a man of about his own age clad in sober priestly robes.

'My lord of Richmond?' the man asked in English.

'Yes?' Henry replied rather curtly. He could little afford another refugee in his tail, especially a priest who could not fight and had no power.

The priest smiled. 'I do not desire your help, my lord, but wish to offer my own to you.'

'Then, I thank you,' Henry said more pleasantly but still non-committally. Help was seldom offered without a price, and the price was usually more than the help was worth or Henry could afford. 'But to whom do I speak?'

'My name is Richard Foxe. It will mean nothing to you now, my lord, but I think you will remember it.'

The assurance made Henry turn his full attention on the speaker, but Foxe did not flinch under that searching stare. 'Indeed I may,' Henry murmured. Then, smiling, 'And what help would you offer, Dr Foxe?'

Foxe's hand stroked the furred facing of his gown. 'You know the orders of the church, it would seem,' he said approvingly.

'Enough to recognize the gown of a doctor of canon law. What do you know of secular law?'

'I have made some study of it,' Foxe replied, pinching his lower lip with his fingers in a way that Henry soon learned was characteristic of amusement.

'Then, riddle me this riddle. Is any act of parliament valid regardless of its wording, and does it supersede any previous act on the same subject whether or not it refers to that previous act or is in direct contradiction of it?'

'You must give me exact particulars, my lord – and even then I will answer you only with more contradictions, evasions, and reservations. When has a lawyer done otherwise?'

82

Both men now smiled. A test had been offered and passed, since Foxe was in little doubt of the subject in Henry's mind.

'Very well,' Henry said. 'In the time of Richard II, my great-grandfather was legitimated by act of parliament – merely legitimated, without reservation. When my great-uncle Henry IV came to the throne, the legitimation was affirmed by act of parliament, but this time a reservation against receiving the crown was inserted. Since the second act stated it was an affirmation of the first yet changed the wording, is that second act valid or invalid?'

'It is of no importance,' Foxe said and held up one finger to check Henry's speech. 'You can come to the throne only in one of two ways – by conquest or by a request from the parliament that you do so after Richard has been deposed. In either case the parliament will pass an act naming you king. Now, if an act of parliament may be invalid because of pressure of circumstances and the act naming you king may be, for that reason, contested as invalid – why, then, the act of Henry IV is also invalid, since it was also passed under pressure of conquest. Then the first act – that of Richard II – is valid and you have the best hereditary claim to the throne and may take it by right.'

Henry nodded, but Foxe's finger went up to keep him silent again.

'But,' the priest continued, 'if any act of parliament is valid, whatever its wording or circumstances, then the act naming you king will be valid and will supersede the act which denied your family the royal dignity. Thereupon, you will be king by law and none may contest that right.'

The answer was as full of holes as an old sieve, but since the Yorkist claim was equally full of holes, resting on a line broken twice by females as well as on deposition, murder, and conquest, it was good enough. Henry liked Dr Foxe, enjoyed his cynical humour and took pleasure in a mind at least as sinuous as his own. He entrusted him with small diplomatic commissions, then with more important and exacting ones. Their mutual admiration and esteem grew. Richard Foxe was more cosmopolitan than any other man in Henry's entourage and less inhibited by hereditary hatred of the French. When even Edgecombe's diplomatic smoothness was marred by distaste and distrust, Foxe never failed.

83

However, neither Henry's winning ways nor Foxe's agile reasonings were able to break the deadlock between Regent Anne and the duke of Orleans. Both professed themselves eager to help Henry win the English throne, but neither could agree on ways and means or, for that matter, endure that the other should have a scrap of credit. Their obstructiveness nearly destroyed Henry's health but also brought him another piece of good luck. In the seven long months of argument, the earl of Oxford, whose connections were wider and whose family was more powerful than Courtenay's, convinced his Yorkish jailer that Richard of Gloucester was a monster and that Henry Tudor was the hope of England. Prisoner and jailer who had, despite their positions, become close friends in the ten years of Oxford's confinement, fled to Paris. Another wedge was driven into Richard's hold upon England.

With the acquisition of Oxford, however, the pendulum had reached its apex and began to swing backwards. Richard had time to work upon the gullible dowager queen, and she sent messenger after messenger to her equally volatile son, Dorset. Seeing no sign of movement in Henry's favour at the French court, Dorset was easily convinced that his best chance lay with Richard. With the ingratitude and lack of loyalty characteristic of the Woodvilles, Dorset deserted, stealing out of Paris at night to ride for the coast. The action did not catch Henry unaware; Dorset had given away his uneasiness and his intentions in myriad ways. Jasper went thundering after him and brought him back before news of his defection could get out and do harm. Under strict command from Henry, Jasper smiled and spoke sweet words, but murder glared from his hot eyes and Dorset returned meekly, uttering glib excuses and protestations of loyalty.

Henry turned his eyes from the window to the papers strewn on the table, but the figures on them were blurred by a mist of unshed tears. Dorset was the first; all too soon there would be others. His men were weary of exile and poverty; the hope upon which they had fed was proving to have little nourishment in it, and their spirit was steadily failing. The mercenaries had long since been dismissed; Henry had no money with which to pay them. England seethed with discontent, but there was no one to organize that discontent into active rebellion. If he invaded England now, Henry thought, would they not surely fail if they had failed when supported by a man like Buckingham? Yet if he did not move now, he would soon have no support at all.

'I am afraid,' Henry whispered to himself, 'oh, I am so afraid. If I fail, I will die.'

The word hung on the air, and Henry considered it with slowly rising anger. Had Edward left him in peace, he would never have been a threat. He could have been won to loyalty. Had Richard permitted Edward's son to rule and resisted the temptation of making a bloody shambles of England's nobility, he would have married Anne of Brittany and lived in peace. What sort of life had the men of York left him? Even if he renounced his claim, would Richard cease to persecute him? To die was better than to live in fear. Henry opened the door to the antechamber of his room and told the servant to summon his council – except Dorset, he added thoughtfully.

'Gentlemen,' he began after kissing Jasper affectionately, 'we can do no more here. As long as we linger in Paris, Orleans and the regent will block each other and do nothing. More important, the spirit of the men fails and the hopes of those in England become weaker. It is time to risk all, for soon we shall have nothing to risk. This, at least, is how it seems to me. Do any of you have reason to believe otherwise?'

From Brandon, Courtenay, Pembroke, and Oxford there were sighs of relief. The negotiations had tried their martial spirit. Poynings, Edgecombe, and Guildford muttered approval. Foxe alone spoke.

'I think if you begin to act, my lord, we will get some help from the French. It will not be what we need – we will never get that – but it will be something.'

'Money?' Guildford and Edgecombe asked together.

'Ah, yes. Well, that outlook' – Henry gestured towards the account-laden table – 'is not overly bright.'

'I can pledge my lands,' Oxford offered. 'Since they are not now mine, that will not bring much, but some banker will surely risk a few thousand crowns.'

Henry smiled. 'You do not speak often, Oxford, but when you do you say something.'

There was no need for anyone else to speak. All were busy stripping off every item of value that remained to them and piling the things on the table. Henry knew that their winter

85

furs, their extra clothing, everything but arms and armour would soon be in the hands of the moneylenders and the coins would come to swell his meagre treasury.

'I will get what I can from the men,' Guildford offered.

Foxe sucked his thin lips. 'You may count on twenty or thirty thousand livres upon my part. You have friends, my lord, and we priests' – he smiled – 'are experts at extortion.'

'And I think I can have the same, or more, from the French,' Henry said.

'How?' Jasper asked. 'You told us but a moment since that no more could be looked for from them.'

'No more freely given help. This money will be borrowed upon good surety.'

'In God's name, what surety have we that is not already pledged?'

Henry laughed softly. 'Dorset.' He laughed again at the general look of incomprehension. 'He is the best. If we fail, Richard must have him back to keep the dowager queen from making more trouble, so he will repay the loan. If we succeed, I will be obliged to ransom my wife's half brother.' A flicker of distaste showed in Henry's face and as swiftly disappeared. He did not relish a marriage with Elizabeth of York, but it was the path to the throne and he knew he must tread it.

'Aye, aye,' Foxe nodded, 'I can make most excellent play with those thoughts. Leave it to me, my lord, and I will have more than you hope for by playing one group against the other.'

'Then, we will leave for Rouen to gather a fleet on the Monday following the Sunday of the next full week. Bourchier may stay to guard Dorset until we have the French gold. After that we need not trouble about him. The French will look to their own surety.'

The plan moved smoothly enough, although Foxe also remained in Paris to squeeze out every penny he could and to keep eyes and ears alert for any favourable or unfavourable sign regarding Henry's cause. Vessels were commissioned, and Henry and his men made ready to move to Harfleur to board ship.

In the bleak north of England, Elizabeth had been no happier than Henry. Although her freezing terror had receded into a

86

little cold core in her heart as day followed dreary day, her boredom and loneliness were becoming almost as hard to bear. Her warm and affectionate nature yearned for a friendly face; her mind yearned for some stimulation. Even in sanctuary there had been people to talk to: the priests, for instance, had often visited her to discuss books and music. Finally, as reports that she was pining drifted back to King Richard from Elizabeth's keepers, some contacts with the world were allowed. Now and again a priest or a friar came to discourse on the will of God and the beauties of submission to that will. One day a lay brother bearing a packet of books and letters from the dowager queen craved and gained admittance. After the letters had been read and the books had been examined to be sure no treasonous matter was in them, the young man was brought into Elizabeth's presence. The ladies stood watching. They were not suspicious, but they had been instructed to overhear all of the princess's conversations.

If the ladies were fooled, Elizabeth was not. Books from her mother? There could not be a more unlikely gift. The cold began to creep outward from its place in her heart, but she could do nothing – only stare at the jewelled missal in her hands. Underneath the rich velvet cover, there was a raised oblong area. She would never have noticed it – as the ladies had not noticed it – if the young lay brother who brought her the gift had not pressed her fingers against it as he placed the book into her hands. After he left, Elizabeth sat silent with the book in her lap. Did she dare open it? If any of the women who served her found the missal with its cover torn, Richard would be informed she had received a message. Trembling with nervousness, Elizabeth began to turn the pages of the book.

When she came to the prayers for the dead, her breath caught and she thought for a moment she would faint. Very small, beside the illuminated capital, in Lady Margaret's fine hand were the four letters: ANNE. It could mean only one thing: her Aunt Anne, the queen, was dead. Elizabeth had to get that scrap of paper. Lady Margaret had dared much to send this to her; she was under house arrest, Elizabeth knew. One of the ladies Richard had appointed to serve her – and spy on her –' had told Elizabeth gloatingly that she need no longer look for succour to her great friend the wife of Lord Stanley. He had barely been able to save her; only his nearly hysterical

87

insistence had preserved Lady Margaret from being sent to the Tower, and Lord Stanley had done himself no good by his devotion to his wife. The king no longer trusted him much, and his eldest son by his first wife, Lady Strange, was in the king's household as a hostage for his father's fidelity.

Clutching the missal to her breast, Elizabeth made her way to her small private chapel. The ladies followed, of course, but they knelt behind her. Holding the missal so that her body shielded it, she began to pray while her fingers fumbled at the back cover. It was fortunate her hands were trembling, for one of the erratic movements of her fingers sent her pointed nail through an almost invisible slit. Suppressing a cry, Elizabeth slid another finger into the slit and slowly withdrew a tiny scrap of paper.

'Dear child,' she read, 'God protect you. Have courage. Try to resist. He who loves us both comes soon.'

Soon? How soon was soon? Would soon be soon enough?

Henry heard the news that Richard's queen was dead and that a strong rumour that he would marry his niece Elizabeth was current only a few days later at Harfleur. His months of frustration and nervous tension erupted in a fit of screaming rage as Jasper had not seen since his nephew's early childhood.

'The murderous, incestuous devil,' he stormed, pounding his fists against the wall. 'I will see him dead or be dead myself. There is not room on the earth for such filth as that.'

'Harry, you will hurt yourself,' Jasper cried, taking his nephew into his arms to restrain him. 'Do not rage so. It is but a rumour. How can he get a dispensation for such a marriage?'

'I swore I would not kill my enemies,' Henry panted, writhing in his uncle's grip as the cramps which accompanied his rage tore him. 'I swore I would not let blood like those monsters of York, but Richard of Gloucester will die.'

'Ay, ay, to that we are all pledged,' Jasper soothed. 'Come, lie down. Even if Richard should contrive to marry the girl by some evil ruse, Edward had other daughters. The girls are all equal as heirs general. You need not marry the eldest. Do not fret yourself so.'

'She is mine, I tell you. He cannot have her.' Henry's voice rose again, quivering on the edge of hysteria.

88

Jasper knew that Elizabeth had written to Henry several times and had even sent him a token of her hair in a ring, but Henry had never given the slightest sign that these advances had more than political significance for him. 'Have you taken a fancy for the girl, Harry?' he asked now.

'Fancy? How could I have a fancy for the daughter of a man who hunted me like a wild beast and whose mother cozens the murderer of her own children?' Henry propped himself against the bolster of his bed and pressed his hands against his flat abdomen. 'What has my fancy to do with these matters?' he said more calmly. 'She is the best known of the princesses, the one who stands for Edward in the minds of the people. Moreover, she was promised to me. She is mine, I say, and no other man will have her.'

Jasper drew a chair to his nephew's bedside and patted his hand. At this point the child Jasper remembered would have burst into tears, but the man merely drew up his knees, pressed the heels of his hands into his eyes and did silent battle with his pain-racked body.

'We cannot wait much longer, uncle,' he said wearily at last. 'Will you tell those whose duty it is to hasten the readying of the ships and supplies.'

'Harry, you are sick. You have not been well for months. You know we cannot leave here until you have your health again. We go to battle, not to a May Day feast in England.'

'I will be ready when men and ships are ready. I tell you, uncle, there will be neither peace for my mind nor health for my body until that dirty beast called Richard of Gloucester is dead.'

Jasper was surprised and uneasy when Henry's mood was unchanged the following day. It was not like him to act in passion nor, because he knew too much of men as a whole, to condemn any one man harshly. Usually Henry was far too tolerant for Jasper's taste; it was not natural for him to be vindictive. Protest being useless, however, preparations were hurried along, and it began to seem as if the low ebb had been reached and the tide would turn in their favour again. Foxe came hurrying from Paris accompanied by Philibert de Shaunde with an armed force of doubtful quality and mules laden with heavy coffers. Then from Wales came a letter from one John Morgan, promising Henry the support of Rhys ap Thomas and Sir John Savage, the two leading figures in Wales. Margaret was still technically a prisoner, but, Morgan wrote, Bray had collected a fine sum of money which was in his hands ready for Henry's use. Bray's activities, although supposedly unknown to Lord Stanley, probably had his concurrence, so there was still good hope that Stanley would change sides.

On August 1st, 1485, Henry stepped aboard the soundest ship of his little fleet. Two thousand men made up his entire force. Most of these were the dregs of the French gutters and prisons, but this unsavoury group, led by Philibert de Shaunde, was bolstered by Englishmen desperate to win back their lands and a decent life. All were ready to embark. There was no confusion, no disorder. The tide began to run out, the evening breeze to blow off the land; the sun set in glory. In Wales, the land of his birth, Henry would seek rebirth as king of England.

This time there was no storm. Each day the sun rose; each day a steady, strong breeze blew. They sailed west, rounding the Pointe de Barfleur, past Cherbourg and round the Cap de la Hague. Henry strained his eyes southward, seeking across the unquiet waters the tiny town on the coast of Brittany that had welcomed him fourteen long years before. He could not see it, but he knelt on the deck and prayed for Francis and for the country that had been so kind to him. When he rose, he looked northward where the coasts of Devon and Cornwall lay. They sailed well west of Land's End, not desiring to be spotted from that point and so give warning of their coming. Then north and east again with the wind backing and changing as if it had been instructed to aid them. No ship was lost, and even Henry, a notably bad sailor, suffered only the slightest mal de mer.

In the forenoon of the seventh day, the kindly green land showed clear. Henry gripped his uncle's arm with fingers that made the newly donned mail bite into the flesh.

'Pembroke, uncle, there is Pembroke.'

'Aye.' Jasper's voice shook and the land was blotted out by the tears that filled his dark eyes. 'You were born there, Harry, and I love it as I love no other place on earth.'

Steadily the land grew near. Quietly, without challenge or opposition, the ships sailed into Milford Haven. Despite restraining hands, Henry broke free and was the first ashore. He dropped to the ground and kissed the earth, bareheaded, indifferent for the moment to the dictates of caution which ordinarily ruled his behaviour. There was little danger, for Brandon, Poynings, and Pembroke had leapt ashore after him full-armed and with drawn swords. For once Henry produced a really startling effect without consciously seeking it. When he lifted his face from the earth, he lifted his voice in praise of God out of the fullness of his heart, and the men picked up the hymn and sang it as they marched ashore.

'*Judica me, Deus, et decerne causam meam,*' they thundered, following Henry's pleasant tenor, and the volume of sound startled him from his dream and made his fair complexion flush.

Henry looked at his three scowling guards and laughed. 'Do not be so cross. No harm can come to me this day.'

Before the words had left his lips, however, a mounted man, fully armed and with drawn sword, approached them. 'Henry of Richmond,' a deep voice bellowed, 'bide where you are.'

As one, Brandon, Poynings, and Pembroke leapt before Henry, but the antics of the man who had accosted them prevented them from attacking. He dismounted, shed his helm and began to struggle, one-handed, to remove his breastplate. This accomplished, he left his audience goggle-eyed by lying down on the ground.

'Come,' he roared, 'step over me.'

Henry shouldered past a stupefied Brandon and Poynings, but Jasper caught his arm. 'It is a trick. He will thrust up at you from the ground.'

'But, uncle,' Henry choked, 'what an uncomfortable and unusual method of assassination.'

Still laughing, he stepped across the body to where Brandon and Poynings, recovered from their shock if not from their surprise, waited for him with drawn swords threatening the giant's unarmed body.

'Ha!' the great voice offered. 'I have fulfilled my oath.' He proffered his sword, hilt first, to Henry and added in a rather lower roar, 'Do you know me, sire?'

Fourteen years flashed away in Henry's mind. He saw again the massive form before the gates of Pembroke, heard the bull-like bellowing voice. Morgan ap Thomas he knew was dead, but this must be his kinsman Rhys.

'You must be Rhys ap Thomas,' he ventured.

'That I am, sire, Rhys ap Thomas.' The man was flattered that his fame had preceded him. 'I swore to King Richard that you would enter Wales only over my belly – and so you have done.'

Henry gurgled and his guardians gasped. 'My dear Rhys,' Henry said in the halting Welsh he had learned as a child as he handed the sword to Pembroke and extended his hand, 'do let me help you rise. Never again shall I say that a Welshman does not keep his oath.'

'You should know,' ap Thomas replied in English. 'You are a good part Welsh yourself – not to mention having been born and raised here. I must go, sire. I have come secretly only to do what I have done. You will hear soon that John Savage and I will fight for Richard – do not believe it.'

'And you will hear that I intend to set Englishmen over the Welsh. Do not believe that, either.' Henry smiled sweetly. 'As a Welshman keeps his oath, I will make you lord lieutenant of Wales if I destroy Richard of Gloucester with your help.'

'Then we will both be content,' ap Thomas growled, 'for you have always wanted to be king and I have always wanted to be lord lieutenant in name as well as in fact.'

'Do you believe him, Harry?' Pembroke asked after he had returned the sword and ap Thomas had mounted and ridden away.

'Of course,' Henry replied. 'What good would it do me not to believe him? But I will trust him when I see his forces fighting under my banner – not sooner.'

The horses having been brought to shore, they rode north to Haverfordwest still without opposition. Here, in fact, Henry was greeted with shouts of approval.

'King Henry, King Henry,' the crowd thundered. 'Down with the bragging white boar.'

Here, too, they received the news Rhys ap Thomas had warned them about and the more cheering message that Pembroke was still faithful and was sending its men to support its earl and king in their struggle. The council met in a convenient field on horseback, since there were no better seats. Henry first called for opinions and listened intently to what was said.

'It is agreed, then,' he summed up, 'that the north will hold by Gloucester, that the south favours me but is fearful of rising because of the bad outcome of the last rebellion, that Wales is largely mine and that the issue will be strongly influenced by the decision of the Stanleys. We must, therefore, give a show of strength and drive the Stanleys to some decision as quickly as possible. Time can only favour Gloucester.'

'We need time, too, sire,' Oxford ventured. 'We must have more men.'

'True, but we are in no state to sit still and wait for them to come to us. We must pick them up as we move. It is the part of wisdom to cut the white boar off from the northern piglets who love him. Those of the south whom he can force to take arms will fight with scarce half a heart. Let us move north, then, but not directly across the mountains for there are not enough men there. Those of the wild tribes who wish to join us will come out of the hills to do so. Let us sleep tonight at Cardigan.'

'It is garrisoned,' Jasper said thoughtfully, 'but not overstrong. I think, sire, it will open to us or fall, providing a decent show of strength.'

Jasper was quite correct. John Morgan and Richard Griffith joined them on the road, Cardigan opened her gates without hesitation, and people lined the streets, chanting in Welsh. It was too much for Henry, but John Morgan translated:

'Jasper will breed for us a dragon.
Of the fortunate blood of Brutus is he
A bull of Anglesey to achieve.
He is the hope of our race.'

'Well,' Henry said in a moderate aside, 'handsome I am not, but no one ever called me a dragon before.'

Nonetheless, he did not fail to make use of the idea. The tailors of Cardigan were summoned, and the famous red dragon of Cadwallader came to life again on Henry Tudor's battle banner. Owen Tudor, Jasper's father and Henry's grandfather, had claimed to be of the line of Cadwallader, the famous Welsh king who conquered and ruled England. Henry was not going to let that go to waste.

Jasper had loved Wales and served her well, and the bread he had cast upon the waters was returning. Henry, for his part, made sure that the bread did not turn bitter in the mouths of

93

the people. The French soldiers were watched as carefully as if they had been prisoners to be sure that they committed no outrages, and Henry paid for every bite of food and drop of ale that was not offered as a free gift. For the moment he had sufficient funds, and he knew the campaign could not last long. If they conquered, he would have all England and an assortment of confiscated rich estates to replenish his coffers. If they failed, he would be dead and free of debt.

News of his moderate and thoughtful behaviour outran him, as he knew it would. The next day Aberayron opened its gates as soon as the van of his army appeared, and shouts of 'King Henry, Harry the king,' echoed through the streets as they passed. Llanrhystyd did even more, for the people carried bread and ale and fish out to the marching men, and the maidens and women bestowed kisses freely, running along the ranks.

Both towns yielded some men, also, but Henry was playing the genial monarch with a none-too-light heart. He rode bareheaded and smiling, the sun glinting from his polished armour and his golden hair. He called greetings in Welsh and praised and promised in the people's own tongue. Not for nearly a thousand years had the Welsh heard their own language on the lips of a king of England; the news spread, as did the tale of the red dragon of Cadwallader, and the bards sang the ancient prophecies of a Welsh ruler on the English throne in each village. Before the end of the day, the fierce hillmen, fighters without match although their individualistic behaviour often defeated them, began to trickle down to swell Henry's forces.

Pembroke took the hillmen under his wing, knowing all too well their strengths and weaknesses and knowing, also, that they would only respond to commands – when they responded to them at all – in their own tongue. It was good; every man helped and the very sight of the Welsh hillmen would spread terror in an opposing force, but it was not enough. Neither sight nor news of ap Thomas had come to Henry, and without him and Savage the only large, trained fighting force in Wales was out of the Tudor's grasp.

Still, not a weapon or voice had been raised against them until they came to Aberystwyth. Here the garrison was strong, for Wales, and the gates were closed. Henry donned his helmet and watched Jasper and Oxford deploy their forces with a sinking heart. If he had to fight Welshmen with Welshmen – if they were delayed in cutting off the northern levies from Richard – they were lost. No blow was struck, however. The gates burst open and the garrison streamed out, unarmed, shouting:

'Richmond, sprung from British race,
From out this land the boar will chase.'

They had turned on their officers, these Welsh troops, when Cadwallader's dragon came into view, and they came to offer their service to their 'own' king. Henry offered his hands to kisses, received a trembling deputation of townsfolk bearing gifts and offers of free quartering for his men with kingly graciousness. The troops rested, but Henry and his council laboured through the night.

Pembroke, Oxford, Poynings, and Brandon argued tactics and planned and replanned with Shaunde the disposition of their scanty forces. They would be at Shrewsbury in two days at this rate, and if Sir Gilbert Talbot chose to fight, they had to win. Edgecombe pored over accounts, reckoning every loaf and fish that had been offered and squeezing the largest measure of ale out of every penny. Guildford examined every stronghold; begged, borrowed, and bought carts; routed out men to lash the small cannon taken from each fortified town to the best of these; marked the cannon and tried to find the gun crews which had worked them, to keep them with their own familiar pieces; tested gunpowder and searched for ammunition. Henry wrote letters – letters of high tone, headed 'By the King', ordering various people who had promised support to meet him to free his 'loving and true subjects' from 'the odious tyrant, Richard, late duke of Gloucester, usurper of our said right . . . as ye will avoid our grievous displeasure and answer it at your peril'. The letters were not conciliatory in the least. They did not beg, they ordered. Henry intended to win or die, and if he won he intended to be a king, not a puppet at the mercy of his nobles.

They marched again at dawn. Talybont opened to them, but Machynlleth was shut tight behind its walls. Henry hesitated; they could go round the town without danger, for time was important. It was also important not to show weakness. A word

95

to Brandon, who rode so close wherever Henry went that their horses seemed tethered together, brought the council galloping up.

'I can reduce it in an hour,' Guildford said scornfully, glancing at his cannons.

'Let us do so,' Oxford snapped. 'It will be an object lesson to others.'

'The Welsh carry grudges for a long time,' Pembroke muttered. 'Shall I parley with them first?'

Brandon suddenly laughed aloud. 'No time. You had better form your battle. Look.'

Henry's face set into the icy calm that covered his fear. From the north came a small army, not as large as his own but apparently well drilled, carrying the banners of Merioneth, Caernarvon, and Denbigh. Pembroke, Oxford, and Shaunde fled towards their various contingents, roaring orders. Guildford rode to his beloved guns; Brandon and Poynings with the rest of the council drew up around Henry. But the North Wales army halted, and the leaders rode forward alone – and as they rode they dipped their banners in salute.

'King Henry,' the voices came across the field. 'King of Wales and king of England! Long live King Henry.'

The lookouts on the walls of the town could not fail to see the captains dismount, doff their helms and offer their swords on bended knees. The gates opened; the captain of the garrison rode out unhelmed and disarmed. He begged for mercy, claiming his fear of Sir Gilbert Talbot as the reason for his resistance.

'We would not have fought if you stormed the town, sire,' he said, 'but when you moved on, we would have been at Talbot's mercy if we yielded without a show of fight. We are so close to Shrewsbury – so close. The townspeople were afraid.'

Henry was mild and gracious to him and to the deputation of townsfolk which followed. He assured them – with far more conviction than he felt himself – that Talbot was his man and would do them no harm. 'But resistance to your rightful king must be punished,' he said, smiling to take the sting from the words. 'Do you quarter and feed my men as your token of yielding.'

His hands were kissed with passionate fervour. The force he had now could have razed the town and looted it bare; yet the Tudor had asked no more than any king had a right to

96

expect, nothing compared with what a conqueror might take. Blessings were cried out as he passed through the streets; merchants came with free offerings of goods and money – only a tithe of what he could have demanded and received had he threatened, but Henry knew that even more glowing reports of his mercy and justice would spread. With each gain of strength, that reputation would be more important to him. If ap Thomas and Savage joined him, if Talbot chose not to fight, if the Stanleys deserted their master – then he would beat Richard. And if he beat Richard, only this reputation for justice and mercy would keep the country quiet for the months he would need to consolidate his victory and seize the reins of government in a sure grip.

If – if – Henry rubbed his smarting eyes and forced himself to eat another mouthful of the excellent meal provided for him. Where was ap Thomas? Where was Savage? What were the Stanleys doing? Where, oh, God, where was his mother? Even she had not replied to his letter, and he was sick with fear for her. Had Richard seized her? Would he murder her out of spite against her son – out of vindictive cruelty so that Henry could not savour his victory even if he won? He broke the food up in his plate, scattered some on the floor, threw some from the window, thanking God for the custom which permitted a king to dine alone if he desired. It would never do for anyone to know that the future king was too terrified to eat.

Too frightened to eat and too tired to sleep, Henry discovered later when at last he crawled into bed. For the past two nights he had been too busy to snatch more than a few hours' rest. Now that there was nothing left for him to do but wait, he could not take advantage of it. He could not even ease his tension by summoning someone to talk to. The mask of calm confidence was the strength that his entire party fed on; it must remain in place. Henry finally slept, but he woke in the morning with a splitting head and a feverish feeling. Let the army march slowly ahead, he thought. I will overtake them easily on horseback when I feel better. The immediate lessening of the pounding in his head made him smile wryly. Harry, he muttered to himself, to use your body as a weapon against others is reasonable; to let it play tricks on yourself is foolish.

A call brought John Cheney and Robert Willoughby with water for washing. Henry permitted himself to be thoroughly

97

scrubbed, since he did not know when he would have another chance, and then to be dressed and armed. Breakfast he waved away except for the ale, which he drank thirstily. It was a torment to mount and ride, and Henry was half-furious, half-worried. If it was really his own cowardice which was making him feel sick, should not the sensation pass now that he was ignoring it? What should he do if he really felt ill? At least that answer was simple. He must do just as he was doing, ill or not.

The hours passed in a daze of pain and unease, from which Henry shook himself to be as charming and gracious as ever to the chief man of the tiny village of Caerwys. They forded the Severn, which was hardly more than a stream at this point, and turned to Newtown. Henry tried to think whether it would be better to travel quickly through the mountains and take Shrewsbury by surprise, even if the army was tired, or whether they should camp and rest in Wales, where they were relatively safe, and come fresh to Shrewsbury, even though the city had more warning of their arrival. The problem seemed insoluble, and Henry's consciousness that he could have decided in five minutes if he was less fearful only served to confuse him further.

Jasper pulled his horse up beside his nephew's. 'The fore riders tell me there is a large force camped around Newtown. Do we fight or try to go round?'

'Fight,' Henry replied without hesitation. 'It is one thing to leave a small town garrison undefeated behind you. It is another to leave an army there.' Jasper nodded his agreement. 'And,' Henry continued, 'send Shaunde and the French round to meet the southern road and come up behind. But bid him remember the lesson of Machynlleth and hold his attack until he hears the fighting joined. We do not wish to fall upon our friends with weapons.'

'You think they are friends?'

'I do.' Henry thought nothing of the sort. He was depressed, certain now the venture would fail, and sick with terror; but he dared not expose his insecurity. 'Nonetheless, form your battle. We must not fall into any trap, and it can do us no harm if our allies know us to be both ready and cautious.'

'Thank God for your cool head, Harry,' Jasper said. 'I would have sent the hillmen to attack without warning. If they are friends, that would have set the fat in the fire.'

98

'No surprise tactics,' Henry snapped. 'We are not here to attack our own people without provocation. Until Richard of Gloucester is in the force opposed to us, we will fight only for passage to where we must go or to defend ourselves.'

Shaunde left with his detachment and the others waited. Worn out by pain and anxiety, Henry dropped asleep, and all who saw him marvelled at his cool confidence. If the Tudor who had the most to lose was so sure, what had they to fear? The word spread through the force, and men laughed and nudged each other and spoke of the good time coming when the white boar should be driven from the land and his ravages ceased; but they spoke softly or at a distance from Henry. One does not wake a sleeping king except for urgent news.

Chapter Eight

So it was that when Henry's prediction proved true and the force camped around Newtown was identified as Rhys ap Thomas's army, Rhys himself found his monarch quietly asleep with his head on William Brandon's thigh. It made a most excellent impression, as did Henry's reaction when Jasper bent over him and said softly, 'Sire, they are here.'

Henry opened his eyes and smiled with the relief that certainty, even of death itself, will bring after long tension. 'Very well, uncle, let's have at them.'

'What, sire,' Rhys laughed, 'have things been so easy that you will fall upon your own supporters only for the sport of a battle?'

'Rhys!' Henry exclaimed, leaping up and clapping him heartily on the shoulder. 'Nay. I told my men we would find no enemies in Wales, but they are so suspicious they nearly convinced me to launch a surprise attack upon you. Uncle, will you send to Shaunde and bid him encamp with his men. I sent him round behind you, you know,' Henry said guilelessly. It would do Rhys ap Thomas no harm to know his king was not a fool.

'Had us surrounded, did you? Even though you thought us friends?'

'It does no harm to be sure – even with friends. Is Savage with you?'

'No.' Rhys shook his head. 'But do not fear him. I parted from him only yesterday, and he is surely your man. I have fair news, sire. Richard has not yet moved to arm himself. Either he does not know that you are here, or he is so sure Savage and I will stop you that he takes no heed of the news.'

'But if Talbot chooses to defend Shrewsbury, we will need every man.'

Rhys shrugged. 'There is a mixture of evils and uncertainties here. Savage, as you know, is Lord Stanley's nephew, as Talbot is his brother-in-law. Savage does not wish to join you before Talbot does – and he says Talbot will – for fear of

100

alarming Gloucester too soon. As long as the white boar trusts the Stanley clan to hold the marches against you, he will not move himself.'

To Henry it was so weak an excuse that it sounded like the knell of doom. That Rhys plainly believed what he said was little comfort. Savage would join Talbot and together they would make a stand against him. To voice his fears, however, might make Rhys turn tail. The Tudor contented himself with flattering the Welshman judiciously and setting Edgecombe to watch his every move. They camped at Newtown that night, planning how best to integrate their diverse troops and their move against Shrewsbury, and in the forenoon of August 11th they arrived before the gates of that city.

The great gates were closed, the stone walls blank. But neither cannonball nor arrow was loosed at them, and Henry forbade attack. The day passed. On the next day, Sir Walter Herbert, kinsman of the Lord Herbert who had been Henry's jailer and another of the men Gloucester had counted upon to defend Wales, brought his men to swell the Tudor's forces. On August 13th, a messenger came galloping from the west. He made no effort to avoid Henry's army and was taken and brought before the Tudor, where he identified himself as Sir Gilbert Talbot's man.

'I will tell you my message,' he said, smiling broadly.

Henry returned the smile and shook his head. 'So much do I have faith in the kinsman of my mother's husband that I do not need to hear it. My men stopped you only so that I could add my assurances to those of Sir Gilbert that no man who yields to me – whether he fought in the past for the red rose or the white – has aught to fear. All men in this nation – English, Welsh, Irish, Yorkist, or Lancastrian – who do me homage will be regarded as loyal subjects and treated alike with justice and mercy. Tell Shrewsbury to open her gates and receive me in peace.'

The messenger knelt and kissed Henry's hand. Half an hour later the great gates opened and the mayor and aldermen came out to greet the king. Shrewsbury, which could have withstood a siege of weeks or months and an attack by a force far stronger than Henry led, which could have destroyed his chance by delaying him until the loyal northern levies reached Richard, acknowledged the Tudor as her master without a struggle.

Instead of feeling better, Henry felt worse. As he looked back over the past two years, he realized he had never really believed in this enterprise. At the time of the Buckingham rebellion, and even after it failed, he had been upheld by some vague, delightful dream of satisfaction and fulfilment. Reality had wakened him in France, and since then he had struggled on because there was nothing else he could do. Whatever he had suffered in the past – shame, anger, and fear – the emotions had been deadened by his overwhelming despair and his sense of the ultimate impossibility of his goal. Suddenly it was possible – really possible – that he would be king of England. Sir Gilbert Talbot had ordered Shrewsbury to open its gates and had promised to join his force on the morrow. There was, also, a letter from Sir John Savage saying that he was encamped some miles east of Shrewsbury and awaited Henry's commands. The actions were a guarantee that the Stanleys would do nothing to hinder him, even if they did not join him.

Ambition, having burst through the shell of desperation, tore Henry as the mythical eagle's beak and claws had torn Prometheus. Henry, too, felt chained to a rock, helpless under that agonizing assault, for there was no action he could take either to further his ambition or to drive it out. The candles guttered and Henry knew he should go to bed – but to lie in the dark and suffer this tearing—

'Tell Poynings to come to me,' he ordered Cheney, who had been dozing in the antechamber, and turned to the window to stare out into the blackness, biting his knuckles until he drew blood.

'Sire?'

'I am sorry to break your rest,' Henry said briskly, having gestured dismissal to Cheney, 'but I wish—' His voice faltered. His eyes went blank, the clear grey now limpid, and empty. 'Ned— Ned, I wish – I want to be king.'

Poynings had no desire to laugh at the ridiculous statement, which was as close as Henry could come to saying he was afraid he would not be king. He felt an intense sense of relief, for he had been wondering how long Henry could feed others on his confidence without absorbing some from someone else to replenish his stock. But confidence had to be administered to Henry carefully. Cheerful assurance, like flattery, invariably brought a negative reaction from the Tudor. Tell him he was wise, and Henry would anxiously search his mind for the last foolish thing he had done; tell him victory was certain, and he would be sure you were covering an expectation of defeat with bravado.

'So you shall be, sire. Either that or dead – and then you will want nothing.'

Sense came back into the grey eyes. 'That is true. I will be king or dead. There will be no more running.'

'Well, at least it is a matter completely within your own control.'

Edward Poynings understood his value to Henry Tudor. He had no wealth, no influence, no special skill. He had also no imagination; he did not catch fire from people or surroundings and his comprehension, particularly of the future, was purely intellectual. He could plan towards the future, understanding that either good or bad could come, but the good raised no thrill of hope and the bad raised no thrill of fear in him. Both were abstractions which could not touch his emotions. What Henry wanted from him was a listening ear that could not be distressed, and a mind which, capable of keeping a goal in sight, concentrated only on immediate practical steps towards that goal. Henry could see long-range probabilities on his own. Often, indeed, these became more real to him than the situation at the moment. He became involved in 'if – thens' and needed to be jerked back to the present.

'I mean,' Poynings continued stolidly, 'that if the battle goes for us, you will be either the king or the hunter. If the battle goes against us, you can refuse to yield and die. This you can decide for yourself. It does not rest upon the whim or decision of another.'

'How long do you think we must wait to come to grips with Gloucester, Ned?'

'It will be soon. He is no coward – whatever else he is. Until now he has trusted others to stop you because he accounted you for little. Now he will come to meet you himself.'

'So I think, also. Gloucester is at Nottingham still. I purpose to move towards Nottingham to meet him rather than trying for London. How sits this with your stomach, Ned?'

'Not ill, except that Nottingham is on the direct road from York, and if there is a man left in England who will fight for Richard with good heart, that man will come from York.'

103

Henry knew that, too. He put a hand to the collar of his tunic and pulled it away from his throat, a gesture he would not have permitted himself in anyone else's company. Poynings watched with a characteristic expression of impersonal concern – concern because he was fond of his master and sorry Henry was distressed; impersonal because there was nothing to fear at present, and he was incapable of fearing the future.

'But I must do something,' Henry burst out. 'I cannot wait any longer. I am choked with patience. It seems as if everything was out of my hands, as if all that happens to me for good or ill I can have no part in. I cannot wait without power to make or mar. I do not even care any longer whether I make or I mar, so long as it is my doing.'

'Ay, sire,' Poynings nodded, 'that is why I said you would be king or dead. You must control. Another would have found a different destiny, perhaps. You will rule or die.'

Henry bit his lip and then burst out laughing. 'Do you care which, Ned?'

Poynings laughed, too; the mood was broken. 'Need you ask? If you rule, I will be fat and rich. I do not say I will die if you die – for that is not my intention – but my lot will not be a happy one.'

The laughter died out of Henry's face, and his eyes fixed on Poynings's as if they would swallow them or bore through them. Ned stood unflinching, relaxed, returning the stare. If Henry could see into the soul, as was rumoured, Poynings did not care. His soul was no cleaner than another man's; but if Henry could see that, he had seen far worse and Poynings had nothing to fear.

'You lie,' Henry murmured softly. 'You lie in your teeth, and you are a fool. You are all fools.' He turned away and Poynings was startled by the bitterness in his voice when he spoke again. 'No, you are not fools. I am the fool. You have but placed another burden on my back and fettered me with stronger chains.'

'No, sire,' Poynings protested. 'Whatever load you carry or chains you bear, you have chosen for yourself. Merely, we would not wish to die with you if you were not the man to so burden yourself. Still, I am sorry you know. We did not intend to add this fear to your others.'

Henry had turned to face Poynings again, and he ran a hand through his fair hair, laughing weakly. 'Oh, no. Why should that trouble me? Why should a man who does not fear to reach out for a sceptre care that every friend he has in the world has sworn to die in the attempt to get it for him? Go to! Go back to your bed. We are all mad together.'

But as the days passed, it seemed less and less mad a venture. Talbot appeared as promised bearing very interesting news. William and John Stanley were Henry's for the taking. William was waiting at Stafford to pledge his faith. Lord Stanley felt the same but could not be so open because his son, Lord Strange, was a hostage in Gloucester's hands. Equally good was the news that the earl of Northumberland, the great Percy who ruled the north in Gloucester's name, had not mustered the northern levies to support the king. Henry, who made a practice of accepting all news with as indifferent an expression as possible, blinked. He had always counted Northumberland as a sure enemy.

'Will Percy come to me?'

'He fears – not only Richard but his own people. But he, like the rest of us, has had enough of Gloucester. The northerners are ignorant of Richard's little ways. Moreover, their necks are not stretched for the axe blow as ours are. Percy dare not fight for you – but he will not fight against you, either.'

Nor were the hopes raised by Sir Gilbert false ones. Henry met Sir William Stanley the next day at Stafford and Sir William knelt to kiss his hand as a subject kneels to a crowned king. Henry was shocked by a wave of revulsion, however, as the reptilian eyes met his own. Not this, he thought; oh God, my mother could not write so favourably of another one such as this. He checked the thought firmly. Brothers were not always alike, and appearances did not always truly bespeak the man within. After all, Henry knew he was no beauty himself and most men did not care to meet his eyes, either.

He listened to the promises of faith and protestations of enthusiasm raised by the reports of his virtues with an unmoved face but a writhing spirit. Nor could the confirmation of Talbot's news that Northumberland had not raised the northern levies give him much pleasure. At the moment he foresaw a lifetime of association with the Stanleys and he wondered briefly if being king would be worth this penance.

'I will give orders for my army to join me here, then, Sir William,' Henry said. concealing his distaste as well as possible, 'and we will drive on to Nottingham and hunt the boar from his lair.'

'You will not find him there,' William Stanley smiled, and it was fortunate that Henry had good control over his stomach because it protested violently at the sight. 'He has summoned my brother and his other men to meet him at Leicester. We would do well to take him from the south.'

'Why?'

'Because, sire, news of your coming has passed through the country now. York has already sent to Richard to ask whether their help is needed – they did not trust Northumberland's soothing letters. If we go north, we will be caught between Richard's army and men who will fight for him without being ordered to do so.'

'But I have information that the southern levies are marching to join Gloucester now.'

'Perhaps. But if you come between them and the king – I beg your pardon, sir – between them and Gloucester, they will sit down and wait. They will not fight unless driven to it. They are Edward's men, you see, and there is war in their souls between remaining faithful to a Yorkist ruler and taking revenge on the murderer of Edward's children.'

Henry twiddled his fingers gently. His instinct was to do the opposite of any action William Stanley suggested because of his certainty that treachery was not only a matter of self-interest but a matter of amusement to Sir William. The reasoning was sound, however, and was heartily approved by the council. Instead of continuing north-east, the Tudor's army marched east by south toward Leicester. Henry still smiled and made speeches to the townsfolk, still ruthlessly and publicly punished any man caught looting or threatening the local population – but he was finding it increasingly difficult to conceal his distraction. Talbot seemed sincere enough, but it was entirely possible that William Stanley had joined his forces only to demoralize them by retreat at a crucial moment in battle.

He told his devoted guard that he wished to ride alone, and dropped farther and farther behind the main body of his army, musing desperately on whether it was more dangerous to take

106

precautions, which would display his doubt of the Stanleys' good faith, and might drive them back to Gloucester, or to pretend trust. It was a dull, lowering day and Henry, who was already so tired that he could feel no increase in his fatigue, did not notice the failing light. When his patient, plodding horse stumbled at last and he was jerked from his reverie, the fields about him were empty. Worse, it was so dark that he could hardly see the next fold in the ground, and it would soon be full night. No star, no moon – where was he? Had he ridden ahead? Fallen behind? Had he wandered off the path of the army to the north? To the south?

Already too thin and feverish, Henry knew that if he slept out all night and was wet by the coming rain, or even by the heavy dews of late August, he would be ill. He urged his mount forward again; he could not stay where he was. Before it grew too black to see at all, he came to a huddle of huts, a village so small that if it had a name at all it was known only to the inhabitants. His hail was not answered, but his sword hilt applied briskly to the door brough a sullen response.

'Open!' Henry called. 'Open, I say.'

The door opened slowly. It was fortunate that Henry had dismounted so that he could thrust his armoured body into the opening or the door would have slammed shut again. As soon as the hind saw that it was a single man and not a troop strong enough to enforce their will, the peasant wanted no part of Henry. The peasant retreated as Henry advanced. For a moment the Tudor choked in the stench; he considered retiring to the open air again. The thought was only a passing one. Here, armoured and with his sword loose in its scabbard, he was safe from the damp and the possibility of being picked up by a roving band of Gloucester's men.

'I am benighted. I seek shelter,' Henry said softly. 'I will do you no hurt. Go. Feed and water my horse. You will be rewarded.'

Dull eyes regarded him without either hostility or hope. Henry blinked in the wavering glimmer of a single rush-light and moved his hand suggestively towards his sword hilt. A slighter male figure detached itself from the gloom and went out the door.

'Whose land is this?' Henry asked.

The man mumbled a name which meant nothing to the

107

Tudor, and Henry then asked how long the landlord had held this land.

'Not long. Never long.'

Henry hooked an uneven three-legged stool from the corner and sat down with his back against the wall. It was as difficult to get speech from this hind as from his dogs, but he was somewhat curious about the dull-eyed despair. The man was not starving. The movements of the boy who had gone to feed the horse were too quick to indicate sickness or weakness. These lands were not as rich as in the south, but they were not as poor as some in Wales, either, and it could not be so bitterly hard to wrest a living from them. Of course, the man's trouble might be personal, but it was hopelessness not sorrow that marked his face. Besides, the longer he tried to pry information from this clod, the less time he would have for his own fears.

'Your landlord is good?'

That was so odd a question from an armoured knight that a spark of interest showed in the labourer's eyes. 'Not bad, but soon he will be gone and there will be another.'

'He is old? Sick?'

A mute negative shake of the head was all the reply Henry received. The door opened, the rushlight flickered; Henry reached towards his sword, and the hind gasped softly and drew back. As it was only the boy returning, Henry dropped his hand again, but the defensive gesture had struck a chord; the older man drew closer again, apparently taking in the pale tiredness of Henry's face for the first time.

'Hungry?'

This time Henry nodded mutely, and the hind grunted something into the shadows behind him. A woman came forward carrying a wooden bowl and a broken heel of bread. The ale in the bowl was little better than water, but Henry drank thirstily and then bit into the bread. Ridiculous it might be, but the hospitality offered demanded a similar courtesy from Henry's breeding. In a man's house, you made suitable conversation with him.

'Will the harvest be good?' Henry asked, thrusting back his hood.

The labourer shrugged. 'The crop is good. The harvest — who knows?'

108

That was a puzzler, and Henry found himself more and more interested in such alien processes of thought. 'If the crop is good, how can the harvest be bad?' he asked.

There was a long silence while the labourer studied his scarred, gnarled hands. Then he lifted his head slowly, as if Henry's intent gaze was forcing speech from him. Anger and bitterness showed on his face now.

'For that the likes of you will trample it down in your war.'

Henry's first thought was that either his own or Gloucester's army must be encamped nearby; his second that it must be his own, since it was unlikely that Gloucester could have moved so large a mass of men so far from Leicester without an alarm. His face showed only interest, however, and its placidity at last unlocked the peasant's tongue.

'There's none but us as suffers. The lord, he hears, and he sets us to harvest his crop and the part of ours which is his, or else he takes his pennies for rent. And the priest, he takes his tithes. And what's left is mine – if the soldiers don't ride it down or graze their horses in the field.'

The Tudor chewed his bread and took another sup of ale. It was useless to speak of intention or necessity to such a man. He knew only his own needs and cared nothing for the general good. To explain that some must suffer so that most would be benefited was a theory beyond his understanding.

'The armies will not fight here,' Henry said at last. It was likely true, unless Gloucester moved incredibly fast. In any case, he wished to offer the comfort to still the man's tongue which he now felt he was unwise to have unlocked. He had worse troubles of his own.

'What matter.' Anger had been replaced by despair again in the hind's face. 'When I was a boy, Henry was king, but then Edward came and with him a new landlord. Then Henry again – again a new lord of the land – then Edward – then Richard. Now another Henry – and each time the lord is new, the rents must be paid again. War or no war, there will be nothing left.'

'Why? You have paid your rent already.' Henry regretted the question, but it was out before he thought.

'I have, and it is written in the lord's book. But the new lord will have a new book with nothing written in it, and a new bailiff who will not remember, or an old bailiff whose affair it is not to remember.'

'So,' Henry said, interested in spite of himself. It was a clever game. He must remember and do something about it if he could. 'You should get a paper from your landlord that says you have paid your rent,' he suggested.

'Who knows what is written on paper? Papers bring only grief.'

Henry almost laughed, partly at the hind's suspicion of the written word and partly at his own consciousness that the remark had a good deal of truth in it. If he had not received letters offering him the crown, would he be here now? The problem as an intellectual exercise was interesting. How could an unlettered man get a receipt and know what he was getting?

'I will tell you,' Henry said. 'You should have a book of your own. Take it to the priest and let the priest write in it the day and the year and the amount of the rent. Then the lord's clerk or bailiff must seal it with the lord's seal when you pay or bring in your crop. You would know the meaning of the seal, as would all other men.'

There was a long, long silence during which Henry's eyes closed and he leaned wearily against the wall. He did not believe that this man or his grandson would dare harm him. They could never explain the horse and armour, and therefore could get no profit from his hurt. Nonetheless, he could not sleep, partly because of his discomfort and partly because the intentions of his stepfather haunted him.

'The priest will not do it for nothing.'

Henry's eyes snapped open. The rushlight was out, but a darker shadow crouched before him in the dark. Henry rolled his head, easing the pain in his neck, and realized that he had been asleep. He checked a hysterical giggle at the thought of the grave matter to which the attention of the king of England was now directed, and also at the tempo of a conversation which permitted one of the participants to sleep between remarks.

'It is worth a few eggs and a chicken or two,' he suggested, and closed his eyes again.

'But will the lord or his clerk put on the seal?'

Was the darkness lighter? Henry looked up through the smoke hole of the roof. Perhaps it was, but the night was not yet over. 'If you go together, the whole village, to pay your rents,' Henry offered, 'and each has his book, then you can pay the priest enough, all paying a little, so that he will come with you. Like enough the clerk or bailiff will use the seal if the priest is there.'

'Like enough.'

Silence fell again. The minutes crawled into hours. Henry slipped deeper into sleep. He did not feel the hand of the labourer steady him as he teetered sideways once. Mostly the rough mud of the walls caught in the backplate of his armour held him upright. Only when the cramp in his neck became so severe that it pierced his fatigue did he open his eyes. The sky showed grey through the smoke hole. Henry raised his hands to his neck and groaned.

'Thirsty?' A filled bowl was offered. Henry took it, drank, and groaned again as he twisted his head this way and that. He stood and a hand was offered to steady him. 'Next rent time,' the labourer said, as if his last remark about the rent book had been made only moments before, 'I will try.'

Henry opened the door and stepped outside. The air was sweet and fresh; he had forgotten the stench of the hut until this moment. The boy slipped out behind him to get his horse from the shed which was really half of the house. Henry lifted the skirt of his armour, fumbled with his underclothing and relieved his bladder. He realized that he was ravenously hungry and that his men would be frantic with worry, but his eyes glowed with pleasure. Anxiety and ambition notwithstanding, life offered him much. He turned and smiled, wishing he had something to give the hind, but he had no purse and to leave a ring or a jewel from his clothing would endanger the man rather than reward him.

'Years from now, yeoman, you may tell your grandchildren's children that Harry, king of England, slept in your house, ate your bread, and drank your ale. And you, yourself, do you remember that King Harry told you how to have justice in the matter of your rents. This I promise you. For the sake of the roof and the bread and ale you offered me – your landlord himself shall place his seal on your book and you shall have no new landlord this harvest time. What is your name, and the name of your village?'

'J-John, lord.' The man was trembling visibly. 'John of Cannock Wood.'

'I will remember it to your benefit.'

Spurs set the horse in motion and kept him at a hot pace. In the light of day, Henry was not afraid of losing his way. Hereabouts all roads would lead to Lichfield where his army was to have camped, and he did not doubt that they would remain where they were until he appeared. His arrival was greeted with near hysteria. Jasper had aged twenty years in that night, and his face was blotched with weeping. William Brandon fell to his knees and seized Henry's hand, breaking into the racking sobs of a man who saw the dead return to life. Even stolid Poynings turned so pale that Henry thought he would faint. All were red-eyed and drawn, so shocked by relief that they could scarcely stammer questions.

'How now,' Henry chided gently, 'am I a child that I may not be gone a few hours without such a to-do?'

'No more,' Brandon gasped. 'You will go out of my sight no more. When you next wish to be alone, you will need to kill me. I will part from you no more. I will not live through such another night.'

'What sort of trick was this, Harry?' Anger could not steady Jasper's voice; he had suffered too much. 'Were you lost?'

To admit the truth would only add to his uncle's anxiety. Besides, it would damage his dignity. 'Of course I was not lost,' Henry said testily. 'If I had been lost, how could I have found you so easily? Do I look as if I have been riding through the night? William, get up, do.'

'Where were you?'

'I—' Henry looked at the red-rimmed eyes, the grim mouths with bitten lips. He had intended to make a jest of spending the night with a woman in Cannock, but he could not give so light an excuse to these tired men. 'I waited in a small village to receive a message from secret allies.' Henry's lips twitched as he thought that he had not lied. Doubtless John of Cannock Wood was now an ally – of some sort – and he had certainly received a message from him.

'I hope you had more sleep than we did, sire,' Stanley said. 'We searched for hours, and even then your council seemed inclined to fix the blame somewhat before they knew harm was done.'

'I am sorry you were concerned over my welfare, but I must retain my freedom of action. What I did not have was food. Will someone see to it?'

112

'My brother would like to speak to you, sire,' Stanley added as Henry began to turn away. 'The message came last night that he would await you at the great manor house in Atherstone.'

'So? Poynings, go you ahead and say I come. My lord of Oxford, you, Rhys, and you, Sir Gilbert, move the army to Atherstone as soon as you may. Brandon, fetch me a fresh horse. The rest of you will attend me.' Orders given, Henry began to laugh. 'For mercy, have none of you a crust of bread nor a sup of ale to give me? I am famished.'

The food was soon brought, but instead of leaving immediately Henry decided to shed the armour which had not been off his back for twenty-four hours so that he would present a less dishevelled appearance. He was washed and shaved while the armour was repolished and, by the time he left, the main body of his army was underway. They had not far outstripped the men when Guildford's keen eyes noted a troop moving towards them at a good rate.

'Back,' Jasper said. 'We may meet our advance guard before they can overtake us.'

Henry wheeled his horse, then reined in. 'Wait. It is common knowledge that the army camped at Lichfield and there are scarce a hundred men in that troop. How could any man know we set off separately?'

'Stanley knew,' Brandon muttered as he set his lance and loosened the battle-axe fastened to his saddle.

A qualm seized Henry, but it was too late now – they had been spotted. The suspense did not last long as two knights pulled ahead, came up, and inquired of the whereabouts of Richmond's army.

'Who are you?'

'Sir Thomas Bourchier. We and our men are from London. We rode north with the constable of the Tower who was summoned to Leicester by Richard, but we broke away—'

'I am Sir Walter Hungerford. I knew the little princes when they lived in the Tower.'

'You have found Henry of Richmond himself.' Henry lifted his visor so that they could see his face. 'I bid you welcome.' He stretched a hand towards Hungerford whose face was bitter between the conflict of his Yorkist loyalty and his hatred for the princes' murderer. 'Be at peace. When I am crowned, there will be no more murdering of babes – no matter what their

113

blood. The army is behind us. Seek out the earl of Oxford.'

'Even wolves do not tear the flesh of their litter mates' cubs,' Jasper snarled.

'Aye, uncle, but a boar sometimes eats its own piglets, which is why, for all their fierceness and courage, we do not honour the pig. The boar that devoured the piglets of England must die. Come. I grow ever more eager to meet my stepfather.'

That was true, but largely in a negative sense. Henry understood ambition all too well, but that his mother should mate with a counterpart of William Stanley— For me, he reminded himself as he dismounted and walked towards the door opened for him. If he is a beast, she has soiled herself for me. In the hall his breath trickled out in a long sigh, making him conscious that he had been holding it. His lady mother had not chosen so ill. Weakness, ambition, and passion marked the face before him, but not the sly evil that dehumanized his brother. Lord Stanley offered to kneel, and Henry caught him.

'A father may not kneel to a son, not even if the son be king.'

'Sire, I—'

Henry made an impatient gesture. 'My mother,' he said, his breath quickening with eagerness. 'How is she? Where is she?'

A softness redeemed Lord Stanley's expression. 'Well. She is well, only very much alarmed over your welfare.'

'Where?'

'Near London. She would have come. She desired it greatly. I had to lock her in her room and give order that she be held most straitly. If all goes well, you will be soon enough in each other's arms. Sire—'

'Call me Henry. You have that right. Why should she not come? I want her.'

'Do you not understand how much your mother loves you? Do you not know what she would suffer if she saw you thus – armed, prepared for battle, for wounds, for— I wished to spare her that. Do you wish her to endure it? She, who can barely give order to beat an erring maid or man?'

For death, Lord Stanley had not said, but he had thought it. Henry dragged his mind away from the unbearable urge to rest in Margaret's arms, to be a child with no fears and no burdens. He nodded acceptance and sat down.

'I am happy, at least, that you care so much for her.'

'Who does not?' Stanley smiled. 'Her beauty and goodness would convert the Devil.'

'Stop,' Henry said sharply. 'You whet my appetite for what I cannot yet have. Let us speak instead of how I can come to her safely.'

Lord Stanley's eyes shifted like a hunted thing. 'I, too, have a son,' he faltered, 'dearly beloved to me. And he is in Richard's hands, close-prisoned, a hostage. Will you call me a coward if I say I am afraid to do what I desire? You, too, will have sons. I pray your heart is not torn apart between their needs.'

'Then you are come here to tell me you will fight for Gloucester?'

'No!' Stanley swallowed. 'You must believe me, sire – Henry – you must. I am trying to free my boy. I have been trying—' He bit his lip. 'The moment, the instant, I know him to be safe, either because he has escaped or because he is too far from Gloucester to be harmed, my men will join you.'

'If you wait for that, you are like to be too late,' Henry said coldly. 'Gloucester's forces are assembled. I doubt not we will meet within the next day or two. Certainly I intend to press for a meeting.'

A bead of sweat ran down Stanley's temple. 'My forces are mustered. They lie to the south. We will march parallel to you. As God is my judge, when battle is joined I will ride to your support. If I had another child here, I would give it to you in pledge.'

'I do not murder children for a father's fault. Both reward and punishment are for the doer, not the innocent without power.' He rose. 'I have business. Farewell until we meet in victory.'

'Sire!' Lord Stanley caught at Henry's arm, and Brandon moved closer, sword half-drawn. Henry gestured impatiently and Brandon drew back. 'I love your mother,' Stanley whispered. 'Do you realize that if I do not keep my word I will not dare enter her chamber nor ride her lands without the fear of a knife in my back or my belly? I will not be able to trust my own priest – so does she bind men to her. If my life could settle the matter, I would spend it. You are not a murderer of innocents, but Gloucester is! I cannot kill my own son – I cannot.'

Quite abruptly Lady Margaret stopped in the middle of a phrase and looked down at her hands, so tightly clasped that the knuckles showed white. She closed her eyes and swallowed hard. What she had been doing must be an offence to God. For the last hour – hours? – she had been mouthing the words of prayers without knowing in the least what they meant, nor even which prayers she had been reciting. She opened her eyes and raised them to the crucifix that hung above the *prie-dieu*.

'Forgive me,' she whispered. 'Your mother would forgive me.'

And then, bitterly, Margaret wondered whether that were true. Holy Mary had not driven her son with her own ambition. Submission to the will of God did not include cajoling a loving and trusting husband into endangering the life of his own son for the advantage of yours. Advantage? What advantage? Would Henry not be in worse danger of his life and his soul as king than in any other state? Margaret tried to moisten her lips, but her mouth was dry as ashes. Her pride. Her sin! And every person who had ever loved her would suffer for it.

The dowager queen of England licked her lips with a wet, pink tongue like a satisfied cat. Soon now, very soon, she would sit in state again, fully acknowledged as royalty twice over. Dowager queen and queen mother both, her position would be unassailable. All in all, this was better, perhaps, than if her son had mounted the throne. Little Edward had always had a mind of his own, even as a small boy. Elizabeth would be much easier to control, and neither the upstart Tudor nor the murderous Gloucester would be able to deny his queen anything. Too much of Edward's blood had been spilled. Another drop and the commons and nobles of England would set Elizabeth herself up as queen.

That thought made the dowager lick her lips again. That might be the end of the matter in any case. If things were manoeuvred just so, it might be possible to rid the country of the hated Gloucester and leave his queen-wife, who was also heir to the dearly beloved Edward IV, as ruler in her own name. Her name and my power, the dowager thought, savouring the concept.

Best of all, it made not the slightest difference who won the battle that was now being drawn up. So long as one of the creatures died, it made not a pin of difference which. They both needed Elizabeth in order to hold the throne, Gloucester because the country hated him and the Tudor because he was only an upstart Welshman, a commoner in fact, with no more legitimate claim to royal honours than the servingman his grandfather had been. A slow smile curved the dowager's lips. Even if both died, it would not matter. Either Elizabeth would be named queen directly or Warwick would be crowned – and Warwick was feeble-minded. He would have to be married to Elizabeth for any kind of security. Thus, I will rule through Elizabeth just the same, she thought happily. The battle and the news of its results – whatever they were – could not come too soon for the dowager.

In the isolated manor house at Sheriff Hutton, where Elizabeth dragged out the weary days, no word of any impending battle was spoken. Nonetheless, the princess knew that something of great importance was about to happen. The women, whose manners had bordered on insolence ever since she had been imprisoned here, had suddenly changed. They now vied for the opportunity to perform any service for her, and their behaviour and speech were fawning.

For a little while after she noticed this change, Elizabeth was almost paralysed with fear. She believed that it portended Gloucester's arrival with a proposal of marriage, perhaps even with a dispensation from the pope for the marriage. Could the pope, the voice of God upon earth, set aside the sin of incest? A niece and an uncle? Elizabeth's gorge rose. Cousins, yes, that was not a great matter, but brother and the daughter of the same man? She would resist, she promised herself; her mother could not force her to obey in this case. She would go to a convent, even die, but she would not marry the king.

But as the days passed and neither her uncle nor any message from him came, Elizabeth remembered the last part of Lady Margaret's message. 'He who loves us both comes soon.' If the ladies feared that the rebellion under Henry of Richmond would succeed and Henry would be king, there was far more reason for them to fawn upon her. They were, after all, Richard's creatures, and she might be able to protect them from Henry. Her mind slipped from that to something more important to her. 'He who loves us both—' Dared she believe that true? Elizabeth wondered. She had often thought of Henry of Richmond in these long, dull months, often thought of how it would be to receive letters such as Margaret had from him. They were marvellous letters, including, among other, more serious matters, gay little incidents poking fun at himself. Once, obviously in reply to his mother's question about how he looked or whether he had changed, he had said that nothing could change or improve him; he was the same, only more so, he said and cited a barber who had refused to trim his hair as short as he wanted it because 'it were better that what it hides remain hidden'.

Elizabeth sighed and choked down a hope that Henry would love her. She had laughed so heartily at that tale of the barber. Lady Margaret was a darling, but she had no sense of humour. She had not thought it funny; she had been angry at the insult to her son even though she freely admitted that he was no beauty. But obviously Henry had thought it funny – so he and I would laugh at the same sort of things, Elizabeth thought. Suddenly she began to sob softly. It would be like heaven to have someone to laugh with. Her father had laughed so easily and so often with her. Since his death she had so seldom laughed. Henry's letters – she had laughed at them— But not his letters to me, Elizabeth reminded herself.

She tried to remember what Henry had written to her, but there was really nothing to remember. The phrases were as proper and polite as the rote speeches she had memorized for certain court situations. How could he love her or she him? Nearly thirty years of bloodshed divided them, and every friend of Henry of Richmond had hated her and her house. The warm, soft breeze of summer stirred the leaves, and they whispered softly. But for a princess there could be no soft whispers of love. Desperately Elizabeth tried to gird her spirit with pride. She would need it to deny Richard and possibly to die if the king defeated Henry. And if Henry won, she would need the pride to live with, to uphold her through the lonely years so that Edward IV's grandson could sit on the throne.

Chapter Nine

The morning mists of a fair, warm August day were clearing slowly. Henry Tudor looked about and sighed softly with mingled nervousness and satisfaction. He was glad it did not rain. He did not like to be wet. The thought brought a smile to his lips. If one must soon be dead, it was better not to be uncomfortable first. He began to laugh softly. Also, if one was to be king, it would be most undignified to accept the crown with a sniffling nose and running eyes – and his colds were always of that unappealing type.

King. Would he be king? Below and to the right of the slight eminence on which his horse stood, surrounded by his council and a band of about one hundred of the most fanatically devoted of the English exiles, lay the main body of his army under Oxford. To the right again was a small group of reserves that Sir Gilbert Talbot commanded, and directly below Henry another small reserve force under Sir John Savage. Left again and almost out of sight were William Stanley's forces, about two thousand mounted men. Sir William had offered to fight in the main body, but Henry had not dared accept. If that snake retreated, the entire force would have been thrown into confusion.

Of course, in his present position Sir William could fall upon the left flank of Oxford's army and destroy it almost at will. That was why Savage held the left wing. Perhaps Sir William would hesitate to ride down his own nephew. Perhaps— South, off to Oxford's right, waited Lord Stanley's force of four thousand, almost as large as Henry's entire army. Oxford's flank was safe enough from them – there was a marsh there – and it was unlikely that Stanley would fall on Oxford's rear unless defeat seemed inevitable.

Henry sighed again. It was the best he could do, for they had been taken somewhat by surprise. After so slow a start, Richard had moved from Leicester with unexpected speed. He had occupied the high ground and the Tudor's men would have to fight uphill, but there were compensations. The sun, brightening into brilliance now, would be behind Henry's force and fully in the faces of Gloucester's host. As Oxford's men fought uphill, they would be able to spread out, whereas if they were forced to retreat, the marsh on one side and the stream on the other would force them to consolidate and permit their officers to rally them. Contrariwise, Richard's men could drift off sideways and desert with the greatest ease. They had better do it, too, Henry thought wryly, for they outnumbered his army two to one.

He closed his eyes for a moment, remembering his speech to the host, in which he had assured his outnumbered troops that Gloucester's army was filled with 'men by fear compelled and not by goodwill assembled'. Please God I have not lied, Henry prayed, and started violently at a crash of thunder. As his eyes opened, instinctively looking heavenward, he laughed again. It was not God's reply, but Guildford whose beloved guns had fired their opening salvo. Perhaps it was God's reply. No answering crash came, which meant that Gloucester had no big guns, and the men massed on the open slope of Ambion Hill were an excellent target. Most of the first salvo had fallen short, but the next crash opened a hole here and there in Gloucester's forces. 'Again,' Henry whispered, 'again, faster.'

The big guns were not really much use in an army battle because, killing friend and foe alike, firing had to be discontinued before the armies mingled. Nonetheless, they had a value. Henry could see the uneasy movement on the hill. Firing the guns spread terror. Now their muzzles were being raised again, and the charges of powders increased. The balls would fall higher on the hillside so that Oxford's men could move forward in safety while the rear ranks of Gloucester's army were rendered unfit to fight by fear.

The trumpets rang out. Now! Rhys ap Thomas's voice, bellowing orders in Welsh mingled with Shaunde's French and Oxford's English. Now! Forward! A flight of arrows rose from Gloucester's vanguard which was under the duke of Norfolk's command. Oxford's archers replied in kind, running forward, shooting, and running forward again. Henry gasped for air as if he were part of the attack, tried to steady his breathing, and then, realizing that all about him men were sobbing for breath, forgot about the impression he was making as the fronts crashed together.

The central curve of Norfolk's force buckled. Henry's fist pounded his saddle pommel as if the blows could push the men onward. Another foot. Another! To the left the Welshmen were screaming like wild things, swirling around the black raven banner of ap Thomas. Rhys himself had discarded his shield and was swinging a sword in one hand and a battle-axe in the other. To the right, Shaunde's men fought low and dirty; they were the scum of the streets and the prisons, and men who had survived that are not easy to kill. In the main centre Oxford's banner, its star seeming to stream light from its bright centre, forged slowly ahead surrounded by desperate Englishmen who were fighting for their lost homes and lands, for the children some of them had not seen in two sad years of exile.

Norfolk's centre gave further, his army bending like the slow stringing of a bow. Henry tore his eyes from the fighting and looked higher up the hill. There, Gloucester was sending a detachment of reserves. Five hundred? A thousand? Henry wiped the sweat from his eyes, glanced left. Sir William held steady. No, it was not time for him; things were neither bad enough nor good enough to demand his unreliable help. To the right Lord Stanley had edged closer, but he, too, offered neither help nor threat – yet.

'Willoughby!'

'Sire?'

'Ride to Oxford. Tell him to disengage if he can or to take care not to be surrounded. Gloucester is sending in reserves and I am sending Talbot.'

Sir Robert Willoughby dug spurs into his horse's sides. Henry did not watch him. Unless he were killed instantly, Willoughby would accomplish his mission. No wound, even a fatal one, could stop him because Willoughby was a religious fanatic – only Henry had taken the place of God. It made Sir Robert useful for clear-cut or dangerous work, but it annoyed Henry because such devotion muddled a man's thinking. Willoughby's judgment was unreliable. He thought too much of what Henry wanted and not enough about the easiest and least painful way of accomplishing it.

'Uncle, send a man to Talbot. Tell him—'

'It is done.'

They watched anxiously as Gloucester's reserve prevented

Oxford from cutting Norfolk's force in two. The French were falling back and would foul Oxford's rear. God, where was Willoughby? Rhys was down! No, there was Rhys, bellowing curses in Welsh at hillmen drunk with blood lust, turning his axe and sword sideways to whack his recalcitrant fighters into giving way. He was holding them together. Oxford was falling back.

Compared with the clang and shriek of battle, the relative silence of the disengagement was shocking. Henry tried to swallow and found his throat achingly dry. In the few feet between the opposing armies, which panted for breath and glared at each other, lay the wounded and the dead. Sickly fascinated, Henry watched them, some moving feebly, some lying still. They mingle their blood, he thought. Can men be closer than that? And yet they strive to slay each other. In these bitter times a mingling of blood meant nothing. Wicked uncle slew helpless nephew, and brother fought brother in the field.

'Talbot is true,' Jasper cried with relief. 'Look how he drives forward.'

The force was small but the men were fresh and eager. Oxford's forces revived as Talbot threw himself forward on the right wing, bolstering the French. The streaming star lurched into action, and the memory of ten years of miserable imprisonment made Oxford's 'For England and Saint George' a scream of lust for real freedom that only a victory in this battle could bring him. Rhys's bellow was almost drowned in the wild battle cry that rose from the Welshmen as, free of restraint, they charged again.

'Harry, Norfolk is down.'

'Move,' Henry gasped, 'move.'

And, as if his will had forced his army forward, Gloucester's men fell back. Somewhere in the back of his mind Henry knew he should check on other danger points, but his eyes remained riveted on the fighting. If he looked away, disaster would come. Gloucester would loose more reserves; Northumberland would have a change of heart and charge of his own accord; the Stanleys would—

'Harry, Gloucester is moving. He will join the battle himself.'

Henry's blood pounded so hard in his throat that he felt strangled. He knew only too well Richard's reputation as a warrior. For a moment longer his eyes remained fixed on Oxford's standard. It was moving, and moving faster.

'Make ready,' he said. 'If Gloucester charges, we must meet him.' He put a hand to his helmet visor.

'Wait,' Jasper cried, his voice rising almost to a scream with excitement. 'He is not charging Oxford. He is coming here.'

'Edgecombe,' Henry snapped, 'ride to William Stanley. Tell him to cut off Gloucester's retreat once he has passed.'

The Tudor was no hero. He would rather have ordered Sir William to fall upon Gloucester and kill him before he reached the hill, but he feared that such an order might be disregarded. Worse, having disregarded it and thereby forfeited whatever reward Henry could be expected to give him for cooperation, Sir William might try to save his oats by joining Richard's attack.

'Sire, Lord Stanley is moving.'

'Savage is engaged.' That was Poynings's calm voice.

'Where the hell is Gloucester?' Jasper snarled.

'There,' Brandon cried. 'There he rides. Murdering pig, he dares wear the crown.' He threw down his shield, grabbed the red dragon standard of Cadwallader, and shook it fiercely. 'England and Saint George! King Henry and Saint George!'

Henry snapped down his visor and drew his sword. It was little enough protection against the murderous battle-axe that Gloucester wielded so effectively, but its longer reach might be of value. To try to meet battle-axe with battle-axe was hopeless. Henry knew himself to be out-classed as a fighter and knew that Richard of Gloucester was seeking him and him alone. Yet now he felt neither afraid nor helpless. He would need to wait no longer. He would never run again. Whatever was to be, would be decided here and now. Henry did not hope to cut Gloucester down; he knew he could not. But if he could hold him off, Brandon and Poynings and Pembroke – in fact every man of the hundred men around him – would gladly give their lives to accomplish that great good.

'Stand and receive,' Henry ordered calmly.

The slight advantage to be gained by the momentum of charging downhill was not worth the danger of becoming separated. A forest of lances tipped forward. The noise of the battle faded under the growing thunder of horses' hooves,

Henry gripped his shield until his fingers ached and tried to swallow the lump in his throat that seemed to be obstructing his breathing. He had fought before, but never when he was the single target of a concentrated attack.

'Stand!' he cried once more as John Cheney broke ranks and charged furiously towards the crowned figure in the centre of the van.

Three – four – men struck out and John went down. There was a crash of splintering lances; but Pembroke on one side and Poynings on the other protected Henry and he endured no shock. Then all were too close for spear work. The unbroken shafts and broken hafts were thrown down. Henry warded off a light blow with his shield and struck out with his sword. He could breathe now, and he was conscious only of a feeling of irritation that Jasper pressed so close to him on his right that he could not swing his sword freely. Brandon, who could hold no lance because he bore the red dragon, now pushed Poynings left, away from Henry, wielding his sword and bellowing his joy in battle and his rage against his enemies. He and Pembroke surged forward, both trying to keep their bodies between Henry and those who sought him, but Henry, caught in the fever of the fighting, pressed on with them.

'Ware! Gloucester!' Poynings screamed, just as he was cut off from Henry's group by Richard's men.

He lay about him furiously, trying to break free, but the crowned figure with armour distorted to make room for the over-developed right arm and shoulder of the battle-axe wielder charged past him straight at Henry. The axe rose. Henry gasped, raised his shield, and drew back his sword arm so that he could thrust forward with the point and keep Gloucester off. With a hoarse scream of rage, William Brandon drew the fiery dragon standard out of harm's way and threw his body between Henry and Richard. Gloucester shouted an oath, foiled of his purpose for the moment, struck Brandon's sword away with his shield, and launched the blow he had intended for Henry at Brandon's unprotected left side. William could have broken the blow with the strong shaft which supported Henry's banner, but the thought never entered his mind. If the pole were broken and the dragon fell, the entire army might panic, thinking that Henry had been killed or had run away. He thrust the shaft into the ground with all the strength of his great body, exposing his neck even more, and shouted 'King Henry!' The axe bit deep.

Blood as red as the dragon of Cadwallader cascaded over the bright armour. Brandon's horse, terrified by the suddenly slackened reins, leapt forward and Henry saw the blow Gloucester had intended to topple his banner whistle harmlessly in the air. He saw Gloucester spur his mount brutally, but Pembroke's shield was there and Courtenay's and Willoughby's. Edgecombe's sword struck Gloucester's shield, rebounding harmlessly, and Richard still strove onward towards Henry.

The Tudor's men were giving back under the insane ferocity of the attack, but the wall about him remained unbroken. Back again. Henry uttered an inarticulate cry as he realized they would lose their standard if they gave another foot. In that moment, Poynings dispatched the last man separating him from his party, threw down the mace he had been using, and grasped the banner. He was weaponless, but he raised the dragon and shook it so that it coiled and uncoiled as if alive.

'King Henry and Saint George!' He cried his defiance in the face of his foes, and 'King Henry and Saint George' came as an answering bellow from behind Richard's men. The cry might have been repeated. Henry did not hear because it was swallowed up in the shrieks of rage and pain that came from Gloucester's men as William Stanley's full force fell upon their rear. Now the simple pressure of the red-liveried Stanley forces broke Gloucester's ranks and, singly, his men were pressed in among Henry's who joyfully cut them down. Henry himself was briefly engaged, protectiing the weaponless Poynings. He was holding his own, actually enjoying himself, when John Cheney, miraculously no more than bruised and muddied, appeared and killed his opponent. Guildford appeared, the guns no longer being of use, and Edgecombe and then Courtenay, who was bleeding from a wound in the side not fatal but serious enough to prevent him from hard fighting. Poynings thrust the banner into Courtenay's hand and drew his own sword.

For a moment as his men closed in around him, Henry suffered the rage of an over-protected child. Then he began to laugh. That was just what England needed; to have both Gloucester and himself slain!

'Sire, are you hurt?' Courtenay cried as he saw Henry shaking.

'No,' Henry gasped painfully, struggling to control the untimely, half-hysterical mirth. 'Where is my uncle?'

'Seeking Gloucester,' Guildford panted. 'I saw him going downhill as I came up to you.'

Henry bit his lip, but it was useless to order the men to ride after Pembroke. If he had found Gloucester, it was too late. If he had not, they would never find him in the wild confusion of fleeing, fighting men. He glanced towards Ambion Hill. No reserves remained there. His own men and Lord Stanley's pursued the remnants of Richard's army. Many were already prisoner; many threw down their arms; some ran away; some still fought because they feared to be slain if they yielded.

'Poynings, bid the heralds offer mercy to all who throw down their arms,' Henry said.

He felt no pleasure now. Looking over the torn fields, the strewn bodies, hearing the groans of the wounded, Henry needed to swallow hard to keep down his sickness. No man disturbed their little group. Courtenay clutched his side and clung grimly to the red dragon which now hung limp. The others watched as the fighting died down. At the foot of the low hill on which Henry was stationed it lasted longest as Gloucester's household guard was subdued. Then there was quiet, broken only by the weeping of those who had lost something or someone dear and by the moans of the dying. One by one, Henry's council drifted back to him, tired, bleeding, awed by what they had accomplished – all except William Brandon. Pembroke came last, riding slowly to dismount and kneel before his nephew.

'I did not kill Gloucester for you, sire. I sought, but I could not find him.'

The Tudor slid from his horse and lifted his uncle. 'Thank God you are spared to me. Gloucester will meet his fate by the headsman's axe if he has not met it already. Indeed, we must thank God for all. It is by His help alone that we have done this. Let us find William. I wish us all to be together in this thanksgiving.'

Brandon was there, where he had fallen, the blood dried to brown now. Henry lifted the visor and looked at the peaceful face, then crossed himself and began to pray. Around him the council knelt, and above them the red dragon, caught by a vagrant breeze, uncoiled and displayed himself, a bloody symbol of victory.

Henry pulled off his gauntlet and touched Brandon's face gently with three fingers. 'Fare thee well, William. We will laugh together no more. Do not let your soul be troubled for any earthly thing. What I promised shall be your son's, and I myself will be father to him.'

He stood up, drew a deep breath, and lifted his head. 'Cheney,' he said briskly, 'do you see that William's body is guarded. He bought my life with his blood, and I will see him buried with all honour.' Henry looked around. 'Oxford,' he paused and held out his hands, which John de Vere grasped. 'I cannot insult you by praising your courage, as if it were a thing new to you, but I can show my trust by placing my safety in your hands. You will be constable of the Tower and lord high admiral.' Henry's lips quivered as he thought – when we have a fleet.

Philibert de Shaunde came forward. 'Sire, you have forbidden looting, but after a battle my men—' He shrugged helplessly.

Henry's face froze. 'Courtenay.'

'Sire?' Edward tried to straighten, still clasping his side with a red-stained hand.

'Nay, I had forgot you were hurt. Oxford, this is work for you, if you are not overweary.'

'I am not rested,' de Vere smiled, 'but until I am dead, I am yours to command.'

'Gather the English troops. Set them to watch the French.'

'They will turn on us,' Shaunde said angrily. He despised the scum he commanded, but they were all the French court would permit him to take.

'Let them strip the dead, then,' Henry said with a bitter grimace. 'But they are not to touch the wounded. If necessary, turn the prisoners loose on them. Ned.' Poynings turned. 'Make search with what men you need for Gloucester's body, and if you do not find it, make inquiry if any saw him flee the field.'

'That is not necessary.' William Stanley stood a little back from the group, smiling. 'I cut Gloucester down with my own hand.' Henry stared, but Sir William did not meet his eyes. 'I can show Poynings where his body lies.'

127

'Go with him, Ned. Gloucester is to be exposed, naked for all to see,' Henry said coldly. 'I desire no rumour that he is alive and free to trouble my reign. Bring me back the crown he defiled. Death has cleansed it – and it is mine.'

'It is here, Henry – sire.' Lord Stanley had been told he might address the king as Henry, but he added the sire for safety when he saw the cold grey eyes.

William leaned over and whispered to his brother sharply as Henry turned his head to look for Pembroke. It was his desire to take the crown from the hands of him who had so long preserved his life; but Pembroke was still faithful to his mad Welshmen, and had hurried away to help Rhys curb the wild fighters before their excesses brought Henry's wrath upon their heads. The Tudor turned back just in time to receive the crown which Lord Stanley set on his helmet with his own hands. His face turned white and set into a mask while a burning rage flooded him. Henry's hand flew up to rip the battered golden circlet from his head, but it was the crown of England and a priceless treasure no matter how it came there. He stayed his hand, just touching the symbolic coronet. It is my mother from whom it comes, Henry thought, the man is but her tool.

'Thank you.' A smile icy-chill, less cheering than a frown, curved his lips. 'He who marries a countess should be an earl. That I grant you, Lord Stanley, henceforward earl of Derby.' He turned away. 'Edgecombe, summon the heralds to me, and some scribes, if they can be found. Call together, also, the chiefs of all the fighting groups – the prisoners, also. I have that to say which must be spread quickly through the country.'

They drew together, the expectant victors and the sullen, fearful beaten. Henry stepped clear of the group which surrounded him. The ranks of men wavered as if a wind tossed them and a murmur rose and fell, 'The king. The king.' The Tudor looked across the sea of faces, wondering at first how far his voice would carry, and then, with a sudden qualm of terror, whether even the words they heard could mean anything to them. Had the struggle between Lancaster and York gone on too long? Could anything heal the wounds? Wash away the bitterness? Weld the nation into one? Why, he himself, whose task this was, needed to force his mind to acceptance when he thought of marriage to the daughter of York.

'Hail Harry, king of England.'

128

The single voice rose from the crowd, and Henry raised his hand to hold back an outburst of cheering. 'My people, we have called you together for this purpose. We are king of England and of the English.' The Tudor paused, raised his voice still higher to say significantly, 'All the English. No longer shall father be set against son nor brother against brother. In this land now, so long torn by strife that it has become the jest of all nations, there is no longer Lancaster or York. Here are Englishmen only. Let us then, as the first symbol of new and better times to come, bind up each other's wounds and give honourable burial to all those slain in this unhappy strife. It is our command, as king of all the English, that no man willing to acknowledge us king suffer any further hurt. When the wounded are tended and the dead buried, let all men depart peaceably to their own place, taking with them their own horse, harness, and weapons. This nation is no more at war. No man is to be prevented from leaving this field with what he brought to it. Any man who loots or harms any of our people may not shield himself behind the excuse of war. The war is over! My people, go in peace.'

There was a moment of shocked silence. The wars of the red rose and the white had been waged with increasing bitterness in the past, the victors despoiling the vanquished, and the lists of proscriptions and confiscated property had run to many pages in the rolls of parliament. Then the roars rose to heaven.

'King Henry! King Henry! Hail the king!'

'Sire, are you mad?' William Stanley, shaken from caution, hissed the question.

Henry raked him with his eyes, and the man recoiled as he had done before. 'Nay,' he replied, smiling, 'merely wiser than my predecessors. What good to wrest a horse and sword from a man who has nothing else? A field or two from a country squire who then becomes both a beggar and an intriguer? A king must strike his enemies, and the commons of England are no enemy to me. Others—' Henry paused, smiled again, and said softly, 'may be.'

Chapter Ten

It was an August-end such as England seldom saw; hot, bright days cooled by a sufficient breeze. The council said, laughing, that the weather had been arranged by God so that Henry's people should see him in comfort and at his best. The prisoners, some score of men of note, ardent supporters of Richard, whispered among themselves that such weather presaged plague and a stern and troubled reign. Even they, however, did not see any quick reversal of Henry's victory.

Many of the leaders of Richard's party had been slain – in battle, not by execution as followed Tewkesbury – and the rest, except for two, were prisoners. Whatever the countryfolk felt, there were now no leaders to support rebellion. And it appeared, as they rode south from Leicester, that the countryfolk were well pleased with the change. They lined the roads and crowded the towns cheering King Henry, and the Tudor smiled and spoke to them, always stressing peace and unity and promising pardon to all who swore fealty to him.

Henry was most splendid, glittering with jewels and cloth of gold which he had appropriated shamelessly from Gloucester's chests. The clothes did not fit so ill; both were slight of form, but the right shoulder had to be made to match the left for Henry. Pembroke had frowned at the borrowed feathers, his own flesh crawling at the thought of wearing a dead enemy's clothes. He even spoke of it, the last night they spent at Leicester, but Henry laughed gaily and said the people would not welcome a beggarly king who could be expected to rob them.

That gave Jasper an opening to an even more important question. 'And what will you do, Harry?' he asked. 'You have refused to execute your enemies. You have set your face against confiscation of Yorkist property. How will you support the royal state?'

Edgecombe and Guildford, who already knew they would be chamberlains of the exchequer, looked their anxiety although they did not speak.

'To rob the poor is a crime,' Henry murmured, staring

130

intently at his own fingers. 'To cut the purses of the rich, on the other hand, enhances the peace of the nation and the stability of the throne. It may be that with judicious trimming of Gloucester's favourites – even though we leave no one bare of sustenance – the crown will not be destitute. Do not forget that Gloucester transferred the property given to Edward's favourites to his own. Most of Edward's favourites, thanks be to Gloucester, are dead. The crown, I think, should resume all the lands belonging to it in the time of Henry VI – with proper exceptions.'

A sigh of relief fluttered through the room. Henry had a craze for the appearance of legality, and the council had feared that he would force the parliament he intended to summon into voting him large subsidies.

'Moreover,' the king added, smiling seraphically on his men while his eyes glittered with amusement, 'confiscation without hope of restitution breeds bitter hatred and enmity. Is it not better to hold in trust property which may be restored as a reward for loyal service in the future?'

'Can you win Yorkists thus, Harry?' Jasper was not easy. He had been bred to a tradition which sought to wipe out its enemies, drowning them in their own blood.

'Some. What would you use, uncle? Can I slay the whole Percy clan – women and children too? What good would it be, if I did not kill them all, to kill Northumberland? And what means would you use to keep Northumberland steady? For others, there will be other reasons to transfer loyalty, but if I hold their purse strings without cutting the purse from their belts entirely, they will think twice before offending me. Cheney, bring the earl of Surrey here.'

Norfolk had died for Gloucester, but his heir, Thomas Howard, earl of Surrey, had been taken prisoner. He now came before his conqueror, a taller man by a head than Henry, dark, his face masklike. He did not bend his knee before the new king, and Henry did not demand it of him, although Northumberland, earlier, had been told to kneel.

'My lord earl,' Henry said gently, 'your father was, I have heard, a man of honour, and I believe that of you, also. You know your life is safe, and I tell you before these witnesses that your wife and mother will not be left penniless. I know too much of that in my own person. Tell me, therefore, without

131

fear, how you could bring yourself to bear arms for so murderous a tyrant as Richard of Gloucester.'

'He was my crowned king,' Surrey replied. 'If the parliamentary authority of England set the crown upon a stock – I will fight for that stock.' He met Henry's eyes boldly. 'And as I fought for him, I will fight for you – when you are established by the same authority.'

Henry nodded acceptance of the reply and gestured to Cheney who led Surrey away.

'That is a good man, sire,' Poynings said.

'Aye, so he is, Ned. He will not rot long in the Tower. Yet there he must go,' Henry laughed softly, 'until the said authority has established me, and until a little trust comes to him from my gentle handling of those he loves. Well, is there aught left to see to before we leave Leicester?'

'Gloucester's body,' Poynings said, consulting a memorandum. 'It is still exposed.'

'Throw it on a dung— No. Let it be decently but quietly interred by the Grey Friars, the grave to be marked in such a way that there will be no doubt – if we should need Richard to give evidence as to his own death, he must be ready to hand.'

Jasper looked away, and fondness softened the cruel smile which had curved Henry's lips. He must remember, he thought, not to distress his uncle with such jests. Momentarily he longed for Foxe, who had been sent for and would doubtless soon be hurrying towards London from France. Foxe would have laughed at the jest, and would have seen the humour of dangling lands and titles before the noses of men as carrots were held on a stick before an ass. He glanced around the room, feeling mortally weary yet knowing there was much still to do.

'What will you do about the Frenchmen?' Guildford asked above a yawn, as if Henry's thought was contagious.

'Send them back to the Regent Anne and Orleans,' Henry said, laughing again. 'That plague belongs in their country.'

'And Shaunde?' Jasper wanted to know.

'Him I would keep if I could. He has done me good service and is a fine soldier. Uncle, will you put that question to Oxford? Ned, are you nodding because you agree, or—'

'I am nodding because I am falling asleep, sire. I beg pardon,' Poynings replied, jerking himself upright.

'You need not. We are all in the same case. If naught else

132

needs doing here and now, let us snatch what rest we can.' As the others left, he held Jasper by the arm. 'Uncle, will Oxford be content with high admiral? I will make no other man but you earl marshal. I will hold the place myself rather than give so much power into another's hands.'

'I cannot, Harry. I told you before. Look at me, child. I am fifty-four years old. I am sore weary. I cannot support the burden of the whole land's defences. Find some younger man.'

Henry's grip tightened fiercely. 'I pray you, uncle, do not say to me that you are old. Who will dare love me now that I am king save you and my mother? I do not need much. You and she are sufficient, but I cannot spare you.'

'As long as God gives me leave, I will stay by you.'

'Oh, uncle—'

'You are overweary, Harry. Come now to bed.'

'There is so much yet to be done.'

'A dead man accomplishes nothing. Come to bed, Harry.'

Henry let himself be led away and was soothed when Jasper dismissed the squires of the body and helped him undress. Jasper's hands were warm and strong, and, though his hair was now nearly white, Harry was comforted because his uncle's back was straight and the flesh firm on his face and throat. He has many years yet, the king thought, but I must not press duty on him to ease myself no matter how sore my need. I must not kill him with overwork. There are others who will labour for gain or for fear. He alone loves me for myself – even when he fears me. Jasper bent above him and kissed him.

'Sleep, child. There is tomorrow for what you wish to do. There will be many tomorrows.'

It was true enough, but each tomorrow was as full as each yesterday. The realm had been so much shaken since Edward's death that nothing ran aright. Henry dictated to clerks as he rode, signed writs before he broke his fast, and worked far into each night after days of speeches and formal receptions. He also drove his poor council to the brink of exhaustion, as merciless to them as he was to himself. He found time, nonetheless, to walk beside the litter which carried Courtenay, for Edward would not be left behind and begged to ride if Henry felt the litter would be too slow. He managed, too, to make much of the council's work light by his jesting. Only it was *his* jesting. Neither Jasper nor Ned Poynings was given to lightness in that

133

way, and the others feared him too much to jape with him even though they loved him. Each day was busier – and lonelier – than the day before it.

Today would be different, Henry thought. Today they would come to Saint Albans and there, at last, he would meet his mother. The sun was midway in its afternoon decline when Henry pulled rein in the courtyard, and he found himself trembling between anticipation and fear. What if Margaret was not the woman he remembered? Could any woman be so beautiful? So good? It had been fourteen years since they had looked into each other's eyes. And now he saw things in people's eyes, things he did not wish to see. They knew it, too. Jasper was sometimes afraid of him. Would his mother be frightened, also?

Henry had intended to go to his own chamber first, to wash the dust of the road from himself and don fresh clothing so that his mother would be proud. Now he said roughly to the man who opened the door for him, 'Where is the Lady Margaret?' And when the servant took time to bow before he answered, Henry could have struck him with impatience. She sat in the hall, he was told. Somewhat else was said, but Henry did not wait to hear.

Unable to abide the slow ceremony of servants and announcements, he flung the hall door open with his own hand. And – she was there. Two steps walking, remembering dignity, the rest running, dignity cast to the wind, brought him past a glory of gowns to fall to his knees and bury his head in Margaret's lap before she could rise. He said nothing, and she only stroked his bright hair, from which the cap had tumbled in his violence, murmuring his name over and over as if it gave the moment reality. It was wonderful; it was heaven. A sob shook him.

'Henry,' Margaret said, 'we are not alone here.' He stiffened as if she had struck him a blow, and Margaret bent low. 'My love, dear love, I do not care, but later – you would.'

Now the real meeting could no longer be delayed. Henry lifted his head, and Margaret's eyes were full upon his. 'May a son not weep for joy when he greets the mother for whom he has longed for fourteen years?' His lashes were wet, but his lips laughed. There was only joy and a burning love in his

134

mother's eyes. If there were other things in her soul, those had been washed away in this moment.

'You are too thin and too tired, but happy?'

'Oh, yes. I am happy.'

'Your fame outruns you. You have done well, my Henry.'

'When did my mother think her only chick other than perfect?'

It was Margaret's turn to laugh. 'I never thought that.' Then she sobered, searching his face. 'Nor are you perfect now, though you have passed through purgatory already.' Please God, she prayed silently, that I have not sentenced him to hell with my ambition for him.

'Send your women away, mama,' Henry urged. 'I have so much to say to you.'

Margaret laid her hand on Henry's mouth, her eyes warning. 'They are not my women, beloved. The queen has come to greet you bearing her daughter.' Her hand increased its pressure as she saw the expression on Henry's face. 'I know Queen Elizabeth will pardon you for greeting me first. She understands a son's affection, longing to greet her own son, Dorset.'

Margaret's eyes still warned, and though Henry flushed red as fire and then grew pale as alabaster, he was silent. He kissed both of Margaret's hands, which now lay over his in her lap, set his cap on his head, and rose to his feet. He should have known. The servant tried to tell him, and he should have realized from the brilliance of the gowns. Margaret's ladies always dressed soberly, as she did herself. True, they were all resplendent in green and white today, but he had passed a rainbow, not a bed of lilies. Margaret had come to her feet, also. Now with tears in her eyes she made ready to curtsy to the ground and kiss the king's hand. Henry caught her.

'No! You shall not bow to me.'

'Will you deprive me of the right of every other Englishwoman, sire?' Margaret asked playfully, but still warning.

Henry hesitated. It was policy, and his mother was ready to do this, as she was ready to do anything else, for him. Yet policy had to stop somewhere or a man would become a monster like Gloucester. For Henry, policy stopped with his mother and his uncle. 'I will not have you bend your knee to me,

135

mother, nor call me sire. Have I done so ill, become so shameful, that you will have me no more for a son?'

That, too, was said lightly, as a jest, but Margaret heard the cry of loneliness. She cupped her hand around her son's face and smiled without speaking. Nonetheless, Henry had his answer. He brushed her hand again with his lips and turned from her. Margaret saw his slight form brace as if he steeled himself to some great trial, but a moment later he had lifted the dowager queen's hand to his lips in such a way that he drew her from her chair to a standing position. He did not bow, did not even bend his head to kiss her hand; he brought that up to his mouth, uncomfortably bent. She had been easy to identify since she was the only woman in the room besides Margaret who had been seated. Now, reluctantly, his eyes scanned the ladies who stood beside her seeking the Elizabeth who was to be his wife.

She was not hard to identify, either, for she was as beautiful as her mother once had been, with a lush ripeness that Henry found faintly repellent after his mother's delicacy. Her huge almond-shaped eyes, blue as the best water sapphire, and her full, sensual lips were her mother's. The fine straight nose, the long upper lip, were Edward's. The coif covered her hair, but Henry knew it to be as golden as his own, and her skin was whiter than milk. He gazed at her, waiting – so obviously waiting that the room was hushed as if no one dared breathe.

Elizabeth, staring back, received several minor and one major shock. Somehow, in spite of what Margaret had told her, she expected a heroic figure. Henry was thin to emaciation, his temples and cheeks sunken, his eyes ringed with the mauve of sleeplessness. Beyond that, Elizabeth was so accustomed to the handsome faces of the men of her family that she was repelled by Henry's plainness. His face was not even redeemingly harsh so that it could be called manly. He had a complexion as clean and fair as a girl's, and hair that was a delicate, golden glory, but the too-long nose, the grim, too-thin lips, the long, heavy, forward-jutting jaw combined to produce a countenance that was not even engagingly ugly but simply unhandsome – plain. And the eyes! Elizabeth felt herself growing cold. One could fall into those too-widely spaced, too-long, too-narrow wells of grey light and be lost forever.

Slowly, reluctantly, as if the eyes had exerted a physical pressure and pushed her down, Elizabeth's knees bent and she

136

went into the curtsy Henry had forbidden his mother to make. And as flowers bend before a wind, every lady sank in obeisance to England's king.

'Madam, we give you glad greeting,' Henry said to the dowager, inclining his head graciously now that he had received his bow. He moved quickly, extending his hand and lifting Elizabeth to her feet before she could rise of her own volition. 'Lady Elizabeth,' he murmured, saluting her cheeks formally in the French style.

Their eyes were level, for he was short and she was tall. Elizabeth lowered her lids demurely; it was impossible for Henry to tell whether she hid hate or fear, or acted merely out of habit. That she could really be shy or demure, he dismissed. She was no green girl; she was more than twenty-one years of age and she had lived in a loose court, intrigue-ridden and sex-orientated, for most of her life.

The dowager queen, recovering from the shock of having been outmanoeuvred, began to make her formal speech of welcome and congratulation. Henry turned to her courteously, noting that his faithful council had filed into the room, that Jasper was kissing Margaret as though he would never stop. Cheney and Poynings were sidling down the room, their eyes fixed on their master. True these were only women, but they were Edward's women; Henry was totally unarmed, and it was not unknown for a madwoman to slide a poniard between a man's ribs.

The speech went on, but Henry's mind was on the weariness of Ned's stance. Henry decided, as he smiled like a wax image, that the additional burden of guarding him must be removed from the council's shoulders. He would employ a guard as the French king did. Not foreign mercenaries, however, nor yet gentlemen's sons who might have their own games to play at. He would use good solid yeomen, English born, English bred, well paid, and with no axe to grind but Henry's own. They would serve both to enhance his dignity and to protect him. Henry felt a trifle better humoured. At least he had been able to employ the time that woman yapped at him to some practical purpose.

'. . . and as our gratitude to you is great, so is our loyalty, which we hope will be rewarded by the restoration to us of what has been reft from us unjustly.'

137

Henry heard that. Loyalty – as exemplified by Dorset's attempted desertion and the dowager's lack of protest when Gloucester planned to snatch his bride from him. Henry felt himself flush with rage, but his sense of humour came to his rescue. After all, knowing what she was, what could he expect? Besides, he held the whip hand and she would get what he chose to give. She would have to have her dower property restored, of course. Gloucester had confiscated that when he declared Edward's marriage invalid and his children bastards on the grounds that Edward had a prior betrothal. Since Henry could not afford to have his wife called a bastard, her mother's marriage had to be valid and the property was hers. It was unfortunate; Henry resented having to give her a penny, but perhaps it was better than trying to support her out of the royal income, and he could not let his mother-in-law starve even if he would like to.

'What was yours as Edward's wife, will be yours again.' That was not what the dowager had meant, exactly, but before she could speak again Henry had turned to Elizabeth. 'And what have you to ask of me, my lady?'

Colour flamed in her face as if milk had been stained with blood. Was it for this that she had withstood Richard? Had she brought insult upon herself by her poor tokens of a ring and a brooch – the only things she had to give at that dreadful time?

'Naught,' Elizabeth said proudly.

She heard her mother's breath hiss inward, and she grew pale as wax as she remembered she had been told to plead for her half brother Dorset's ransom. The dowager had not wished to mention Dorset's name, since she had been involved in his desertion and she did not want Henry to be reminded of that to her discredit. Characteristically, she had pressed the task upon her daughter. Elizabeth had agreed willingly, for she was fond of Dorset in spite of his selfish weakness. In fact she hardly noticed a trait so common to her family as to be a natural thing. It was only that she had been so deathly weary last night when her mother had harangued her on the subject. Two hundred miles she had come in four days, all the way from the prison at Sheriff Hutton in Yorkshire where Gloucester had hidden her. From one prison to another, she now feared, another perhaps more terrible, although she might not

138

be physically confined. That and her anger had made her forget poor Dorset.

'Except—' she faltered, as Henry began to move away.

He turned to her again, courteously, his head thrust slightly forward as with the intensity of his listening. 'Except?' he encouraged, his thin lips curved mockingly and his bright grey eyes filled wtih contempt.

Was she to endure this? Elizabeth wondered. A swift glance showed her her mother's fury. She would be scolded, shrieked at, reviled. Elizabeth was not a physical coward. She had faced with courage the possibility that Gloucester would kill her and marry one of her sisters. She had ridden south with Robert Willoughby at breakneck speed without a murmur. Her cousin, the young earl of Warwick who was really her father's heir to the throne now, had wept and trembled at the pace Willoughby set. The boy had to be carried across Willoughby's saddle at last, but Elizabeth had faced ditch and fence without fear. Only she could not endure loud voices, angry quarrelling, or endless nagging. It made her sick and weak to be told that she was unkind, unnatural, and selfish.

'My brother Dorset,' she whispered, her face red as fire again. 'I would beg you to – to recall him homc.'

'I am pledged to do so,' Henry said smoothly. 'I am not likely to break my word, however, like others are to do so.' He raised her hand and kissed it, properly, icily. 'And now, I beg your pardon all for so brief a greeting, but I have much to do.'

Henry worked for the rest of the day in his own chamber. He did not come down for the evening meal, sending Oxford, Edgecombe, and Courtenay, who was much improved, with smooth-tongued excuses. Before the second set of candles had guttered and been replaced, however, Jasper entered without ceremony. Henry glanced up and smiled, but Jasper did not respond.

'Harry, your mother wants you.'

Henry laid down his pen at once. 'Is she alone?' Jasper nodded, and he rose. Poynings and Guildford stood, also, but Henry gestured them back. 'Keep on with those lists of men suitable for commissions of the peace and sheriffs. I am in no danger here.'

He found Margaret pacing her room, and the glance she

139

turned on him was neither awed nor admiring but frankly angry. 'What made you use such discourtesy to the queen and Lady Elizabeth?'

'I thought I was most courteous – compared with what they offered me.'

'Elizabeth Woodville is a dangerous woman.'

'True. Would you have me ruled by her? There were women enough in that room to spread word of how the king of England bowed meekly before her while she remained seated. Is that what you desire? Why the devil is she here?'

Margaret's angry expression faded to one of weary worry. 'Because I dare not leave her out of my sight or hearing. I think she already had made some plan of setting Elizabeth up as queen. It could not succeed. England will not accept a queen, particularly when the state is so reft apart, but it could have made more trouble for you. Oh, Henry, I am so afraid.'

He caught her hands. I am not afraid. If it were not God's will that I be king, I would have been slain on Bosworth field. Richard came within one axe blow of it. Nay, Mother, do not weep. Here am I, unhurt, with Gloucester's crown fastened to my helm. I tell you this is God's work, not man's. He has set me on the throne, and He will preserve me there.'

'God's will be done,' Margaret sighed. 'Perhaps you are right. Perhaps it is better to outface the Woodvilles. But why did you insult Lady Elizabeth? What hurt has she done you? Henry, she has ever favoured you. She even sent you tokens when she had little enough to send and it was a danger to her if the messenger was taken. She is a good girl.'

Henry dropped his mother's hands. 'Edward's and Elizabeth Woodville's daughter! Good? Good for what? Lust and luxury are what she is good for.'

'Henry.'

'Oh, I will wed her, and bed her, and doubtless she will breed me heirs – they are fecund mares, those Woodville women. I know where my advantage lies. But I will be king of England of myself, not by Lady Elizabeth's courtesy. In this country and in my own house, I will be master.'

'Henry, listen. She *is* a good girl. She was in my husband's keeping for near a year, and I came to know her well. Her looks are like her mother's, I admit, but her nature is more like her father's.'

'I do not see that there was much to choose between them.'

'You are growing bitter, Henry. There was much good in Edward. His temper was sweet.' Margaret smiled almost pleadingly. 'Sweeter than yours, my love. And at first he was temperate and not vengeful.' Her voice dropped to a fearful whisper. 'It was the kingship that destroyed him. All men say it. Little by little, he rotted.'

'There is not enough of me to rot,' Henry said gaily, slapping his lean belly. 'I can only dry up.'

Margaret would not let him shift the subject. 'Be kind to her, Henry.'

'I hope I will be just,' he replied coldly. 'If she is a good wife, she will find me an irreproachable husband.'

He kissed his mother and left, and, though he was irritated by her defence of Elizabeth, he was happy. Margaret had spoken her mind freely, had come close to scolding him. All was well. His mother was still his mother and not afraid. He returned to the problem of setting men faithful to him in both major and minor administrative posts with the least disruption and dissatisfaction possible. Margaret stood staring at the closed door, then turned and dropped to her knees before the elaborate crucifix that hung on the wall. My knees have become calloused with praying, she thought, but they will bleed with it before my Henry is safe. Later she rose and crossed the hall. She scratched at a door, opened it without waiting for a reply, and went in swiftly.

Elizabeth was not asleep. She was sitting upright in bed, her hair a golden cascade around her shoulders, two bright red spots on her cheeks, and her eyes sparkling like gems in her rage.

'I did not announce myself for fear that you would turn me away,' Margaret said, smiling.

'You have always been a kind friend, madam,' Elizabeth replied icily. 'How should I turn you away?'

'Elizabeth, just because Henry has disgraced himself, must you be angry with me?'

The full lips quivered, the blue eyes misted over. 'I am not angry.'

Margaret laughed. 'Now you will have to confess that you tell lies. You are angry and, indeed, I would think you a simpleton if you were not. Dreadful boy, he has no sense at all.'

'On the contrary, he has, it seems, an overwhelming sense of his royal dignity – being new to it.'

'Oh, dear,' Margaret said, plaintively humorous, 'I never knew you to be so waspish.' Then her face became grave. 'But it is not true. Henry wears dignity like a cloak to hide the man underneath. Elizabeth, you must be patient with him. You and he will spend your lives together. Is not a little patience a small price to pay for a happy life?'

'Happy! A princess does not expect to be happy. She does not expect to be insulted, either.'

'But Elizabeth, you can be happy with Henry. This is why I beg you not to harden your heart against him because of a sharp word or two. He loves few, but he loves with his whole being. It is worth much suffering to see the cloak cast aside and gain such a love.'

'Doubtless it is given already.'

That was the thing Margaret feared. She had not had the courage to ask her son, and now she did not dare lie to Elizabeth for she knew not whether hardship might have bred cruelty in Henry. If so, he might tell Elizabeth just to hurt her – to wound the only thing that was left of Edward who had driven him into hardship.

'He is so good,' she said desperately.

Elizabeth's expression softened. 'Indeed, madam, he is good to you. Who could fail to be good to you?'

Margaret seized eagerly on the sign of weakening. 'You cannot forgive him now, but only let me tell you what I heard from Pembroke so that you may understand. Henry has not slept three hours a night for ten days. Think what it is to set to rights a kingdom so torn by war and hatred. He has made a hundred – mayhap a thousand – pretty speeches, and listened to as many. Then he comes, overworn, overweary, to a place where he thinks there will be no need for fine words. Who needs fine words for a mother? This relief denied him, he struck out at those he felt tore his rest from him. Elizabeth, he is so frail. He was never strong. That is why I said he has no sense. He pushes himself beyond his strength.'

'A very dangerous thing to do. Dangerous to himself as well as to others.'

The faint warmth was gone from Elizabeth's voice. Margaret could only hope that the girl would remember what had been

142

said when she was less angry. She turned the subject to Elizabeth's studies, for both of them loved learning, and before she left she had the satisfaction of seeing the princess's complexion and expression return to normal. Nonetheless, Margaret was deeply distressed. Aside from being Edward's heir, Elizabeth had seemed a perfect match for Henry. She was beautiful, pious, sweet-tempered, and very intelligent. Her conversation was witty and she was an accomplished musician. What could be more perfect to delight a busy man in his few hours of leisure?

If Elizabeth did have a fault, aside from the very womanly ones of being easily excited and easily reduced to tears, it was pride. She was very conscious of being a king's daughter. Still, Margaret did not believe that Elizabeth wished to rule. She had never shown any sign of interest in political matters except those which affected her personally. Her pride was centred in outward things – very like her mother she was in the love of show – in being treated with honour. Henry would be battling a chimera if he classed Elizabeth's desire for recognition for its own sake with her mother's desire for recognition, which could be used to wield influence over government. If he fought to keep her in the background so that she would not interfere with his kingship, he might wound her pride mortally and make her his enemy.

Chapter Eleven

In spite of Margaret's renewed expostulation, matters mended very little between Henry and Elizabeth. He unbent so far on the second day at Saint Albans as to wear the ring and brooch she had sent him and to present her with some pretty trinkets lifted from Gloucester's baggage. He had also been perfectly courteous, but unfortunately in a cold and distant manner that contrasted sharply with his warm playfulness to his mother. Perhaps Elizabeth would not have taken that amiss, since she was very fond of Margaret herself, and Henry's sportiveness, even when addressed to someone else, was very appealing. She could have forgiven his coldness. After all, they were really strangers, and Henry was reserved in his manner to all the women there, only he struck at her pride again.

Sir Robert Willoughby, who had taken Warwick on to the Tower which was to be his home for the rest of his short life, reappeared. Unsmiling, single-minded, lacking the diplomatic polish which could have eased, although nothing could conceal, Henry's purpose, he told the ladies that he was to escort them to London before dark. Elizabeth did not need to ask why. It was plain that the new king wanted no relation of Edward's to distract the Londoners' attention from him when he made his triumphal entrance the next day. Edward had been London's darling, and Henry meant to win the city for himself independent of any association with Edward's heiress.

The dowager queen had made a scene. Willoughby, interested only in fulfilling Henry's command, Lancastrian to the core, indifferent to the dowager's past status, said briefly, 'Madam, I will bind you and gag you, throw you into a covered cart so that none will see or hear, if you do not ride with me willingingly.'

He meant it. He herded them into one room and stood guard over them while servants packed their things. Through the window they could see waiting armed men in the green and white Tudor livery.

'Where are you taking us?' Elizabeth asked fearfully. Were

144

they prisoners? she wondered. Would they, too, be lodged in the Tower, never to emerge into the light?

'Why, to your mother's house, my love,' Margaret's voice replied. 'Oh, do not mind that grim escort, and do not mind Robert's coarse ways – he was raised in a stable, I think. I am going with you, and my son has suddenly decided that I am not old enough to care for myself. Moreover, we will watch the procession from the lord mayor's house. Really, sometimes men are too foolish when they think a woman needs shielding. Henry says the mob may turn dangerous when it becomes drunk. The lord mayor's house will be safe.'

The excuse was pitiful, but Elizabeth received it in silence. Her mother had brought this upon them with her constant shifting of purpose. No, her birth had brought it upon her. She could not be angry at Lady Margaret, although she realized that Henry's mother was now her jailer. Doubtless Margaret had taken the thankless burden upon herself out of kindness, to spare them the fear and discomfort of a real prison.

She had indeed done so, coming near to quarrelling with her son again over the question. 'I will not have them running about loose, concocting God knows what plots to annoy me,' Henry had snapped when Margaret had protested his decision to put them in the Tower with Warwick.

'Elizabeth will concoct nothing – unless you drive her to it.'

'It will not be for long, mother,' Henry pleaded, weakening. Prison was no place for women, even women like the dowager queen. 'Two months or three at the most. Once I am crowned and parliament has acknowledged me, they may bide where they will. By then my own men will hold every key position in the country.'

'And you will have ruined your life and have a wife who hates you. She does not hate you yet, Henry. She is not at fault for what her mother and father did to you. Do not do this.'

'Your mother has a point, Harry,' Jasper said. 'I am no friend to the Yorkists, but if you will not kill them, you must not enrage them by treating Edward's wife and daughter this way. The whole country will take you for another Gloucester if news of this leaks out.'

Henry dropped his head into his hands. 'What am I to do with them, then? Will the country like it better if I set armed

145

men to watch them, or seclude them in some distant manor?'

Jasper looked troubled, but Margaret smiled. 'Leave them to me, Henry. I know how to deal with the dowager, and there is no reason why a son should not set guards about his precious mother. I would be a fair hostage in your enemies' hands.'

'But I want you with me tomorrow. You have laboured as hard as I to achieve this.'

'No, dear. The triumph must be yours alone. You must bear the burdens alone, and you must stand alone in the eyes of the people.'

And Henry's entrance into London was a triumph. He had been worried; Londoners were independent and strong-willed, and they had supported the Yorkist cause in the past. They greeted the Lancastrian king, however, with a burst of enthusiasm, the mayor and aldermen of the city dressed in their scarlet robes pressing forward to kiss the hands 'which had overcome so cruel and monstrous a tyrant'. The citizens were out in force, too, and echoed their approval of the mayor's sentiments with cheers and strewn flowers. Henry was relieved. It was not unknown for London crowds to stand sullenly silent or to express their disapproval more vigorously with stones and refuse. Some day that might be his fate, Henry thought wryly, but today they loved him, and he made sure to move at a snail's pace, turning first to one side and then to the other so that all might see him well.

At each major crossroad the procession stopped completely while a pageant of some sort unrolled. Laudatory speeches were made in verse and in prose, in English, in French, and even in Latin, and Henry prayed he would not stumble hopelessly in the confusion of languages as he made his replies. If he did, no one seemed to notice, and Henry was too excited to worry for long. On the steps of Saint Paul's Cathedral the lord mayor came forward with still another speech and, even more pleasing to the practical king, a free gift of one thousand marks from the guilds of the city. Within the church the banners which Henry had carried at Bosworth were dedicated to God and a Te Deum was sung.

Henry found himself trembling and close to tears. He knew it was hunger and exhaustion, but he also knew that his apparent emotion was making a most excellent effect and he exerted no effort to check himself. Fortunately this was the

146

end of the ceremonies, for the Tudor's exhilaration would not have supported him much longer. He was permitted to withdraw to the bishop of London's palace where he would have collapsed in the main hall had not Pembroke and Poynings held him upright. Henry went immediately to bed at his uncle's almost hysterical insistence, but a flagon of wine and a simple meal revived him. Having slyly waited until Jasper could be convinced to go out and tell Margaret about the portion of the ceremonies she could not see, Henry sent for his council. The first man to enter the door was a priest, and the king was just about to offer a tactful excuse for not attending to him when he recognized the face.

'Foxe!' he cried joyfully.

'Sire,' Foxe replied, bending to kiss his hand.

'How I have missed you! You are hereby appointed as my principal secretary. Are you too tired to work?'

Foxe pinched his lower lip. 'I am a cautious man, Your Grace. Knowing you, I had a good night's sleep before I presented myself. I am ready for anything.'

'You are a sensible man. Get from Poynings a list of Gloucester's men who were slain and another of those who are prisoner or fled into sanctuary. Their property is to be used to reward my men, but – I wish no heir to be stripped naked. Enough is to be secured to the wife and children of any man killed to support them in decency although not in luxury. You can estimate such needs?'

'I can.'

'Good. When there are no direct heirs, of course, the whole may be distributed.'

'Fortunately, Gloucester was more generous than wise in the distribution of his favours,' Foxe murmured. 'There will be sufficient to make many feel rewarded.'

'The matter is not so simple. In the case where there are heirs, or where the men are prisoner rather than slain, I do not wish to take from them all hope of recovering their property. Richard, I vowed I would not bathe this land in blood. Since I will not slay them, I must find a way to make these men accept me.'

'Not difficult, Your Grace. If the property goes to the crown – where, of course, it will be most useful – but is not deeded elsewhere, two purposes will be served. Now, while commerce is at a standstill, you will have use of the revenues. What the crown holds, however, it may always return; and when the custom returns and other yields have grown greater, it will not harm the crown to regrant the lands.'

Henry nodded. That was exactly what he had decided himself.

'Then they must bide prisoners until the realm is securely in your hand. Not long, mayhap six months or a year, and the imprisonment to be honourable – not hard or shameful. I will speak with them from time to time, and Your Grace should do so, also, making plain, but without promise, that their honours may be restored for loyal service. Then release, one at a time, the least dangerous or most trustworthy first, with title restored and sufficient land for comfort but not for the hiring of mercenaries—'

'Richard, I will make you chancellor as soon as I can find you a see to support the honour. Your mind and mine are as one.'

Foxe shook his head sharply. 'No, Your Grace, I beg you. You will clip my wings too close. There is a man better fitted for that place – Morton, the bishop of Ely.'

'I do not know him.'

'I do. Moreover, he has served your cause well. If it suits Your Grace, I would hold the privy seal.'

Henry burst out laughing. 'Richard, you wear the garb of a priest, but I suspect a serpent underneath.'

'If I must be that to strike your enemies, that I will be.' Foxe yielded his place beside the bed as the remainder of the council filed in and came to kiss Henry's hand.

'We are come to the dividing of spoils, gentlemen,' Henry said merrily. 'Ah, that whets your appetite, but I fear you will be displeased with me. Not only will I swallow the lion's share, but what you receive will be widely dispersed.'

'If I have back my own lands which Gloucester reft from me, I desire naught else,' Courtenay said roughly. 'In truth, sire, I would rather have nothing at all than that you should fear I would use your gift ill.'

'Now, Edward, this nonsense is not like you. You nearly died for me. How could I suspect you of disloyalty? The dispersal is not to guard against a concentration of your power but to make it possible for me to set you in authority in many places. We will have to spread ourselves thin this year. Later you may sell or exchange as you see fit.'

There was a murmur of approval, and Henry moved on to discuss arrangements for collecting the customs duties.

'You may leave that to Thomas Lovell, Dynham, and myself,' Edgecombe said when Henry had passed from outlining the rules to be followed to the appointment of collectors to take the place of Gloucester's men. 'We have been working on the lists and will submit them to you as soon as they are ready.'

'You mean to collect before the subsidies are revoted by parliament?' Foxe asked.

'They were voted to the king. I am the king.'

There was a silence while eyes shifted uneasily to stare at the floor or the walls – anywhere but at Henry.

'Do you mean to rule without a parliament, sire?' Edward Poynings asked quietly.

Henry examined the faces. The earl of Oxford seemed ready to burst into tears. Guildford and Courtenay were pale. Edgecombe was wringing his hands unconsciously, and Foxe had sucked his thin lips right out of sight. Henry shook his head and began to laugh.

'I would like to know what reason I have ever given you to believe me a fool. How long do you think I would hold this land if I offended its people more than Gloucester? He, after all, only murdered a king and his brother – so many kings have been murdered in this land that had they not been children little notice would have been taken of it. The parliament is an institution no king may make light of.'

The sigh of relief in the room was universal. Henry had discovered what he wished to know at small cost. If these devoted supporters were shaken at the thought that parliament would not be called, the country as a whole would have gone mad. Henry did not pretend to himself that the common men or even the petty landed gentry, outside of Wales, had flocked to his banner. But had they loved Gloucester or even favoured him, Henry could never have marched to Lichfield unmolested. His troops would have been harassed; the towns would have shut their gates and refused to sell him food. There were many ways to support a king. If he offended the people and a challenger

149

rose to claim his throne, they would not support him, either. Actually he was relieved. He was fond of an appearance of legality, at least. It would be best to summon a parliament and have that body affirm his title. But affirm it was all they could be permitted to do. It would not be wise to foster the notion that parliament could make – and therefore, perhaps, unmake – kings.

'No,' Henry continued, 'I intend to call parliament as soon as is practical. Obviously, however, that must wait until our supporters grasp control of the shires. It would be – ah – unfortunate – if Gloucester's creatures filled the Commons.'

There was a hearty burst of laughter. Naturally one called a parliament. Also naturally the parliament should be filled with men who wished to do the king's will. Where was the sense of having there men who would merely impede legislation?

'I think it would also be well for Your Majesty to be crowned before the summoning,' Foxe suggested.

Henry could have kissed his henchman, for that was certainly what he intended; but now he could purse his lips and thoughtfully take stock of his gentlemen's faces. They would be honest in their reaction since the suggestion had not come from him. Guildford, Edgecombe, and Courtenay now looked eager, and Oxford looked serious but not disapproving.

'It is the custom, Your Majesty,' Poynings said flatly. 'When the king dies, his son is crowned and then summons parliament.'

Oxford's face cleared. 'So it is. It has been so long since a son inherited from his father that I had forgot. Your Majesty had best follow custom.'

'Well, I will, and that gladly, but would you please stop calling me "Your Majesty" and "Your Grace". It is quite enough to do so in public, but when I am near naked and propped upon singularly hard and uncomfortable bolsters I can be neither majestic nor graceful – hardly gracious. Sire will do nicely, if you can no longer bring yourselves to call me Henry.'

It was the right thing to say; they were all pleased. Day by day since Bosworth Field a gulf had been opening between them. Henry's reminder had thrown a bridge across that gulf, yet he knew with a faint sinking of the heart that none of them would ever cross the bridge. No, that was not correct. When

150

they had grown old together – if they were both spared that long – Foxe would call him Henry, even Harry. A pair of faintly compassionate brown eyes met his. Henry restrained a shudder. He did not look forward to the day when Ned Poynings would call him by name, although he knew it would be a comfort to him at the time.

'It would not be wise to delay the summoning too long—' Foxe let his voice trail off.

'No, by God, there is scarce time to chew what we must swallow. Oxford – no – your back will break beneath what I am loading on it. Courtenay, gather some of your relatives and see if some plan for a coronation can be found. Wait – take council with my mother. She took part in Gloucester's crowning. Keep in mind that my crowning must outshine his as the sun outshines the moon. Next?'

'The dowager queen—'

'Thank you, Ned. I forget her so regularly that I fear I wish to do so. Foxe, her dower property must be restored – but that is all. Neither stick nor stone, brooch nor bracelet beyond what Edward deeded her for dower is to be hers.'

'It will be done.'

Henry flashed a smile. 'I am sure it will. Oxford, the Tower is in your charge. I want to know what lies within. John Radcliffe will be lord steward. You can set him on to Windsor and the other royal houses. I want it all – plate, jewels, coin, prisoners, animals – all.'

'It will take time—'

'Henry!'

'Gentlemen,' the Tudor said wryly, 'you must retire. It would be most unsettling to my dignity in your eyes for you to hear me being scolded like a naughty child. Yes, uncle, I know. If I work so hard I will be sick and unable to work at all. But I have not been working hard. I have merely been setting hard tasks for others.'

Jasper opened his mouth to scold further, and then shut it. What Henry said was plainly true. He looked revived, not more fatigued by the conference he had had. As the days went by, Jasper and Margaret agreed that their fear that Henry's driving spirit would wear out his frail body was far from the truth. Kingship sat lightly upon him, although he took his task most seriously and worked away at it from dawn till late night. If any were to be pitied it was the tight-knit group around him who worked until they reeled from exhaustion and then were flayed by jests into renewed strength so that they could labour more.

Others were now added to the original group. Reginald Bray, who had done so much to forward the cause, was transferred from Lord Stanley's household to Henry's; William Berkley, Thomas Lovell, Lord Dubeney, and Dynham, who had not merely a talent but a genius for money, all were absorbed and set to work. William Stanley and Lord Stanley were both given high posts close to the king – high posts which would keep them at Henry's side constantly, and which had nothing whatsoever to do with the armed forces of the nation. It soon became a clear fact that the king's love was directly proportional to the burdens a man bore for his sake and totally unrelated to the honours he bestowed. Those who worked were rewarded with land and power; those he suspected were praised and patted and given high-sounding, empty posts of honour. Once that was plain, any man given a task completed it to the best of his ability as quickly as possible and ran back to ask for more work.

While the gentry of England laboured, the Commons played. Henry declared a period of thanksgiving and, having assured himself that the treasury could bear it and that the income from customs and confiscated property would soon cover the expenditure, he ordered the distribution of free bread and meat and wine. Minstrels and play actors were paid to perform in public, and in London where the king's largesse flowed most freely, men danced and sang in the streets praising Lancastrian Henry who had freed them from the Yorkist tyrant. They forgot – it was easy to forget when ale barrels stood on the street crossings and wine ran in the fountains – that they had stoned the last Lancastrian Henry when he rode through the lanes and wept with joy when Yorkist Edward came. The Tudor did not forget, but he deemed it necessary to court the people.

The celebrations were cut short by tragedy. A new and terrifying plague scourged joy from men. They called it the sweating sickness, for in it a man sweat his life away while his body was racked with shuddering chills. The lord mayor, who had kissed Henry's hands, died; his successor died. Not one in a hundred escaped the disease, although its course was short and if a man lived through a day and a night he did not die at all. Those who did not love Henry swore the plague came with him, and predicted ill for the reign and the realm, but Henry himself remained untroubled. Although he fled from London and took refuge at Guildford, he laughed at the fears of his followers, saying they were fortunate that the plague had tamed the people. He would not have known, he confessed, how to curtail the merrymaking and bring them back to business without angering them otherwise.

And, plague or no plague, the work of the kingdom went on apace. By September 15th the summons to parliament had gone out into the shires naming the fifth day of November as the time for assembly. None could claim that the king was neglectful either of law or of the comfort of his subjects. Less than a month had passed since his victory at Bosworth; there had been no unnecessary delay in the summons. Moreover, a month, or near that, was needed for a man called to parliament to set his house in order and travel – sometimes the full length of the kingdom – to London.

Arrangements for the coronation moved even faster. Henry's agents scoured the city for cloth: rich velvets and silks; for furs: ermine, miniver, and vair; for jewels and gold chains. They bought wherever they could get the best price, bargaining unmercifully, but – miracle of miracles – they paid for what they bought. When that news spread, the prices dropped a little. It was better to sell to the king's agent for a low profit and know that the claim would be settled at once than to sell elsewhere at a higher price and face a lawsuit which would swallow the profit before the money was forthcoming.

The only thing which seemed to lie forgotten was Henry's courtship and marriage. Margaret had given up urging the matter because Henry had turned her aside with loving jests and japes so often that she realized he simply would not discuss it. No one else dared mention the subject since Jasper, prodded by Margaret, had been snarled at for bringing it up. Anything which could make the king lose his temper with his dearly beloved uncle was a topic to be sedulously avoided. As a matter of fact, it was shocking to find anything at all which could overset Henry's good humour. Never, the clerks and lesser gentlemen marvelled to each other, never had there been a better-tempered king.

It was true enough. Long buffeted by fate, Henry had given up blaming men for the blows dealt him by circumstance. If a river was in flood, he did not berate the messenger for coming late. Nor even when the fault was man's did he grow angry. He could flay an erring servant better in a freezing, level voice, wearing only an icy expression of gravity, than anyone else could do while bellowing like a bull with a black scowl. All the more terrible to see him frown. Elizabeth, the white rose of York, was a forbidden subject.

Henry had not been able to avoid his destined bride completely. Margaret, being as stubborn as her son, soon refused to come to visit him. Her message had been stern; if Henry wished to see her, he could command her presence as king to subject or he could come to her as a proper son to a mother. Meekly, Henry arrived, entering the room with his hat in his hand and a look of such false humility on his face that both Margaret and Elizabeth, who stood by her, had burst into surprised laughter. Henry had lifted his lowered lids at the bell-like trilling which was very different from his mother's soft laugh, had seen the unguarded loveliness of the princess's face, and had been surprised himself into a fleeting expression of avidity.

The mask of a chastened and dutiful son dropped again, but Elizabeth had seen. When Henry finally stopped making the most extravagant and ridiculous apologies to his mother and turned to converse with his future bride, his manner was particularly frigid. Margaret could have wrung her hands in despair. She had hoped that meeting Elizabeth when the dowager queen was absent and the girl's manner was more natural would soften him. That plan had failed dismally, but Elizabeth did not seem to be taking offence at Henry's chill courtesies. Her replies were proper, but her glance was inviting and she displayed both her lovely hands and her charming profile to their best advantage.

Elizabeth had not been raised in the court of Edward IV for nothing. She had seen many men enslaved by women, weak men like her brother Dorset, and men who had once been strong, like Hastings, and, she flinched at the memory but faced it, like her father. Insult her, would he, this upstart Welsh adventurer? Before she was done, he would regard her lightest sigh as a command. However, Elizabeth had no opportunity

154

to test the quality of her opponent. Within a week of Henry's visit, he was besieged by troubles which made it impossible for his mother to think of bothering him about the feelings of a single girl.

Scotland was England's hereditary enemy in the north, as France was her enemy across the Channel. James III was no strong king, for his nobles were powerful and often defied him, but England's troubles had given him ideas. If he could fall on the war-torn country and defeat it, his prestige and power would be greatly enhanced. As soon as it was clear that Henry's attempt at the throne would not be easily crushed, James had begun to assemble an army. When Gloucester was defeated, his opportunity seemed golden indeed. The north had been deeply devoted to Richard III and had made it plain that, although Londoners kissed Henry's hands, they would greet him otherwise. It would take little effort, James believed, to swarm down over those counties and annex them to his kingdom. What could Henry do? He had disbanded most of his army, sending the Welshmen and the mercenaries home for fear of offending the proud English. The gentlemen of the northern shires would make no resistance. Was not their chief lord, Northumberland, in prison? Had they not publicly deplored Gloucester's defeat?

Reginald Bray, who had an efficient network of spies throughout the country, brought Henry the news of James's intentions on September 20th.

'We should have kept the Frenchmen and Welshmen under arms,' Oxford said tensely.

'Shall I mass the guns and begin moving north with them?' Guildford asked.

'Rhys and I can summon the Welsh to arms again,' Jasper offered.

'We should have no trouble in raising an army from the southern shires,' Devon suggested.

Henry smiled on them. He had just eaten, but his belly felt suspiciously hollow and his hands were icy, although they rested quietly, lightly clasped on the table. 'Gentlemen, gentlemen,' he protested gently, 'are you my friends or my enemies? The men of the north know they have done me great disservice. What would be their feelings if I marched upon them with an army of French, Welsh, and Southrons? If I brought great

155

guns from my southern strongholds? Would they fear me or Scot James more?'

'Often it comes about that a man's worst enemies do him more good than his best friends,' Foxe said softly. 'What will you do, Your Grace?'

'I will do what is the custom of this country. I will warn the northmen that they must defend themselves, and I will tell them that the rest of the nation will be called to arms to support their effort if need be.'

'That is a dangerous gamble, sire,' Poynings said doubtfully.

'Not so dangerous, I hope. Agreed that the men of the northern shires do not love the slayer of Gloucester, at least I have done them no hurt as yet, whereas the Scots have been their enemies all their lives. They will fight. Moreover, I will give them reason to fight and reason to love me at the same time. I will give them a free pardon for the crimes I might have charged against them.'

'But—'

Henry shook his head, stilling Oxford's protest. 'I always intended it, but to pardon an enemy without reason merely makes him think you weak. James has done me a good turn, all in all. It is most reasonable to pardon men who must fight for you.'

He had not convinced them, but they were accustomed to following his lead, and his appearance of easy confidence removed any tendency to panic. By September 24th hard-riding couriers had warned the sheriffs and principal gentlemen of the north of James's intentions. By October 8th a formal pardon was written to the men 'who have done us of late great displeasure, being against us in the field with the adversary of us, enemy of nature and of all public weal.' It was issued, said the pardon, because they repented of their faults, because they were descendants of those who had fought loyally for Henry VI (in Henry VII's opinion that proved they were merely loyal idiots and not to be blamed for following Gloucester), and because they 'be necessary and according to their duty must defend this land against the Scots'.

As soon as Henry was sure the pardon had been published and the northern shires would not suspect he was raising an army to retaliate against them for their support of Gloucester, commissions were issued to assemble men in the London counties and the south-western shires. Courtenay and Edgecombe rode to Devon and Cornwall; Guildford and Poynings to Kent, and Oxford covered the midlands. Henry went calmly on with his preparations for his coronation, seemingly impervious to his danger. Had Margaret seen him she would have noticed that he was losing weight again, but his servants knew only that ample portions were missing from the meals they brought him. He ate seldom in public at state dinners, citing the pressure of his work as excuse. No one commented that his dogs were growing fat; his men were kept too busy to attend to such minor matters.

Four days of terror, well-concealed under an almost-gay exterior, were ended when messengers galloped in bearing the welcome news that everyone was responding promptly to the call to arms. There were no disturbances; there was no resistance. Henry VII was king of England. When he called on his people, they were ready to fight for him.

By dawn, October 20th, Cheney was riding into Norfolk and Suffolk with orders that the men were to be ready to march north at an hour's notice. If these counties responded when their duke had been killed in battle against Henry and their earl was his prisoner, the king felt he would have little to fear from the Scots. It was not necessary to wait to find out. That same afternoon word arrived from Bray's spies that the Scots had withdrawn. James was not strong enough to engage in a full-scale war. When he realized that the northerners had been won by a combination of Henry's clemency and their hatred of his people, that the remainder of the nation was ready to fight under their upstart king, the venture became too dangerous. If James failed, his own rebellious nobles would turn on him. Any excuse to throw off authority was a good excuse to them.

That evening Henry sent his thanks to the gentlemen of the northern shires and his permission for the sheriffs to disband their forces. He ate his first decent meal in almost a month, and slept through the night without once waking in a cold sweat of fear. In the morning he attended almost passionately to the two masses he always heard; knowing that his prayers had been faint and doubting, he intended his thanks to be full and fervent. Christ would pardon his doubts, he hoped. The Lord God would understand that he was human and very frail. And no sooner had he come from mass to break his fast than his hopes were confirmed. Cheney sent word that the sheriffs and gentlemen of Norfolk and Suffolk were ready to obey him at an hour's or even a minute's warning, and Foxe came smiling with the news that London was clear of the plague which had racked it and readying itself with joy for the coronation.

Chapter Twelve

The barber snipped, patted, smoothed, snipped again. He ran careful fingers over the king's face from which every vestige of fair beard had been removed. Then he handed Henry a mirror and stepped back proudly. The squires of the body stood by tensely; the council watched the face of the king gravely. Henry studied his appearance, sighed, and laid the mirror down. The gentlemen stared at the barber. The barber's face worked with fear.

'It is most unsatisfactory,' Henry said softly. The barber made an animal sound of terror and the gentlemen made feral sounds of rage. 'It is most unsatisfactory,' Henry repeated somewhat louder, 'to have a face like mine. I can see that nothing – and your efforts have been heroic,' he said, turning to the barber with a slight bow as to one who has laboured beyond the call of duty, 'can make me into a beauty.'

There was a roar of laughter, and Pembroke strode forward. 'Harry, you are a devil. You nearly frightened this poor man to death.'

'Well, you have all frightened me nearly to death. I admit that a coronation is a weighty matter. I agree that I wish to make as agreeable an impression as I can. But you have been looking at me and attending me like mutes going to a funeral. Have I never had my hair cut or been shaved before?'

There was more laughter and a buzz of talk as the barber withdrew and the half-circle of watchers broke up. The squires came forward now with the royal hose, but Henry shook his head briefly and turned towards a curtained alcove in the room which held a crucifix and a cushion. He sank to his knees, but offered no formal prayer, merely staring up at the suffering face of Christ and seeking calm. A silent, nervous laugh shook him. Those men of his would have torn that barber apart with their bare hands if he had really been displeased. Who could believe that ten days of concentration upon clothes, hangings, and an order of procedure could so shake men who had faced death calmly? Henry passed a hand across his forehead. He was shaken himself. It had been easier to arrange the battle of Bosworth than to disentangle the orders of precedence. There had been glares of hatred exchanged over who was to carry what, and in what order the object should be carried.

Henry, soothing, adjusting, jesting, and frowning coldly by turns, had kept them from each other's throats, but he admitted one night to Edward Poynings who had come to give him a game of chess, that he had been less unnerved by Gloucester and the Scots than by his own nobles. 'They are a greater danger to you than Gloucester or the Scots,' Poynings had said judiciously, and Henry had been so startled by that plainspoken truth that he had mismoved his queen and Poynings had checked his king.

He had understood, however, the real necessity for the rigid protocol which had annoyed him so much at the French court. Pembroke and Oxford, for example, who were genuinely fond of each other and had worked together as one man before and after Bosworth, turned frigid to each other over the fact that Oxford's earldom was far older than Pembroke's. That had been easy. Henry had created his uncle duke of Bedford at the same time he created Lord Stanley the earl of Derby and Edward Courtenay earl of Devon. There were only two other dukes in England – John de la Pole, duke of Suffolk who sat shivering at home, and young Edward Stafford, son of the dead Buckingham. Neither of those would attend the coronation in any official capacity, and that left Bedford free to carry the crown which Henry felt he deserved. Oxford had been given his choice of sword or spurs. To Henry's surprise he had chosen the spurs. And, displaying a sense of humour Henry had not suspected in him, said that for Derby to carry the sword, which he had been so late in bringing to Henry's aid, would make a merry jest.

Henry shook himself sharply and rose from his knees. The arrangements had been made; he could only hope that permanent animosities had not been raised among his supporters. Now when the royal hose were advanced, he let them be smoothed over his legs. Then came the doublet, cloth of gold with green and white satin. Henry looked again in the mirror, this time with approval. He was not as tall as some, and he was still too thin, but he was well made and the full-sleeved, full-bodied style of the doublet was flattering. The squires were

160

holding his long gown, royal purple, furred from neck to hem with powdered ermine. Henry stroked the fur while John Cheney knelt to adjust his emerald-studded garter and Poynings fitted the sarpe. After glancing once more into the mirror, Henry turned.

'Well, uncle?'

Tears ran down Jasper's face. He could find no voice, and he kissed Henry again and again, forehead, cheeks, and lips. William Stanley, rewarded with the position of grand chamberlain of the household, watched this display with ill-concealed disfavour. The mutual affection of uncle and nephew and of the band who had shared Henry's exile, and to whom he now was offering his lips instead of his hands to kiss, blocked his way to the influence he sought.

'Look, Your Grace,' Stanley said. 'God surely favours you. For so mild and sunny a day on the thirtieth of October, one must have special dispensation.'

Henry smiled pleasantly. His spirit still recoiled from Stanley, but he had conquered any outward manifestation of that. He had also learned not to look into Sir William's eyes, and he glanced sidelong at him now.

'It is time, Your Grace,' Derby suggested.

The courtiers trailed after the king as he moved down to the courtyard where he mounted the stallion trapped in cloth of gold and held the horse steady as Guildford, Edgecombe, Poynings, and Willoughby raised the golden canopy over his head. He glanced back. Cheney was leading the seven squires of the body, all attired in crimson and gold, who were to follow. The fifty yeomen of the guard, that body of permanent soldiers Henry had introduced, were resplendent in their green and white liveries, their longbows slung over their shoulders, their quivers of goose-feathered arrows full, glittering pikes upright in their hands. The trumpeters forming ahead also wore the Tudor green and white. The heralds behind them – Henry could see Garter, Clarencieux, and Norry – made splashes of brilliant colour. The others were hurrying up. There were the pursuivants now, *Rouge Dragon, Rouge Croix, Portcullis,* and *Bluemantle.*

A quick glance upwards where large white clouds hung so still in the peacock-blue sky that they seemed painted, and Henry touched his mount very gently with his golden spurs.

The horse had been thoroughly exercised at dawn so that he would move quietly. Henry did not mistrust his horsemanship, in that he knew himself to be the equal of any man in the kingdom, but he wanted no tragedy to mar this day. If an overbold citizen pressed his stallion too close, a fresh horse might rear and do harm.

It was as well that the Tudor had taken the precaution. His appearance called forth even more violent enthusiasm than his first triumphal progress through London. Thus far the two-month reign had been a miracle of peace. The king had saved his nation from a new war with Scotland. He had given lavishly to the church and the poor; he had provided free meat and drink for a thanksgiving not equalled in memory. No heads rotted on the Tower gates. The bodies that swung from gibbets were those of criminals, not men who fought for Richard of Gloucester. The yeomen of the guard were a new innovation, true, but they had already proved their usefulness by being sent to the lord mayor's assistance when a party of celebrants had become too merry and the party had degenerated into a minor riot. Henry VII, a chronicler wrote, 'began to be lauded by all men as an angel sent from heaven'.

There was some dissatisfaction, but that was in high places – the people felt none of it. The dowager queen cursed the slender figure of the king silently as he entered Westminster Abbey. William Stanley bore his rod of office high, but he resented the paucity of his financial reward and Henry's imperviousness to his advice that harsher measures should be used on Gloucester's supporters. Elizabeth bit her lips, pale with rage. She should be walking beside the king. She was her father's heir; she had a right to be crowned – certainly a better right than a Welsh adventurer, scion of a bastard line.

Henry walked slowly up the aisle between the rows of magnificently clad noblemen and gentry. Waiting for him was the aged Thomas Bourchier who had, as archbishop of Canterbury, already crowned two kings – Edward IV and Richard III. Henry's hands, the right resting on Richard Foxe's arm and the left on John Morton's, struck cold through their vestments. He had been king for two months, had thought of this coronation only in political terms until this moment. Now the Tudor was awed in spite of himself, and he trembled as he knelt before Bourchier while the old man anointed him with the holy chrism.

The correct responses were coming from his lips; he heard his own voice, clear and sure, ringing through the abbey, a happy contrast to the thin, reedy tones of the archbishop. Henry was not thinking of what he was saying, but when the coronation ring was pressed on to his finger, he shuddered. 'I am wed – no, more than wed – I have become England,' he thought. 'This land and I are one. When she prospers, so shall I, and if her body is torn, blood will run from mine.'

Seated in the great coronation chair with the orb and sceptre in his hands, he looked out at the crowded abbey. They are my children, the thoughts continued. A few – a very few are grown men who can be trusted. A few more are in early manhood. They, too, may be trusted once the way is shown them, but most are mere boys to be taught and corrected when they err. Then the news that the crowning was complete must have spread to the crowd outside, and the people greeted the word with roar upon roar of delight. The sounds came dimly to Henry who was startled until he realized the cause. He smiled, thinking that those were the infants of the realm, to be protected and told firmly what they might and might not do. A large and rebellious family, Henry decided, abruptly putting away the sentimentality he had been indulging himself in, to be well whipped when they were wicked.

From the balcony where Elizabeth sat with Margaret and her mother, Henry VII of England looked almost buried beneath his regalia. Elizabeth could see him shift his arms so that the weight of the orb and sceptre should be partially supported by the chair. She looked at her own delicate, white hands. They could not hold so heavy a weight, she realized, and with the realization came a revulsion of her earlier feeling. Indeed, she did not wish to be a crowned queen. She did not wish to pore over accounts and legal matters all day long. They sat close enough, although high, so that she could see how pale Henry's face was. He is frail, she thought, remembering what Margaret had said, and the thought made her glance at the Tudor's mother.

The countess of Richmond and Derby was not gazing at her son with pride nor was she considering what honours and gains would accrue to the mother of the king. Elizabeth turned towards Margaret with concern, for she was in a state bordering on collapse. She held her mantle across her mouth to silence

163

herself, but she was crying hysterically. Elizabeth put her arms around her future mother-in-law. Margaret's trembling communicated itself to her body. Memories, all bad, turned her cold. She remembered her father changing from the gay, sweet-tempered man of her childhood to a debauched, frankly lecherous, and sometimes even murderously suspicious person. And Uncle Richard, what had happened to Uncle Richard? He had never been gay, but he was gentle and wise and kind. He had been loyal to her father, risking his life again and again. Was that the same man who, as king, had murdered her mother's brothers without even a trial? Had murdered her own brothers, the nephews with whom he had played so gently when they were babies?

Oh, God help me, she prayed. I do not wish to be queen. I do not wish to be the wife of that man who hates me already. I do not wish to be like my mother who had to smile into the faces of her husband's whores; who one moment was queen and the next was crouching in sanctuary stripped all but naked. I do not wish to see my sons murdered. God help me. Let me be as nothing.

A roar of ovation cut off her thoughts. Henry had risen and was making his way slowly from the abbey. The throng swayed as men bowed and women curtsied low. Elizabeth could not restrain a twinge of pity for the frail man who would now have to sit through a banquet that might last as long as ten hours. She had resented bitterly not being invited; now she was glad. Perhaps he did not mean to marry her, now that he had seized the power and been crowned without her. Perhaps he would permit her to become a nun.

Had Henry known of Elizabeth's sympathy, he would have been highly amused. It was entirely misplaced. The Tudor was enjoying himself immensely. It gave him the greatest pleasure to see people having a good time, and he did not mind being isolated from them, an onlooker. He had been isolated for so long that it seemed quite natural, and he had lost the art of mingling easily. In fact, compared with his state as an exile, he was now rich in friends. Moreover his life in his present position as king was no more precarious than it had been as a hunted enemy of Edward IV and Richard III, and it was a great deal more comfortable. Henry loved luxury, loved music and feasting. He was completely happy and beamed impartially on friend and past enemy alike.

The celebration lasted far into the night, but Henry's poor council was routed out of bed by his messengers just after dawn. The Tudor laughed heartily at the half-opened eyes, the pale faces, the muffled groans, but he set them to work drafting and refining the bills which were to be presented to parliament. They moaned, but there was no resentment. Parliament had been called for the fifth, but that was a Saturday so the session would actually open on November 7th. They had only eight days before all must be presented in perfect order, and they were new to this work. Henry's fondness for and gratitude to Richard Foxe grew by leaps and bounds. Not only was he personally invaluable, but the men he recommended, particularly John Morton, were equally so. Morton was perfect. He was astute, cautious, and reasonable, nodding imperturbably as Henry explained that he had named Alcock, bishop of Rochester, to be chancellor because he did not wish to seem to favour only those men who had been exiles. As soon as parliament was prorogued, Morton should have the chancellorship.

It was Morton who worked with Henry over the final polishing of the drafted bills. He had parliamentary experience and could teach the king the proper forms. It was Morton whose fine hand guided the House of Lords where he sat quite legitimately as bishop of Ely. Not that the parliament needed much handling. Henry's firm and merciful rule was much appreciated, and when Alcock referred to him as 'a second Joshua, a strenuous and invincible fighter who was to bring in the golden age', the king received a standing ovation. Henry's lips twitched a bit at the reference to himself as a warrior, but he rose and bowed silently. After all, he fully intended to bring in a golden age if any effort of his could do it, and he hoped he would not need to prove himself as a fighter. War never brought gold.

On Tuesday, Henry did not attend parliament. He did not wish it to seem as if he influenced the election of a speaker for the House of Commons, which was the business of the day. The speaker was bound to be one of his favourites anyway; parliament would not wish to arouse the displeasure of the king any more than he wanted to irritate them. Thomas Lovell was chosen and it was he who welcomed the king to the session on

165

the third day. Henry made a sober speech, lacking the high-flown oratory of Alcock but claiming firmly that his right to the crown rested on 'just title of inheritance', which might have raised some doubts had he not added, 'and upon the true judgment of God as shown by the sword on the field of battle, giving me victory over my enemy.'

The reminder was sufficient. The king's business proceeded apace. The very first bill stated that 'to the pleasure of Almighty God, the wealth, prosperity, and surety of the realm, to the comfort of all the king's subjects and the avoidance of all ambiguities, be it ordained, established, and enacted by authority of the present parliament, that the inheritance of the crowns of England and France . . . be, rest, and remain and abide in the most royal person of our new Sovereign Lord King Henry the VIIth and in the heirs of his body lawfully comen perpetually . . . and in none other.' Henry was king by law and right as well as by might.

Henry returned to parliament only once more before the end of the session. On November 19th an act which might have provoked resistance, an act to limit the practice of noblemen and rich gentlemen of hiring what amounted to private armies of their own, was pushed through. In the presence of the king, they dared not protest, and one after another they swore 'not to . . . retain any man by indenture or oath, not to give livery, sign, or token contrary to law or make, cause to be made, or assent to any maintenance, imbracerie, riots, or unlawful assembly, not to hinder execution of royal writs, not let any known felon to bail or mainprize.' Whether the Tudor could make them keep the oath remained to be seen; at least he had the power to make them swear it. The remainder of the king's bills passed without a whisper of opposition.

With nothing to argue over, and the nation still in urgent need of its gentlemen on their own lands, parliament did not sit long. On December 10th Henry attended again to prorogue the session. Before he could do so, however, the speaker rose to present a petition from the Commons direct to the king. Henry gave permission, and Thomas Lovell asked, in the name of all members, that Henry take the Lady Elizabeth of York as his wife. As soon as his voice faded, the lords, spiritual and temporal, stood. They bowed their heads as a token of submission, but as one man they repeated the request. Henry smiled largely.

Visions of Elizabeth's ripe beauty had not been completely absent from his moments of leisure and grew more appealing each time they came. Also, the subject was dealt with most correctly. Parliament had requested, not demanded, that he make Elizabeth his wife, not his queen. Briefly, but most positively, Henry assured them that he would accede to their request very willingly. He would wed the Lady Elizabeth with all decent haste – as soon, in fact, as a dispensation could be secured since he and his intended bride were within the forbidden degrees of kinship.

Messengers were sent at once to Rome, but Henry did not intend to wait upon the reply of the dilatory Curia. His most pressing political problems were settled. There would be a lull before new needs beset him, and in this lull he had time to think of himself as a man. He harried council and servants unmercifully so that the preparations for the wedding might move swiftly, and he went often and often to the queen dowager's house to glance sidelong out of his narrow eyes at Elizabeth as he talked with his mother.

Margaret was appalled at Henry's method of courtship, and she explained to Elizabeth that he was shy with women. If the princess heard, it made no difference in her demeanour. She seemed numb to all feeling, although for what reason Margaret could not fathom. When Henry requested her presence, she came; when he addressed a remark to her, she replied. She was docile and dull, completely unlike her usual vivacious self, but Henry did not seem to mind. He seemed satisfied to absorb her physical beauty in quick, bright glances, content with insipidity so long as she made no active protest. He never mentioned the forthcoming marriage to Elizabeth, reserving all questions, even those concerning the readying of his bride's gowns for which he provided generously, to his mother.

On December 22nd, Henry sent a formal invitation to all the ladies of the household to move to court for the Christmas celebrations. Even the dowager queen could find no fault with the apartments assigned nor with the furnishing of those apartments. She did protest that Elizabeth's rooms were so widely separated from hers while Margaret's adjoined them, but the lord chamberlain, under strict instructions from the king, was immovable. When Henry himself was approached, he looked startled and asked in an indignant voice whether he could be suspected of wishing to dishonour his intended bride – and in his own mother's presence, too? Elizabeth retained her privacy, and Margaret's respect for her son increased yet again as the girl came slightly more alive.

It was hard to pinpoint the exact cause that was bringing colour back to Elizabeth's cheeks and an occasional smile to her lips. Perhaps it was the brilliance of the court, which reminded her of her happier youth. Perhaps it was the effect of Henry's attentions, which were becoming steadily more particular. Margaret guessed, however, that freedom from her mother's complaints, demands, and nagging was in part relieving Elizabeth's depression.

Certainly Henry was putting himself to pains to make the season merry. Each night the feast was grander; each night the courtiers appeared in new and handsomer clothes; each night the music was gayer and the dancing lasted longer. Elizabeth could not complain of her betrothed's attentions now. Henry danced well and he danced every dance with her. Even more surprising, his eyes were for her alone. Unfortunately, what looked out of those eyes on the few occasions when Elizabeth was able to catch their expression unveiled was not love but curiosity, caution, and – hunger. Still, it was better than hate or indifference, and since her mother could not plague her to make demands of him, Elizabeth did not need to see again the contempt and distaste with which Henry had regarded her at their first meeting.

Twelfth Night brought a culmination of the festivities. The entire day was replete with excitement as gift after gift arrived to be examined, ohed over, and set up for display. As the hour grew later and later, however, Elizabeth began to wonder whether the favour Henry had shown her was merely a gambit to make her vulnerable to a more cruel insult. Plate and jewels and gold had arrived for Margaret; a similar gift with a correct, although impersonal letter, had been delivered to the dowager queen. For her – nothing. Elizabeth was trembling between rage and terror when the king himself was announced. He dismissed her women and his gentlemen with a quick gesture, and Elizabeth drew in her breath and braced herself. Henry, however, did nothing more alarming than to bow over her hand and kiss it.

'Madam', he said, his eyes sweeping her from head to foot, 'you are in truth a white rose.'

Was it a compliment or a cruel gibe? 'I endeavour only not to shame your own magnificence, sire.'

Henry laughed, and Elizabeth felt a trifle better for the sound seemed natural. 'I am a pretty popinjay these days,' he admitted, 'but it is necessary, and, in truth, I love fine things. I wished to bring you your New Year's gift with my own hands.' He withdrew from his voluminous doublet a purse and a box. 'I brought you no plate, madam, for all that is in the royal residences will be yours. This,' he laid the purse in her hand, 'for your charities or your pleasure.'

Elizabeth curtsied and set down the purse, which was very heavy.

'This,' Henry continued, opening the box, 'for your eyes and to grace your white throat.'

Once more Elizabeth bent her knees. She could feel Henry looking at her directly for once, and the speeches were both pretty and proper, but her relief had blossomed into resentment rather than gratitude. The very appropriateness and beauty of the diamond and sapphire necklace he was extending towards her fed the sensation. Did he never make a mistake? Never say an incorrect word or display an improper emotion? The silence was now becoming marked. Henry was waiting for a proper expression of thanks. A flush stole up Elizabeth's throat as she realized that he was perfectly prepared to stand there and wait forever for the response he desired. Apparently nothing could disconcert the king.

'Thank you,' she said in a gasp as she took the box and laid it beside the purse.

'And this is my last gift – one to be shared between us.'

A rolled parchment, heavy with seals, had appeared from nowhere. This time Elizabeth took it without delay, having no desire for another engagement with this imperturbable man which could only lead to her discomfiture. Henry's eyes were veiled, but the slight curve of his mobile lips seemed to indicate an expectation of amusement. A glance at the document was sufficient. Elizabeth paled. She was not even to have respite until the pope sent a dispensation; Henry had procured one already from the papal legate.

'When—' she faltered.

'I am happy to see you so overjoyed by the imminence of our wedding.' Henry lifted his right hand so that it drew her attention and twisted the ring she had sent him which was prominently displayed on his forefinger. 'Any day this month will suit me, madam. I give you the honour of naming the day.'

Did he expect to plead for more time? She would plead for nothing. Did he believe he could taunt her into rejecting him? The parliament had asked him to marry her; it was her duty to the people and to her father that the legitimate line remain on the throne. It was God's will that she be the sacrifice for this purpose.

'The eighteenth would be a good day,' Elizabeth said at random.

'The eighteenth it is,' Henry approved. 'I will announce it to the court at once.'

He did so simply and without apparent pleasure, holding her hand in his own and, when the cheering stopped, turning to touch her lips with his, to bring on a new ovation. Elizabeth, not to be outdone, did not shrink from his salute, and no one but Henry knew how cold and passive her lips were under his brief caress. She extended herself for the first time to be gay and witty with the courtiers. Perhaps it would seem to them that she had been sullen in the past because of Henry's delay in setting the date. Her pride was hurt at that notion, but her fate and the Tudor's were now linked. For the sake of the children she would bear, the grandchildren of Edward IV, the rightful heirs to the throne, it must be her purpose to support her husband. There were plenty of ways to salve her pride and show him what she thought of him in private.

'That was well done, Henry,' Margaret said when he came up to her in his progress through the room.

'I could still wish that it need not be done at all, but needs must is soonest mended with willing compliance.' He smiled when he saw his mother's troubled face. 'Nay, I am not all ill-pleased. She is beautiful – and that much is sweet to me.'

'There is goodness and warmth as well as beauty in her.'

'I have seen none of it.'

'For that you may blame only yourself.'

Henry's mouth set hard. 'What she desires, I cannot give.'

'You are mistaken, my son. She desires only what all women desire – love.'

'Perhaps.' Henry's eyes slid away. 'But I cannot love Edward's daughter.'

'Oh, my God,' Margaret whispered, 'will you never cease to hate? What black sin do you feed in your heart? It is God's law that we forgive and even love our enemies.'

'Edward and Richard are dead. I do not hate the dead – nor even the living – I hope. But I cannot trust Edward's daughter. Think, mother. I love you. What could you ask of me that I would not give? Is it safe to put such power in hands other than yours or my uncle's? I dare not—'

'Sire!' Foxe was slightly breathless, and Henry turned to him at once. He whispered; Henry smiled.

'So? God bless Morton that he made me see the reason in sending those gifts to James. Mother, a Scots embassy is here with New Year gifts. I must away to receive them at once. This means a truce with James that will permit me to settle with those damned rebellious northerners.'

Henry kissed his mother's hands and left, hardly knowing whether he was more pleased by the political significance of the event or by the fact that it gave him an excuse to be busy. His recent constant contact with Elizabeth was unsettling him. Although he was willing enough to acknowledge his physical desire for her, he had found himself recurrently battling the temptation to make her smile at him, and to discover whether he could bring out the warmth that his mother promised she had and make it replace her cold passivity. It was no safe wish. Henry knew he had no skill to dissimulate with women, to draw affection from them without being trapped in it himself.

His unease grew as the days passed and his wedding drew nearer. It was a shock to find himself with pen idle in hand wondering what colour Elizabeth's eyes would turn when they were passionate or pleased. He buried himself in practical details, estimating how much increase in expenditure a suitable household for her would mean, poring over the lists of crown lands to determine which would be best to assign as her dower property. All too often, however, Henry found himself in the state apartments which were being readied for Elizabeth's use, meddling with the choice of hangings and furniture – particularly those for the bedchamber.

His uncle laughed at him openly, and Courtenay innocently brought Henry's wrath down on his head by proposing to fetch him a wench to ease himself upon. Henry apologized and kissed his startled friend, rather startled himself by the violence of his reaction. It would not do, he told Courtenay, to affront his bride and the court with such behaviour; but he knew the matter could have been kept secret and would really affront no one but Elizabeth. He closed his mind to the real reasons for his refusal and worked harder than ever on the Scots truce. That night he cursed himself heartily as he turned and twisted, inflamed and unable to sleep. A few days more, he told himself, but whether in hope or in fear he could not decide.

Chapter Thirteen

The Tudor's luck held for the day of his wedding. Henry had decided that the thing must be done decently, but in no way rival the brilliance of his coronation. Compliantly, the skies were grey and the cold more than sufficient to keep any large crowd from gathering. Unfortunately Henry was too far gone to appreciate nature's willingness to fall in with his plans. His temper was so bad that his squires of the body slunk out of sight the moment their particular task was finished, and Margaret and Jasper could do nothing but stare at each other in despair.

Elizabeth, on the other hand, was perfectly calm. She had come to terms with her personal sacrifice. She did not expect any pleasure from her relationship with the Tudor, whom she still found rather unattractive, but she did not fear him, either, for she knew herself to be valuable property. There were also advantages to come from her marriage. She would be relatively free of her mother, and, God willing, she would have children. Elizabeth's lonely heart yearned towards that day. Even Henry's passionate desire for an heir could not overmatch her need to have something to love.

Of the two, therefore, Elizabeth's voice was the steadier in the exchange of vows, her hand the warmer of the two when they clasped. She grew positively merry at the wedding feast, capping jests, teasing the fools, and laughing heartily at the bawdy farces presented. Elizabeth was a virgin, but her mind was not in the least virginal and her body had long since been ready for love. She was accustomed to the lewdness which had been a regular feature of her father's court and was unashamed of her own sensuality. If her husband was no beauty, she had no reason to doubt that he was a man; and if he did not desire to amuse her, at least he had reopened to her the court that she loved. When the feasting was ended and the dancing was done, however, she grew a trifle nervous. Henry had been unusually silent and she detected tense glances cast at him from the men who knew him best. There was nothing to be

173

read in his face, but were his lips thinner? Was there a cruel glint in the half-lidded grey eyes? Elizabeth did not fear the natural consummation of marriage, but she wondered if Henry could mean to take his revenge on her family by misusing her personally.

Margaret was quick to see the changed mood, quick to respond to it by beginning preparations for the bedding. Henry's temper had not improved, and it was useless to delay longer and permit the girl's apprehension to increase. All in all, it was not a merry bedding. Henry's intimates had more than a suspicion that the king was something of a prude, and the remainder of the lords and ladies were too much in doubt and awe of him to be free with their jests. They stood in a formal semicircle as Elizabeth was led to the huge bed and ensconced in it, wrapped in her bed robe. The dowager queen whispered urgently in her ear, but Elizabeth stared straight ahead, frightened more by her own imaginings than of Henry. In all honesty, he did not look a fearsome sight when the knights of the body and the gentlemen of the bedchamber escorted him in. He was paler than Elizabeth, and Margaret, who had never dared ask, wondered if he were as much a virgin as his bride. He also was assisted into the high bed, and in a most unnatural silence, the bed curtains were drawn closed.

Usually that would have been a sign of dismissal for all except the ladies and gentlemen who slept by turns in the royal bedchamber to attend to chance wants in the night. Tonight, however, the courtiers merely drew back a little and waited. It was their duty to be witness of the consummation of the marriage, as it would be their duty to watch the birth of Elizabeth's children to be sure that the queen had given birth to the child, and that the child presented to them was the child that had been born. In spite of maidenly modesty – of which, in truth, she had very little – Elizabeth was suffering far less acutely than Henry. She was accustomed to the lack of privacy in which royalty lived, having endured it for most of her life.

Henry felt paralysed. He could hear a low buzz of whispering, but he knew that every ear was cocked for a sound from the great bed. Desperately he untied and shrugged off his bed robe. Elizabeth turned and regarded him with her blue eyes gone almost black in the dim light that filtered through the bed curtains. For a long moment Henry sat still, allowing her to examine him, his chest rising and falling quickly with his short breath. Then, as she made no move, he reached slowly towards the fastenings of her bedgown.

For once Henry's iron will failed him. His hands trembled, and his fingers were so clumsy that it seemed hours before he had the robe loose. In fact, when he thought he was done and made to slip it off Elizabeth's shoulders, he found to his chagrin that a lace bow remained. Forgetting himself completely, he uttered a resounding oath and tore the knot free. Sudden silence fell outside the bed curtains, and Henry blushed as red as ever Elizabeth could. It was impossible, Elizabeth found, to continue being afraid of a husband who blushed like a girl. Her sense of humour was tickled and she giggled. The silence in the room remained tense. Henry glanced distractedly from the bed curtains to his bride's face. A fine impression of his virility he was giving both his court and his wife.

Elizabeth's movement, however, had shaken her robe open. Tantalizing glimpses of a breast even whiter than her throat appeared. Henry ceased to worry about either the watchers or the impression he was making. Very gently he thrust the robe from one shoulder, then the other and drew it off. Such delicate fairness! He traced the line of throat, shoulder, and arm with his fingertips, then the curve of the breast. Elizabeth's eyes widened and she drew a faintly shuddering breath, but Henry seemed entranced by what he was doing and he paid her no heed. Self-absorbed in the pleasure he was taking, for he lacked experience with all but bawds who made the advances and scarcely gave him time for this slow titillation of the senses, Henry did not realize he was giving as much pleasure as he was receiving.

He closed his eyes and the flesh was like velvet beneath his fingers. Soft to touch, he soon found it sweet to kiss, also, sweet and scented with roses. Desire stung him sharply, but he resisted, for to take what he desired would quench desire. Elizabeth slid down on the pillows and lay flat, breathing in gasping sobs. Vaguely aware that there was some reason to maintain silence, Henry stopped her lips with his own – and then he could wait no longer.

Now I am truly a wife, Elizabeth thought, and wondered if it would be safe to move. She did not wish to wake her husband who was sleeping heavily, lying half across her. She frowned, trying to piece together the things she had been told with what had happened, but she found her mind muddled by the sight of Henry's blond hair, now dark and lank with perspiration, and his lean shoulder. She knew he had been drunk with pleasure, and that there were ways of using that intoxication; only her mind kept wandering away to the fact that he was too thin and that feverish spots burned in his cheeks when he was excited.

The room was quiet now. No doubt the courtiers had finally withdrawn. Did Henry— Elizabeth paused. She had never called him by name except once during the wedding ceremony. It was odd that the name should come so easily to her mind. Did Henry know he had cried out? She had not. She was proud of that. But there had been little reason to cry out and none to fear; he had been very gentle. Childbirth would be worse. Elizabeth's frown returned. She had been eager for Henry's love-making because it would eventually bring her a child, yet she had not thought of the child, not since— She twisted her head to look at her husband's long-fingered hand. Beautiful hands he had, and his face – it was not so very ugly. Plain— One could grow used to plainness – perhaps – even fond—

Some hours later Henry stirred, flexed an arm which was numb, and parted his lips to call for a drink. He lifted his head so his voice would carry through the curtain, and his half-open eyes fell on the mass of yellow hair spread over the pillow. Henry shut his mouth with a snap. He had fallen asleep in Elizabeth's bed. It was not surprising – he had slept very little the past few nights – but he must not do it again. If he called out— Henry felt himself blushing at the thought of one of his gentlemen pulling back the curtains and seeing Elizabeth, who was partly uncovered, naked. It was a good deal darker now, but her fair skin showed white. He should go. There was that accursed business of the recorder of York to attend to, and the damned Irish— It was a great pity she was so sound asleep. It would doubtless be wrong to wake her. How soft her skin was. Henry bent lower. How sweet.

In the end it was broad daylight before the Tudor slid out of his wife's bed and returned to his own apartments. His gentlemen were discreet, for Henry gave them no openings to

176

congratulate him on his prowess, but they were vicariously proud.

'Frankly,' Courtenay whispered to Poynings while Henry was being shaved in the next room, 'I was worried. I know he is a great king, but I sometimes wondered whether he was a man or a monk.'

'I think he is only fastidious.'

'Yes, but the way he trembled when we brought him to her—'

'Have you never seen a hound – not to compare the king with such, of course – trembling with eagerness while held on the leash? It does not signify lack of courage or strength.'

'Yes, but still— Was it three times or four?'

Poynings and Courtenay had been the gentlemen of the bed-chamber on duty that night, but their duty did not forbid them to sleep and occasionally they had done so.

'Edward, you are incorrigible. You know His Grace does not like that kind of talk about himself – or anyone else, for that matter. You got the back of his tongue for it just the other day. Have done. He is a young man, and she a fair maid—'

'Maid no longer, not by several— Good morn, Your Grace.'

Ordinarily Henry did not encourage talk about his sexual habits. Perhaps, he thought with wry insight, because there had not been much to talk about, but this morning he smiled blandly. It was not mere pride in his performance, he told him-self. It was a matter of policy that the court know – and, through their gossip with their servants, the people know – that any failure to produce an heir immediately was not for lack of effort on the king's part. Moreover, the news that he was so well pleased with his white rose might pacify some Yorkists who could continue to hope for favour through Elizabeth. That thought gave him a quiver of alarm. He had been well pleased with his white rose; it was something he must guard himself against or what he wanted the Yorkists to believe would become true in fact.

Not that he intended to discriminate against any man who could be useful, whatever his past political affiliation. It was merely that he must not be blinded by affection and thereby leave himself open to treachery. But the idea that Elizabeth could influence him should be fostered if it was possible to do so harmlessly. It would give him a breathing spell before the Yorkists became actively dissatisfied. Rather absently, Henry

177

chose green hose, a white doublet brocaded in gold, and a dark green velvet surcoat embroidered with gold and trimmed with ermine. From trays he picked rings and jewelled gold chains. As his squires were dressing him, he came to a sudden decision.

'John, I want Lovell, Dynham, and Edgecombe.'

John Cheney handed the shoe he was about to slip on to Henry's foot to another squire and left on his errand. Henry's eyes rested speculatively on Poynings and Courtenay. Neither spoke, but both stiffened and waited expectantly. Devon was of higher rank, but he had the looser tongue, and Henry needed a rumour spreader at court. Poynings would have to go. Henry tapped impatiently on the arm of his chair. He did not relish sending Ned on a winter journey across the Channel. His mind ran over his other trusted men. The financial wizards would have to stay. He was pinched for money and yet had to spend more. Guildford was working on the armoury; Oxford was absolutely necessary in case of a rising in the north. Damn! Ned it would have to be.

'Edward,' Henry gestured to Courtenay, 'I wish to speak to you privately.'

The earl of Devon's face whitened as he followed the king into his bedchamber. 'Sire, if my hasty tongue—'

Henry took his arm and winked at him broadly. 'It was four times, since you find the matter of such interest, and would have been more had not the lady begged off. For which I cannot blame her, indeed, she being a maid most surely when I had her first.'

'My felicitations, Your Grace. I cannot deny you have out-stripped me.'

'You see, Edward, it does no harm to be a little saving in a good cause. Nor can it do harm – though in a general way I do not like lewd talk – to let it be known that Her Grace pleases me well. You know, Edward, that money never comes amiss to a king. Go lay me some wagers about the court that Her Grace will be with child before the year is out – doubled, if she be brought to bed before that time.'

Courtenay swallowed nervously. This was out of character for Henry. He knew that the Tudor often laid traps for the unwary, but he had never practised that game with his inti-mates before. 'Yes, Your Grace,' he said hesitantly, wondering

178

if he could have fallen so far from favour for a few words. It was not likely, but Henry had been most peculiar in his behaviour of late.

'And, Edward, I do not like to take money from my friends. See then that the bets are laid with those who still lean towards the house of York. They will be happy to lose, for it will mean that Edward IV's grandson will sit on the throne.'

Devon's wits were not as sharp as most of Henry's intimates, but he was by no means stupid. A broad smile illuminated his features. 'Aye, sire that they will. Also they will not be loath to believe you likely to fall under the spell of the white rose. I think, perhaps, I will go calling this morning. It should not seem that I am so free as to say these things where your ear might pick them up.'

Henry clapped him on the shoulder companionably and they came out together, Devon only to make a parting bow and leave. Henry looked thoughtfully at the door which closed behind him, grimaced with distaste at the necessary exposure of intimate personal details, and shrugged. The king's body was as much a political tool as the king's mind.

'Ned.'

'Sire?'

'I need you to go to France for me. How soon can you be ready?'

'Tomorrow. Today, if the matter needs haste.'

'It will not be so soon as that. I want you to arrange for the ransoming of Dorset and Bourchier, and I will need time to find some money. In any case it will be impossible to repay the whole debt at once. You are to do your best to get them both free, but if the French will release only one, it must be Dorset.'

'Dorset!'

'Aye. Would you have said of me that I prefer my Lancastrian friends to my brother by marriage?'

'Oh.'

'This is no secret matter. It may – should – be talked of freely. And, if it should be hinted that Her Grace had some influence on my choice – do not deny it.'

Poynings nodded. 'How long will this hold the wolves, think you, sire?'

Henry shrugged. 'A little time. For some not longer than it takes the queen's mother to ask me for something I will not

179

give. Others, more reasonable, a little longer. Every day is a gain, Ned.'

The Tudor's voice sounded tired suddenly, and Poynings met his eyes with sympathy. To his mind the most incredible feat Henry performed was his constant appearance of confidence. They were all tense, overworked, and all too aware that the stability of the realm was no more than a thin sheathing of ice over turbulent undercurrents of rebellion. Yet Henry, who not only directed but checked and corrected all the work done by the others, could show neither fatigue nor fear. The first sign of weakness in the king would crack the ice and they would all be swept away by the flood. Poynings was about to speak when the yeoman of the guard at the door announced Lovell, Dynham, and Edgecombe. Henry smiled at them and held up a hand.

'No, I did not rest well last night, as you will all be glad to hear. And, yes, I am strangely invigorated by that lack of rest. Ergo, I am ready to set you all to work harder than ever. Dynham, I need money – a really large sum – and soon.'

The treasurer passed a hand over his weary face. 'Your Grace, there is no money. You know it, and you know where every penny that we have found and collected thus far has gone.'

'Lovell?'

The chancellor of the exchequer sighed. 'We can hold back some disbursements to merchants. Your credit is very good, sire. A few hundred pounds here and there – perhaps. What will come in in revenue the next month or so is hard to estimate.'

'Edgecombe?'

The comptroller of the household grinned. 'Well, if you go on progress, sire, you will have low household expenses since you will be living off the nobles and cities you visit – not to mention the gifts you can expect. Tell me how long you will travel, and I will tell you how much I can pare from the household.'

'Something, but not enough and not soon enough. Well, Dynham, can we borrow?'

The treasurer's face lighted. 'Aye. There will be no trouble in that.'

Henry's lips tightened. He had strong principles about either

180

the government or the king personally being in debt. He had even redeemed some of Richard III's pledges, but there had not been time enough to fill the exchequer. Commerce had been disrupted by Richard's reign and by his own conquest so that customs were not up to their usual amounts and the collection of revenues from confiscated property was a slow business. Moreover, disbursements had been unusually great. The coronation and wedding expenses were enormous; the cost of new clothing for himself and his impoverished followers not far behind. Time – if he only had a little time. Between economy and the encouragement of trade he could fill the exchequer and— But time was the essence he did not possess, and money could be obtained first and then repaid, as much as he disliked that manoeuvre.

'Very well, Dynham, borrow. As much as you can get that you also believe I can repay in a reasonable time. But do not borrow from foreign sources.'

'That will cut sadly into what I can obtain, Your Grace.'

'I know, but there are enough things to juggle without foreign pressures being added.'

'Very well, Your Grace.'

Henry smiled ruefully. 'How you must hate me, Dynham. All I do is ask for the impossible, and then interfere with your efforts to obtain it for me.'

An answering smile relieved the treasurer's worried expression. 'Indeed I do not, sire. At least you do not lose your temper when you ask for the moon and I bring you a silver plate. There is also the matter of time. The longer I have, the more I can raise.'

'This money is for the ransom of Dorset and Bourchier. There is no special haste, but I would not want it said that I was delaying apurpose.'

A sudden burst of animated talk about the appropriateness of the move exposed the hidden fear that, married to the daughter of an extravagant king and queen, Henry had been about to embark on a course of extravagance of his own. He found it funny, but hid his amusement. In a way he had given cause for the fear by the magnificence with which he surrounded himself. All had agreed that the expenditure was necessary to provide a proper awe for royalty, but it was not unknown for a political gambit of this type to grow into a habit or even a disease with kings. As a matter of fact, Henry did like lavish surroundings, gorgeous clothing, and beautiful jewels – he loved all beautiful things – but he knew himself in no danger of succumbing to the vice of extravagance. The habit of counting each penny and balancing that against value received was too strong. It was useless, even dangerous to protest, however. Protests merely fixed suspicions. His men would learn soon enough that he would spend only what he could afford.

He was about to send Poynings for Foxe so that a draft of official instructions and letters for the French court could be started, when an altercation was heard at the door. A woman's voice, shrill with anger, rose above the rumble of the yeoman of the guard's protest. Henry raised his brows and gestured at Poynings, who opened the door. A young and highly agitated lady burst in, her complexion bright with rage.

'Her Grace, the queen, desires that you wait upon her at once.'

Henry turned red, fixed his suddenly blazing eyes on the maid of honour, and moved forward a step. Edgecombe, who was nearest, laid a hand gently on the king's arm. He could not, of course, restrain Henry if he was about to strike one of the queen's ladies, but—

'Sire!' Poynings said warningly.

The colour faded from Henry's face as the girl sank to the ground, trembling. 'You do not know your work, my dear,' the king said softly. 'When the queen says to a maid of honour: "Tell that damn bastard I married to get over here on the run," it is your duty to say: "Please, Your Grace, my mistress being taken suddenly ill begs your presence as soon as may be." Or, "Please, Your Grace, my lady the queen is in the greatest distress. We can do nothing with her. Will you not come before she makes herself ill?"'

Beside him, Henry heard Edgcombe choke, and his own lips quivered. Still, clear as the understanding on both sides was of what was hidden in the formal messages, the formality could not be dispensed with. It was the grease which made easy the rubbing together of two people who could not afford to sever relations with each other no matter how divergent their desires or personalities. Elizabeth either needed some schooling or more experienced ladies. However, he could not lesson his wife

182

as he would like to because that would destroy the edifice of her influence he was building so carefully.

'Now,' he said cynically, 'you may return to Her Grace and tell her either that I am sorry for her sudden illness or that I am most concerned for her distress – whichever seems more appropriate – and I will come to her as soon as I can discharge the weightiest and most immediate of my state duties.' He nodded dismissal. 'Ned, tell the yeoman to see this lady safe to her mistress's chamber.'

There was a silence during which Henry tried to decide whether the girl understood his warning and whether it was wise to have so clearly exposed his contempt. He heard a gasp and looked up to see his men convulsed with laughter and struggling to hide it. Poynings was looking out the door, as if to watch for the yeoman's return, but his shoulders were shaking. Edgecombe was leaning against the bedpost, his eyes closed, and his lower lip caught fast in his teeth. Dynham was wiping his lips rather harder than necessary, and Lovell was staring at the painted ceiling as if he had never seen it before. Henry sighed. There was not a man in the kingdom who would dare— And yet a chit of a girl— He yielded to his sense of the ridiculous and gave himself up to the laughter which released his companions from their agony.

'What,' Poynings gasped, 'do you suppose could have upset Her Grace?'

'Now, Ned, Her Majesty would be more appropriate. There was nothing graceful about that message at all. Bless me if I know. That will be all, gentlemen,' he said to the three others. 'See what you can scrape off the bottom of the pan for me. But really, Ned,' he added when the door closed, 'either she must have more experienced ladies or learn to control herself. This was funny, but a message like that delivered in the wrong company—' The Tudor's voice trailed away and his eyes became hard and remote.

'It could not have been so planned, sire,' Poynings protested, suddenly feeling sorry for Elizabeth. 'She is too young. Why, the very fact that the maid was sent to your chamber rather than to the public rooms—'

'We do not know she came here first. Had I not been so late in rising, I would have been in the audience chamber by now

183

– a room full of courtiers and envoys, not all of whom love me. Young? She is two and twenty, and was raised in a royal court.'

'Your Grace, have patience. A woman—'

'Oh, I will have patience. Did you expect me to use a whip to tame her?' Henry snarled.

Poynings dropped his eyes. Perhaps a whip would be kinder. Henry's methods could be more excruciating to the soul than torment to the body. 'Do you go now, sire?'

'Oh, no. My message should have time to sink in. Fetch me Foxe, and we will get to work upon the Dorset business.'

The instructions to be prepared were complicated, and in the end Morton joined Foxe to draft them. Henry, meanwhile, went to give audience in his usual way. He was particularly gay and genial, as a happy bridegroom should be, although his eyes kept watch for the irruption of another of the queen's ladies. None came. Elizabeth had not, of course, meant to do any political harm; however, unlike Henry, she had no use for the grease of formality between two people who had to live together. She believed they would rub off each other's rough edges by contact, and the sooner it was done the better in her opinion. She was, therefore, annoyed by the condition in which her maid of honour had returned and even more annoyed by the message she received. Surely her husband could not expect her to wait upon him in person. If he did, he could expect in vain. She was sure he would prefer to discuss the matter she had in mind in private, but if he did not come she was willing enough to make the affair public. She would see him at dinner, certainly, and raise the subject then. Indeed, he might frighten a silly maid by a stare – for from what Elizabeth could discover he had done no more than look at the girl, had not even raised his voice – but he would find Edward's daughter less timid.

An hour before dinner, the king was announced. He came forward, kissed his wife's hand formally, and then looked at the room full of highborn ladies. 'I was sorry to learn,' he said gravely, 'that something had given you cause for distress. A private matter?' He did not wait for a reply but tightened his grip on her hand which he had not released. 'Let us go into your bedchamber,' and he moved so quickly that he was able to shut the door behind them before Elizabeth's mother, or his own, who had both made to follow them, could enter. 'Well, madam?'

'You shut the cause of my distress outside the room.'

For a moment Henry was puzzled. 'One of the ladies?' Then he frowned blackly. 'My mother?'

'A list of names on my desk,' Elizabeth replied sharply.

'A list of— Pray seat yourself, madam. What list of names?'

'The men you have assigned to my household. That list of names.'

Henry's brows lifted. 'That was submitted to you at least two weeks before our marriage. You had time to—'

'Time!' Elizabeth gasped. 'I was so pulled about by dressmakers and cobblers and jewellers that I had not time to breathe. You planned that. You knew I would not be able—'

'If so, it would do you no good to protest, would it? Let me warn you, madam, to make no plans to counter mine. In fact, I planned no such thing. The list was submitted in good faith. If you had taken five minutes to read it— If you would give over half an hour a day from your pleasuring—' That was a stupid thing to say, Henry thought, checking himself. He did not want Elizabeth attending to business.

'Pleasuring! What pleasure do you think it gives me to mouth empty courtesies to—' Elizabeth checked herself, also. Even she did not dare sneer at the wives and mothers of Henry's intimates although most of them were rather unsophisticated, never having been at court before.

'I repeat, the list was submitted in good faith. If you had objected, I would have sought to find others more pleasing to you. Now it is too late. The appointments have been made public; those men waited upon you at the wedding feast. To remove one from office now would be a deep insult. However, if one of the gentlemen has displeased you in some particular way, I will certainly reprimand him and caution him against any fault in the future.'

'Reprimand!' Elizabeth barely restrained herself from shrieking. 'Do you think me so poor a thing that I cannot reprimand my own servants?'

Henry had not wished to make too much of the maid of honour's behaviour. It might have been an accident and, if so, to belabour the point might give Elizabeth ideas. However this was too good an opportunity to miss, since Elizabeth did

185

not seem to have understood his first plainly spoken warning.

'Can you, madam?' he asked coldly. 'Then let me suggest that you do so to the maid of honour who bespoke me so pertly this morning that I was forced to rebuke her myself. Another such mishap, and I will be forced to select your ladies for you as well as your gentlemen.'

Accustomed to the screaming passions of her mother and father, Elizabeth miscalculated completely the danger behind Henry's calm. Fortunately, Henry did not realize that his wife was unimpressed by a manner which reduced brave men, who knew him better than she did, to quivering terror. He took the pallor and speechlessness of rage for fear and said, more kindly but still firmly, that a king's daughter should know it was impossible to alter honorary appointments without good cause. This insult from an upstart so completely tied Elizabeth's tongue that Henry was able to lead her back to the company in the other room before she was able to collect her scattered faculties and launch another attack. Henry bowed briefly to the company, offered a particular bow to the dowager queen, kissed his mother's cheek, and retired.

With a look of total unbelief, Elizabeth stared at the door that had closed behind her husband. She uttered a gasp, and fled again into her bedchamber whither, this time, her mother and Henry's followed her.

'You did not quarrel with Henry, did you, dear?' Margaret asked anxiously, for she had been frightened by his eyes which had gone cold and opaque as a wintry sky.

'Quarrel? With your son? It is not possible to do so, I must presume. If one presents a grievance, it becomes clear at once that *he* is the injured party and that *you* must beg pardon.'

Margaret bit her lip. It would not do to laugh, although the king's daughter sounded suspiciously like any young wife. She knew nothing of what had happened earlier, having just arrived to pay Elizabeth a wedding visit and dine with the court. Nor did she care much. Whatever Henry felt, he was handling Elizabeth well now. A few quarrels between young people served to draw them together. So long as Henry did not expose Elizabeth to public ridicule – and he had certainly guarded against that – no harm would come of an argument or two.

The dowager queen was now speaking softly into Elizabeth's ear, and the girl shook her head angrily. 'Why, whatever did

186

my poor Henry do to enrage you so much?' Margaret asked. If the dowager was behind this quarrel, the humour was rapidly evaporating from the situation.

'Poor Henry! Of course. I must be at fault to you since everything Henry does is perfect.'

'Dear, dear,' Margaret remarked mildly. 'I cannot think how I could have gotten such a reputation for stupidity. First Henry accuses me of thinking him perfect, and now you do. Being Henry's mother, I should think I was the last person in the world to believe that. Come, Elizabeth, Henry is not in the least perfect. He is not even particularly sweet-natured, but he does mean well and he is basically very kind. What has he done?'

'It is of no consequence,' the dowager queen said smoothly.

'It is, too!' Elizabeth denied hotly, violating a cardinal rule about not contradicting her mother, for which fault she had been whipped several times in her girlhood.

'Elizabeth!' her mother snapped.

The queen quailed, then drew herself up. One does not beat or scold a queen. If it was necessary, she would dismiss her mother from her presence. Then the intensity of the old queen's anger broke through the mist of Elizabeth's own rage. Something was amiss here. Of course she had been told again and again that Margaret was her enemy. This she could not really believe. Margaret had been consistently kind. Elizabeth had even overheard her once, having responded more quickly than usual to Henry's summons, reprimanding her son for his cold behaviour. In any case, now that she was Henry's wife Margaret could not injure her without injuring her son. Her own mother, on the other hand, had no such scruples with regard to the king's welfare – not even mine. Elizabeth thought sadly.

The silence was lengthening painfully, but Elizabeth was not ready to break it or to have it broken. She needed time to think. Margaret could wish to keep Henry and herself divided so that her own influence would remain paramount with her son. But Elizabeth, remembering Henry's quivering passion, knew she had one major weapon Margaret did not possess. In any event, to seem to have a secret would play directly into Margaret's hands. If the countess ran to her son hinting of plots— Why had her mother complained of the gentlemen Henry had selected for her? True, they would not add to the

187

gaiety of her household, being sober and mostly elderly. True, also, they were Henry's supporters. Her mother said their purpose was to spy on her. Spy what? She could have no intention of harming her husband. Whatever she thought of him, he would be the father of her children. His throne would be their throne.

'Just a moment,' Elizabeth said. She went to her desk and returned with the list in her hand. Probably she would never have so good a test case of Margaret's or her mother's intentions again. 'See this, madam,' she said placing the list of household officials in Margaret's hands. 'Every one an ardent Lancastrian. Every one attainted – at one time or another even if later forgiven – by my father. Aside from the insult – I am grown accustomed to that – I had hoped to make provision in my own household for gentlemen who lost my Uncle Richard's favour and were impoverished for defending me and my brothers.'

'Elizabeth,' the dowager queen said sharply, 'this is a matter for you to settle with your husband yourself. What sort of wife needs to run to her mother-in-law for help?'

Margaret would have given a year or two off her life to see the substitute list she was sure had been prepared, but she dared not ask because she did not know what game Elizabeth was playing. It had to be a game; the girl was acting stupid, and Margaret knew she was not that.

'You have put me in a fine position,' she said to Elizabeth's mother, laughing. 'If I offer to help, I will be an interfering mother-in-law, and if I do not, I will be condoning an action which does seem, on the surface, to be a trifle high-handed. Henry is a superb administrator, but sometimes he does get carried away by his own efficiency. What do you want me to do, Elizabeth? I will speak or be silent, just as you wish.'

'It is no use to do either. The king says that appointed officials may not be dismissed except for just cause.'

'Oh dear,' Margaret sighed. 'That does sound like Henry on his high horse, doesn't it? Perhaps you did not explain that you were not asking for their dismissal but merely a shifting about. Perhaps if you chose a better time than just before dinner when he is hungry, and tired, and irritable—'

'I tried to reach him in the morning, but he was too occupied by "weighty matters of state" – his words – to spare his wife a moment.'

188

'Oh dear,' Margaret said inadequately, wondering in her ignorance what could have made Henry act so idiotic. Apparently his behaviour had not improved. Now that list might be lost forever. If the dowager queen and Elizabeth were plotting something, the names offered after this discussion would not be the same as those which would have been offered in the morning. Margaret felt sick. Could she have been fooled by Elizabeth's sweet face? Poor Henry. What had she done to him by making him king, by making this marriage? She did not even dare warn him. If there was no plot and Elizabeth's game was merely the normal womanly one of wishing to rule her husband, it would be a dreadful sin to reinforce the suspicion already in Henry's mind. A sin against Elizabeth, and a deathblow to Henry's personal happiness – if a king could have personal happiness.

Chapter Fourteen

No one could have thought from the placid behaviour of the king and queen at dinner either that they were newly wed or that they had just had a nasty quarrel. Their conversation with each other and with the courtiers around them was correctness itself. After dinner, perhaps, neither was quite as calm. Henry fidgeted away the long evening in his own apartments quite unable to work or play or to allow his companions to do so. Elizabeth tinkled the keys of her virginal, making so many errors that her ladies felt like screaming. However, except for the few who knew what had happened, all pardoned the young couple readily, seeing so obvious an excuse for their behaviour that they sought no further.

'For God's sake, Harry, sit still,' Jasper growled as Henry rose for the tenth time from the dice table and tripped over his uncle's feet.

'A young husband,' Oxford whispered indulgently.

Jasper, not liking some of the rumours he had been hearing about the court, and seeing in Henry's behaviour only too sure a confirmation of them, felt even more irritated. 'Then why the devil does he not go and pace around in her chamber. Perhaps she would take the hint and go to bed.'

Those who had been present at the scene with the maid of honour stiffened apprehensively, but Henry chose not to hear. He looked steadily out of the window, wondering what he would do if he knew Elizabeth had gone to bed. What was the correct tactical move? Should he continue to show displeasure by staying out of her bed that night? A distinct sensation in Henry's loins indicated that he might be giving himself more displeasure than his wife if he chose that method of displaying anger.

Anyway the quarrel was over and he had won. It would be wrong for him to continue angry, being the victor. That made the quarrel over for him, but what about Elizabeth? He had been pleased with her demeanour at dinner, but he knew it had no meaning. A king's daughter was rigidly trained not to make scenes in public. What if the quarrel was not over for her and she refused him? Unconsciously Henry pressed himself against the window frame, pulled surreptitiously at his hose which seemed suddenly binding, and flushed when he realized what he was doing. It was her duty to bear him children; there could be no refusal. That sounded very fine, but what if she refused to do her duty? Henry had a vision of himself retreating like a dog with his tail between his legs. He suffered a flash of fury and then began to laugh. His tail was certainly not between his legs now.

Yet it was no laughing matter because it was not essentially a question of his sexual satisfaction. Perhaps he should not press the matter. If Elizabeth were allowed a few days to get over her temper and consider what being on bad terms with her husband meant, she might be more amenable in the future. It might worry her as to his next move if he withdrew himself and she believed him still angry. Oh God, this was where he had started out. Well, then, he would force her if necessary. Show her there was no defence against him either as a man or as a king. Henry swallowed nervously and admitted to himself that he would not have the least notion of how to go about it except to threaten her with violence. He was revolted by the thought; for once the threat was made, it would be absolutely necessary to follow through if she did not yield. It was distasteful to him to use violence upon men; to use it on a woman – to mark Elizabeth's beautiful flesh— Well, then, he simply would not go to her until he was sure—

Henry uttered a violent exclamation of disgust as he realized he had come full-round to the beginning of his thoughts again. The exclamation made his gentlemen glance uneasily at each other. At least half of them, not knowing the cause of Henry's annoyance, still mentally damned the woman who had managed to overset a temper that war could not affect. Jasper sighed, glanced at the clock, which Henry had been so sedulously avoiding, and levered himself to his feet. The entire nation envied him his position as the king's uncle who had only to ask to receive, but they never remembered that to him fell the tasks no one else would dare undertake.

'Harry,' he said plaintively, but low enough so that Henry alone heard, 'it is eight of the clock. In mercy to us, if not to yourself, go make ready for bed. I will send a message to Her

Grace to be ready to receive you at nine. Good God, it is no shame to be eager. If anything, Her Grace must be flattered.'

A short and quite unpleasant bark of laughter was all the answer Jasper received. He was, however, sufficiently annoyed with what he considered his nephew's infatuation that he continued to stand and wait for a reply.

'Perhaps she will not be so flattered as you think,' Henry replied irritably at last. 'I have had some sharp words with her. She thinks to be queen instead of the king's wife.'

'The devil fly away with all the blood of York,' Jasper muttered. 'Why I heard a story just opposite – that you were enamoured. Who knows of this?'

'Only a few who will hold their tongues, unless she has been fool enough, or desirous, to spread the tale. I spread the first rumour, or rather Devon spread it on my order.'

'Then she must receive you tonight, even if you need to gag and bind her. Go make ready. I will go to her myself.'

Jasper could not decide, as he accepted Henry's mute nod and went on his errand, whether he was more pleased or distressed. He was certainly relieved to know the rumour that Henry was falling into Elizabeth's power was false, but it was scarcely better that there should be real enmity between them. First of all it would make Henry unhappy, for he was an affectionate soul. Worse, however, it could not be hidden long, not hidden at all if Elizabeth wanted it to be known, and would turn the Yorkists against the king. Jasper was prepared to offer both blandishments and threats, but Elizabeth's reception of him was so pleasant and placid, that he merely gave her the message and waited for her reaction.

'Very well, Bedford,' she said calmly.

Either Henry had vastly magnified the affair, which was not his way, unless – heaven forfend – he was enamoured of her and did not realize it, or she was pure Woodville and up to something. Jasper bowed deeply, murmured a few conventional commonplaces, and took himself back to his nephew. He waved Henry's gentlemen away, as only he was privileged to do, and began to undress the king with his own hands.

'Well?'

'You are sure you had words with Her Grace?' Jasper asked as he went down on his knees to remove Henry's shoes.

Henry put a finger in his ear and shook it as if to clear it.

'Did I hear you aright? Do you think I can no longer tell when I am involved in an argument?'

'Very well, then. Is Her Grace so stupid *she* does not recognize a quarrel?'

'Uncle, I am not in the humour for jests, not even yours.'

'Harry, I am not jesting.' Jasper slipped off his nephew's doublet and untied his shirt. 'When I gave her the message, she said, "Very well," without a shadow upon her face. Either she does not remember that—'

'I tell you she was all but shrieking at me, and not half an hour before dinner.'

'Then beware. I have told you before that Woodville blood is not to be trusted. York I do not love, but Woodville reminds me of something that creeps on its belly.'

Henry pulled his robe around his naked body, pretending he was shivering with cold. His mother and his body urged him one way; his uncle and his mind urged him the other. The trouble was not that he distrusted Elizabeth. He distrusted almost everyone except his few faithful, tested friends, and he found no difficulty in living with his distrust. The trouble was that he did not want to distrust Elizabeth. If he had married little Anne of Brittany, he would not need to watch every word of his own and listen for double meanings in every word of hers. He was a trifle early because he could bear the suspense no longer, but Elizabeth was ready and waiting. If she did not smile at him, she did not frown, either.

Actually Jasper was not far wrong when he asked Henry if Elizabeth remembered the quarrel. In fact she was so absorbed in the new problem of her mother's and Margaret's intentions that her only feeling about the argument with Henry had been an anxiety that it would prevent him from coming to her that night. First and most important was her need to test her sexual weapon against him. If she could use that to make Henry appoint the men she wanted appointed, she could use those appointments to discover why her mother wanted them to have positions at court. She knew, however, that she was not expert in the use of her weapon. Her mother advised her to refuse him access to her body until she had her way. That was the technique she had used herself, but Elizabeth was not at all sure either that it would work with Henry, or, even if it did at first, that it was a good idea. After all, her father had found

193

other willing bodies soon enough. For some obscure reason that made Elizabeth think of Henry when he had lain asleep against her, and she felt indignant at the notion of sharing him. It was the fate of queens, perhaps, but certainly she would do nothing to encourage the practice.

Well, then, should she ask him before, during, or after? Not during. Of course she intended to use the intoxication of pleasure to get her way, but at that point he would be too drunk to hear. Not before either, that might break the mood and anger him still more. After? He had fallen asleep so quickly. Between would be best, if she could be sure there would be a between tonight. It was, after all, not the first time of having. There was no use worrying any more. He was here. Elizabeth looked gravely at her husband. It would not do to be too warm, that might be suspicious.

'You will take cold if you stand there long,' she said prosaically.

Could she be an idiot? Henry wondered. No, no, his mother had lived with her for a year and said she was clever. Besides, Henry knew Elizabeth could speak several languages and keep up a brisk repartee. He opened his mouth to say something complimentary about the sweetness of a temper that could so soon forget a quarrel. Then he thought that would sound condescending or sarcastic. The forgetfulness had to be planned, but there was no reason why he should not enjoy the fruits of that planning even if Elizabeth did not. A gesture drove the ladies from the room; his gentlemen had been instructed to wait outside. Tonight Henry was determined he would have no audience.

Elizabeth opened her eyes and tried to steady her breathing. Her first surprised thought was that she could not have asked for anything, including her life, from the moment he had begun to caress her. It was something she must remember. The sexual weapon was a double-edged sword, and Henry seemed to have as good a grip upon it as she did. Perhaps that was why her mother had refused all contact with her father until her desires were granted. Elizabeth's lips curved softly. Now that seemed even less good an idea than it had before. There were compensations to sharing a weapon. Her husband was still gasping, but she caught the infinitesimal tensing of his

194

muscles which meant he would soon move away. To sleep? To leave her? He did neither. He turned partly on one side and regarded her from the corners of his long eyes.

'Henry,' she said softly, 'why were you so angry at my sending for you? Do you consider that improper?'

His lids dropped lower, but Elizabeth guessed he could still see her. 'It was the way you sent that was improper, not the sending.' His voice sounded sleepy, relaxed, not as if he was carrying a grudge. 'The maid was rude.'

'But I was not responsible for that,' Elizabeth protested. Then, realizing that defence was untenable she added, 'Oh, perhaps I was. I was angry and said— Perhaps I spoke sharply. Henry—'

He responded with an interrogative grunt which sounded even sleepier. If she asked him now, would he remember? As if her thought had disturbed him, he opened his eyes a slit, licked his lips, and mumbled, 'What?'

'I was not angry because you chose the men. It was only that I hoped to give some old friends of my father's employment. Gloucester—' her voice faltered on the word, but she steadied it and continued, 'stripped them of everything. They lost all for my sake. It seemed only right that I should help them.'

Henry's eyes were closed again, but after a moment he turned on his back, yawned, and asked, 'Who?'

Elizabeth gave him five names, but instead of replying he moved so that his body lay against hers and his head rested on her breast. 'Will you change the appointments?' she pleaded softly, her fingers playing with his hair.

'Cannot,' Henry mumbled, and was satisfied because he could feel the slight stiffening which took place in her body although her fingers continued to toy gently with his hair. 'Cannot – insult old friends.'

'Please – Henry? I will ask no more of you. Please?'

'Give them other places if you want. Not your household – mine – always room in mine.'

The words were so slurred he sounded drunk. Elizabeth could only pray he would remember. She stroked his hair again, whispered, 'Thank you. Thank you, Henry. You will not forget, will you?'

Henry laughed sleepily. 'Never forget anything – anyone

195

tell you that. Henry never forgets anything—' And he allowed his voice to drift away in a long sigh and his breathing to fall into the pattern of sleep.

Yet the Tudor had seldom been more wide awake or more puzzled. Elizabeth was satisfied with his taking the men into his own household – of that he was sure. He had been pressed against her from head to toe, his ear above her heart. When he refused to change the appointments he could hear the quickened heartbeat, feel the tension of her body. When he agreed she had gone back to normal with relief – yes – but not with the total relaxation she should have displayed if the matter was of really great importance. Did that mean that it did not matter where the men were appointed so long as they were at court? If she wanted the men to have appointments in his household, why not just ask? Why the quarrel? To ask simply was probably too obvious. There was a Woodville. Take a tortuous path over a straight one at any time because there was a better chance of covering the trail whether it needed to be covered or not.

Very well, if she intended them for his household all along – why? Probably as spies. Tit for tat. Henry had a violent impulse to laugh, and relieved himself by coughing. His wife's hand, which had fallen still, began to stroke his hair again. He sighed and nuzzled closer. There was no fear that his body would betray him. He had years of practice in breathing smoothly and keeping his muscles flaccid while his mind scurried round like a trapped rat in a cage. There welled up in him a warmth and a sympathy for his fair, young bride. She did not know what sort of an opponent she had – and she must never know. If she knew, his pleasure would be destroyed and she would become dangerous. At present she was such easy prey. She played right into his hands – at one and the same time bolstering the impression he wanted to give of her influence with him and marking out clearly the men who were violently Yorkist and would need to be watched.

There was a continuing sense of puzzlement under the satisfaction, though, because Henry could not understand what she was trying to accomplish. Any danger to him must be a danger to her. She was his wife, but not crowned queen – and England would not accept a ruling queen anyway. Surely her position was better as his wife than of – say – the aunt of Warwick if

196

he should be put on the throne. Unless she hated him enough to think the whole world well lost for the sake of revenge—Henry's body did betray him. He shuddered involuntarily, and Elizabeth who was half-asleep herself tightened her grip on him and murmured, 'Hush,' as to a restless child.

No, not that. It was not the Woodville way to sacrifice person or profit to any purpose. Henry relaxed again, but with an effort. Unconsciously, seeking solace, he began to rub his lips against Elizabeth's breast, sucking the fragrant skin gently. Still half-asleep, she sighed and turned a little towards him to facilitate his caress. The sickness which had been rising in Henry's throat dissipated. Woodville she was, and lustful as her mother. Thank God for that. Even that adder, the dowager queen, had never struck at the man who satisfied her lust. As long as he contented Elizabeth in bed, she would never hate him enough to harm him. Only when Edward strayed out of his matrimonial bonds had his wife formed factions counter to his purpose. Edward must have been mad, Henry thought as his caress became more ardent and more purposeful. Who would wish to stray when passion and profit were so intermingled?

Henry had not meant to spend the night this time, but dawn was lightening the sky when he rose to leave. 'I have given you little rest,' he said as Elizabeth sat up, too. 'Lie abed. When it is warmer we will rise together so that you may hunt with me.'

'I hope I shall have as little rest then,' Elizabeth laughed.

It was frank sexuality – a thing of which she had never been taught to be ashamed – but Henry took it for a warning. 'You will never have more rest than you desire,' he replied lightly. 'I try to suit the feeding to the appetite.'

She laughed again, but grew grave quickly and touched his hand. 'We spoke last night – do you remember?'

'Henry never forgets anything,' he repeated, and gave back her list of names.

That, too, was a warning, but Elizabeth either did not care or did not understand. She clapped her hands delightedly. 'Oh, you do not. Wait, Henry,' she said, reaching for him as he turned to go. 'Will you come to me every night?'

'Every night?' His brows rose.

Elizabeth blushed a trifle and shook her head at him merrily. 'Nay, I know there will be times when you or I are too tired,

197

or when I cannot receive you – that way. I did not mean that as it sounded. Only – there is never any other time when we may be together to talk privately. At other times, if we send our courtiers away, they wonder what we are saying to each other.'

He leaned forward so swiftly to kiss her that Elizabeth did not see his eyes. When their lips parted, the Tudor's expression was merely tender. 'I will come every night that it is humanly possible. There will be times when we are parted by necessity.' He leaned forward again and touched her face gently. 'At such times I will write you a letter every night – or a little every night if I have not time for a whole letter.' The more she believed him to be in her power, Henry thought coldly, the harder she would strive to keep him there and to keep him king.

Elizabeth lay back when the door closed behind her husband. She was both spent and content. Henry was certainly kind, as Margaret said, when he was well used. That message yesterday had been a bad mistake, but fortunately his hurt had been easily salved – more easily than she deserved for her carelessness, Elizabeth thought. It was natural that the scion of a Welsh adventurer would stand more upon his dignity than trueborn royalty. She must take care never to offend that sensitive and only half-buried sense of unworthiness. Her pride could afford to bend – privately. She was the daughter of a king and of a line more legitimate even than that of the original Lancastrian usurpers.

It would also be necessary to have a care not to ask for too much nor to ask too often. Not that Elizabeth feared it would drive Henry from her bed just yet – his pleasure was too intense and too new. This power must be wielded cautiously, however, lest the victim become aware of the trap and reluctant to fall into it. Her mother had made that mistake. Elizabeth's contentment vanished at the thought of her mother. She had been feeling sleepier and sleepier and putting the feeling off. Now, wide awake, she wished she were asleep. What would she do if she found by her mother's reaction that something beyond simple charity lay under the wish to appoint these men to her household? Tell Henry? Her every instinct revolted at letting a stranger – satisfactory lover and husband notwithstanding, Henry was still a stranger – see the washing of dirty family linen. No, she would handle her mother herself.

198

However, long before Elizabeth rose to break her fast, her family's linen was being firmly thrashed against the rocks of policy by Henry, Foxe, and Reginald Bray.

'Where did you get this list, sire?' Bray asked, plainly unhappy.

'I think I will keep my own council on that,' Henry responded with a smile. 'You know them?'

'I know them because it is my business to know such things. Mostly they are believed favourable to you, but Brodrugan will be in – or start – the first rebellion against you, sire. Broughton, the Harrington brothers, and Beaumont are a trifle more cautious, but will not be far behind.'

'Gloucester's men?' Foxe asked.

Bray shook his head. 'Oh, no. They hated Gloucester sore, which is why they are accounted your friends. But they are legitimists – or that is what they call themselves – Yorkist legitimists.'

'Would they accept Her Grace as a ruling queen?' The question seemed almost idle, for Henry still looked very sleepy as he lounged beside the fire in furred slippers and bedrobe.

'I do not think they are mad enough for that,' Bray said. 'They would elevate Warwick. Indeed, it would ease my heart, sure, if you would say who proposed these men to you. They are dangerous. Whoever named them should be watched.'

Henry laughed. 'Do not trouble yourself for that. Are they dangerous to me personally – would they use poison or a knife to rid the land of me?'

Bray hesitated. 'In an ordinary way I would say not. They think of themselves as honourable men – but I would not wish to be responsible for vouching for them in this case. Why not order their arrest?'

'On what charge?' Foxe asked.

'I am a lover of justice,' Bray replied with a troubled frown. 'Yet if I had a shadow of a cause, these men would already languish in a safe prison or be even safer in their graves.'

'God forbid!' Henry exclaimed. 'It is sheer foolishness to slay the goat that leads the sheep to the slaughter pens. Foxe, find me appointments for each of them – nice safe employment which will keep them in the court but not too close to my person. Do you not find yourself in urgent need of assistance,

Richard? How about Morton and Edgecombe and Poynings? Are they not all overworked? And you, Bray?'

Two grim faces reflected no image of Henry's half-smile. 'You play at a dangerous game, sire,' Bray protested.

Henry's smile broadened, and he stretched and yawned. 'When I was six, Edward summoned me to court. If my mother had taken me – I would have died. When I was fourteen, my uncle fled with me to Brittany in the teeth of a gale which promised to drown us because death was more certain if we stayed. When I was eighteen Edward offered my present wife as bait – and sent two murderers to fetch me. When I was twenty-six, Richard bribed Landois to slay me or send me hither to slaughter. I do not count the assassins who came, tried, and failed. What did you say about danger?'

'There are more lives than one hanging on the single thread of yours now, sire,' Foxe said reprovingly, pulling his lip. 'Mine is one. I would like to see you use more caution. Nonetheless, I can see the merit in this move. Strict watch will be kept.'

'They will make five little windows to see into many more dark hearts,' Henry murmured. 'Bray, let me have a list of whoever else leans this way.' His breath caught at the appalled look in Bray's eyes, but he changed the tiny sign of fear easily enough into a choke of laughter. 'The ringleaders, man. I do not expect you to list the name of every non-Lancastrian male in the country.'

'There are women, too,' Bray replied miserably.

'Women, too, then,' Henry agreed easily, though a weight seemed to be pressing his breath out of him. 'For now, Reginald, that will be all.' When he was gone, Henry said softly, 'My little Foxe, you will check him. Bray is a lover of justice with too many scruples and too many fears. Eventually you must take over his work. Kings cannot afford scruples.'

'He will be better testing and watching the judges,' Foxe agreed. 'He will do you much good, for it will give him pleasure to ferret out that kind of corruption, and you will get a name as a lover of justice.'

'Richard, I love you,' Henry murmured. 'So often you save me from needing to speak my own thoughts.'

'And I you, sire, because great affairs are as meat and drink to me, yet I could not be patient to lead a stumbling, blind

200

ruler. But speaking of justice, is it not time for another visit to the prisoners in the Tower?'

'Yes. It is time also to free Northumberland. How goes the truce with the Scots?'

Foxe understood. As soon as that was signed, Northumberland could be released. Any treachery he contemplated – if he should be untrustworthy – could then be nosed out sooner and reported by Henry's spies in the north and at James's court.

'Near done. The envoys are very agreeable.'

'Too agreeable?'

'I think not. They do their king's will in this, and James is a peaceful man. Sire, I would say orisons for his good health.'

'You think it in danger?'

'From a slipped word here and there, I think his son will have the throat out of him – and then out of you – if he can.'

Henry stared into the fire. 'A viper in the bosom is good reason for peace abroad,' he said lightly, turning and turning the ring Elizabeth had given him on his finger.

Some hours later, Elizabeth invited her mother to breakfast. This, in itself, was offensive because the dowager queen believed she had the right to walk in and out of her daughter's apartments whenever she wanted, and this seemed a clear indication that Elizabeth did not intend to permit such freedom. Elizabeth, she concluded, arriving in high dudgeon, was an ungrateful, unnatural child, and if ill befell her she would deserve it. Her once-beautiful face was drawn into ugly lines of dissatisfaction and self-pity. The children who loved her were all reft from her, and she was left with mean-spirited daughters. Elizabeth, grown so high and mighty since she married the bastard Welshman that she needed a whipping, and also those two puling younger ones who clung to their sister, ignoring their duty to their betrayed mother.

'I suppose I should curtsy right down to the ground to you,' she snapped after she haughtily dismissed the queen's ladies.

Elizabeth made no protest at the dismissal. They were better off alone. 'Not to me, mother,' she replied. 'If you curtsied at all, it would be to my office.'

'Well, I will not. Even that – that—'

'The king, mother?'

'Call him what you will – he is no king to me. Even he forbade his mother to bow to him.'

Elizabeth's eyes dropped. She was ashamed – not for teasing her mother about curtsying, but for the difference in the relationship which permitted Henry to fall on his knees before his mother without fearing the result. Perhaps she was doing an injustice. Her mother's life had been so bitter, flickering unsteadily between too-great brilliance and too-dark obscurity.

'Nay, mama, it was a naughty jest. You know how light of wit I am. Indeed, I have tried my best to accomplish your will. I begged the – my husband – softly, and I received what I asked. The gentlemen will have appointments. Henry's own secretary, Dr Foxe, brought the warrants.'

The queen's mother grasped the parchments, saw that they were signed and sealed, and began to read. 'You fool!' she gasped.

'Fool?' Elizabeth paled, her worst fears confirmed.

'I said appointments in *your* household, you idiot, not his!'

'But what difference can it make? They have a livelihood now. Is that not what you desired?'

'What I—?' The dowager saw her daughter's mouth quivering, and she softened her expression. How she and Edward, who both loved power, could have been cursed with such weak-minded children she did not know. She must, however, soothe her daughter or the puling fool would be idiot enough to tell her bastard husband that her mama did not approve the appointments. 'Elizabeth, my love,' she said patiently, 'your husband was forced by the love the people still have for your father into marrying you. Do you not see that his one desire must be to rid himself of you? Therefore, he has set your household full of spies.'

'I am not afraid of spies, mama,' Elizabeth said sturdily. If this was her mother's reason, she was relieved. She did not fear Henry; she had seen his face all soft, his eyes swooning with passion. The lips which touched her breasts so eagerly, the hands which sought the secrets of her body so gently, would never be used to order her away. 'I shall never do anything which a spy could report to my disfavour. What is there to fear?'

'Idiot!' her mother spat, losing control again. 'Cannot evidence be made? Besides, how can you be sure you will

202

never receive a person or give charity or a gift to someone who is secretly disloyal? You must begin again and free yourself of these watching eyes. I will find some other men suitable to your service.'

'I can ask for nothing more just now,' Elizabeth said slowly.

The dowager queen groaned. 'Now is the time – now, before he tires of you, before he fills his bed with whores. Refuse him until he grants your desire. He cannot bed a mistress yet. Even his own men would frown if he did so before you were with child. They need a Yorkist heir to bolster their worthless claim to your father's throne.'

You have just outargued yourself, Elizabeth thought. Henry can wish me no harm if he needs a Yorkist heir. If the men in my household are spies, are they not here, perhaps, to protect me from the dangers you threaten me with? In any case, to rid myself of them – would that not prove me guilty of evil intent? Tears welled into Elizabeth's eyes and rolled down her cheeks. She did not know whether her fear that her mother could be right or her renewed fear that she was hatching another conspiracy was more dreadful.

Chapter Fifteen

'What do you think of the temper of the Londoners?' Henry asked John Morton who was now archbishop of Canterbury, the winter having slain the aged Bourchier.

'Towards you, Your Grace?' Morton nodded at Henry's smile. 'The priests tell me there have never been so many unpaid prayers so fervently said for any man's health before. I dare believe that if an enemy to you fronted this city, it would close its gates and fight.'

Henry sighed. 'A tribute I pray it may never need to make me.'

The archbishop contemplated the raindrops coursing down the small, glazed panes of Henry's private closet. It was a small, pretty room behind his bedchamber, fitted with sybaritic splendour and meant for confidences. Henry used it when he wished to work alone or to confer privately with someone. All in all, the time he spent in it was not much, but it was invariably important.

'There is no reason to delay your progress, except, of course, the weather.' Morton paused, then said slowly, 'You should go. You need the change. You are tired, my son.'

The word was a reminder of the confession Henry had just made. The king bit his lips. 'Am I overanxious? Elizabeth is not herself.' How could she be, he thought. What sort of a marriage is it? I watch her. She watches me. 'I dare not take her,' he added tensely, 'and I dare not leave her behind.'

'You are tired,' Morton repeated. 'You must leave her here, sire, both for your health's sake and for policy.'

Henry stirred restlessly. He knew it was not Elizabeth's physical demands upon him that were dangerous, in spite of Morton's reference to his health. 'She desires to go. I do not wish to offend her.'

'Promise her the next progress. It is necessary that this time you appear alone as king. The north is—'

A quick gesture of irritation curbed the repetition that the north was too strongly Yorkist and might greet Elizabeth as queen rather than Henry as king. 'How goes the business with the French?'

Morton showed no surprise at the switch in subject. 'I have not yet received word, but I expect daily – nay, hourly – to hear that the treaty is ratified.'

'And they will surely free Dorset?'

'It is the second condition.'

'I wish to know at once, day or night – whatever the hour. Send to Her Grace's chambers for me if you cannot find me in mine.'

Now Morton was surprised. All discussion of affairs of state were sedulously kept away from Elizabeth's quarters. 'Yes, Your Grace. Is there aught of speciality in this treaty of which I am not aware?'

'No. It is the draught of honey to make the bitter purgative go down. When we first met, Her Grace desired that I free Dorset. She has respoken that request more than once, having a great natural affection for—' Henry paused, 'her family. When I have news that he is free, I will tell her I cannot take her on progress and offer her her brother's presence as consolation.'

The archbishop stifled a sigh of pride and relief. All of Henry's advisors had set their faces against Elizabeth's accompanying him. As ever he had listened patiently to them, but until this moment he had refused to commit himself as to whether his wife's desire or his ministers' advice had more influence. In fact, the news came three days later, most conveniently when Henry was transacting the normal business of the day. There was a letter from Dorset in the packet, also – just the right kind of letter, filled with glib thanks and meaningless protestations of good faith. It would please Elizabeth; that was more important than the nausea it raised in himself, in Henry's opinion.

He brought the letter with him when he made his customary visit to his wife that night. Love first and news after, or news first and no love, Henry wondered. There was no physical urgency in the thought, for Henry's sexual cravings had been fully gratified for nearly two months. He merely would have liked to know which pattern would be least likely to irritate Elizabeth. She had become increasingly nervous the last few weeks, increasingly prone to break into shrill argument over nothings. If this was the sweet nature Margaret had praised,

Henry found it hard to imagine what his mother would consider shrewish. When he complained to her, however, Margaret had looked blank and advised him, most infuriatingly, not to annoy his wife.

The question of news first or love first never arose. As soon as she saw him, Elizabeth sat up and gasped nervously, 'What is wrong, Henry? What is the matter?'

'Nothing is wrong. I have news for you. Some will disappoint you, but some is very good.'

'Bad news?'

Her voice trembled and her eyes stared wide, showing their whites like a terrified horse. Henry wanted to scream at her that she should confess and relieve her soul, that he would pardon her whatever she had done. Instead he said soothingly, 'Not bad news – good news. I have made a treaty with the French. In a few weeks your brother Dorset will be home.'

Elizabeth shook her head. 'No, that is not what is in your face. Not unless – you do not mean harm to Dorset, do you?'

Henry closed his eyes and took a deep breath. 'I do not mean harm to any man or any woman who does no hurt to me. Do calm yourself, madam.'

'Madam! Madam! I have a name. Can you not call me by name?'

'Elizabeth, control yourself. If you wish the sour mixed with the sweet, then here it is. I have decided not to take you on progress. It is clear to me that you are not well—'

'I must go! I will go! Henry, you cannot leave me behind. I want to go.'

White-faced, she slid from the bed and came towards him, opening her robe to expose her body. Before he was conscious of the emotion and could master it, Henry's face displayed such revulsion that Elizabeth screamed and shrank away. Instantly the door sprang open, Cheney and Willoughby appearing with half-drawn swords. As swift as they had been, Henry was quicker. He had twitched Elizabeth's robe together and put an arm around her. He turned his head towards the door and smiled.

'Her Grace is a little overcome at hearing of the French treaty and her brother's release. Send in her ladies.'

'No,' she whispered, clinging to him, 'no. Henry, do not go. I want to talk to you.'

'We will have time enough to talk when you are more composed. I do not leave tomorrow.'

'Henry. I did not mean it. I was not thinking of what you thought. I am so cold.'

That was true. She was trembling, and where her fingers clutched his robe Henry could feel them like ice above the velvet. He gestured and the maids of honour and ladies-in-waiting withdrew again.

'Perhaps if you told me why you are so anxious to go with me—'

'I do not know. I am afraid.'

'Of me or for me?'

She acted as if she did not hear, but her eyes were fairly staring from her head. 'They say you never change your mind once you have made a decision.'

'That is not quite true, but I will not change my mind about this.'

His certainty seemed to calm her. Elizabeth drew a shuddering breath and said, 'Come to bed.' Henry's hesitation was infinitesimal. It was a small price to pay, he thought, if it would keep her from making a scene, but when he began to caress her automatically she caught his hands. 'Oh no. Please. I could not.'

'Then what is it you want of me, Elizabeth?'

'Hold me. Hold me. I am afraid.'

Henry complied, but his efforts to conceal his relief and his real, if temporary, distaste for her were apparently not successful, although he could see nothing different in his manner. Elizabeth wept anew, quarrelled bitterly with him, and sent him away. Henry restrained his fury and braced himself for several weeks of hell, but the scene had an effect he did not expect. In the three weeks he remained in London, Elizabeth never again raised the subject, and thereby caused him more mental distress than she had at any time in the past.

Elizabeth turned suddenly dull and docile, as she had been before they married, neither inviting nor rejecting his attentions, and Henry began to learn how much he had depended upon her witty tongue and gay manners to enliven state dinners and formal entertainments. He even missed her waspish quarrelling, for there had been a stimulation in it, a blessed change from political conferences in which no one dared quarrel with

207

the king. An argument against his opinion might be presented, but it was offered logically and without passion. Elizabeth was never logical; she was often hardly coherent and always totally impassioned when she argued. Too often, now, his nightly visits ended after an exchange of formal courtesies, but Henry's growing resentment could not blind him to the fact that Elizabeth was suffering some terrible strain. She grew daily paler and thinner.

It was both agony and relief to kiss her goodbye on March 10th, to mount his horse and know he would not have to come to her that night. His enormous entourage baited their horses at Ware and took refreshments. Henry drank deeper than usual, and his spirits soared. He teased Ned Poynings and John Cheney, who was almost as strong as William Brandon, into a quarterstaff match, and he tried his own skill with the longbow against Oxford. Both of them were so bad, neither having had much use for archery in his military preparation, that the professional archers dissolved into mirth.

Royston received them that night with a right royal welcome. Bonfires blazed, the people cheered; Henry and his entourage ate at someone else's expense, and Edgecombe chuckled and counted up what the household had saved. The next morning brought them to Cambridge. Both the town and the university did the king honour, but Henry's easy courtesy did not hide the fact that it was the colleges which attracted him. He went from one to the other, listening to the professors, examining the facilities, and agonizing Dynham and Lovell by promising liberal financial help. They spent an extra day at Cambridge, and the court energetically cursed whatever or whomever gave Henry so ardent an interest in education, for the next day it poured rain. Since they could stay no longer in Cambridge without bankrupting their hosts, perforce they rode on.

Not one whit were Henry's spirits dampened. He rode through the downpour merrily swinging his sodden hat at anyone who braved the rain to see him, and laughed at his uncle who tried desperately to keep him dry by changing his cloak as often as a new one could be procured for him. His teeth were chattering with cold by the time they reached Huntingdon, but Henry even found that amusing. He demanded his hot wine in a silver goblet, refusing the fine venetian glass one his hosts proffered. The man was frightened, for silver was supposed to be a remedy or a warning against poison. Henry clapped him on the shoulder and laughed some more. He might have bitten a hole in the glass, he explained, his teeth having grown suddenly rebellious against the majesty of his cold head.

Fortunately the storm abated that night. It was still drizzling the following day, but they moved forward. Henry said the rain was not enough to disturb a true Englishman who was born wet, baptized wet, and usually drowned if he left his country. By March 16th they were in Peterborough where Henry spent hours examining the architecture of the cathedral with Bray who was, as a sideline, devoted to the subject. They attended several masses, Henry listening enraptured to the voices of the choir which seemed to be wafted heavenward through the great arches. He marvelled, too, at the flat land, having been born among the hills of Wales and seen little since his conquest beyond the rolling country of the midlands.

In any case it seemed as if nothing could displease him. Everyone received smiling and courteous attention, from the masters of great corporations, who knelt before him to offer a rich purse, to the poor woman who humbly and timidly brought him a nest of baby rabbits. She had seen him in church, she said, her voice so low with awe that Henry had to bend above her to hear, and she thought if the king so loved God he would not scorn to receive even this poor gift in thanks for the peace he had brought. Henry found a gold coin for her, knowing with the cynical part of his mind that the hope of reward and not his love of God was what brought her. Yet he carried one of the baby rabbits about with him for hours, stroking its soft fur and feeding it tidbits of greenery. That night he dispatched the rabbits with the letter he had faithfully been writing, a few lines at a time, to Elizabeth, particularly recommending the little bits of fluff to her care.

Stamford and Ely were more of the same. Henry was still happy, but very glad, by April 4th, to get to Lincoln where they would spend a week and he would have some privacy. He was growing a little tired of being constantly on exhibition at grand ceremonies. Easter was celebrated in Lincoln with due solemnity. Henry heard several masses and then went to the porch where, gorgeous raiment notwithstanding, he knelt and washed the feet of twenty-nine beggars. He passed on foot through the worst parts of the city, giving alms to the poor, to the prisoners, and to the lepers for whom he prayed. The acts were traditional, but the king's sincerity and lack of self-consciousness won hearts. Lincoln loved him.

The feasting a few days later was no less impressive. Henry never drank much, but that night he drank enough to make him cling to Poynings and Cheney as they escorted him to bed. None of the party was too steady, and there was much laughter before Henry's clothes came off. With the bedcurtains drawn, he was just beginning to enjoy a slightly frightening sensation of floating when his uncle was shaking him.

'Harry, Harry, wake up. There is news you must hear.'

Such news could only be bad. Henry sat up slowly and blinked as if he were not completely awake to gain time. 'Very well,' he yawned, 'what is it?'

Jasper gestured and Hugh Conway strode into the room. His bow was brief, but indicated no disrespect. 'Sire, Lord Lovell and the Staffords have left sanctuary.'

Henry licked his lips and passed his hand across his face. 'Did you have to wake me up to tell me that?' he asked mildly. 'Can no one beside myself give order that attainted traitors be taken on sight?'

'Harry, wake up,' Jasper repeated irritably. 'Those men of Gloucester's have sat still for more than half a year. We have applied no new pressure to them. If they have fled sanctuary it is to join a rising, and the only part of the country which would support such a rising is where we are going – Yorkshire.'

'I am awake. Do you come from Colchester, Conway?' Colchester was where the rebels had been in sanctuary.

'No, sire.'

Henry closed his eyes as if the light hurt them. He did not want to ask the next question. 'Where did you have this news then? I left you in London.'

He heard the thud as Conway went down on his knees. 'Pardon, sire. I have been your man since I first came to you in Brittany, but I swore I would not betray my informant. I am faithful. I rode as fast as I could. I have given you the message exactly as I had it, but I cannot tell you who bid me come to you.'

'So?'

'You may rack me apart, sire. I swear I will not speak.'

'When have I given you reason to expect me to put my

friends on the rack? Now that you are here, Conway, stay. But go to bed, man, and do not talk nonsense.' Henry reopened his eyes and looked coldly around at his anxious gentlemen. 'I must say that I cannot see why God has seen fit to saddle me with such a pack of fools. I will not inquire as to who proposed this harebrained scheme of waking me in the middle of the night to tell me it is necessary to go where I am going anyway. However, I suggest that it should not happen again. Uncle, you are not included in this rebuke. I know all too well they make you do what they are afraid to attempt themselves. Good night.'

They went; they could not do otherwise. Then they found that the situation did not seem as serious after talking to the king as it did before. Cheney apologized in a shamefaced fashion to Bedford, but Henry's uncle told him he had acted just right and that he should do the same in any similar situation.

'This time, of course, His Grace is right. What can we do in the middle of the night? And we are headed for Yorkshire anyway. But another time there may be need for action at once. Come to me any time. I will take the responsibility.'

Henry did not hear his uncle, for the walls were thick and the door well-fitting, but he knew what Jasper was saying. There was no need to fear that his rebuke would breed future carelessness. He pulled the bedclothes tighter around him, but it was useless to pretend to himself that his shivering was caused by cold. She knew, he thought, unable to bring himself to give Elizabeth her name. His shivering increased until he was afraid the bed would creak and bring his gentlemen.

The real question important to him was not Elizabeth's knowledge but her complicity. Knowledge was nothing. Perhaps she did not understand that with adequate warning a conspiracy could be nipped in the bud, and doubtless she was trying to shield those dear to her. Henry did not assume that Elizabeth's sexual response indicated any fondness for him. She was merely made that way; she would respond to any man who was strong enough to satisfy her. After all, he enjoyed her himself without any—

With a muffled groan, Henry turned and buried his face in the pillows. Curse her and rot her and damn her, her white body and her quick wit and her sharp tongue – she *was* dear to him. The acknowledgment made no difference. What he had to do would merely hurt him a little more. Even if she was not implicated in the plot— How could she be? She was watched by a covey of hawks. Even her ladies were spied upon. Nonetheless, she must be taught a sharp lesson. Good God, what was wrong with him that he constantly sought excuses for her? She was implicated by her own actions, even though the spies could find no evidence against her. Were they trustworthy themselves? Her charm could blind a man. It was blinding him. Doubtless this was the reason for the hysterical insistence on travelling north with him. She would have slipped away to join the rebels, perhaps even taken him prisoner or murdered him in his bed. Plainly the spy system was not adequate. Elizabeth would have to be confined.

But the next day Henry could not bring himself to do it, nor the next. Aside from Conway's report, the country seemed quiet. Wherever Henry went people lined the roads and cheered him; the nobles and country gentry came readily to kiss his hand and repeat their oaths of loyalty. Henry sent out the lesser gentlemen of his suite to seek news secretly and prepare to move from Lincoln to Newark. Outside this city, however, the deputation met him in tears. There was plague in the city, they said. He was welcome, more than welcome, but for his own safety he should move on. Henry made no attempt to test the truth of the statement. He returned the gift of money the city offered, to be used to aid the sick and pay for masses for the souls of the dead, and he moved on to Nottingham.

Here on April 11th he was greeted with almost hysterical relief. There was definite news of a rising in Yorkshire. Lord Lovell had raised a strong force around Middleham – the castle which was Richard of Gloucester's favourite home – and the Staffords were planning to attack Worcester. Henry looked around at his stricken suite and shook his head.

'No one would ever believe you raised rebellion for me and swore to die on Bosworth field if we did not succeed. Chicken-hearted – that is how you look. Can eight months of authority have so weakened you that you cannot hope to put down the mistaken enthusiasm of a handful of fools? Guildford, we will need no heavy guns on this venture. Ride back to Lincoln and raise a force there. Devon, ride to Northumberland and tell him to raise a levy of men and come to me. Oxford, you will command as usual, organizing the men as they come in.'

There was some embarrassed laughter. Of course they were more anxious now than when they had nothing except their lives to lose, but Henry, who had the most to lose, did not seem anxious at all. He continued to designate tasks calmly until only his uncle and Ned Poynings were not assigned.

'And for God's sake,' Henry said at last, 'do remember that this is a matter of no account whatsoever. The whole of a loyal country is at our backs. Keep your heads. Ned, go get some rest. You will have a long ride before you. Uncle, remain with me. To your business, gentlemen.'

When the others were gone, Jasper put his arm around his nephew's shoulders. 'Are you as easy as you seem, Harry? You lie abed, but I see from your eyes that you do not sleep, and you have not been eating well.'

'Oh, this rising does not trouble me. They have not a real leader to follow nor even a straw figure to put up as king. I think I know who is behind this, also, but I am not sure how to move.' He shook his head as Jasper was about to question him. 'Nay, I am so unsettled in my own mind that I would rather not speak of it. Now, uncle, we will have to divide our forces. As soon as some men arrive, you will take them and march on Lovell. Oxford and I will remain here, ready to come to your support or to protect Worcester.'

'You know I never dispute your commands, Harry, but— I would rather bide with you, child.' Jasper walked away to stare out a window. 'Once I came too late—'

Henry joined his uncle and embraced him affectionately. 'There can be no fear of that. I will have the stronger force and, I think, will never be engaged at all. It is you who are going into whatever danger there will be. Frankly, I do not wish to fight if it can be avoided. Therefore, as you move, you will proclaim full pardon for any man who lays down his arms and proceeds peaceably to his home. This is why you must be the one to go. The entire country knows the love that lies between us. They will believe that what you promise I will perform – and they might not believe that if another promised.'

'Very well, Harry, you are right. You have an older head and a steadier heart than I.' His face flushed. 'Stupid, rebellious fools! They do not realize what a treasure God has given them.'

'Aye,' Henry laughed, 'a treasure am I.' Then he sobered.

'But you spoke aright. They are foolish, not evil apurpose. Be gentle. It is not wise to beat a foolish child to death.'

When Jasper left him, Henry went to his bedchamber and asked to be left to himself. He lay down and tried to sleep, putting off the inevitable. At last, consideration for Ned Poynings, who would have to ride through two nights if he did not soon act, made him nerve himself to the most unpleasant task he had yet faced. The command he wrote was short and to the point. He wrote in his own hand, so that there could be no doubt, signed and sealed it with his personal seal. Ned Poynings who came alone into the bedchamber when summoned found his master in an unaccustomed attitude of despair. He was much surprised, since he had not believed the situation serious, although he was sure, knowing Henry, that part of the king's confidence was assumed.

'Sire?'

Henry lifted his head from his hands. 'You must ride to London, Ned.'

'You have had more bad news?'

'No. You carry an order to commit the – commit my wife to the Tower.'

'What?'

Ignoring the startled exclamation, Henry went on. 'It is to be done as -- as gently as possible. Try to make her believe it is for her protection in a time of danger, but her ladies are to be separated from her. My mother, to whom I have also written, will recommend to you new ladies suitable to Her Grace's service.' Henry put his clenched fist to his mouth and bit the forefinger. Somehow he had said quite the opposite of what he had intended. If Ned carried out these orders, Elizabeth would hardly receive much of a lesson.

'Pardon, sire, but— Indeed, Her Grace could have no part in this matter. You have had her watched. There is nothing, no reason—'

'She knew,' Henry said dully. Poynings opened his mouth to protest again, but the king cut him off. 'Do not reason with me. I mean Her Grace no harm, but I mean also that she can do me no harm. Here is the order; here the letter for my mother.'

'God keep Your Grace,' Poynings said, not liking either the look on his master's face or the sound of his voice.

214

'God go with you, Ned.'

The next day, Henry moved on to Doncaster, giving no reason to his men but admitting to himself it was a superstitious fear. Nottingham had been the city in which Gloucester waited for news of his attack. The levies from Lincoln came in swiftly and, to the king's great satisfaction, Northumberland arrived promptly with a well-armed force. Henry kept him, but detached some of his men to swell the army from Lincoln which permitted Jasper to start off at once with about three thousand troops. Information about the movements of the insurgents kept pouring in, and, as it seemed that Lovell was far more dangerous than the Staffords, Henry moved north again to Pontefract castle. He arrived on April 20th, establishing his base in that strongly fortified place so that he could move upon York at the slightest indication that the rebellious city planned to attack his uncle from the rear.

Here he waited, the spirits of his party rising constantly higher as the local magnates rode in to profess their loyalty and the willingness to fight for their king. Henry's attitude remained solidly confident, his temper as even and his readiness to laugh as great as during the first days of his progress. If his eyes were heavy and blue-ringed and he toyed with his food rather than eating it, that was only because he was very busy with the preparations for offence and defence which were added to his normal business. The whole entourage knew that the king sat up late working every night, so when Poynings arrived, mud-splashed and grim-looking, he was shown into Henry's presence at once.

The king looked up, then looked away almost as if he wished to ignore the obvious. He checked the childish impulse, however, put down his pen, and gestured for the room to be cleared. 'Well?' he said, and his voice was harsher than any Poynings had ever heard him use.

'I— Sire, I—'

Henry leapt to his feet, his face contorted. 'Is Her Grace safe?'

'Safe, safe, but not where you ordered her.'

Poynings was pale and for the first time really frightened of Henry. He had seen the king emotionally disordered before. He knew Henry displayed his feelings more freely in his presence than in that of other men, but he had never seen him in such a state as this.

215

'Where?' the Tudor shrieked. 'Where?'

'Where you left her, at Westminster palace.' There was an immediate slackening of the insane rage, and Poynings took a good grip on his courage. 'I pray you, sire, have patience to listen, then do with me as you will.'

'Speak.'

'When I came to London, Your Grace, my heart failed me. I never knew myself for a coward before. Tell me to face armed men, and I trust for courage even to die, but what I should do if Her Grace wept or refused, I did not know. To order her moved by force was beyond my strength, and I knew it.'

Henry turned away. He was not sure he would have sufficient strength for that himself.

'It seemed to me that women deal best with women, so I went first to your lady mother. Sire, she was . . .' Poynings hesitated. The king's back was not expressive and his stolidity was near cracking. 'She was much overset at my news. She – she straitly forbade me to carry out your order. She said she did not believe it, and demanded to see it. Sire, I could not— Could I lay hands on your mother? She broke the seal – and she destroyed the order.'

He waited for doom, for a recurrence of the king's rage, but Henry stood still, with his back to him, leaning on the table.

'Sire, I know I should have obeyed you. I have no defence. I am guilty. The countess of Richmond wrote you a letter and sent me to Dr Foxe. Here is the letter.' He came forward and laid it on the table. 'Dr Foxe follows. He will be here tomorrow or the next day, not having the strength to ride as I did.'

The seal of Margaret's letter was broken before the last words were out of Poynings's mouth. 'Dear my dread Lord King and son,' the letter read. 'I have done that which in another would be treason, and in doing it, I have subverted one of your most loving and loyal servants. Please, my lord son, if wroth you are when you understand the whole, that your wrath fall upon my head and not upon his. I could not permit your order to be carried out. In truth, I would have called the guards and caused Poynings's imprisonment if he had insisted. Your lady wife is with child, and not well with it. You believed her to have guilty knowledge and to have been distressed thereby. I dare not swear as to her knowledge, but her tears and terrors I believe to be caused by her breeding state. It is common in women. To have added further to her unhappiness by the removal of servants to whom she is accustomed, and to fright her by sudden imprisonment, I am sure would cause the loss of the hope she carries. I, myself, am moving to the palace, and I promise upon the life that gave you yours I will so guard her that she can do naught. Pray forgive the disobedience of the mother who loves you more than life – nay – more than the hope of Heaven, and believe that your mother acts only for what she believes is your greatest good.'

'Do you know what is herein?' Henry asked in a rather stunned tone.

'Nay, sire.' Poynings wavered on his feet with exhaustion and nervousness.

'Sit down before you fall down,' Henry said more naturally, and pushed him into a chair. 'Thank God you went first to my mother. The queen is breeding. I might have slain my own child had you carried out my order.'

'The queen with child!' Poynings's tired face lit with joy.

The true union of the houses of Lancaster and York would settle the Wars of the Roses once and for all. If the Yorkists wished to accept Henry with the mental reservation that he was really regent for his son, that was their affair, so long as they made no more trouble. Poynings would have said more, but Henry's eyes were again fixed on his mother's letter. He found the sentence he sought. 'Your lady wife is with child,' but now the next words, less significant before, leapt out at him, 'and not well with it.' Was Elizabeth not well or not holding the child well? It came to the same thing and either interpretation was possible from a rereading of the remainder of the letter. Henry sank into a chair, one wave of emotion pushing another out until he felt dizzy.

'Can you stand, Ned?' Poynings came to his feet at once. 'You are a better man than I, or your surprise is less – though I suppose it should be more. I never thought— Fetch me some wine and come back alone.'

Why the king should be distressed at this news, Poynings did not wish to imagine. He pressed a full glass into Henry's hand and set the decanter beside him on the table. Often the Tudor's reactions were different from other men's, but about this?

217

'I think, perhaps, as good as this news is we should not speak of it yet. It seems that my wife is not anxious for me to know. No doubt she has reasons of her own. More significant, my mother writes that she is not well. If she miscarries— Perhaps the fewer that know, the better.'

'I am sorry.'

The fervour of sympathy might refer to Henry's political problem, but the king suspected it was directed to his personal hurt. He gave Poynings a half-smile of acknowledgment, filled his glass and drank again. 'Sit down,' he said after a long silence, then glanced up quickly and smiled. 'Oh, no, how unkind. Go, find yourself a bed. You will need to ride back to London tomorrow. I must write to Elizabeth. Also, if by some happy chance she has not heard of what has happened here, she must be guarded from the news. My mother, I know, will take every care of her, but if there is something I can do – or send. How foolish! What could I find here that is not more and finer in London? I am talking nonsense for the sake of talking. Go, get to bed. You are dropping off your feet.'

Poynings, however, was to get little rest that night. Soon after he dropped asleep, he was awakened by the sound of re-joicing. Another messenger had ridden through Pontefract's great gates. This time John Cheney did not hesitate to open the king's bedcurtains himself.

'Your Grace,' he cried, 'the duke of Bedford sends good news.'

Henry shielded his eyes from the sudden light of the candles Cheney bore, but he sat up so quickly it was plain he had not been sleeping. Cheney proffered the sealed message, but Henry, still covering his eyes, said thickly, 'Read it.'

'To His Most Royal—'

'John! The message, not all that.'

'Yes, sire. Bedford says: "You were right, as ever, my dearest Harry. The proclamation of amnesty took the heart from the rebels. Many made submission at once and many simply stole away. Lovell fled, deserting his men like the rene-gade coward he is. I do not know whether this be bad or good, however. Certainly it means there will be no engagement, but I am afraid we may not be able to take the traitor, for there are many bolt holes here in the north in which he can hide. I bide hereabouts until it is certain that all will be quiet and to make search for the traitor. Dear my king and my most dear nephew, I await further orders." '

After signing himself devoutly and murmuring a prayer of thanksgiving, Henry smiled at Cheney. 'Tell them in the castle.'

Chapter Sixteen

On April 22nd a fitful sun shone through occasional light showers of rain. The weather was no more uncertain than the mayor and aldermen of York who came five miles from the city to greet their triumphant king. They knelt to him in the road, muddying their scarlet robes, but they could not ask for mercy because they had never confessed to rebel sympathies. Nor did Henry accuse them. He graciously bade them to rise and thanked them for their greeting. Then he spoke of the rebellion, but in terms they had scarcely hoped for. He spoke not as their wrathful sovereign but as an aggrieved father, pointing out how fruitless any rebellion was against the power of his authority, how quickly the remainder of the nation had sprung to arms on his behalf.

'I have not sought to punish this foolishness,' he said in closing the subject, 'because I understand that men may be led astray by a few wicked persons who prey upon their fears. Some thought because they were the staff of my enemy in the past that I would use them hardly and unjustly in the future. That is not true. The past is past. All Englishmen, Northron and Southron, from the east or the west, are alike in my heart as my subjects. Therefore, this once, have I shown soft clemency and loving forgiveness. This once! But it is needful for the innocent and the guilty alike to know that clemency is not weakness, that what was regarded as foolishness once cannot be so regarded again.'

He bade them mount and ride with him, and he turned the subject to the immediate interests of York, asking of their trade and what was needed on the king's part to help the city flourish. The mayor was cautious in his replies, but he sensed the sincerity in this king who, unlike past Lancastrians, did not scorn the merchants but called them the sinews of the nation. They went very slowly, for fore riders needed time to warn the city of Henry's good intentions. All had been prepared for a great celebration, but there were two sets of speeches for every pageant – one of praise and thanksgiving, another more humble, pleading for mercy.

The relief the people felt at finding the king so merciful – after all, York had publicly announced its grief at Gloucester's defeat – brought forth a burst of enthusiasm for Henry which solid loyalty probably could not have awakened. The streets were so thronged that Henry could scarce make his way through. 'King Henry! Hail King Henry!' they cried. One brass-lunged individual, perhaps not close enough to see well or of poor vision, bellowed, 'Our Lord preserve that sweet and well-favoured face', and this cry was also picked up and followed Henry about until he found himself laughing helplessly instead of smiling with dignity. It was only the eyes of blind love – however temporary – that could name his face either sweet or well-favoured.

It was necessary to compose himself, to respond to the pageant speakers. After all, when King Solomon stated that he was a 'most prudent prince of proved provision, sovereign in sapience', it would not be proper to laugh like an idiot and be incapable of reply. Nor was it possible to allow the sudden constriction in his throat to interfere with his speech when a man dressed as a red rose and a maid dressed as a white one appeared lovingly intertwined.

In spite of the streets newly flushed free of filth and the houses hung with tapestries and garlands, Henry saw signs of bitter poverty – ragged clothes, pinched faces, and, more important, for the poor were everywhere, empty and tumbled shops and warehouses. Times had been hard for York since Richard's reign. In constant fear of retaliation the merchants had done little business. Goods they sent out might be confiscated, and merchants of other cities hesitated to trade with those who might be called traitors at any moment. Henry strove to reassure the city fathers, giving a practical demonstration of his favour by telling them he would not expect the customary gift of money; it should be used instead to restore foundered merchants and generally to increase commerce.

For this he was thanked without high-flown phrases but in natural forthright speech, which bespoke more real gratitude and sincerity than anything that had gone before. The city voted him instead a generous supply of provisions, and these

Henry accepted, knowing that no one likes to be thought of as a poor sister, and knowing, also, it would permit him to ease the strain of the smaller towns in supporting his vast entourage. He retired at last to the archbishop's palace where, to his joy, he found Foxe waiting for him.

'Our Lord preserve that sweet and well-favoured face,' Foxe said merrily, kissing his hand.

'Richard! Not you, too!'

'Such are the rewards of good policy, Your Grace. I cannot compliment you on how this matter was treated, for you are always wise, but it was well done to pardon them. This was no more than the foolishness of a few desperate men. There was never—'

'Yes, yes, I know. How is it with Her Grace?'

'If she had any part in this, it is beyond my fathoming. The five we watch knew nothing of it, though their souls are guilty for they were all much frightened and made preparation to escape.'

'That is not what I meant, Richard,' Henry said impatiently.

'I can tell you little. I have not seen Her Grace much of late, for there is nothing to bring us together. She is pale and weary, very quiet at the state table. Certainly it is not generally known that she is with child. I did not know, but your lady mother is sure.'

'I thought to have some news from you.' Henry hit the table sharply, and Foxe calmly righted an empty goblet which toppled under the violence of the blow.

'I have no bad news,' he soothed, 'and in this case that is as good as you will get until the appointed time passes.'

Henry began to pace about nervously. 'Oh, sit down,' he said at last. 'There is no reason for you to be weary because I cannot rest.' There was a long pause while the uneasy king wandered about the room fingering the hangings, uselessly lifting and setting down any loose object, and irritably kicking at the furniture which came into his path. Foxe carefully withdrew his feet as Henry passed, and the king stopped suddenly and laughed. 'I do not kick my friends, Richard, even when the Lord does not see fit to make special provision for kings and shorten the time of breeding. I am a fool.'

'No, sire, you are a man.'

'Yes, but I have no right to that. A king cannot afford to be

222

a man. Enough. I am a fool. Now, York has troubles, and if I can mend them or ease them I will have less need to worry about their loyalty.'

Without command Foxe moved to the table which was provided, as every room the king used was ordered to be, with paper and writing materials. He made notes as Henry spoke, first of the manner of election of the mayors of York and then of various concessions to the guilds of the city which would stimulate trade. Later Foxe would draft the charters, adding any ideas of his own. The draft would be checked by Henry, rewritten with the necessary changes and omissions that the king suggested, checked again, and – if no new ideas had occurred to either of them or to any member of the council or the city fathers who were consulted – put into final form on parchment for the king to read once again, sign, and have sealed with the great seal.

On April 28th Henry sat through his farewell feast in York. On the twenty-ninth he returned to Doncaster to show himself in triumph after the tenseness of his previous brief stay in that city. Nottingham was revisited for the same purpose, and then the king moved west and south to Birmingham, beginning the return swing of his progress. He had heard regularly from his mother and Elizabeth – but nothing to the purpose. It was necessary for him to be content with Foxe's cold comfort that no news was good in this case. Thus far he remained in official ignorance of his wife's condition. He had had sense enough, even in his first excitement, not to betray his knowledge. If Elizabeth discovered someone else had given him the news, she would be mortally offended. It was wearing on the nerves because Henry had to reread every letter he wrote to her three times for fear he would give himself away. Unfortunately, this also made his letters very stiff.

On May 11th, the day before they were to leave Birmingham, Henry received his release. Elizabeth wrote at last, in her own hand this time, that, having missed three fluxes, she was sure she was with child. She hoped, she said, that this would please him, it being plain from his manner of writing that something had caused him discontent. Henry uttered a string of blasphemies which caused his attendants to shrink back against the walls. It was the first indication he had received that Elizabeth was dissatisfied with his letters. He should have known, he thought. At first her replies to him had been dictated to one of her ladies. After his gift of the rabbits, however, she had written to him herself until he had broken off communications when he heard of the short-lived rebellion. There was a hiatus, since Elizabeth only wrote in response to his letters, but after the note he sent to her with Poynings her replies had been dictated again. Henry thought nothing of it, except for worrying whether she was too ill to write. Now he realized he had hurt her.

Paper and pen were at hand. Henry dashed off a reply full of apology, concern for her well-being, and joy at her news. It was most unfortunate that the habit of re-reading everything he wrote was ingrained in him. He blushed at the naked emotionality of the composition and destroyed it. Then he re-read Elizabeth's letter in an attempt to find a starting point for a second try. That was a mistake, he realized later, for his instant reaction was fury. How dared she protest at anything he did when she was probably neck-deep in conspiracy against him. She could thank the child in her womb – his child – for the fact that she was not languishing in the dank confines of a prison. That reply was not sent, either, Henry having recovered his temper enough to remember that she was probably unconscious of his suspicions and might even be innocent.

The third draft was rather the worse for the effect of the other two. It was careful and considerate, containing proper sentiments of joy, proper questions regarding Elizabeth's health, proper puzzlement as to what she meant by writing of discontent in him. He certainly had no cause for complaint now, and hoped he would have none in the future. If he was brief, she must consider the very small time at his disposal for personal matters.

Elizabeth's dictated reply to his masterpiece was its equal in propriety; but Margaret's, which began 'Even a mother dare not call a king an ass', would have ignited the paper if ink were flammable. Miserably, Henry tried again; struggle as he might, however, he fell between the two stools of love and hatred. If he permitted any feeling to warm him, it ran away with him completely. He cursed himself in French, Welsh, and English, in languages his gentlemen had never heard on his lips before and did not realize that he knew, all to no avail. Cold propriety was the only salvation he could find. He could

224

not declare a love he would not acknowledge nor acknowledge a hatred he dared not declare.

Work was another salvation. Never had the cities Henry visited enjoyed such minute attention to every piece of business presented from any previous king. The Tudor was ready to receive deputations at all times, and his advice was practical and precise. No problem was too small for his consideration, and nothing was forgotten. Wherever the king touched, he left golden opinions of him behind – mixed with a good deal of awe. Word spread of his real interest in his nation's welfare, and when he rode into Bristol women leaned from their windows to throw wheat, the symbol of fruitfulness and plenty, down to him.

Now Henry heard more speeches of complaint than empty phrases of exaggerated praise. Bristol cried of her decay, blaming the decline of the navy and the falling off of the cloth trade. The king listened and promised help. Every king did that, but the mayor and aldermen were agreeably surprised when they were summoned to an audience. With Henry sat Lord Dynham, the treasurer; the earl of Oxford, who was lord high admiral of the defunct navy; and Dr Foxe. The table before the king, however, was no neat and formal sight. It was covered with papers and calculations. This was not to be a session of more empty promises, but of real business.

Let the Bristol merchants start to build ships, Henry said. He would lend so much, and so much he would contribute for shares in the profits. He would provide guns to arm the ships from the royal foundries, but in return he must have an agreement that the ships would be available for naval purposes free of charge for a certain length of time and upon proper notice. He spoke then of the cloth trade. He could make no promises, he admitted, because it depended in part on the will of other nations, but he would strive to bring life to that cold body with all his power. In parting, the lord mayor kissed Henry's hands with tears in his eyes, and said, 'They have not heard this hundred years of a king who was so good a comfort.'

Then Henry could bear no more. He rode in one day from Bristol to Abingdon, and on the next from Abingdon to London – right across the width of England. The small party which had kept pace with him arrived very late, but for once Henry allowed himself the wisdom of not thinking. Splattered with mud and streaked with sweat he went directly to Elizabeth's apartments. He did not intend to waken her. He merely wanted to see how she looked with his own eyes. He had forgotten that certain ladies slept in her chamber to attend to her wants in the night when he did not come to her. One young fool shrieked with terror at the sudden sight of a man in riding clothes.

'Be quiet,' Henry snarled at her, and then, knowing it was too late to withdraw, called out, 'Do not be afraid, Elizabeth, it is I, Henry.'

He moved quickly to the bed and pulled the curtains back. She had been startled by the shriek, for she clutched the bedclothes nervously and her lips trembled. The shock had been very brief, however; she was already recovered enough to stretch out a hand to him.

'I am so sorry,' Henry said softly. 'I did not mean to wake you.'

Puzzled, Elizabeth asked simply, 'Then what did you come for?'

'To look at you. I—'

'Oh, Henry!' She drew him down to her and offered her lips. 'Welcome home.'

'Are you well, Elizabeth?'

'Much better now. I am not so sick any more, and I am growing heavy,' she said proudly.

'Is that good?'

Elizabeth looked at her husband's anxious face, burst into a trill of laughter, and threw her arms around his neck. 'Henry, you write the most dreadful letters. I swear I came to believe that you were angry with me for getting with child.'

'Bess,' he said softly, using the tender short form of her name for the first time, 'Bess— I— My mother wrote that you were ill. I did not know what to say. I did not wish to frighten you by asking—' For the moment it was true. She was so lovely and so warm. He had forgotten the rage and the suspicion. He wet his lips, suddenly dry with desire. 'Bess, may I come back?'

'Where are you going now?'

'To wash and change my clothes.'

'You certainly need it,' she said, laughing and wrinkling her nose. 'You smell of tired man and hot horse.'

'I am not too tired,' he insisted. 'I want to come back.'

'So eager, Harry?' Elizabeth smiled and touched his dry

226

mouth with her forefinger. 'Does this mean you have been true to me?'

'By God, I have – for three long months.'

Elizabeth was fairly sure he spoke the truth. Possibly he had slipped once or twice with an unknown chambermaid; but that was not important. In the reports about his progress – not the official reports, but the rumours and stories which had filtered back to her – not the least of the virtues for which the king was praised was his chaste manner with the wives and daughters of his subjects. Perhaps she would not need to face the humiliation her mother had endured. The next few months would tell. When she was heavy with child and could not satisfy him: that would be the crucial time. His behaviour on the miles of the progress boded well, but there was no sense in putting an unnecessary strain on his virtue.

'Come back then – I have missed you, too.'

He kissed her eagerly and went to the door, then returned slowly. 'Elizabeth, will it be all right? Could I do you – or the child – any harm?'

'It never did my mother any harm, and I know she was not celibate when she carried my brothers and sisters,' Elizabeth answered frankly.

'Thank God for that,' Henry replied with heartfelt sincerity.

For Elizabeth, the succeeding months passed in peaceful contentment. Henry was unfailingly tender and considerate. No matter how busy he was – and international affairs were beginning to press upon him just as he seemed to have subdued domestic rebellion – he always had time to respond to Elizabeth's demands for attention. He took to breakfasting with her, often rising before dawn to do the work he could have accomplished in a more leisurely fashion if he'd had the extra hour or two to devote to it. The activities in which she could no longer partake, such as hunting, he curtailed drastically, going only when she urged him to do so. And Elizabeth blossomed under his kindness. Her nervous irritability disappeared. As she grew more unwieldy and the weather grew hotter, Elizabeth was sometimes fretful, but Henry's patience never failed. And if he could not jest her into good humour, the thought of the child within her soon brought her peace.

Henry was not so contented, and it was fortunate that his

227

wife, self-absorbed as breeding women so frequently are, did not realize how much the ideal husband was really the politic king. His spies had been ineffective; very well he would watch her, himself. He watched, and he learned. He was almost certain that Elizabeth knew of the rising in the north. When he told her of it, her reaction was not natural.

That knowledge did not please him, but other things did. She did not seem to be an accomplished actress, and he did believe now that she had no active part in the rebellion – more, that it was probably she who had sent Conway to warn him. He thought he knew the seat of the trouble, too. If ever hatred glared from a woman's eyes when they fell upon him, that woman was the dowager queen. What profit she could find in such behaviour he could not guess; but he could do little to seek the answer because she avoided him. The information was not of much value, either. He could see no way to separate Elizabeth from her mother completely – especially at this time. Fortunately, she seemed much attached to his mother, too. Henry could only hope that Margaret's influence would counter the dowager's, and he applied himself to keeping Elizabeth faithful by coddling her in every way he could think of.

They moved from London when the heat made the stench of the filthy city unpalatable, travelling by water to Richmond and then very slowly south until they settled in Winchester on September 1st. Henry remained for a week and, seeing Elizabeth particularly peaceful and in good health, he told her he would have to leave her for a time.

'How long?' she asked, setting down her mug of ale suddenly.

'A week or two – not more.'

Elizabeth looked away. She was hot and uncomfortable, and felt herself to be ugly and misshapen. She could hardly bear to wait until she was free of the burden she carried, and at the same time she was terrified of dying in childbirth.

'You want a woman,' she said harshly.

Henry flushed, conscious of the queen's ladies whom he was sure were listening, although they were not close. 'Bess,' he said softly, 'you know I do and I know I do, so I would be a fool to deny it. I swear that is not my purpose in going. I will swear, also, if it will make you more content, that I will not. Have I given you any cause to accuse me thus?'

228

'You have been under my eye too much, but you are a man – do I need any other cause?'

'I certainly hope I am a man,' he rejoined lightly. 'I have surely given you reason to believe so. Elizabeth, I cannot help it. I have delayed and delayed, seeking a place where you would be happy, and I dare wait no longer. I wish very much to free the earl of Surrey from prison, but first I must be sure that Norfolk and Suffolk are quiet. They must not inflame him and, if I have guessed wrong with regard to his loyal intentions towards me, he must not be able to inflame them.'

So seldom did Henry mention a political matter to Elizabeth that she blinked in surprise. Then she was flattered, for his explanation showed how earnest he was to pacify her.

'If you must—' she said uncertainly, and then, swallowing nervously, said, 'but I am so near my time. You would not leave me alone then, would you?'

Regardless of the watching eyes, Henry rose and put his arms around his wife. 'You will not be alone, Bess. Your mother is here and mine.' Not to mention, he thought, a dozen court physicians, midwives, and God knows who else.

'But I want you.'

Filled with remorse for his unkind thought, Henry kissed her hair, and then her eyes and mouth. 'I will be here, I promise. I will be here.'

Leaving behind him any man who could not ride like a centaur, Henry galloped two hundred miles in two days. The horses were not too much wearied, for they were changed at every town, but the men were half dead with fatigue. He arrived at East Dereham on the ninth, concluded his business in that day and rode thirty miles more in the dark to Brandon Ferry. Here he made arrangements for Charles Brandon, William Brandon's son, to be transferred to his care to be raised with his child. The next day he was in Downham, twenty miles north, and here problems of trade and administration delayed him for three days. By the fourteenth, however, he had ridden to Greenwich where he spent two days with foreign deputations from France, Brittany, the Empire, and Spain, and two nights with Morton and Foxe outlining what could and could not be suggested to the foreign envoys when he was away. At dawn on the seventeenth, a messenger arrived to say the queen had been taken ill. Henry dressed, mounted, and

229

rode the nearly eighty miles to Winchester in six hours, only to find that the signs had disappeared. Elizabeth was so grateful that he could not be angry. She pressed him to her swollen breast.

'I am glad I sent for you. You are half dead with work. You must not go back to London. You must stay here and rest. Henry, please! Your mother says it will be any time now. Please do not leave me.'

'No,' Henry said thickly. 'No, I will stay.' Misunderstanding, he gestured for a chair to be brought to the bed, but Elizabeth shook her head.

'Not here.' She lifted a hand to stroke his hair. 'Indeed, I would be glad to take you into my bed, but you could not sleep. Go and rest, my love. I will try not to disturb you too soon.'

Henry slept the clock around and then spent the afternoon of the eighteenth nervously prowling about the palace, expecting to be called at any moment. The day, however, was completely uneventful and the evening, which he devoted to Elizabeth, seemed to prove her condition unchanged. He grew extremely irritable. It appeared as if she would not deliver for a week or a month and that he would be imprisoned among these chattering women forever. In fact, he came so close to quarrelling with his wife, that Margaret was forced to drive him away.

Unfortunately, Henry had reached a state of nerves where nothing but a rousing quarrel could content him. Margaret was too occupied with preparations for the lying-in to be bothered with him. Jasper totally misunderstood the problem and absolutely refused to be drawn into an argument, no matter what Henry said or did. No one else dared quarrel with the king, and everyone slunk out of his path with such fearful glances that his temper was further exacerbated.

Henry approached Elizabeth at breakfast on September 19th with a surface calm which covered emotions approaching those of a raving maniac. The day was warm and she was flushed and short of breath. Her hair was dark and oily because her skin had grown very sensitive and she could not bear to have it brushed properly. She was sitting sideways near the open window, the light outlining the grotesquerie her body had become. Henry was revolted.

It did not take him five words to insult her and Elizabeth,

230

who was even more miserable than he, was soon screaming like a fishwife. When her ladies tried to interfere, Henry drove them from the room. Half fled to Margaret, the other half to Elizabeth's mother, but by the time those ladies had thrown on enough clothing to be decent Henry was gone and Elizabeth was in hysterics. The king then flung himself on a horse, cursing women, children, and his own misfortune in having a wife who was such a fool that she did not know when her own baby was due.

Ned Poynings saw him careening towards the stables alone. He grabbed two cloaks and a purse and followed at a discreet distance until Henry, seeming to have galloped off the worst of his temper, reined in his mount. Poynings approached cautiously, but Henry wanted none of him or anyone else and fled again, westward across the downs. They played the game twice more. It was nearly noon and the unseasonable warmth showed every sign of building up into a thunderstorm. By two of the clock the storm broke, pouring such sheets of rain that Henry had to stop for fear his horse would stumble and throw him. He sat still, his head hanging. Poynings covered him with one of the cloaks and was about to withdraw again when Henry spoke.

'I have ruined five months of hard work in five minutes.'

'You mean you had a fight with Her Grace, sire?'

Henry nodded.

'Women do not take such matters amiss.'

'I suppose,' Henry sighed, 'I must go back and make my peace.'

'If that is what you have decided to do—' Poynings left that hanging and caught Henry's look of inquiry. It was clear that the king was filled with remorse but still in a state of nerves in which a rejection of his peace overtures would rapidly cause a reversal of his feeling and precipitate another quarrel. 'I am no expert on such matters,' Poynings suggested, 'but I know what Devon would say.'

'What?'

'That you must first let her cool well, and then eat humble pie.'

'But I cannot go back and not go to her at once. I am sure that would make matters worse. And—' Henry laughed, 'I would be glad to eat any sort of pie. I am most damnably hungry, having come away without my breakfast. I have not a

231

groat upon me, Ned. Do you think anyone would believe I was the king in this draggled condition and give me a bite to eat?'

Poynings jingled the purse, blessing his foresight in having brought it. 'You will not have to test your people's charity, sire.'

They rode slowly together until they found an inn where, covering their too-elegant clothing with cloaks, they ordered and ate the ordinary dinner with great pleasure in happy anonymity. Their horses were tired from the wild ride of the morning so that it took a good deal longer to return to Winchester than it had to come away from it. Nonetheless there had not been enough time to permit Elizabeth to cool. When Henry presented himself, all dripping with rain, he was turned away. He did not press the point; but when he returned at night, he was again denied admittance. He hesitated. No one would dare keep him out if he insisted on entering, of course, but he decided it was too soon to force himself upon Elizabeth. He went to bed, feeling rather at a loss. This was the first time in their marriage, when they were in the same house, that he had not had some conversation and a parting kiss from his wife. It was an odd sensation and a very disagreeable one, Henry decided, as he stared at the pattern of the bedcurtains. He did, however, fall asleep eventually, only to be shaken awake some time after midnight.

'Sire.'

'John, if the palace is not on fire or under attack, I will have your head for waking me.'

Cheney did not blanch. Necessity was necessity. 'Sire, Her Grace's woman begs you to come to her.'

'Oh, Lord!' Henry said irritably.

The bedrobe was slipped around him skilfully, slippers slid onto his feet. Henry moved quickly, but he really did not expect anything more than a fretful Elizabeth who could not sleep. Still, he had made the quarrel and it was only right to mend it when Elizabeth desired. The impression was reinforced when he found her alone, except for her regular attendant, although when he came to the bed and took her hands they were cold as ice and trembling.

'I am so very sorry, Elizabeth,' Henry said contritely. 'Indeed, I do not know how to explain nor excuse myself. I—'

232

'Never mind that now, Henry,' she replied in an odd, gasping voice. 'I have teased you enough in these past months for you to strike back once.' Her grip on his hands tightened. 'It is started. I am sure it is started.'

Henry glanced wildly around the room, wondering where all the people were whose work this was. He did not realize that his constant kindness had made him Elizabeth's symbol of security and comfort, and that, for all her piety, he was a greater source of consolation to her than God. As princess royal, her will and whims had been pandered to, but she was clever enough to realize that, after her father died and her family was deserted, those people were all self-seeking, interested in the advancement, wealth, or favour she could bestow. To her it seemed as if Henry alone, for he had her absolutely in his power, was good to her because he loved her. He never said he did, not even in their most passionate moments, but he had proved it in these last five months, thousands of times in thousands of ways. She knew she was Edward's daughter and of value to him, but that alone could only have ensured her of courtesy and not of the unfailing tenderness he displayed.

'Let me call the physicians and your mother, Bess.'

'No,' she cried, clutching his hands more desperately, 'I want you!'

The king of England, who had fought for his life and his crown at Bosworth field against superior odds and faced rebellion with relative calm, broke into a cold sweat of terror. 'I will not leave you,' he said, trying to speak steadily, 'but I do not know what is best to be done. Let me send for someone.'

'There is no need.' The marchioness of Dorset, who was in attendance and had been sleeping in an adjoining room, came forward. 'Her Grace was uneasy and asked for you, sire, so we thought it best that you give her your company. It will be some hours yet before aught need be done.' Elizabeth closed her eyes and tightened her lips. 'Lead her to talk,' Dorset's wife whispered in Henry's ear, 'of the child or of anything that will hold her mind. She is frightened.'

So am I, Henry thought. Holy Mary have mercy on me, so am I. 'Bess,' he said seating himself on the bed, 'if it is a manchild, what do you wish to name him?'

'Henry.'

'Thank you, but I think there are Henrys enough, do you

not? I am the seventh already. Let us give England a rest from Henrys. Do you wish,' he said reluctantly – but at this moment he was ready to give her anything – 'to name him Edward?'

Kind, kind, he was so kind. Elizabeth heard the reluctance, thought of her mother's triumph, and shook her head. She was glad when she saw her husband's relief that she had denied herself the small victory. Then her hands tightened spasmodically on his again.

'A new name, Bess? A British name?' Henry said hastily. 'Arthur? He was a great hero and a great king.'

'Yes, Arthur. That should please everyone.'

That ended that subject. Henry cast wildly about for another, but his mind was utterly blank. Elizabeth herself saved him.

'Will you be very angry if it is a girl, Henry?'

'Of course I would not be angry. A pretty girl like her mother would be a great joy to me.'

She found a small smile. 'Oh, that is not true, but it is good of you to say it.'

'It is true, Elizabeth. We are both young. There will be many other children. What matter whether there be a girl or a boy at first?'

It did matter to him, of course; it mattered desperately, but Elizabeth could do nothing now to change the sex of the child. Her eyes sought his, and he saw the fear in them. Not fear that he would care, but the fear that she would die and, for her, there would be no more children nor even the joy of this one. His hands grew wet in her grasp, and he knew sweat was standing on his forehead again.

'I think,' the marchioness of Dorset said smoothly, 'that Her Grace should walk about for a little. If she sits too long in bed her legs will cramp.'

They slipped on her bedrobe and Henry put his arm about her, and they walked together. When Elizabeth grew weary, he placed her in a chair by the fire and knelt at her feet, talking, talking. Twice the marchioness suggested that Elizabeth's mother be called, but Elizabeth wept each time and clung to Henry, and he had not the strength to deny her. Dawn lightened the sky, and Elizabeth's gasps grew more frequent, louder, and more regular. Now her nails bit into Henry's hands when she clutched him. The women came and went quietly about the room and Henry vaguely heard sounds of great activity in

234

Elizabeth's sitting parlour, but still sometimes they walked and sometimes they sat and Henry talked until he thought the sound of his own voice would craze him. He knew not what he said and he did not think it mattered for he was sure that Elizabeth did not understand a word. She wanted to hear him, however, for if he fell silent for a moment she would gasp, 'Yes, Henry?' and he would have to begin to speak again.

When it was full daylight Elizabeth's mother sailed into the room. 'You are not needed here,' she said coldly to the king. 'We will call you at the proper time.'

'No!' Elizabeth screamed, clinging fiercely to her husband. 'You promised you would not leave me. You promised.'

Henry leaned his head against the arm of the chair, grateful that they were not walking because his legs were shaking so, he thought they could not hold him. 'I will stay as long as I do you no harm, Bess.'

'You do me good, only good.'

About ten minutes later, although it seemed eons to Henry, Margaret approached them. She said nothing at first, merely kissed Elizabeth and began to comb and braid her hair, which was tangled and damp with sweat. After that she insinuated one of her hands between Henry's and Elizabeth's.

'Elizabeth dear,' Margaret said, 'look at me. Yes, love, look here. You must let Henry go and put on some clothes.' She paused while a pain came and went. 'Come love, look at him. He is soaked with sweat. You would not wish him to take cold. See how he shivers.' Some awareness came into Elizabeth's dilated eyes and Margaret reached for her other hand.

Elizabeth thrust her away. 'No,' she cried hysterically, 'I will die. I want him.'

Exhausted and overwrought, Henry began to sob. Margaret did not even spare him a glance, but she kicked him good and hard.

'Nonsense, love. Why I bore Henry when I was only thirteen years old. It was hard, but I did not die. And you are like unto your mother. Think how many children she had, and here she is, hale and hearty.'

The dowager queen bent over Elizabeth on the other side of the chair. 'Of course you will not die, Lizzy my love. If every woman died in childbearing, there would soon be no more women and no more children.'

235

'Henry is afraid,' Elizabeth wept. 'I have never seen or heard that he was afraid before. I know. Even at Bosworth he was not afraid.'

Margaret aimed a look at her son which should have struck him dead, only he was too terrified to notice. 'That is only because he is a man and knows nothing. In truth, Elizabeth, you will not die. Soon you will have a fine child to hold in your arms. Send Henry away. You are frightening him because he does not understand what is happening, and he is frightening you because,' Margaret looked daggers at her trembling son, 'he is a fool.'

Between them, Margaret and the dowager queen broke the grasp Elizabeth had upon her husband. They hated each other, but they worked together now as if love had bound them from birth. They crooned and cuddled and comforted until Elizabeth ceased to cry for Henry with each pain. He had not moved, but little by little the women pushed in front of him until at last Margaret whispered, 'Go.'

'I cannot,' Henry gasped.

Margaret cradled Elizabeth's head against her bosom and turned to hiss over her shoulder at Dorset's wife. 'Fetch Bedford to the king.'

She did not so far forget herself as to call him the snivelling idiot she thought him, for Margaret was really enraged at Henry. He commanded a whole country, but he had not sense enough to be firm with his wife or, if he could not summon so much resolution, at least insist that someone who could handle Elizabeth be called. In Margaret's opinion Henry had allowed Elizabeth to work herself into a state of hysteria which might endanger her delivery for no good reason at all. She was also annoyed with Dorset's wife, who should have known better than to leave them together for so long before she summoned the elder ladies even without permission. But the marchioness was excusable, being much in awe of the king and not overly clever.

Jasper arrived in the marchioness's wake. He kept his head averted from Elizabeth, but at Margaret's whispered command helped Henry to his feet and started to lead him from the room. 'Wait,' Henry said faintly, his head on Jasper's shoulder, 'that chamber must be full. I cannot face those people. I cannot.'

'Here, then.' Jasper spied the door to Elizabeth's dressing-room. There was a chair, and Henry sank into it gratefully. 'Child, do not worry so. It is the way with women. God, you are wringing wet. You must change. Will you be all right if I leave you alone, Harry?'

'Yes.'

To be left alone was exactly what Henry wanted. He sat with closed eyes, fighting to bring his breathing to normal and his body under control. The door opened and closed, but he did not turn, only cursed his uncle's tender vigilance under his breath. After a time, when no one spoke and Henry realized that no attentive eyes were boring into him, he looked cautiously about. Ned Poynings was standing at the narrow window looking out. Henry sighed with relief, then stiffened as a long, low, animal-like moaning came through the closed door. He was a little comforted to see Ned's shoulders jerk. It was good to know he was not the only one distressed by so natural a thing as childbirth.

Muted sounds of increased activity made Henry tense, but no one troubled his retreat. Eventually Jasper returned with his clothing. As he opened the door, Henry heard his mother say, 'Do not cry out now, Elizabeth, you will only waste your strength. Take a deep breath and try to push it out downward.' Jasper closed the door hurriedly and began to be very busy making Henry change into his clothing. There was no clock in the room, the day was overcast so that one could not see the position of the sun, and Henry became desperate for a measure of time.

'Does it always take so long?' he asked at last.

'Yes,' Jasper replied briefly.

Truthfully he had no idea, the only other childbirth he had attended having been Henry's twenty-nine years earlier. There was another long silence, broken twice by the animal-like moaning from the other side of the door. Henry picked at his clothing and bit his fingers; Poynings stared out the window; Jasper looked into space with blind eyes, clenching and un-clenching his fists rhythmically. Suddenly a shriek rent the air and then another. Henry leapt to his feet, overturning the chair. He put his hands to his ears, but neither that nor the door could block the moans and screams which alternated with agonizing regularity.

237

'I cannot bear it,' he sobbed. 'If she must die, let her die. Let her suffer no more. Cannot something be done for her? I cannot bear it!'

Jasper put his arms around Henry. 'Poynings, tell the countess of Richmond to come at once to the king.'

Ned had no desire whatsoever to enter that room, but a command was a command. He made his way through the scurrying women and, inadvertently catching a sight of Elizabeth, he stopped, shocked. The queen was unrecognizable, her face swollen and distorted, her eyes bulging, her mouth open. Poynings choked, recovered, and tried to speak, but his voice was drowned in a heart-rending wail and Elizabeth's hand, clawing for support, caught in Margaret's dress and ripped the sleeve away, leaving a long red weal on the countess's skin.

'Madam,' he said desperately, as Elizabeth gasped for breath and clawed at Margaret's hand, 'the duke of Bedford begs you to come to the king.'

Elizabeth's next shriek drowned the first part of Margaret's angry reply, and Ned caught only, 'old ass Jasper,' and then, 'rarely lose fathers in childbirth, Henry must do as he can.'

Even with that unsatisfactory reply Poynings was glad to retreat, but the situation in the dressing-room was little better from his point of view than the one outside it. Henry was white and shaking, retching without result because he had eaten nothing. With no remedies at hand, Jasper and Poynings administered as best as they could to him. The door sprang open.

'Your Grace, come at once!' a woman cried.

Henry staggered to his feet, shook free of Jasper and Ned. A path opened before him in Elizabeth's bedchamber, which now seemed incredibly full of magnificently dressed people. Henry, however, saw nothing. He was blinded by the peal upon peal of Elizabeth's screams. Suddenly, as if the sound had been cut with a knife, there was silence, then a series of long-drawn whimpers, and then, after a breathless thirty seconds, a thin squalling.

Margaret appeared before her son. Blood was dripping from her hands where Elizabeth had clawed her skin away, her hair hung loose in disorder, her dress was in tatters, and her arms and shoulders were lacerated with scratches, but her eyes shone with triumph and her voice was like a paean of victory.

'A man-child, a princeling, a fine, lusty boy!'

'Elizabeth?' Henry croaked.

'Magnificent,' Margaret replied proudly. She had said Elizabeth would make a fine wife – and she had been right. Then she looked at her son with a faint return of her original disapproval. 'No thanks to you for frightening her into such weakness. But when we had undone your work and she understood what was needed, she was wonderful. You can go to her in a little while and thank her for your son.'

'Thank God,' Henry whispered, but in the next moment he was laughing half-hysterically, going down on his knees to assist Poynings, Poynings the stolid, Poynings the imperturbable – who had fainted.

Chapter Seventeen

Richard Foxe paused with his hand on the door he had just opened. A sweet tenor voice was singing a lilting French air, and he knew the king was supposed to be alone in the chamber. Foxe stepped forward quietly and his shrewd eyes softened. The Tudor was singing. He was dressed with the magnificence customary even in his least formal clothing, but he was not – as Foxe usually saw him – bent over his table working. He was standing with one foot on the window seat, looking out into the garden at the blaze of autumn flowers, singing.

Why he should have been surprised, Foxe did not know. Henry loved music, sang well, and had good cause to be happy. His heir was strong, and his wife was recovering well during her lying-in. Moreover, the woman would cause him no more trouble. The entire court knew, and soon the entire country would know, how she clung to him. It was a shame to break his peace with problems. Foxe was tempted to leave Henry with his joy, but the king expected him and, in truth, the problems would grow no lighter for being put aside.

'Sire.'

Henry turned, smiling. 'Come in, my little Foxe, come in.'

'I have come to trouble you, Your Grace.'

'You are mistaken. Nothing can trouble me. You may be able to make me work, but trouble me, you cannot.'

'So I hope. First, sire, you must return to London. The enmity between Brittany and France grows worse. Both demand you support them, and Morton's fencing can hold them no longer.'

'God curse the French and all their greed. They swallow one duchy after another until all Europe will be one large France. They grasp at a helpless old man and two girl children – no mercy, no justice, only greed.'

'We cannot afford to make an enemy of France, Your Grace. And the Regent Anne has some cause for dissatisfaction. Duke Francis has given refuge to the duke of Orleans whom Anne has finally driven out.'

Henry sighed. 'Oh, I know. I cannot wish that Francis was less kind because, perhaps, I would not be alive and certainly I would not be king if that were so. Still, for him to give France any excuse for war is so foolish— Nay, do not begin to tell me what he hopes to gain from Orleans. He should be able to see— Very well. I will come. Perhaps there is some way to save Brittany, but I fear— I can do no more than I can. It is, as you say, impossible for me to challenge France – as yet.'

'There is worse.'

'Yes, Richard, I know.' Henry grinned. 'Knowing each other as we do, I did not believe you would think I could be troubled by war between France and Brittany.'

Nonetheless, Foxe hesitated to speak. He knew to his sorrow how unnatural Henry's attitude about death for political purposes was. After the rebellion in the north, the Stafford brothers had been caught. It was not a matter of suspicion; there was certain knowledge of treason. They had raised an armed force against their king. Yet the council had needed to argue bitterly all through one long night – the duke of Bedford had even gone down on his knees to plead with his nephew – before Henry could be convinced to order an execution. Even so, they could not make him condemn the younger brother, who, Henry insisted, had been led astray. And on the day of the execution, the condemned had been calmer than the king. Not that Foxe was planning to ask to have anyone executed. Still, the entire subject was a very sensitive one with Henry.

'Well, little Foxe?' Henry prompted.

'There is a good deal of talk suddenly about the earl of Warwick, sire.'

The king's face darkened. This was a sensitive subject. His conscience smote him for keeping that child in prison, yet he dared not free him. Even in a secluded and well-guarded place, Warwick would be a desperate danger to Henry. If the child had been free or in the hands of the king's Yorkist enemies, the rebellion he had put down so easily might have become a very serious threat.

'What is being said?'

'That you will become another Gloucester now that you have a son of your own and murder the boy.'

'Murder? I?'

Foxe recoiled from the sudden blaze of rage. 'Your Grace,

no one who knows you could believe such a thing. What is important is who began the rumour and for what purpose.'

Even though he knew it was not directed at him, Foxe found the cold hatred in the king's face frightening. 'It should not take so astute a mind as yours much effort to find the answers,' Henry said with a calm that made Foxe feel worse instead of better. 'Is there not a direct trail from the rumours in London to this place?'

'No – not direct.'

'Do not seek to salve me with double words. Nor do not try to make me tell you what you should tell me.'

Foxe bowed in acknowledgment of the rebuke. 'When we have found a source, it is true that the source is the court.' Henry had turned away, but Foxe was raked with the familiar sidelong glance. His voice faltered. 'The gentlemen are – are related in some manner to the – the ladies of the court.'

'In other words, since they seem to clog your tongue, to my wife.'

'The Queen's Grace! No!'

'The king's wife, not the Queen's Grace, Foxe – and do not forget it. Elizabeth has not been, and is not like to be, crowned.'

'I am sorry, sire. That is not what I mean. Forgive me, but I have seen Her Grace look upon you. I cannot believe it. To read men is my business, sire—'

'Women, too, Foxe? Surely your cloth should preclude that.'

For the first time in his relationship with Henry, Foxe was confused. The king was fond of very few people, but to those he showed a steadfast loyalty. Foxe had not been in Winchester at the time of Elizabeth's delivery, but word pictures, graphic as reality, had been furnished for him. The king's distress, amounting to near hysteria, at his wife's sufferings could not have been feigned. Moreover, he had been a personal witness of the intimate tenderness Henry had displayed during her pregnancy. Could any man be such a mass of falsity as the Tudor appeared at this moment?

'Perhaps the cloth which protects me from personal involvement permits me a clearer vision. Her Grace's ladies were her mother's choice, not her own.'

The expression in Henry's long eyes was veiled; his face was perfectly immobile. 'Do you also conclude that Elizabeth is deaf and blind – or just mentally feeble?'

Foxe swallowed and then said stoutly, 'I conclude that Her Grace has been otherwise occupied in her thoughts – a thing not uncommon in breeding women. Sire, you confessed you had been wrong in your suspicion of her in the spring rising. If you have some proof against her of which I am ignorant, I beg I may hear it so that I may consider this matter more fairly.'

'There is Arthur,' Henry said very softly, 'not three weeks old, but lusty. There is the daughter of Edward IV. If Warwick should die, and the king who was blamed for that should be repudiated by his people – as Gloucester was – who is most like to rule this country as regent?'

Cynical and unemotional as Foxe was, he still cried out, 'I cannot believe it! I tell you I have seen Her Grace's eyes when you were in her vision. Set the source further back and, if you desire, I will help you use a garrotte with my own hands. It is Edward's wife, not his daughter, who hates you.'

Henry's mobile lips twitched and then tightened. 'So I hope and pray, but do not forget the influence of the mother upon the daughter nor neglect the daughter while you hunt the mother.' He turned away sharply, and his voice was strained when he added, 'For God's sake, Richard, find me some proof one way or the other.'

So that was it, Foxe thought with relief. The king was not seeking false cause to put away his wife now that he had a son out of her. He could not suspect her and feared that he should. 'Innocence in deeds is one thing, and easy to put to the proof. Innocence of thought and hope is another matter.'

'Let us make deeds available then. Free Surrey – under the usual terms. You have people in his household now?'

'It is well seeded. If he blinks an eye, writes a letter, or twists a ring on his finger, a crop of information will grow.'

'Take care it grows wheat, not broom.' Henry smiled unkindly. 'I like Surrey and you do not – just remember, little Foxe, I know that, too.'

'That is true, but yet I am not unjust. Surrey is a poor trap. Even I, who do not like him, acknowledge that he is a man of honour. Only a fool would try to involve Surrey in treason.'

'And so,' Henry purred, 'I will have my proof. Look you here. For nigh on a year I have had Her Grace under my eye. If she has aught in her mind except womanly things, she is

243

far, far cleverer than I have guessed, and I believe her clever. Her mother, on the other hand, is a fool. If Surrey runs to us affrighted by something he has heard, sure as death it will not be Elizabeth's doing.'

'So much is true, but if he is not approached that does not prove it was Her Grace's doing.'

'I know.' Henry walked to the window and looked out at the garden again. 'Is there something more, Foxe?'

'A pile of charters and bills for parliament which you must approve, sire. I left them on your worktable.'

'Anything you must go over with me?'

'No, sire, all are plain enough.'

'Do you stay?'

'Not unless you specially desire it, Your Grace. When can the meetings with the ambassadors be set?'

'Oh— The first week in November. By then we should be in residence at Greenwich or Westminster. If not, I will ride to London alone. Foxe – you have set guards on Warwick?'

'Need you ask? Two men sleep with him, two guard the door. His food must be tasted by the cook as it leaves his hands and by the server as it is set on the table. They, too, are watched.'

'Yes, well, I do not know what more we can do for him. Poor child, poor child, happier had he never been born. Very well, Richard, you may go.'

Henry went into the adjoining room shortly after Foxe left and glanced at his worktable. In addition to the pile of material his secretary had left for him there were household accounts, business ventures, petitions by the dozen. He made a sound of irritation, went out the door, and up a flight of stairs. As he passed the door to Elizabeth's apartment, he hesitated a trifle, but she would be startled – or suspicious? – if he came at this time of day. Besides, Henry wanted soothing, and just now the very sight of Elizabeth made him dangerously excited.

The guards at the nursery door drew up their pikes and Henry passed through, already smiling. He was greeted with a bubbling cry of joy as the two-year-old Charles Brandon spied him and came toddling forward. The king seized the sturdy youngster and tossed him in the air until he shrieked with pleasure, then kissed him soundly, put him down, and coyly turned away. That brought another crow of laughter for Charles

244

was a clever child and recognized the game Henry was playing. He caught at the king's surcoat and burrowed beneath it, attaching himself firmly to one of Henry's legs.

'How now, by what am I held and hampered?' Henry asked in a loud, wondering voice. He bent to run his hand over Charles's head and back, tickling the child's ribs and pinching his small buttocks. 'Why it is a small man. Help! Help! I am a prisoner.' Now Henry made deliberately futile attempts to free himself, raising and lowering his leg so that Charles was jounced gently, and bending over to lift the child up by the legs and swing him around. 'Alas,' he cried, 'I cannot get free. I am your captive. I yield me. Name my ransom and I will pay.'

'Plum,' little Brandon replied with commendable clarity.

Henry laughed with delight, for he had taught Charles the word himself, and brought forth a piece of dried fruit covered with crystallized honey. Charles released his leg, popped the sugarplum into his mouth, and sucked contentedly. He trotted after Henry hopefully as the king moved towards the inner chamber where his son lay. The nurse immediately moved aside from the elaborate cradle. Arthur was cared for by relays of women who literally did not take their eyes from him for a moment unless his father or mother were present. Henry bent over the cradle and touched the petal-soft, jelly-smooth cheek with one forefinger.

'He is certainly ugly enough to be mine,' he said fondly.

'Oh,' the nurse gasped, forgetting her awe of the king in her indignation at the slur cast upon her nursling. 'He is a beautiful child, just simply beautiful.'

'My experience with babes is limited,' Henry acknowledged, laughing. Charles pulled impatiently at his gown and he bent and lifted the child to his shoulder. 'I will accept your assurance as to his beauty, but I must say that he looks like a little red ape to me. Let us hope, for his sake, that he grows up to resemble his mother. He is well?'

'Oh, yes, Your Grace. He takes the breast greedily, and his bowels—'

Holding up a restraining hand, Henry laughed again. 'I beg of you, no details. Ouch! Charles! You must not kick the king in the back nor pull his hair.'

'Horse,' Charles exclaimed.

'Very well, let me kiss my son and I will be a horse.'

The royal horse galloped out into the antechamber, twice around it, and through an adjoining door where, rather breathless, he set Charles down. He then brought out another sugarplum and gestured to little Brandon's nurse who came forward with a favourite toy to lead the child away. A boy of seven was standing near a table, but he had pushed away his books and papers and was smiling expectantly. As soon as Henry turned to him, he bowed low and kissed the hand which the king extended.

'Well, Buckingham, how goes it?'

Young Edward Stafford, duke of Buckingham since his father's execution by Richard III, sighed. 'Sire, I will never learn all these things. No one but priests speak Latin. You do not mean to make me a priest, do you?'

'No, indeed. I would not like that at all, unless you desired it very strongly yourself. But it is not true that only priests speak Latin. I speak it and men who go on embassies often need Latin to speak to others who do not know their tongue.'

'Do they need to know mathematics and music also? And French and history and—'

'It only seems hard in the beginning, Edward. Men of great place do need to know these things. I am sure you will find it more interesting as you go on.' Suddenly Henry smiled. 'Perhaps you are kept too hard at it, child. It is a fine day; the sun is shining. You will study better when it rains. Come, I will take you riding.'

Edward Stafford jumped forward to hug the king impulsively and Henry returned the pressure, but there was disappointment in his face. Perhaps the child would improve, but his tutors were not sanguine. The boy was decidedly slow, not hopelessly stupid but disinclined towards learning. It would have to be sufficient to bind his love and forgo the hope of making him contented by making him useful. Perhaps it was better that way. Young Buckingham had a violent and uncontrollable temper. It is my fault, Henry thought. I am not firm enough with him because I cannot love him as I love Charles.

By the time they returned, Henry was better satisfied with Edward and with life in general. They boy, if he would never be a scholar, certainly rode well and was fond of him. It was now possible to concentrate on bills, accounts, and petitions, and Henry did so until he had to dress for dinner. Elizabeth dined alone. She was gaining strength rapidly, but was still disinclined to don the elaborate robes and undergo the strain of formal dinners. Frankly, Henry missed her, for she was not upset by the malicious asides he was prone to make, as Jasper was, nor did she lack a sense of humour, as his mother unfortunately did.

Once he started thinking about her it was difficult to stop, and Henry grew morose and silent. It had been a great error to make that promise about visiting her each night. Henry was not naturally lecherous, but his normal appetites had been whetted by Elizabeth's demands and response. The source of supply had been cut off for some time, however, and Henry was growing very hungry. Ordinarily that would not have been a serious problem, but Elizabeth was not behaving reasonably. She was jealous even when he was innocent, and the one time he had not been – very soon after Arthur's birth – she had played him a scene he did not wish to repeat. It had ended for him in a raging headache and for her in a fever that lasted two days. How she discovered his small slip from virtue was a mystery which the most exhaustive inquiries could not solve, and Henry had come to the extremely uncomfortable conclusion that it was something personal about himself that had betrayed him.

If he could stay away from her it would not be so bad. Henry had very little to do with the ladies of the court. During the day he worked or played with men and, as he was not overly sensual and his gentlemen knew he did not like lewd talk, he never gave women in general or sex in particular a thought. But those nightly visits to Elizabeth! She was lovelier than ever, a little plumper, her breasts a little fuller, altogether inviting. And she invited! She dressed, deliberately Henry was sure, in her most revealing bedrobes. She often received him when she was in bed, and she flirted with him – yes, that was the only word for her manner.

He went to work in his closet after dinner, to the relief of his gentlemen who were free to gamble, listen to the musicians, or laugh at the fools without being conscious of the king's irritability. He worked very late, hoping that Elizabeth would be asleep by the time he arrived. She was not. She was tense and frightened and looked as if she might have been crying. As soon as Henry appeared the ladies curtsied and departed. It was

247

understood that the king and queen were always to be left alone at this time even if it was impossible for them to sleep together.

'I am sorry to be so late, Elizabeth.'

Her eyes devoured him, saw his slide from her face to her throat to her breast – and her face lightened and she stretched her hand to him with a smile. 'I would wait all night, if need be.'

The remark was scarcely a consolation to the king the way he felt just then. 'I was working,' he said rather sharply. 'I have had some unpleasant news.'

'Really? Come sit on the bed, dear.' Elizabeth's expression remained perfectly calm and she ran her hand over the collar of Henry's furred robe so that one finger caressed the back of his neck.

'There is a rumour that I intend to murder Warwick.'

'That is plain silly,' Elizabeth said placidly. 'You are the most unmurderous king this country ever had. I heard your uncle complaining to your mother that you do not even kill the people you should. Henry, I would like to adorn the chapel here somewhat. Could I give that big chalice Lincoln gave me for a wedding present to be consecrated for it and those gold candlesticks I received from—'

'Elizabeth! The rumour about Warwick is not silly. It can do me much harm.'

'Well, I am sorry for that. If I hear it, I will contradict it. Is there more I can do, my love?'

'It has been traced back to your ladies.'

There was a sudden silence. Elizabeth's hand tightened on her husband's gown. 'Do not, Henry,' she whispered, turning pale, 'do not frighten me. Dismiss the guilty ones – dismiss them all if you like.'

Henry was furious with himself. He had given away a valuable and dangerous piece of information, and had received in return no more than a reaction as unrevealing and predictable as an opening gambit in chess. What was wrong with him?

'I do not blame you, Bess. Perhaps it is natural for some people to believe that since I have an heir I would smooth the way for him with blood. Perhaps I would – for Arthur – but blood never smooths a path, it only makes it slippery. Nor did I mean to frighten you. Only watch your ladies more carefully, and if there is something I should know – even only suspicion or

248

rumour – tell me. I am not like to act unjustly or in anger.'

'I know nothing – nothing! Send them away. I could not look at them, knowing they tried to hurt you.'

She was shivering now and would not meet his eyes. Henry took her hand. 'Do not make yourself ill over this, Elizabeth. I do not wish to dismiss your ladies. Indeed, if they are guilty of deliberate malice instead of careless gossip – which is all I believe this to be – it would be dangerous to send them away. If you wish to help me, you must control yourself and seek out the culprit.'

Elizabeth gasped as if he had stabbed her. 'I cannot – oh Henry, I cannot. Set spies on them, on me, do what you like, but do not ask me to betray – to—'

'Very well, do not fret yourself so.'

He set himself mechanically to soothe her, partly because he did not wish to bring his mother's wrath on his head for upsetting her, and partly because her mention of betrayal rather than protests of innocence or accommodation to his will seemed genuine. It could not be easy for a daughter to betray her mother. He was being unjust and unkind to Elizabeth who had just given him a son. His caresses grew warmer, then rather less comforting and more passionate.

When Henry left his wife's chamber, he smiled at the ladies dozing in their chairs. He had stayed a good deal longer than anyone, including himself, had expected. Lips pursed in a soundless whistle, the king let himself out without disturbing the sleepers. He had not had what he wanted really, but a sufficiently adequate substitute had been furnished so that he was more at peace with the world. It was less important that some of those dozing ladies were innocently or deliberately conniving at treason. They were known and could be watched. As long as the treason was not Elizabeth's. The whistle burst from his lips, a fluting, musical birdcall that he had learned as a boy in Wales and had forgotten until he uttered it.

Elizabeth lay very still. She could not hear her ladies stirring, and the soft opening and closing of the outer door did not reach her. Was Henry still out there? Questioning her ladies, perhaps, in that cold deadly voice she had heard him use although, thank God, never to her. At least, not yet. Why was he so angry about the rumour concerning poor Warwick? It was an ugly rumour, but there would always be rumours. She wished it was not the middle of the night so that she could ask to have Arthur brought to her. Then she could hold his pliant little body and examine his perfect, miraculous toes and fingers, let his tiny hands aimlessly grasp her hair – and forget that her ladies – her ladies—

If there was a rumour which could hurt Henry, Elizabeth knew from where it came. Henry knew, too, but he was too kind to say it to her, too kind. Was it kind to place the burden of controlling her mother on her? Why did not Henry, who seemed to know everything else, know that she was still terrified of her mother? Why did he not do something? Anything. Anything except ask her to face her mother down. Not face her down in one argument – Elizabeth knew she could screw up her courage for that, but it would not end there. There would be scene after scene, tears, shrieks, nagging, spiteful remarks in public – until at last Elizabeth would be worn down, reduced to compliance and deliberate blindness.

The ladies were appalled when Elizabeth insisted on rising and dressing the next day. She looked feverish, with dark smudges showing beneath tired eyes. They could not refuse to help her, but one sent a page scurrying for the dowager queen and another for the countess of Richmond. This was what Elizabeth expected, and she tried to concentrate on her dressing so that her mind would not run ahead and become so enmeshed in fear that her tongue would be paralysed. Margaret reached her first. The countess's apartments adjoined the queen's and she, herself, was more slender, quicker to dress, and perhaps more anxious about the cause for Elizabeth's behaviour.

'Why, love, what are you doing out of your bed?'

Elizabeth tried to smile. She had to be rid of Henry's mother as soon as possible, but Margaret's hands still bore the scars they had received during Arthur's birth, and Elizabeth was more than ever attached to her mother-in-law. Her own mother refused to be clawed. She had been kind and reassuring and steady during Elizabeth's ordeal, but she offered twisted silk scarfs for Elizabeth to tear at, not her own hands. And Elizabeth needed flesh then, warm, human flesh that returned her desperate grip and flinched in sympathy with her pain.

'I am tired of it. Do not scold me, madam. I have been up and about for a week, and today I had a desire to dress. I am not ill. Now I do feel tired, but I will rest awhile. If I do not regain my strength, I promise to go back to bed. There, is that sufficient?'

'It would be, dear, if I thought it was true. You must learn how to lie from Henry. He is much more convincing. What has he done? Did he tell you it was time to return to your duties? You must not allow him to force you to do things that will hurt you. He does miss your company, but he does not understand that—'

'No,' Elizabeth laughed shakily. 'It is not his doing. Dear madam, I never saw a mother so eager to blame her son for her daughter-in-law's waywardness. Henry is very good to me.'

'Yes, but he never cossets himself and he drives his men until they drop. You must not let him do that to you.'

'Madam, he is so gentle to me. How can you accuse him—' She began to laugh more heartily. 'Oh, madam, how silly we both are. Do you remember before we wed you told me Henry was kind and gentle? I did not believe you then, and now I tell you the same and you do not believe me. Do not worry about me. I will soon return to bed, I promise. I only wish to sit awhile so – and – please – to be alone.'

That was a dismissal, however kind, that even the king's mother could not ignore. Margaret was unconvinced by Elizabeth's protests, but she decided to leave well enough alone. Plainly, whatever her trouble, Elizabeth did not wish for intervention. She felt that her understanding with Henry was good enough to dispense with his mother's— Dispense! Margaret was horrified, both at her own use of the word and the real meaning of it. I must not, she thought, biting her lips, I must not come between them. She had a momentary exultant flash of satisfaction, knowing she had the power to destroy her son's relationship with his wife and remain the only woman in his life, and then she sank to her knees and began to pray frantically for strength to resist such desires and for forgiveness for having them.

Meanwhile the dowager queen had entered her daughter's bedchamber and found her, surprisingly, alone. It was one of the things Elizabeth's mother was growing to hate about her daughter – the habit of never permitting private conversation.

'Elizabeth,' she said, 'you are growing sillier instead of wiser as you grow older. You are ill. Go back to bed.'

'I wished to talk to you without summoning you, mother, and this seemed the best way. When I have said what I wish to say, I will go back to bed.'

'That is not the proper tone to use to your mother, Elizabeth.'

'That is not the proper tone to use to the queen, mother.'

'The queen!' The older woman laughed harshly. 'You are no queen nor ever will be. Your husband will use you to fulfil his political purposes and then cast you aside like a dirty clout.'

'Do not speak ill of Henry to me. You do not know how tender of me he is. You purpose to do him ill, mother, and he knows it; but for my sake he holds his hand and will not even complain of it. I have heard of the false tale that is being spread about Warwick.'

'Who says it is false?'

'I do. Henry is no murderer. The distinction of being a murderer of children is reserved to the truly royal family – ours! Do not try to inflame Henry's subjects against him. Sooner or later my power with him will fail to protect you.'

'Your power with him! It is the power of a carpet which asks only to have feet wiped on it.'

'More, then, do I love and honour my husband that he has never used me so.'

'Elizabeth, you are a tender-hearted fool. I do not deny that he cosseted you during the time of your increasing. But you think it was for your sake, and I know it was only for the child. Oh, I see in your face that because he is still amiable you do not believe me. He desires a few more sprigs from the royal tree. I tell you he hates us all, branch, stock, and root, because we are of the true tree of royalty. You have a chance now. Let the country be rid of him, on Warwick's account or any other, and your child will be king and you – you will be regent as I should have been had not that monster Gloucester—'

'Stop!' Elizabeth's face was deathly pale, beaded with sweat, and she panted with terror. She saw every fear she had ever had before she married Henry, before his confidence brought some security to her, becoming a fact. 'You are mad,' she choked, 'mad or possessed of devils. I will tell Henry. I will—'

'What will you tell the suspicious Tudor? Who would dare plot to make you regent for your son without *your* encouragement?'

252

Elizabeth uttered another choked cry and slumped sideways in the chair. Her mother stared at her for a moment and then rose to call the ladies. When the Tudor, that ugly growth in her daughter's heart and mind, was removed, Elizabeth would be as wax in her hands.

Chapter Eighteen

'. . . on shore or on float, in England, or export or import goods, merchandise, etcetera, from abroad, according to their liking.'

'Henry!'

The king looked round, startled. He had been dictating a trading charter to one of his clerks, and it was an hour of the day when he was known to dislike interruptions.

'What is it, mother?' he asked, smoothing the frown from his face.

'Come to Elizabeth. Come at once. Never mind that business. Come, I say.'

The frown returned. Henry snapped his fingers and the clerk disappeared through the outer door. 'I know you are fond of Elizabeth, mother, but I cannot be constantly interrupted by her tantrums. She is safely delivered now. You must calm her yourself, or her ladies must, or she must learn a little self-control. I have a whole kingdom to govern. I cannot stop to attend to one woman.'

There had been more bad news about Warwick. A box of poisoned sweets had been smuggled to him, and thus far Foxe's attempts to discover the culprit had been vain. It was the more frightening because explanations of the danger in accepting and concealing mysterious gifts seemed beyond the comprehension of the feeble-minded boy. When told that the sweets were poisoned, Warwick had replied, 'They were not. You wanted to eat them yourself.' Henry sent Foxe a blistering message about providing Warwick with every delicacy he craved until he was glutted, but that did little to relieve his anxiety. And now this sudden distress of Elizabeth's so soon after the news about Warwick was doubly suspicious.

Actually Henry was sorry for his wife. He knew her position was not easy, but he felt that she must choose her side and struggle for its success. That his would be the side she chose Henry was almost – an agonizing almost – certain. In fact, his reluctance to go to her just now was less a result of personal anger against her, he told himself, than fear that he could not control his temper and would upset her more by displaying the disgust he felt at the attack on a helpless, feebleminded child.

'This is not tantrum, Henry. Or if it is, you alone can stop it before she becomes desperately ill. Do you think I would intrude upon you for nothing? All of us have been trying to calm her, but she already has a high fever. I hope we have not delayed too long. I hope she still recognizes you. She is gone back into the past and keeps crying of Gloucester and her mother and their struggle over the regency for her brothers.'

A chill raised the hair on the nape of Henry's neck. If his mother had heard about Warwick, she had not connected the news with Elizabeth's illness. The wandering of his wife's mind, Henry realized, was distinctly apropos. If he went to her for no other reason, he had to silence her.

'Very well.'

Forewarned and angry as he was, Henry could not help feeling alarmed by the pitiful woman who huddled shaking under heaps of covers while her face and eyes burned with fever. However, if she had been wandering previously, which Henry doubted, she was not now.

'Send everyone away,' she whispered. Henry's gesture cleared the room. 'Do not let anything happen to Warwick,' she continued in the same breathless whisper. 'Pray, Henry, let nothing happen to Warwick.'

'I told you I was no murderer, Elizabeth. I am doing my best for the boy. Now you must calm yourself. I will be angry in earnest if you continue to make yourself ill. First you fret over my — infidelity — and now about my intentions towards your cousin.'

'Not your intentions. Not yours, Henry.'

'Whose then?'

Her mouth opened and closed twice, and her eyes grew so wild that Henry put his hand on her forehead. 'I cannot say it,' she gasped. 'I want to, but I cannot. You would not believe me, anyway, and it is so horrible that even when I think about it everything goes around inside my head. Where are you?' Elizabeth whimpered suddenly. 'Where are you? You are gone away.'

Really frightened, Henry lifted his wife, covers and all, into his arms. 'No, I am here. Bess, I am here, holding you.'

It was so inconceivable to Henry that his mother's interests

255

and his own should ever differ, that he had never before considered how he would feel if he were placed in Elizabeth's position. Not realizing that his wife had cried out against the cold remoteness of his expression, not his physical absence, he was afraid he had unsettled her wits by demanding that she be the one to accuse the woman who had given her life – given her life with the same incredible suffering she had endured not three weeks past to give life to her own son.

'Hush, Bess, hush. Do not trouble so. Everything will come right.' A hand found its way out of the cocoon of coverings and fastened on to Henry's jewelled collar. 'Bess, speak. Can you understand me?'

'Let me see your face.' She pulled away, looked at him, and allowed her head to drop on to his shoulder. 'Do not go away again.'

'No, I will stay here until you are better.' Henry gave a distracted thought to the piles of work in his closet, to the coming session of parliament which necessitated that the work be finished, and tightened his grip on Elizabeth. 'You must not fret. Do not think about this matter any more. Bess, listen. Do not be afraid. I will not hurt you nor anyone dear to you. I will never ask you another question about such matters. Nor will that harm me, for I think I know what you are unable to tell.'

Her shivering seemed to be decreasing and Henry's arms ached horribly so he laid her down on her pillows. Elizabeth made no protest. Henry stood patiently by the bed holding her hand and watching for her eyes to close.

'If Warwick dies, Henry,' she said quite clearly, no longer speaking in a gasping whisper, 'will you kill me?'

'Good God, Elizabeth, where did you come by such an insane idea?'

'You misunderstand me. I was not asking whether you would wish to do that, I was asking you to do it.'

'Bess,' he sighed wearily, 'if you do not stop raving and get well, you will kill *me*. I will die of worry and exhaustion. Will that content you?'

'No, because then Arthur would be all alone, and someone would kill him the way my uncle killed my brothers—'

'Be still, Elizabeth!' Henry bellowed.

They had quarrelled bitterly, but he had never raised his

voice to her before and the shock brought a realization of what she had done. Elizabeth had lived with the idea for so long that its horror had paled with familiarity, but that it had never crossed Henry's mind was clear from his suddenly ashen face. I must be half-mad, she thought, to add this terror to his other burdens. If it would have given her husband any satisfaction, she would have torn out her tongue. But there was a compensation she could make. She could remove herself as a burden to him.

'I am sorry, Harry. It is only the horror of a sick mind. It could never happen. Do you believe Bedford would let anyone hurt your son any more than he allowed you to be hurt?'

'That is a comfort! That my son should run like a hunted beast as I ran.'

Elizabeth did not flinch at the reference to the persecution her family had visited on him, although he had never openly mentioned it before. 'Harry, come closer.' She stilled the shaking of her body with an effort of will she did not know she possessed and pulled him so that he sat down beside her. 'That is not what I meant, as you well know. Nothing had happened to your Uncle Henry when he was a child although he was only nine months old when the king, his father, died. His uncles were not like mine. They cared for him and protected him. Would Bedford hurt your child?'

'Jasper is old.'

'Oxford is not so old, nor Foxe, nor Devon, nor Nottingham. Must I name all your friends? Sick minds have sick fancies. You said yourself I was raving.' She pulled him down against her breast, hoping he would not notice how hot she was. 'You see, I am better now. Did I not ask you to kill me? What could be worse for you, even if you hated me – and I know you do not. How much madder could a question be?'

Elizabeth could not mend the breach she had made in Henry's wall of confidence, but she babbled on until he was able to fill it temporarily with the more cheerful ideas she presented. Finally she sent him away, assuring him of her complete recovery, apologizing for the nonsense she had spoken and the trouble she had caused, and begging him not to work half the night to make up for the time she had cost him. She repeated several times that she knew how much there was to be done and, slyly, when the fixed expression of fear he wore was a

257

little overlaid with a different, lighter concern, she asked for a promise that he would not rush off to work. He would not promise and Elizabeth felt a little relief. She knew her husband's ways. If he could work, he would soon put aside his fear. Perhaps he would never forget it, but he would lock it into a small dark chamber of his heart and the longer he lived with it, Elizabeth felt, drawing on her own experience, the less agonizing it would be.

She tried desperately to keep the bargain she had made with herself. She obeyed faithfully all the instructions the physician gave; she strove to quiet her mind. Henry knew and Henry would take care that no harm came from her mother's plotting. No harm ever came from her mother's plotting, she reminded herself. It had always been easy for cleverer plotters to circumvent her, and surely Henry was the cleverest man alive. When nightmares woke her screaming, and her ladies found her burning and shaking she whispered only, 'Do not tell Henry,' although it seemed to her that there was no price too high for the comfort his arms would have given her.

It grew easier when her actual illness had passed, and still easier as the fear that clouded Henry's clear eyes dissipated a little, for then her guilt also lifted. There was always sufficient shadow, however, to spur Elizabeth on. She dressed beautifully and made her conversation as gay as possible. When she was able to invite Henry to her bed again, she was more passionate than ever, making sure that her husband would be too tired to lie awake and worry once he left her. She bit her tongue when she was fretful, and if she knew she could not keep her temper she closed her mouth altogether and played the music that Henry loved, which never failed to keep him silent, also.

Fortunately, Elizabeth was not perfect. She did try to soothe her husband when he was irritable, but when he continued to snap at her sweet rejoinders, she was human enough to regress to normal and give him the satisfaction of a rousing fight. She found, too, that if she used language vulgar enough to make him blush she could usually reduce him to laughter. For her effort, Elizabeth received the reward generally accorded to wives who struggle to make themselves over to their husbands' satisfaction. Henry spent every minute he could spare from his demanding work with her, never noticed the effort she was making, and complained bitterly when the effort failed and she was not perfectly in accord with his mood.

They moved from Winchester on October 25th, and it took them seven days to cover the distance Henry had galloped in six hours. There was no need to hurry. They had four glorious, bright days out of the seven when Elizabeth insisted on mounting her horse and riding with her husband, although Henry then refused to move faster than a walk. They could not go much faster, anyway, because the great covered cart which carried Arthur and Charles Brandon moved very slowly over the rutted roads in spite of the six horses that drew it.

Even the three rainy days were delightful. On two they did not travel at all but stayed in a bare old castle where Henry gave sudden vent to a burst of high spirits. He organized all sorts of wild games – to keep them warm, he said, for the old keep was damnably cold and damp. On the last day it only drizzled and Elizabeth rode in the cart with her son and little Charles, to whom she was growing as attached as Henry was. It was delightful to cuddle Arthur, tell Charles simple stories, watch Henry dismount and swing in to join them, slapping Charles with his wet hat and making him shriek with joy. It was delightful until Charles fell asleep in the middle of a rough-and-tumble as happy, energetic babies do. Then Henry took Arthur from Elizabeth's arms, and suddenly he looked old and tired and very grim.

Elizabeth was stricken cold and mute as she watched her husband's beautiful long fingers run over the fuzz of baby hair not covered by the cap and trace the delicate curve of a tiny ear. Then Arthur's aimless hand struck his father's, and his little fingers closed by instinct over Henry's thumb. The king turned his head aside, but neither of his hands were free to cover or wipe his face and Elizabeth saw the shining tracks of tears on his cheeks. She had destroyed his joy in his son and given him fear to live with.

'Why does your mother refuse to come to London with us?' Elizabeth asked in a shrill, peevish voice. 'I have begged her and prayed her, but she will not attend to me. Oh, Henry, give Arthur to me and wipe your hair. It is wet and dripping all over everything.'

'She said to me that she was tired and wished to rest.' Henry's

259

voice came muffled and husky from the cloth he was using.

'And to me' – Elizabeth sounded even more irritable and aggrieved – 'when I said it was not fair to leave me with the babies and all the state dinners, too, that she did not wish the world to say that the king took suck from his mother still.'

Henry had started to clear his throat and he choked on a laugh. 'Bess, she said no such vulgar thing.'

'Well, it was very like. I wish you will speak to her, Harry, and make her change her mind.'

'If I can, it would be the first time. Would you have me give commands to my mother? And for all she pretends humility, it would not do the slightest good. You know she really pays me no mind. Besides, it would be very embarrassing if she refused my order outright. What would I do?'

'I do not know, but you should be able to do something. And I wish you would do something about Devon, also. That odious countess of Northumberland was complaining that he is trifling with her daughter.'

'Devon and Northumberland's scrawny—'

'Oh, so you have been looking her over, too! Perhaps I am grown too stout for your taste.'

'Elizabeth!'

'And while we are on this subject, I must say I would have to be blind not to see how particularly you stared at Dorset's wife—'

'My God, am I to look nowhere but at the floor or the ceiling? She spoke to me and I answered her. Where should I look?'

'There are looks and looks.'

'You must have eyes in the back of your head if you saw the one I gave her. We were behind you.'

'I have eyes all round my head, and in my behind, too, where your looks are concerned.'

'Elizabeth, you have a filthy mind.'

'And what is yours like, since you always know what I am thinking?'

Henry was half-laughing, half-furious, well aware that he was being managed, prodded away from useless and dangerous thoughts. He was almost grateful, but wary, too, of the growing self-possession in Elizabeth. Something had made her aware of him in a way that increased his difficulty in hiding his thoughts from her. In fact, he was no longer sure he could hide them at all. That would make her a dangerous opponent – one whom he grew less sure of defeating daily. Arthur gave the series of muffled squeaks which preceded the onset of a lusty wail, and Elizabeth bent her head towards him. Suddenly Henry was not sure he was willing to combat her even if she was an opponent. Certainly she belonged to Arthur body and soul, no matter how she felt about him.

'Go away, Henry,' she said. 'Arthur wants his third breakfast or second dinner, and I would not like you to get ideas from looking at what the nurse has to offer him.'

'How vulgar you are, Elizabeth,' he laughed, and her eyes twinkled at him.

The arrival at Greenwich solved the problem that too much idleness for Henry bred too much thought. It brought him, instead, concrete worries. No sooner did a courier or ambassador from Brittany arrive than one from France was hard on his heels. Obviously neither could say anything to the point while the other was listening, but to receive one while the other waited was a serious affront. To Henry's horror none of the envoys would willingly accept Morton or Foxe as a substitute for himself. They knew all too well that neither of these gentlemen could be influenced away from the king's position, and that neither would try to exert any influence upon him. If they could not have the king's own ear, they clamoured for Bedford, Margaret, or Elizabeth.

Henry could not permit Jasper to become involved. He was useless for diplomatic work. His likes and dislikes showed too plainly on his face; he was an unconvincing liar, and his sympathies were too easily worked upon so that he might, conceivably, make an awkward promise. Henry tore his hair and wrote to Margaret, who replied that she knew nothing about such matters, cared less, and wished to be left in peace. That left Elizabeth. She at least had sufficient training of court life never to make a definite promise, and if her sympathies were engaged, and she tried to influence him, Henry knew himself to be impervious.

Setting Foxe at her elbow, Henry tried the experiment one afternoon when he really needed freedom to talk to the Breton envoy. Francis of Brittany was proposing that Maximillian, king of the Romans, and – far more important to Henry –

regent of Burgundy and the Netherlands for his infant son Philip, should marry his heiress, Anne. Henry had to remain on good terms with Maximillian, since England's greatest trade was with the Low Countries, but he felt obliged by past favours to warn Francis that Maximillian could not even control his own dominions and would be a weak reed to lean on for help against France. He felt also that since there were two other suitors for poor Anne's hand, Francis's purposes would be best served by keeping them all dangling and offering the girl as a reward to the one who provided the most practical help instead of the most grandiose promises.

If only, Henry said, Francis could keep out of an actual war for a year or two, he might be able to provide a more palatable alternative as a suitor for ten-year-old Anne than Maximillian, a widower, or Gaston d'Orleans, who already had a wife, or Lord d'Albret, who was older than either of the others and widely known for his cruelty and his vices. England was building ships as fast as the old shipyards could turn them out and as new shipyards could be built. Soon there would be a fleet capable of making Henry's wish to help his benefactor a practical possibility. There were boys in England, like Buckingham – masters of great estates which could provide enormous wealth and many men. Private armies had been mustered from such estates in the past and could be so mustered again, especially with the king's permission. Let Francis delay until England's naval strength was greater, and much might be done to ensure Brittany's safety.

And all the time that Henry talked, he wondered what Elizabeth was saying, for a page had whispered in his ear that she was with the French ambassador, who arrived soon after Henry, and the envoy from Brittany were closeted together. Foxe, of course, could keep her from making any drastic mistake, and Henry did not care whether the French envoy thought Elizabeth had power either as the king's wife or through her Yorkist influence. The more sure France was that Henry had domestic problems, the less closely she would watch him and the less likely she would be to press him for active intervention against Brittany. Henry simply did not like Elizabeth to come into close contact with anyone who could awaken pretensions to majesty in her.

He was somewhat surprised when Foxe arrived to give him

262

a synopsis of the interview, as close to giggling as a dignified churchman and the principal secretary to the king could get. Henry said blightingly that he did not see anything in the situation which could provoke mirth, but Foxe refused to respond to his master's mood.

'Sire, that is because you were not there. I had much ado to maintain my gravity, but fortunately I was not called upon to open my mouth even once. Her Grace has the finest ability to say nothing to the point that I have ever seen in my life in man or woman. Yet she never wandered from the subject nor gave the impression that she did not understand it.'

Henry's lips twitched. He had suffered not infrequently from this ability of Elizabeth's.

'Take the question of Anne's betrothal,' Foxe continued. 'When the envoy complained that Duke Francis wished to use it as a weapon against France, Her Grace replied that she did not like Anne and hoped she would not be betrothed at all.'

'Why should she dislike Anne, whom she has never seen?' Henry wondered, distracted for the moment from the main point.

'Oh, she made that clear enough. Do you not remember, Your Grace, that you were nearly betrothed to Anne?'

'By God,' Henry exploded, 'that woman's mind travels the same rut—'

'And a very useful rut it is. The envoy is convinced now of two things – that it is useless to talk of political matters to Her Grace, for she sees all in a personal light, and that she will use her womanly influence upon you against Brittany. The track of her mind made another point even more important – that it is utterly useless to think of her as a focal point for any conspiracy against Your Grace.'

But Henry ignored that and said, 'Oh, she will use her influence against Brittany, will she?'

Foxe looked at his master with concealed annoyance. It was ridiculous the way anything relating to Elizabeth upset him. It was no more than annoying, no cause for alarm; practically, the queen had no influence on Henry's decisions at all. He did not permit what he felt towards her – whether it was fondness or anger – to becloud the practical situation, but whenever she was involved he was testy and irritable. Still, Foxe knew that – for a time, at least, until Henry became better known to the envoys

263

– she could be endlessly useful. He was not inclined to forgo that usefulness because it induced bad temper in the king.

'I think,' he said, 'you should try her on the Breton envoy next time. Francis must know your sympathies are with him. Aside from your personal attachment, any aggrandizement of France must be to your political disadvantage. If Her Grace is hostile to the envoy from Brittany, it may make Francis less sure of your ultimate support and more willing to listen to present advice.'

After some further argument and hearing an outline of the complete interview, which made him laugh in spite of himself, Henry agreed. When he went to Elizabeth that evening for an hour or two of music and conversation before going to bed, he thanked her somewhat ungraciously for her help and told her he would require it again. Elizabeth put down the cap she was embroidering for him with an ill-tempered thump.

'Really, Henry, I do not know where you expect me to find time for this nonsense.'

It was the first time in any court that Henry had heard international affairs called nonsense, and he blinked. 'If France swallows Brittany, it will make her that much more powerful and, perhaps, that much more dangerous to us.'

'If France swallows Brittany, she will find herself with a disturbance of the bowels which will keep her busy for some time – and I have that just being made to listen. Oh, yes, I know the matter is important, but it is not important to me. This is your work, not mine, Henry.'

'It is a wife's duty to obey and help her husband,' Henry snapped, and then wondered if he had been manoeuvred into pressing her to do something he did not want her to do.

'Very well. Tell me what I am to say to the envoy and I will say it with as many simperings as I can manage. But I tell you plain, I would like to spit in his face and I may not be able to hide it. Also, you should consider that if you keep pressing these unwomanly duties on me, your son and Charles will be raised by chambermaids. Is that what you desire?'

As if she realized that her suspicious husband had doubts of her display of unwillingness, Elizabeth returned to the subject later when they were in bed. Henry was resting for a few minutes before he left her, looking very peaceful and relaxed, flat on his back with his clasped hands behind his head.

264

'Harry, why are you making me deal with state matters? I do not like it.'

'No?' He did not move, but his eyes slid sideways towards her.

Elizabeth stretched out a hand to play with the sparse hair on his chest. 'No. And that is the truth. I am fit for certain things and not for others. I am fit to raise your children, to make them love and fear God, to teach them simply of right and wrong. I am not very brave nor very wise. Harry, I have such a terror of saying the wrong things—'

'Make no certain promises and no certain denials, and you cannot do much amiss. Foxe will be there.'

'It also leads to things I do not like. The ambassador sent me a fine pair of jewelled gloves – for my help. Harry—'

'You did not send them back!' Henry exclaimed, jerking upright.

'Of course not. I am not a complete fool, although since you plainly think me one I cannot understand why you place me in these situations. What I do not like is that it was no official gift. He wants something, and I have nothing to give.'

'Give him – give them all – your sweet smile and your assurance you will speak well of them to me. And do so, if you like. It will make no difference.' Henry's narrow eyes peered more sharply at those words, but if Elizabeth was offended she showed nothing. 'The cards are thrown on the table,' he added, softening what might seem contempt for her opinion, 'and must be played to advantage, not for liking or disliking.'

So, will she nill she, Elizabeth was temporarily drawn into international intrigue. True, the envoys soon gave over trying to interest her in the actual affairs, but they plied her with personal attentions and Henry slyly made them dupes by smiling more particularly the next day upon those who had courted Elizabeth the day before. The rumour grew that Her Grace could not be relied upon to introduce any particular idea into her husband's mind, but that she could incline him to listen more favourably after pillow talk to this man or that who pleased her.

Unfortunately this growing conviction among the ambassadors was no longer growing among the Yorkists. Henry had taken no revenge on them – yet. But every day he grew stronger, every day he drew more threads of government into his own

265

hands, strand by strand stripping the local magnates of their powers. The king's writ was growing in force, the local magnate's strength decreasing. Soon a man would be unable to ignore the king's order to summon troops or come to court to be punished for what Henry decided was a misdeed. Then the snake would turn and strike them, when they were powerless.

Little rumours from the court fed this. Before the queen had delivered, she had begged her husband in frantic terror not to be angry with her if she bore him a girl instead of a boy. The king had pretended to expect her to die in childbirth and had nearly frightened her into doing so. And when the queen was ill with an ague after her delivery and her husband had been called to her, she had begged her ladies not to call him again, no matter how sick she was. If Henry oppressed his wife, would he not oppress them when they were equally in his power? And the poor earl of Warwick, the rightful heir to Edward's crown, was he not shamefully mistreated?

With the new year came new rumours. Lord Lovell had escaped and – marvel of marvels – had contrived the escape of Warwick. Here was proof that Henry was not all-powerful and might still be challenged. If the mighty Tower could not keep so important a prisoner, there was wide disaffection towards the king close to the throne. Warwick was safe. Warwick was in Ireland and had been recognized by men who had seen him in childhood.

Henry tried at first to keep the rumours from Elizabeth, but to control the tongues of the court was to try to restrain the buzzing of wasps by blocking the opening of their nest. Elizabeth struggled valiantly and she did not succumb to hysterical terrors, but she grew so pale and thin that Henry rode to Richmond himself to beg Margaret to come to her support.

'I am taking her to Sheen where there will be less formality, but she needs someone, mother.'

'She needs only you, Henry.'

An almost overwhelming desire to throw himself down and weep in his mother's arms stopped Henry's tongue, and he rose and walked away. If only he could confess, speak out of the vision that stood before his eyes, perhaps it would leave him. He did not dare. Not because his mother would think him weak or betray him to others, but because he might transfer his

266

fear to her. He could not even give her the real reason why her presence was so necessary, that his terrors were infecting his wife and hers him, so that they could barely endure sight of each other. Only if Margaret believed him confident would she be able to comfort Elizabeth, and Elizabeth's comfort was now more necessary to him than his own.

'I can be with her so little,' he said calmly, returning to his mother's side after seeming to have examined a missal which was lying open on a table. 'Any disturbance of this kind makes sore labour for a king. There is another reason, also. Elizabeth is not on good terms with her mother. I fear they quarrel about me. And she does not trust her ladies because of some things I had to bring to her notice.'

'Then this is a good time to get her new ladies she can grow to trust and be rid of her mother's agents.'

'Alas, it is the very worst time. There are already tales that I am cruel to her. I dare not dismiss those chattering women lest they say I make as much a prisoner of my wife as of Warwick. Mother, you must come. Elizabeth will go mad if she has no one to talk to and no one to drive out her silly fears. You know how hysterical and fanciful she is.'

Margaret riffled the pages of the Bible she held. Lay persons were not encouraged to read the Bible, particularly the Old Testament. but Margaret had permission. The book fell open, as if by long usage, at the story of Naomi and Ruth. 'Very well,' she said softly, 'I will come to Sheen.'

Chapter Nineteen

On February 2nd the king called a full council of forty men to decide what was best to do about the growing recognition of the false Warwick in Ireland. He seemed, himself, to have shockingly little interest in the matter, saying merrily that he would need to be king there as he was in England before he could make them obey, and then suddenly bringing his restless nobles up short by adding, 'And this will make me king there – without the cost of transporting Englishmen to fight them.'

Then, frustratingly, he would not enlarge upon that fascinating theme, turning his attention to measures to ensure the peace in England. The first decision that was reached, after considerable argument, was that arrangements should be made to take Warwick from prison and display him. He was to be ridden through the major streets of London and taken to High Mass at Saint Paul's Cathedral where any who wished to would be allowed to speak to him, assure themselves that he was truly Warwick and that, except for being confined, he was well treated.

The second proposal met with even more argument. It was Henry's customary gambit of offering a free pardon to anyone implicated in the affair so long as he took no active part in it.

'Pardons, pardons,' Oxford muttered. 'They will think us too weak to fight.'

'No one who knows I have you to lead my armies could believe that, John,' Henry soothed.

'Do not such pardons encourage men to conspire?' Nottingham asked unhappily.

'No,' Foxe offered. 'They keep men from becoming desperate. Men who have perhaps done no more than listen to loose talk or received letters urging them to join the rising. If they feared punishment they might indeed join, thinking to be hung for a sheep instead of a lamb.'

'A thousand well-wishers who will not lift a hand to help my enemies are less dangerous to me than a thousand friends who will not lift a hand to support me,' Henry said pointedly.

268

There was some unhappy stirring among certain of the councillors who had been wondering whether they could get away with just that game. Henry's eyes swept the faces before him. There was no more protest.

'Then we all agree that this is best?' asked Morton, the archbishop of Canterbury, glancing around.

'Let the proclamation be written, Dr Foxe,' Henry stated.

'I must bring to Your Grace's attention that there are certain men who have already taken action in stirring up sedition, although they have not yet taken up arms. Are their names to be mentioned and specifically excluded from the terms of the pardon?'

'Mentioned, yes. Excluded, no. They must yield up their persons into my power, but with the assurance that their lives will be spared and their punishment, if any, will be light.'

'Sire.'

'Yes, Lincoln?'

'I would like to hear the names of those who will be proclaimed rebels.'

A faint frown marred the serenity of Henry's countenance, but he nodded curtly at Foxe.

'Sir Henry Bodrugan. Sir Thomas Broughton. Thomas Harrington. James Harrington. John Beaumont. There are one or two others, but they are of less account.'

Lincoln stood up. 'I have somewhat to say, but I desire assurance that it will be taken in good part by Your Majesty.'

'Pardon is offered to all, even to those who have already offended. Why should you be excluded, Lincoln?'

'I need no pardon. I have done nothing and intended nothing ill. I have tried only to shield Your Majesty from pain, and now that I must be the one to give that pain I do not wish the matter to be held against me. What I have to say touches the Queen's Grace.'

A horrified murmur ran through the room. Henry was not murderous by nature, but if he could have caused Lincoln's death by any means at that moment, he would have done so.

'I will vouch personally for Her Grace,' Henry said gently and warningly, but he knew it was too late.

Perhaps the warning did more harm than good. Henry never knew in fact whether it was a deliberate act of malice or whether it was the result of fear, but Lincoln poured out a

269

sordid story. Rebellion was to be raised in the name of the false Warwick. The real Warwick was to be murdered and the false one repudiated after Henry was dead. Then Arthur was to be declared king and Elizabeth regent for him.

The king rose to his feet, white-faced, his mouth so tight with rage that his lips had all but disappeared. 'We commend your courage if not your good sense in retelling these rumours of filth. We had heard them. Why do you not also explain why Her Grace finds it necessary to take this step? I beat her; I am slowly poisoning her; nay, I tear strips off her body with my knife and eat her flesh. Bedford, go summon Her Grace here to us.'

'Sire, I beg you to reconsider. You will frighten Her Grace to death with such a summons. Let us wait upon her if necessary, but do not order her appearance here. No one can put credence in this tale.'

There was another murmur of approval, but Lincoln threw a packet of letters on the table. 'There for your credence,' he cried.

Henry could grow no whiter, and he put his hand on the table for support while the room whirled around him. No man reached for the white packet lying bright as a serpent's eye on the dark, polished wood. They regarded it with expressions of fascination, horror, and loathing, seeing instead of the small white patch burning cities, starving people, and fields soaked with blood. There was the end of the hope of healing the rift between red rose and white. The white rose had shown her thorns, and the red must incarnadine her with blood.

'Sire,' Ned Poynings's placid voice broke into the stillness. 'That is not Her Grace's seal.'

A series of quivering sighs broke the dead silence. Without asking permission, Poynings opened the packet and glanced through the first letter, the second, the third. Henry stood like a figure carved from marble, white and perfectly expressionless now. Around him the councillors shifted their eyes uneasily from place to place, as unwilling to look at the king or Lincoln as they were to see their hopes dashed by a change of expression in Poynings's face. That, at least, Henry did not fear. As quietly as he had picked up the letters, Poynings refolded them, laid them down with seeming casualness but in such a way that the seal was hidden.

'Pass these, please, to Her Grace,' he said, handing them to Foxe. 'There is nothing in them at all to reflect upon the queen except that her name has been taken in vain.'

'Bedford, Northumberland, Oxford, Surrey, Canterbury, and Dr Foxe will read those and decide whether their contents need be made public.' Henry had deliberately chosen an even number of his own supporters and Yorkists, with the two churchmen who were relatively safe from his retaliation as leaven. He looked around, saw the relief in the other faces, and nodded. 'Can we do more at this meeting?'

A ragged series of nays answered. In truth they were all too shaken to do more, even had the need been urgent.

'Lincoln,' Henry gestured him forward as the men he had designated moved into a corner to read the letters and the other men left. 'If I spoke sharply, I regret it, and I am grateful that you brought this information – at last. I wish to warn you, however, against such publications in the future. I prefer to receive information of this genre privately – and if I am not available, Dr Foxe or Canterbury will be. See to it that your zeal does not outrun your judgment again, or I may take that zeal for something quite different. And, since you have kept silence about these letters so long, keep silence still. You may go.'

'Harry.'

'Yes, uncle?'

'Thank God Poynings is a sensible man. Let us hope no one else recognized that seal.'

'For God's sake, tell me.' Henry's voice was ragged with tension.

'The dowager queen.'

'No! Her own seal? Not in cipher? It is impossible. She could not be so incredibly stupid.'

'Your Grace is correct. There is something wrong here.' That was Foxe, smooth and soothing. 'This matter must be concealed. It is more than possible that these letters are forgeries sent to enrage you against your wife and her mother so that you would act against them and, in so doing, destroy the Yorkist and Lancastrian reconciliation.'

'Surrey?' Henry snapped.

'I lend my aye to Dr Foxe. The peace you have made in this land should not be broken – whether the letters are forgeries or not.'

271

'Northumberland?'

'I agree.'

Having asked for the opinions of the Yorkist members of the group, Henry waited only for the nods of the others. He held out his hand for the letters and Morton gave them to him.

'That is all, gentlemen. Hold yourselves ready to attend council tomorrow to make final decision on what is to be done in this case.' He saw Jasper look at him uncertainly and, needing desperately to be alone, added, 'Uncle, will you find Ned and thank him for me?'

They were gone. Henry stood quietly for a few minutes longer, fearing someone would return to the room, and then sank into his chair and put his head down on the table to fight the waves of dizziness and nausea which rolled over him. The letters dropped from his hand, and when his vision cleared he moved his head a little so he could look at them lying on the shining floor. Had Elizabeth agreed to this thing? He would never know, no matter what she said; she had been different since that night when he tried to make her accuse her mother. But for what? Was it the power she wanted? For Arthur's life? Had she been convinced that his hold on the throne was so frail, that the rebellion would surely be successful, that she had offered to be the Yorkist pawn to save Arthur?

And if the letters were forgeries? Then the plot was more widespread than the wily Foxe or he suspected. The only purpose for such forgeries would be as a deathblow to an already shaky alliance. Was the welding together of Yorkist and Lancastrian so utterly hopeless? Should he have listened to Oxford and Jasper and the others who argued for severity and tried to wipe out his enemies? If he had been wrong, the country would fall apart, and Arthur would die. At least he was too little to be frightened. At least he would not need to know the terror those two poor children in the Tower felt. Henry put his hands to his eyes as if to shut out a scene he had never witnessed, but it was not the death of the princes he was trying to block out. It was the vision of Warwick, empty-faced, helpless, with his head on the block, that hung behind his tight-closed lids. If Warwick were publicly executed for his part in this conspiracy, after due trial, of course, so that the king could not be accused of being another Gloucester— Henry retched and

272

clapped a hand across his mouth, swallowed the bitter gall. There must be no sign of the king's disorder of spirits.

No sign. Henry thought bitterly that he could not even do what any other man could. He could not send his wife and son to a place of safety. Oh, no, that would bespeak lack of confidence in his own cause – and that would mean defeat before he started. Henry bent and picked up the packet. There was no mirror in the chamber, but he had not wept so his face would be clear. He smoothed his hair, set his hat at its usual angle, and left the room wearing an expression of mild gravity most suitable to a monarch emerging from the council chamber.

When Henry entered her apartment, Elizabeth rose with a gasp. Margaret assumed at first that it was merely surprise at seeing him there at a time when a visit was very unusual, for there was no particular expression on Henry's face. She did not even feel apprehensive when he asked the ladies to leave, although that naturally meant he had something either serious or private to say. Elizabeth's face, however, had turned the colour of cheap wax, and Margaret could not help but be frightened in spite of Henry's calm aspect.

'Is this your mother's seal and your mother's hand?' Henry asked, mildly extending the letters.

For a moment it seemed as if Elizabeth would refuse to take them, but she did. She glanced at Henry mutely and he nodded, so she unfolded the paper and began to read.

'I wish to assure you, Elizabeth, that I am merely curious. It will make no difference what you say. Whether or not she is innocent this time, she has been guilty so often in the past that this is a mere straw to add or subtract from the wagonload.'

'Do you believe this?' Elizabeth whispered.

Henry glanced at her sharply, but she showed no sign of wandering wits or hysteria. 'Believe it?' he said impatiently. 'It does not matter. It is of no importance. I merely—' His voice died away and suddenly he had an answer he had not expected. There was such a look of agony on Elizabeth's face that he could feel his heart contract in response. She was innocent! She had no part in this because she was not afraid; she was only flayed by his indifference. 'Bess,' he exclaimed, 'I did not mean—'

'It does not matter to you that I may have plotted your death?' she asked dully.

273

'No, it does not – not to me.' Henry's relief was so great that he was almost amused. 'So much do I love you, Elizabeth, that I do not care whether you want me dead or alive. I cannot hurt you. Why should I torment myself with wondering what your intentions towards me are? I do not think you *can* encompass my death. I do not wish to believe you desire it. For me, that is sufficient.'

'You will never trust me.'

'Probably not. Does it matter, since I love you?'

'Only to you, Harry,' she replied, and tears started to run down her cheeks. She wiped them away impatiently. 'As for the letters, I know it is my mother's seal – or a very good imitation. The hand I am not certain of. She does not write to me often. It looks like. More I cannot say.'

Margaret stretched out a hand. 'Let me see. I know the dowager queen's hand well.'

To her surprise Henry looked inquiringly at Elizabeth. She bit her lip, but nodded her permission. 'It cannot be hid. Madam, do not hate me. I will die of shame.'

'Nonsense, Elizabeth. Why should I hate you for your mother's doing?' But when she had read the letters her eyes grew cold. 'What will you do, Henry?'

'Oh, I must be rid of her. There is too much chance for mischief as long as she is loose, and I am tired of being stung by this wasp.'

'Henry, you would not – kill her?' Margaret gasped while Elizabeth, wide-eyed, sank back into her chair.

'A woman? No. I will strip her naked, so she can buy no more spies and support no more rebels, and I will thrust her into a convent where she will be well cared for and well guarded. Is this too harsh, Elizabeth?'

'No, my Lord, you are ever kind. What will you do with me?'

'I will beg you to recover your complexion, my dear, and to believe that the great need I have of your company would make me overlook anything short of a dagger in the ribs.'

'That is not a funny jest, Henry,' Margaret snapped, but she should have saved her protest because a faint smile appeared on Elizabeth's pale lips and she stretched her hand to her husband, who took it kindly.

274

'When I see your ribs, Harry,' she said, 'it is I who expect to be stabbed.'

'Elizabeth! For shame! You will corrupt my innocent mother,' Henry said, pretending to be shocked.

'Why, sire,' she rejoined, attempting to maintain a bantering tone while her lips trembled, 'what could I mean except that you are too thin?'

'Try not to fret, Bess.' Henry bent to kiss her. 'I must go now.'

Taking the packet of letters from his mother's hand and giving her a significant glance, Henry left them. Elizabeth maintained her composure until the door closed behind him, and then she thrust her hands against her mouth and began to weep. Margaret rose and came towards her, but the sight of her mother-in-law's frozen face brought no comfort. Elizabeth fell on her knees and pressed her face against Margaret's gown.

'I did not,' she cried. 'I did not know.'

'Control yourself, Elizabeth. Your ladies will be here in a moment. Do you want the whole world to think you accused and guilty? Does Henry deserve this?'

'Deserve? He deserves to be canonized for his patience,' Elizabeth gasped, laughing hysterically. 'Who, except he, will not think me guilty? You think so. When this news flies abroad who will not withdraw the hems of their skirts from me – the leper. I will be spat upon like that Isabella who contrived her husband's murder and took his murderer into her bed.'

'If Henry stands by you, that cannot happen.' Margaret lifted Elizabeth to her feet and mechanically patted her shoulder. 'You should at least strive to deserve his loyalty. You must not make yourself ill. Henry has enough troubles without adding your vapours to them.'

But the news never was sown broadcast, although political considerations, not personal ones, dictated keeping the secret as well as it could be kept. The next day a reduced council met, consisting of those who had read the letters and those of whose loyalty Henry was most sure. All agreed on the necessity of maintaining the appearance of solidarity in the royal family. The dowager queen was to retire to the Abbey of Bermondsey, resign her dower lands to her son-in-law, while retaining only

275

a pension of 400 marks, and the lands would be transferred by act of the next parliament to Elizabeth to demonstrate publicly Henry's trust in and affection for his wife. Elderly women often retired to convents, not to take the veil but to end their lives in peace and comfort. The move would fool no one who knew the dowager queen, but to the local squire who lived on his lands and never came to court it would seem natural.

And to Henry the opinion of the local squire was of great importance. The great magnates he had under his eye and hand. Henry would never make Gloucester's mistake and trust his 'supporters'. He was constrained to 'trust' the lesser men because he could not keep his eye directly upon them. Yet, in the last analysis Henry knew it was the local squire who had defeated Gloucester. Had every man Richard summoned to his standard responded, his army would have outnumbered Henry's by ten to one instead of two to one, and the decision of the Stanleys would have been irrelevant. Had even the men who did respond fought wholeheartedly, instead of yielding and deserting during the early part of the battle, probably the decision of the Stanleys would have been different.

Then they waited. Henry conducted the business of government, played with the children, rode out with Elizabeth. The pardon was published and Warwick was exhibited. At the end of February the first blow fell. Lincoln fled to Burgundy, openly joining the rebellion. From merchants who doubled as spies, Henry learned that Edward IV's sister, Margaret of Burgundy, had acknowledged the false Warwick and was contributing heavily to his cause. Through her means, Lincoln and Lord Lovell were hiring Flemish mercenaries.

Henry responded by appointing commissions of array to guard the east coast against invasion from Flanders. As if to mock his black fears, England had burst into magnificent spring. The king was blind to beauty, however, as he rode through the country, checking the defences and showing himself to the people. He veiled the horror in his eyes, and he gave justice and laughed away the concern of others.

Fortunately there was much to encourage his supporters so that they did not need to lean too heavily on his confidence. The commissioners responded promptly to his orders and did their duty conscientiously – and many of them were men who had shirked similar duties for Gloucester. The people cheered

276

Henry wherever he rode. But Henry's own spirits would not lift, and the strain was telling on him. Thus far the only one who realized how oppressed the king was, was the unfortunate Ned Poynings who, because he suffered unshaken, was exposed to Henry's worst moods.

Kept in attendance almost night and day, Poynings was wearily watching Henry being fitted for clothes. The king was very hard on clothing because he always dressed in the most elegant fabrics. The delicate silks, velvets, and brocades did not last long under the wear and tear of much riding and hunting. Moreover, Henry believed in distributing his custom, for it was much to the mercers' and tailors' benefit if they could say that the king purchased from them. Whenever he stayed more than a week in one area, Henry bought clothing. Now he was clad only in hose and a white shirt which was open halfway down his thin breast. Poynings frowned as he watched the too-quick pulse in Henry's throat and saw the flesh sucked in between the prominent ribs.

'The white silk brocaded in gold for the doublet. That green for hose, but it must be clocked in gold, and the darker green velvet for a surcoat. That should be trimmed in the ermine you showed me earlier. All to be ready the day after tomorrow – for Easter.'

One of the tailors closed his eyes and muttered a prayer under his breath.

'You can make up the yellow, orange and brown for Sir Edward, who is watching with so sour an expression,' Henry added. 'What is it, Ned? Do you disapprove of my taking pleasure in my dress?'

'I think Your Grace dresses as befits your station,' Poynings replied, unmoved by the lash of the tone under the light words.

'Oh, you—' Henry had begun, when a very flustered and very young page interrupted him to crave audience for the marquis of Dorset. Henry's lips parted, closed tightly, and then softened into a smile. 'Sirrah, come here.'

The child's knees knocked as he approached, but Poynings relaxed momentarily. Henry was never cruel to children, and this was a very new addition to the household.

'What is your name?' the king asked.

'Boleyn, Your Majesty, Thomas Boleyn.'

'Sir William's son?' The child nodded. 'Yes. Well, you must

277

never interrupt the king, even when he is merely jesting with an old friend. Now, you must have known that, so tell me what has frightened you so much as to make you forget your manners? Surely I do not look to be an ogre?'

'No, sire, but the marquis said I must go to you, even when I told him it was not my duty. I was afraid not to obey him and also afraid to come where I do not belong.'

A clever child, Henry thought, fixing his name in memory. 'Ah, the marquis insisted, did he? Very well. Tell him I will receive him here. Do you happen to know where the earl of Oxford bides, Thomas?'

'He is just below in the great hall, sire. I was serving wine, and—'

Henry touched the boy's nose with his forefinger. It was a smooth-tongued, talkative child – very good. 'Hush. When the king asks a question, you answer as shortly as possible – yea or nay – unless you are asked for an explanation. Conversation comes when you are older. Run away then, and after you have given my message to the marquis of Dorset, tell the earl of Oxford to come hither to me at once.'

Poynings studied the embroidery on the cuff of his sleeve with great interest. He did not like what was going to happen. He did not like what had been happening to Henry day by day over these past two months. He took a quick glance at his master, who had cleared the room of tradesmen and servants and was watching the door sideways out of his long eyes with a touch of smiling expectancy. Probably, Poynings thought, he could stop what was about to occur with a few words, but that would be dangerous. Not dangerous to him, but to the king. Henry needed an outlet; he also needed a lesson, and it was far better for the king to administer that lesson to himself than to be told what might have happened by someone else. Ned returned to the involved stitchery of his cuff. If matters went too far, he could appeal to Bedford or Elizabeth – he hoped. Anyway Dorset was worthless, so it would not matter.

Dorset entered, his fingers playing nervously with the edge of his surcoat. 'It came to me quite suddenly, sire, that I—'

'I thought you were in London,' Henry said with deceptive mildness. 'Did I send for you or give you leave to come here?'

'I beg your pardon, Your Majesty.' The marquis's face went

278

pasty. 'I did not know I was required to remain in London. I will return at once.'

'So you will. But now that you are here, what is it that you desire of me?'

'Nothing. Nothing at all.'

If only the man were not such a coward, Poynings thought with exasperation. Then he stopped himself before he shook his head in wonder, realizing that, although it was true Dorset was yellow livered, Henry had a similar effect on men who were brave as lions. Oxford and Devon sometimes stumbled in their speech when under the king's eyes. It was most puzzling because Henry was ordinarily both reasonable and just. Poynings suffered a moment of doubt as to whether the change he saw was really temporary, and stifled it.

'It only seemed to me that I had never explained to you properly what had happened in France.'

Poynings uttered an involuntary exclamation of surprise, and Henry looked startled. 'But that was more than two years ago, and you have been at court, seeing me nearly daily for a year— Ah, come in, Oxford. Dorset has decided to explain what happened in France.'

'That I would like to hear. Thank you for summoning me, sire,' John de Vere said drily.

Dorset's face was now shiny with sweat, as well as being pasty. 'It did not seem important before, but now that there is doubt about my mother's loyalty, I wish to assure you of—'

'What doubt? The dowager queen, my most beloved wife's mother, has retired from court to rest and see into her own salvation. If you doubt her loyalty to me, Dorset, you are alone in it.'

The icy words dropped into a frozen stillness. There was a small sticky sound as Dorset's lips parted, but whatever he wished to say was congealed in his throat. Slowly, as if Henry's eyes were exerting pressure upon him, Dorset went down on his knees. Henry waited, watching the sweat form beads and then rivulets that ran down his face, waited while he began to tremble, waited until even the hardened soldier Oxford turned his eyes away from what was on the floor. Such wanton cruelty in the king was a strange, savage pleasure. It released the tensions bred by months of smiling and guarding his tongue.

'John,' the Tudor said to Oxford, 'Dorset desires to return

to London. Would you be so kind as to see that he arrives safely. Perhaps, since he is so timorous, he would do better for a feeling of security. See that he is lodgéd safely in the Tower.'

Dorset cried out for mercy, but Henry's narrow eyes merely signalled Oxford to remove the prisoner, and he turned away. The room was still. Henry took a half-step towards the door and stopped. He clasped his hands together, pulled them apart violently, and let them hang loosely by his sides. Poynings could see a vein pulsing in his temple.

'I am so beset, I know not where to turn,' he said suddenly. 'Is it only a king that has no right to strike out at his enemies?'

'Is Dorset your enemy, sire?'

'He would be if he had sufficient courage.'

'Well, you have struck him. Do you feel more at ease?'

'I might as well have beaten that child that pushed his way in here. Dorset is weak and a fool, but he has done me no harm.' Henry stretched out a hand blindly, and Poynings grasped it. 'I will send after him and remand the order. Oh, God, I cannot. I have frightened him so much now that he is likely to turn on me and do something foolish for which I would really need to punish him.'

'Dorset is nothing. No one cares for him because all know what he is. Leave him in the Tower as a symbol of your power and your caution.'

'But he will be in torment. Do you think I wish even that half-man to suffer what I feel myself?'

It was the opening Poynings had been waiting for. 'What is it that troubles you, Henry? I know the whole kingdom is feeding on your flesh and drinking your blood, but that is nothing new. We have eaten you for years, and you have withstood that drain on your substance without weakening. Something else is eating you now. It is time to speak of it, to gain a companion to fight the danger before it swallows you whole.'

'Does one speak of sick fancies?' the king asked faintly, aware from the use of his name that Ned was offering himself as a friend to a friend rather than as a man to his ruler.

'Devils fly out through the mouth,' Poynings said calmly. 'You should spit yours out.'

'To you?'

Poynings shrugged. 'I know my worth. Sick fancies and

280

fears for the future hold no terror for me. I do not know why, but that is true. Just as it is true that tales and players hold no pleasure for me. Perhaps an inner eye is needed for these things – and I have it not.'

'I have.' Henry fingered the cloth he had chosen for his doublet, holding its rich substance as if to cling to reality. 'Do you know how the princes died?'

Startled, Poynings did not answer for a moment. He could not see the connection between this subject and the last and wondered whether Henry was rejecting his offer of help. The fixed expression on the king's face, however, led him to believe the question was somehow important.

'Many things were rumoured. It was said most often that they were strangled or smothered in their bedclothes.'

'They looked doubtless like hanged men then.'

Ned swallowed down a momentary sickness. 'Henry—'

'It would take long to die thus. So much terror for such young boys.'

Poynings wondered wildly if the king had some secret knowledge, some secret guilt concerning the princes. But he had not been in England—

'Ned, when this invasion comes, if we fail, what will you lose?'

The illogical leaping of Henry's mind was more alarming than any burst of passion. 'I will lose my livelihood and my head,' Poynings replied stolidly. 'You can lose no more, Henry.'

'You are mistaken. My baby, like Edward's sons, would be heir to the throne. He knows me now. He smiles to me and stretches out his arms to be taken. And I see him with a blackened face, with bulging eyes and a protruding tongue—'

It was fortunate that Henry was staring wide-eyed into nothing, for Poynings blanched. The king's mind was not wandering. Its logical path was all too horribly apparent. Poynings, too, played with little Arthur, and the word picture was so vivid that his tongue cleaved to the roof of his mouth. He pulled it free.

'Then obviously, we must not fail,' he said, but no effort of will could keep his voice steady.

'Have I frightened you too, Ned?' Henry asked, meeting his eyes.

'You have that,' Poynings admitted. 'You have also given me the strength of ten. With that vision to spur me, I will doubtless continue to fight even if I be struck dead.'

'I, too. But will it be enough?'

Poynings shook himself violently. 'Ugh! Henry, we are both fools – begging Your Grace's pardon, but it is true. Not even the direst enemy, the worst monster, would dare. There has been too much murder of babes in this land. I think the very beasts in the fields would rise up and cry against another such act. Prison, as you prison Warwick, yes, but not murder.'

'That is cold comfort,' Henry said, but it was not. While there was life, there was hope. The vision had faded. It was still there; it would come again. But what Ned said had logic and the force of practical politics behind it. 'I know what I will do about Dorset,' the king remarked in a much more natural tone. 'I will write him a letter and say that some have spoken against him – which is true enough – but that I believe him my friend – which is less true – so that I have placed him in safekeeping and whatever befalls he cannot be blamed for it. There, a weight has fallen from me.'

Chapter Twenty

The thorn was in bloom. The white petals made clouds of hedges, carpeted the ground, filled the air with sweetness. The last sharp chill of April had been vanquished by the balmy mildness of May. Rain fell sweetly and then the skies cleared and the sun made rainbows in the pearly drops caught on spider webs and blossoms. Even old Kenilworth's grey walls looked welcoming to the party returning from a morning's hawking.

The king smoothed the feathers of his falcon and turned to his wife who held her white mare close to his stallion's side. 'Now you will have to take all the jewels off these gloves. You should never have presented them to me this morning and then tempted me to ride out in them. They are all marked with blood.'

Elizabeth leaned over to see, disturbing her own bird which batted its wings irritably. 'It is only the cuff. I will cut it off and sew on new ones. Who could suspect that you would wear white gloves ahawking.'

'You made them and they suited my clothes admirably.'

'And now I will have to remake them. Silk gloves, Harry, ahawking. It is a wonder the falcon has not torn your wrist. You could keep the glove-makers of the entire kingdom working with such extravagance.'

'You see, even my bad habits are to the nation's benefit.'

Elizabeth was about to make a tart remark on not permitting such reasoning to extend to other vices, when a rider came pounding towards them from the castle. Henry's mouth grew grim, and he set spurs to his horse so that he met the messenger halfway, leaving his entourage behind. His wife was the first to reach them, and the colour came back into her face when she saw Henry's expression.

'Is it good news, Harry?'

About to say yes and tell her, Henry reconsidered. It was unlikely that Elizabeth would think the news good, and half the courtiers were now surrounding them. Too many would see the matter in the same light as Elizabeth without having her distress to spark their fears. Nor could the methods by which Henry hoped to soothe his wife in private be used in public or upon those others. Henry looked sidelong at Elizabeth.

'It depends,' he replied with a curl of his mobile lips, 'upon how one looks at things; but it is a good omen that the news comes now when I am ready to work instead of breaking our pleasure.'

The council assembled in their sweat-stained riding garments, for Henry's patience was strained by preparations which led to nothing. He was eager for action, and woe betide the man who was late when he summoned. He threw the letter on the table, tapping on it with the fingers of his white-gloved hand. The bloodstains from the hawk's talons showed red.

'From Lord Howth in Ireland. Lovell and Lincoln with two thousand Flemish mercenaries have landed there. They brooked no waiting. The false Warwick has been crowned Edward VI in Dublin Cathedral.'

'This news you do not think bad?' Bedford muttered.

'They are fools. Will the English love the crowning of their "king" among the barbarian Irish? Setting that aside, we are ready for them now. If they do not come soon, the need for watchfulness and defence will last so long that none will really watch or defend.'

'If a trial of strength must be made, it is better to come to it with fresh spirit,' Oxford agreed.

'You have it, John. You have the command, also, which you will share with my uncle, as always. Bedford, write to Rhys to raise the Welsh. Devon, go at once to raise the south for me. Guildford, see to your guns. They must be fitted to travel far and fast.'

Devon had not waited for the end of Henry's instructions. He was already out of the room and they could hear him bellowing at pages to summon his men and order his horses saddled as he closed the door behind him. Henry raised his brows. Guildford, who had thought of following, sat still. There would be much riding for him, also. The artillery of key cities all over the country would need to be inspected and mounted for offence as well as defence.

'Dynham' – the treasurer looked up – 'I need not tell you that our resources will be strained. It is unfortunate that I sent

284

Foxe to London and that foreign matters keep Canterbury there. You must tell them that I expect the Church to contribute to maintaining the quietness of the realm also.'

There were firm nods of approval from the nobles around the table. It seemed to them very often that the Church profited alike from peace and war while they paid the piper. Thus far no demands had been made of the Church and many had wondered, because of Henry's piety, whether he planned to excuse the prelates even their ordinary contributions to national defence.

'Ormond, write to your Irish relations to hold off from this foolish business. Tell them how strong we are, how happy the nation, how unlikely any revolt is to succeed. You know what you must say.'

'Sire, they will not obey me.'

'I know, but a word that shakes a man's courage or plants a single doubt in his mind is of aid to us.'

'What of Northumberland and Surrey?' Bedford asked, but his eyes asked about the Stanleys who were seated at the table and whom he dared not name.

'Surrey is to raise no men but to come himself to serve with me. He is a mighty man of his hands. Northumberland— He showed himself loyal enough last spring. Let him go about his duties. Nottingham, you had better help him. Sleep in his bed, if you must, but see that he gets into no mischief. The rest of you gentlemen who are officers of my household will bide with me. I cannot spare you from attendance upon my person.'

There was a significant silence. This king would not be put off with excuses of illness, nor would he be content to take children for hostages – his softness to children was well known. The men themselves would remain in his hands – their seals and signatures available to his will. Dorset was in the Tower, but all knew there would be letters in his hand and sealed by his seal ordering his tenants to obey Devon's or some other of the king's faithful lieutenants' commands.

'Since you need me, sire, I will order my people to obey your deputy,' Derby offered quickly.

'You are as generous as a loving father should be to his son,' Henry approved, smiling. 'Give your commands to Willoughby – oh, I beg your pardon, Robert – to Lord de Broke.'

285

'And to whom do I give my commands, sire?' William Stanley asked smoothly.

That there would be nothing to read in those reptilian eyes Henry knew, and he did not bother to meet them. He knew also that this was the last time he could work this trick upon Sir William. If there was another time, it would be war to the death between them. It was almost a relief. Henry had never quite prevented his skin from crawling when he had dealings with this Stanley, although he suppressed any outward sign of the sensation most successfully.

'To the earl of Nottingham. He will be in that part of the country anyway,' Henry said without the trace of warmth in his voice which had softened the order to his stepfather. Derby was no prize in staunchness perhaps, but he was a loving husband to Henry's mother, and Henry would pardon him any weakness for that. 'Edgecombe, you will see to the victualling of the host. You all know my general orders. There is to be no forcible levy of provisions, no rape, no arson, no fighting among different retinues in the host. There is to be no disturbance of the country at all. Every man not called to arms must continue in his regular business. Any questions?'

There were none. Most of the details had been worked out long before, and it was now clear that this conference had been called largely to close the trap on the Stanleys.

'Very well,' the king continued. 'Those of you who leave here for duties in the shires will send me a written report of day-to-day progress – every day.'

There were muffled sighs, but no protests, as Henry dismissed them and they left. They only had to write one report a day; the king would need to read dozens.

'Ned,' Henry added softly, 'remind me to write to that literal idiot Devon that he must do the same. Perhaps,' he laughed, 'he thought to escape by rushing off, but I cannot forgo seeing that crazy scrawl of his. And his spelling is the delight of my life, even though I often cannot make out what he means at all. There must be some lightness to be found in this. Pray God Devon never thinks to hire a clerk.'

Word came from Ireland day by day. The bishops of Armagh and Clogher were faithful and preached against the usurper. In the southeast, where the Butler influence was

286

strong, the orders of the earl of Ormond, the head of the family, were heeded to a certain degree. Kilkenny, Clonmel, and a few other towns shut their gates and would contribute nothing to the insurrection. Waterford offered a bold defiance to the earl of Kildare, who was one of the false Warwick's major supporters. But these were mere drops withheld from the bucket which was filling rapidly.

On June 4th the pretender landed near Furness with two thousand Flemish and nearly six thousand Irishmen. Henry did not attempt to stop the landing, largely because there was no fleet to stop it with. He made plain, however, to the men with him when the news came on the sixth, that he was not ill-pleased, reminding them that he had once told them that the activities of the Irish against him would bring them under his power.

'There will be none to return to Ireland,' he said coldly, 'or one in a hundred, perhaps. The Irish will not play this game again, nor any other. When I send an order bidding them obey or the English will come and slay them – they will believe me.'

Some thought that it would be safer to talk after the battle was fought and won, but most were carried along by the king's conviction. There was another satisfaction also to Henry's men in his manner. All of them deplored his softness to his enemies. They simply could not comprehend the king's willingness to forgive those who injured him. Many when they first came to power offered amnesty, but as soon as the first murmur of protest came there was retaliation. Henry's attitude was un-natural, and no king had continued to pardon and pardon as long as Henry had. This time, instead of speaking of foolish children and gentle handling, the king spoke of killing, and his eyes were hard and cold as steel.

It was impossible to shield Elizabeth from the news of what had happened. Details might be kept secret, but the main fact, that an invading army had landed in England, could not be concealed. Henry went most reluctantly to bid his wife good night and farewell at the same time. He knew that Elizabeth could pierce his mask of confidence and read the half-mad horror that lay below it. She had set the horror there, and while he did not blame her he was afraid to face her fear. Nor was it his promise, nor any thought of Elizabeth's comfort, which brought him out into the long corridor leading to her

287

apartment after the whole castle slept. He had, in fact, decided to spare himself the scene, had written a long letter of excuse and love. Habit, stronger than his will, would not let him sleep, and, lying awake with nothing left to do, Henry saw his child's dead face hanging in the dark.

He glided noiselessly by his sleeping men on soft felt slippers, past the silent salute of the guards, and, as soundlessly, woke Elizabeth's lady and sent her from the room. If Elizabeth slept, he might still be spared. To kiss her or just look at her might give him some ease. No one would harm Elizabeth, except to mew her up in a convent, perhaps. She would not be unhappy there once she had recovered from her losses. She could play her music and study and pray and love God. Perhaps the sight of her peaceful face would block that other vision— His hand touched the curtains.

'I thought you would never come, Harry. Is it true? You leave tomorrow?' The tense whisper destroyed his hope, and he bent and kissed her. 'Oh God, why are you so cold?'

'I have been sitting still too long, I suppose. Yes, I will leave with the dawn tomorrow. I have come to say farewell now.' Henry braced himself. Now would come the burst of tears, the wails and prayers. Elizabeth had been very good this past month, but to expect self-control now—

'Come into bed and I will warm you.'

He had intended nothing of the sort. Henry was physically tired and mentally depressed, and he was not the kind who enjoyed love under those circumstances. If that was what Elizabeth needed, however, he was prepared to try to satisfy her, although he had a sudden frightening doubt of his ability. He was cold; his body seemed frozen, stiff in movement. It was extremely pleasant to discover that Elizabeth had meant what she said literally. She folded him in her arms and held him close along her entire body, but she made no gesture of ardent invitation. A little of her warmth seeped into him and Henry stiffened apprehensively.

'Harry, what is it? Are you angry with me? For Mary's sweet sake, speak out. I will not cry nor complain. I could not bear to part from you in anger – not tonight.'

'Of course I am not angry. What cause have I for anger?'

'No cause of which I know, but who can tell what tales of me are whispered into your ear?'

288

'No one speaks aught to me of you except of your goodness. You have even won my uncle, and that is no mean feat for Edward's daughter.'

That hurdle was passed. A few more minutes, Henry thought, and he would be able to go. He continued to hold himself rigid, feeling as if the cold that was now leaving him had been armour, that when the coating of ice melted he would crumble to pieces if he relaxed. Suddenly Elizabeth's arms tightened around him.

'Please, Harry, let us comfort each other.' A little half-sob, half-laugh escaped her. 'I am so frightened already. Nothing you could say or do could frighten me more. Is it so very bad?'

'No, it is good. You must believe that. The country replies to the muster nobly. There was a little trouble in the east because they desired to fight under Surrey, but they have come – Paston, Boleyn – all of them.'

'Then why are you afraid, Harry?' It was the faintest, most tremulous whisper. He would not have heard it, had it not been breathed into his ear.

'If you must have the truth, because I am a coward,' he snarled, prodded beyond endurance. 'You once said I was not afraid before Bosworth. Well, you were wrong. I would have shaken with fear then as I would be shaking now if I did not hold my body still by my will. I am afraid to fight, to die—'

'Oh that.' Elizabeth laughed very softly, very tenderly, and kissed the ear she was whispering into, then his cheek and his chin and his lips. 'You mean you are a man, like other men. There is no harm in that.' And she snuggled closer, more comfortably, as if her fears had been relieved.

'I do not know why it is that you can see into my heart as if my face and body were glass,' Henry said resentfully. 'None other can.'

'Only because I love you as no other does. I do not mean,' Elizabeth explained, more as if she were making the matter clear to herself than to Henry, 'that I love you more than others. Not more than your mother or your uncle. No one could love you more than that. I love you in a different way. They have come almost to worship you, I think. But a wife— I know you have a mole on your belly and a scar like a half-moon on your thigh. Did someone bite you there, Harry? I have thought of that and longed to bite you there myself.'

289

'I fell against a stick.' He was trying to find the familiar argument, the familiar laughter, to cling to the escape Elizabeth offered, but his voice broke and he turned his face into his wife's breast and began to sob.

'Did you so?' Elizabeth asked softly. 'But you see, with such wonderings, how a wife cannot worship and cannot be shocked to know her husband is a man. How can I fail to know you weak and mortal? Have I not seen you tremble with desire and heard you cry out in fulfilment? So feel I, and I am weak and mortal.'

Long tremors shook Henry from head to toe, but the sobs were subsiding and his hands were growing warm. Elizabeth continued to speak of the little things that bound them, the quarrels and the laughter, the personal peculiarities. Henry's neck was often stiff from long hours bent over accounts, and Elizabeth rubbed it sometimes with mustard pounded into a scented cream to ease the muscles. How could a woman worship a man with a stiff neck, she asked him, laughing, or fail to find the plain – not to say ugly – face on top of the stiff neck more beautiful than any other countenance she had ever seen.

'You are beautiful, Bess,' Henry said clearly, suddenly finding his voice. 'Even your kneecaps are beautiful. They are like oval jewels. But you have a crooked toe.'

The thought of that tiny imperfection made her so dear, so much more precious than all her beauty, that Henry nearly wept anew. He might never see that bent toe again. It might be lost to him. He sat up and threw off the light covers. Elizabeth smiled, offering up to him her perfection and her imperfection. And he knelt naked in the bed and kissed the crooked toe, the oval kneecaps, the milk-white thighs. He was trembling afresh, although for a far pleasanter reason, and Elizabeth matched his passion with an abandonment even she had never shown before. Henry never went back to his own bed. They clung together through the night wringing the last thrill from the pleasure that might be torn from them by death.

Their mutual comforting posed a pretty problem for Henry's gentlemen, however. This had not happened since his wedding night. No one even considered daring to intrude upon the king and queen, but the hour assigned for departure was drawing closer. Ladies and gentlemen alike stood in the antechamber silently wringing their hands, wondering whether the

290

king had finished his pleasuring and, if not, what they were to do about it. He would be furious if they did not leave on time because he had made rendezvous with Devon; doubtless, however, he would be even more furious at being disturbed. Henry, whatever they feared, was all too aware of the passing time, even as he came up from a last drowning wave of pleasure.

'It is full morning,' he said as soon as he could control his gasping. 'I am already late.'

'Yes.'

'I must go.'

'Yes. You will not do anything foolish, Harry? You will not take it into your head to lead the battle or—'

'I wish I could,' he replied sharply, bending to pick up his robe which had fallen to the floor. 'I get so angry when I fight that I do not feel afraid. You need not worry. My guardian angels – my uncle and the others – would probably restrain me by force if necessary. A king is too precious a thing to risk, you know.'

'So is a man,' Elizabeth murmured, rising and coming to the door with him.

'Thank you, Bess. I am a man again – although a weary one. I was not when I came here last night.'

'You are always a man. Your trouble, Harry, is that you wish to be more than that.' She saw him pull the door open and braced herself for one more effort. There would be time enough and to spare for weeping when he was gone. Bringing a bite to her voice, she exclaimed, 'And for heaven's sake, if you get wet change your clothes. I do not want you coughing and sneezing all over me when you come back. A stiff neck I can bear, but being sniffled on is disgusting.'

So Henry's men saw him come laughing from his wife's chamber. The king's eyes showed he had slept little, but when he was hurriedly dressing they saw the marks on his body that provided obvious reasons for his wakefulness. John Cheney, although tactfully silent, could not restrain eyebrows raised in surprise when, drawing on his master's hose, he saw teeth marks over the little scar on the king's thigh. What if there be an invasion, a rebellion, a war? It could not be too great a matter if this was how His Grace spent the night. He had prayed before Bosworth.

Fortunately, since Henry was totally exhausted, they had not far to go. Even so, he almost fell asleep in his saddle before they rode the few miles to Coventry, and he shocked Devon who was encamped there with the southern levies by yawning in his face all the time he was making his report. Henry commended his zeal sleepily and staggered off to bed, leaving Devon openmouthed with amazement until Cheney enthusiastically recounted the probable doings of the previous night.

'I will never understand him.' Devon shrugged and laughed. 'He is simply not made like other men. To bid one's wife a tender farewell, this is reasonable, but to play such games— All night, you say?'

'It must be so, for he was still at it in the morning, and we standing outside, knowing it was time to leave and not daring to enter. We listened at the door, of course, and it was plain that— You should see him. Bitten and bruised all over—'

'No wonder he fears war so little. He is wounded worse abed. Ah, well, if he is so lighthearted it will be like last spring in the north. I do not know why I went to the trouble of gathering troops.'

But it became more and more apparent that this was to be no repetition of the rising in the north. Henry was determined to fight. No pardon was offered now to those who would throw down their arms, and the king spoke to his council only of tactics and weapons and discipline. They had to wait three days at Leicester for parts of the eastern and western forces to join them, and two days at Loughborough for Guildford to remount some of the guns that were not travelling well. At Nottingham there was good news. The cities of Lancashire and Yorkshire were closing their gates, refusing to supply the false Warwick's army, and the people of the countryside were fleeing into the cities rather than join the pretender's force.

'They will soon starve,' Bedford said with satisfaction. 'Let us sit here and wait.'

But Henry retained his superstitious fear of Nottingham, and the next day the host moved on to Newark. Here there was more good news. The northern shires had not only refused to join the invading forces but were rallying to the king. From Northumberland, Cumberland, and Yorkshire the English Borderers came, leading their hard-bitten troops. They were few in number, barbarously dressed and armed, but rich with experience of endless raising by and against the Scots. Now

292

Henry was ready to drive westward and cut off the invaders, but he found it was not necessary.

Lincoln and Lovell, hoping to take the king by surprise, had come very swiftly east. It was not easy, however, to take by surprise anyone with as good an intelligence force as Foxe had established. It was as if Henry 'was in his bosom and knew every hour what the earl did'. When the pretender's army tried to reach the great Fosse Way which led south from Newark, they found the royal force blocking their path. Henry was delighted to hear that they had come to him. His army was well-rested and well-provisioned. When he led them to battle the next morning they would be fresh and well-fed. It could not have been better planned had he done it himself.

At the council called that night, however, it did not seem to Bedford that Henry was being reasonable about this battle. It would be better, of course, if they won it; but it would not be a major tragedy if they lost. Both Edward IV and Henry VI had lost battles without losing the crown. Richard III's loss was only fatal, Bedford explained patiently, because he, himself, was killed. Whatever the outcome, Henry should not involve himself personally. The king listened politely; he always listened politely to advice, and sometimes he even took it. In this case he shook his head.

'It will not happen often that I come to battle in my own person, but when I do I will win or die. It is foolish, perhaps, to discuss this matter before a battle in which the victory is so certainly ours. Nonetheless it should be said that when I am present the principle of running away so that one may fight another day is abrogated. The man who runs away from any field I am on will be my murderer as surely as if he struck the blow himself.'

'No man of us will leave the field while you are on it, sire, and I for one will not leave it at all until your voice commands me to do so,' Oxford said.

'So say we all,' came the murmur around the table.

'Let us hope, then,' Henry replied merrily, 'that I do not lose my voice shouting commands, for this will be a barren place – and noisome, too – for a victory celebration. Will you accept a note in my hand, Oxford, if my voice fails?' He paused to let the laugh die, and then continued seriously, 'Look you, they cannot win. Only two thousand are decently armed or trained. The others are barbarians, wild and ungovernable, ill-armed. They may be brave, but they will be useless.'

'What arrangements shall I make for prisoners?' Edgecombe asked.

To the universal surprise, Henry turned pale and seemed to lose his confidence. He looked around the table at his council as if for help, but before anyone could respond his lips thinned into an ugly line. 'None. There are to be no prisoners. No quarter is to be given except for Linclon. Every effort is to be made to take him alive. I intend to find out from him who was part of this conspiracy.'

There was a moment of shocked silence. In the past the council had struggled against Henry's leniency. They scarcely knew how to protest against this complete reversal of policy.

'Is this not a little hard, Your Grace?' Jasper asked.

'I am always "Your Grace" when you are displeased with me, uncle, I know, but this is not wanton cruelty – I hope. We have now a remarkable opportunity to accomplish a multiplicity of purposes. Think first of the effect on the country if these rebels are slain to a man. Who will be tempted to rebel again? At the same time, we can arouse little hatred amongst our own people by this slaughter for these are not Englishmen with brothers or cousins among our own forces. They are foreign mercenaries and Irish barbarians, unconnected to our folk. Third, think of the effect on the Irish, who set out so bravely to plunder or conquer England, when their great army does not return – or perhaps a man or two to tell a tale of English invincibility. When next I send a lord deputy to Ireland, they will come on bended knee and kiss his hand.'

Smiles flashed round the table; heads were shaken in mute admiration. Henry never forgot anything, never permitted passion to sway him. Never had there been such a king.

'Now, the order of battle,' Henry continued. 'There is no need for much prearrangement for we know not what they will do. Oxford will take the first shock. Devon and Nottingham will hold the flanks. When the time is ripe, I will give order that Devon and Nottingham encircle for the kill. When the reserve is needed, it will come in with Bedford as leader. Understood? Very well, let us to our beds. Tomorrow we will have them.'

'One thing more, Harry.'

294

'Yes, uncle?'

'We think one or perhaps two other men should wear your colours and arms as like to yours as possible. Remember how Richard charged at Bosworth.' Henry considered for a moment and then shook his head negatively. 'Harry,' Jasper said sharply, 'it is better to be a live king than a dead hero.'

'I am no hero,' Henry laughed, 'as you all well know. If any one of you around this table could wear my clothes, I would agree. In fact, I have seldom regretted my lack of girth and inches more, for such a device would give me much freedom of movement. Not one of you could be mistaken for me, even in the heat of batttle. Every man is a head too tall or a yard too wide. Who else dare I trust with such a thing?'

They suggested this and argued that, but at last Henry's viewpoint prevailed. The meeting was ended, but Ned Poynings remained behind as the others rose to go. Henry looked at him, looked aside, and forced a smile.

'Are you checking on your investment in head and livelihood, Ned?'

Poynings laughed. 'In a way I am, I suppose. I wish to ask a favour.'

'Ask.'

'I wish to be your standard-bearer.'

'No!' Henry paled again. 'William was cut down because he had no way to guard himself and would not loose the pennon. No. I cannot spare you, Ned. I cannot.'

'I am no hero, either, sire, but I have a reason. I heard a most interesting tale this afternoon. One of the yeomen came most anxiously to me and asked where you were going all unguarded towards the enemy host. I, having but that instant left your chamber, told him to mend his eyesight and that you were within. He insisted, however, that a man of your looks, manner, and bearing had left the city.'

'Were extra suits of my colour ordered?'

'Aye, two. They are still here. I checked at once, but if the tailor knew the style and manner of the emblem, what should stop him from designing still another suit?'

'What indeed? Well, there is nothing to be done.'

'We could find out from the tailor.'

'Which tailor? Do you expect me to put twenty men and all their assistants on the rack to discover if one extra suit of

295

colours was made? Do you think whoever ordered the work done came himself to do so? And what if the same man did not make all three, but three men one each, or no tailor we used but some private person did the work? There is not time enough in this one night. To ferret out such answers needs days or weeks, not hours. No, let it go.'

'Then will you let me hold the pennon? If another Henry should appear and the standard-bearer grow confused—'

'No, Ned,' Henry said softly. 'If I have another fear or another worry, I will run mad. I could not bear it. I would see you lying dead like William. I will give the banner to John Cheney. After dressing me and undressing me, he is not like to take me for another. Besides, if they have another "king" will they not have another dragon also?'

Chapter Twenty-one

Messengers rode in every half hour through the night to report on the movement of the false Warwick's army, but it lay quietly encamped and no one needed to wake the king until the time he had ordered. The force was still encamped when Henry rose at dawn, heard two masses, and marched his men to Stoke, a small village about a mile from Newark. It was certain from this position that they would intercept Lincoln, Lovell, and their pawn unless they retreated.

The royal army was drawn up into its usual three battalions. Oxford commanded the main force, with Devon and Nottingham to support him, while the reserves held the men of doubtful loyalty mixed with some who were fanatically devoted to the king. It was the best arrangement that Henry could make to ensure against treachery. He had placed in command the formidable Bedford, who would not hesitate an instant to order the loyal troops to kill any man who seemed about to falter. Jasper did not like it because he did not like to be separated from Henry, but he understood the necessity and made no protest. The king, surrounded by the faithful group which had come from France with him, was slightly to the rear. The fact that there was no sufficiently rising ground had forced him to take a position a good deal closer to the actual battle lines than he had at Bosworth.

He had to be seen and to make his orders known, of course, but his station made Jasper even more acutely uncomfortable. To his mind, Henry was strangely excited. The king did not seem to be fearful or bad tempered, but he was certainly under more tension than appeared in him at Bosworth. He seemed much concerned that the invaders would not fight, and all he spoke of to his captains before they separated was the need to engage. In fact, Henry was very nearly out of control. The battle had become an obsession with him. He was convinced that if he won, the beloved son who gurgled at him so lovingly would cease to appear with a dead, bloated horror as a secondary image.

297

The battle, like Bosworth, had begun with the crash of Guildford's guns. Like Bosworth, too, there was no answering crash, but Henry took little joy in the swaths cut in his enemies' ranks or in their cries and waverings. For once he had a desire to fight hand-to-hand on his own. His months of fear and frustration had risen to a crescendo, which could only be satisfied by violence. He was also concerned that the enemy would break and run, being largely undisciplined barbarians, that he would be denied the bloodbath he craved personally and politically, and that the invaders would spread through the land spreading sedition with them.

Long before the proper effect had been achieved by the bombardment, Henry had sent a curt order to Guildford to raise the muzzles and concentrate his fire upon the reserves. That action was Oxford's sign to advance and, if he thought the time of firing short, he did not question it. The king had ordered it; there must be some reason he could not see from his position. A glance right and left across his line. All was right. 'Archers!' he bellowed, and the cloud of deadly wasps rose humming. Shields went up along the line as the volley was returned. The pennant with its streaming star was shaken out and surged forward.

Henry edged closer. The household guard obediently followed. Those who knew the king were surprised, for he had not shown the slightest inclination to join the fighting at Bosworth. He had been courageous enough when the battle was brought to him, but his tendency was to direct, not to engage. Now the signs were plain on him: flushed face, eager eyes, the hand that crept to the sword hilt and was pulled away. Henry knew that what he desired was foolish. If a chance arrow should strike him, the battle would be over regardless of strength, skill, or superiority in his forces. Still he moved closer. The exchange of arrows was nearly over and Oxford's men were fighting hand-to-hand up and down the line. John de Vere himself struck out mightily, bellowing encouragement and orders whenever he cleared a space and had time for them.

Personal bravery and encouragement notwithstanding, Oxford's men were no more than holding their own. The line wavered forward then back. The accursed German mercenaries were fighting not only with precision but with a determination Henry had not expected of men who were paid by the day like

298

labourers. The Irish, too, although ill-armed and paying a heavy toll for it, showed a stubborn bravery. At the moment the virtue was lost upon Henry who cursed them aloud. To the right and left, Devon and Nottingham were less engaged. Henry felt like cursing them, too, but he knew their tactics were correct and what he had ordered. The enemy showed no signs of panic or breaking. Their force was still far too large to be encircled and too great a pressure on the flanks might buckle Oxford's line.

A quick glance at the sun told of an hour's fighting. An hour, and they had not gained a foot. The streaming star still waved bravely, but it had stalled. Oxford could not advance and he would not retreat. If Henry could have reached his hair, he would have torn it with the agony of his desire to throw himself forward and end the stalemate. He actually raised a hand to his helmet as if his head hurt him. Cheney, bearing the red dragon standard, pressed closer to see his master's face. It had not changed except that the eyes were madder, more eager. The knowledge that his personal entrance into the battle would be more a danger than a help to his army had less and less power to hold Henry back. He wanted – more than he had wanted anything except to be king – to strike with his own hands, to kill those who threatened his child.

Then Oxford's banner dipped. Henry did not care that it might merely be the effect of the standard-bearer dodging a blow or that, even if he were wounded or killed, someone else would snatch up the banner. With a scream of joy he drew his sword. 'Forward!' The household guard with their retinues, the yeomen of the guard, and a troop of Londoners, above five hundred men in all, followed. They crashed into the lines. Henry's sword swung and bit and the scream of the wounded man tore loose the remaining strands that anchored the Tudor to sanity. He was not conscious of the men fighting to keep beside him, exposing their own bodies to shield his. He only knew that he could strike and strike, that his sword grew red, that screams followed his blows.

The duke of Bedford watched with bulging eyes. He had cried out with fear when he saw his nephew charge, and now he bit a bloody gash in his lip as he fought the impulse to follow him into the fray. He was an old soldier and he knew his duty. What had driven Henry to such an act of madness he could not guess, but it was certainly not tactical considerations. To bring in the reserve at this moment would be madder than what Henry had done. He fought back tears, not because he was ashamed to weep but because he had to watch the rather small figure in green and white and could not allow his vision to be misted.

'Harry, Harry,' he muttered, 'Harry, be careful! Watch what you are about. Guard yourself. Child of my heart, oh God, protect him.'

But Henry felt perfectly capable of protecting himself. His charge had done some good, the shock forcing back Lincoln's men and giving breathing space to Oxford's. It had not broken the enemy, however. They closed their ranks and held, but not as firmly as they had before. Here and there a bulge of the Tudor's men pressed forward, and at the head of one such bulge, Henry fought with a ferocity foreign to his nature — blind, deaf, and desiring only to kill and kill and kill.

Lord de Broke, Poynings, Cheney, and, surprisingly, the earl of Surrey fought beside him desperately. Cheney, hampered by the standard, had enough to do to protect it and himself. Lord de Broke followed fanatically wherever Henry went. If the king wished to go forward, forward they would go, whether it was reasonable or not. Surrey, personally knowing little of the Tudor, was fired by admiration. He had not thought that the quiet, studious monarch, always surrounded by papers, always concerned with personal adornment, had this fire. He warded blow after blow from Henry's body with steadily deepening appreciation of his bravery, although he could not greatly commend his fighting skills. He had never doubted the Tudor's wisdom; now he would never doubt his courage again. If Henry did not fight, Surrey thought, it was because it was wiser not to fight, not because Henry was afraid. Edward Poynings alone had a glimmer of what drove the king. He would, if he could, have stopped him, but he was far too busy keeping Henry and himself alive to speak or try to manoeuvre.

Forward again, still forward. Shaking with terror, Jasper moved the reserves closer. If Henry did not stop, he would be encircled by the enemy. What was wrong with him? On the flanks, Devon and Nottingham had not seen the sudden charge. They knew the king was engaged because they could see his standard in the thick of the press, but neither would believe that the cautious Henry, who remembered everything, would have gone into battle without leaving orders for them. Both knew it was time to begin the flanking movements, but each hesitated because their orders were to wait for Henry's command. All three strained their eyes, watching for a gesture from the king or for a messenger riding towards them. It was growing harder and harder to separate Henry from all the men – friend and enemy – around him. He was small to begin with, and his colours became more and more smirched with dirt and blood as he penetrated deeper into the enemy lines.

'Harry,' Jasper groaned. The standard was there. Foot by foot it still moved forward, but as far as Jasper could see the king was gone. He remembered suddenly with an even greater thrill of terror that John Cheney was the kind that became drunk with fighting. He had charged, against the king's orders, at Bosworth. What if Henry was no longer near the banner? What if Cheney had forgotten that his first duty was to stay by the king so that the men would know where to rally? What if Henry were alone on the field?

'Harry, come back!' he screamed suddenly.

Far off to the right – a lone figure in green and white, unhelmed to show golden hair whipped by the wind – was fleeing away, galloping off the battlefield.

'The Tudor flies!'

'The king flees!'

'Henry the bastard runs from us!'

The cries rose from every quarter of the field, and the royal army wavered, hesitating whether to strike again or take to their heels. In the few seconds of relative quiet, Jasper's agonized scream pierced the blood-stained mist in Henry's mind.

'Harry, come back!'

'I am here,' he called, raising his bloody sword, but he was small and his voice was not loud.

'The king is here!' A voice like a trumpet rang out, as Surrey let loose the power of his lusty lungs. 'Here in the midst of his enemies! To the king! To the king! Here! Here!'

'Devon! Nottingham! Forward!'

Henry wondered whether his voice would reach them, whether others would take up the cry. He could send no messenger. There was not a man around him that he dared part with because he had so few. A fine mess he had gotten himself into, he thought, but he had no time for self-blame. The pretender's forces had taken heart and the royal ones were shaken. It was most necessary to address himself to staying alive.

On the evening of June 17th, the king's wife and mother sat silently together in the garden of Kenilworth Castle. They did not sit together for comfort, for to each other they had no comfort to offer. They said nothing to each other, for neither had anything left to say. That morning a scrawled note in Henry's hand informed them that battle would be joined on the sixteenth. They knew the battle had already been won or lost, but they did not know which. Margaret's strength was exhausted. She had prayed until her mind was blank, and now she sat with the slow tears streaking her cheeks, indifferent to everything but her own agony.

Elizabeth had been no help to Margaret and no good to herself. She only struggled for composure in Henry's presence. When he was not there to be protected, Elizabeth gave way without reserve to her fears. She had been embroidering new cuffs for the white gloves Henry had ruined hawking when the message came, and she had thrown the gloves away and fallen into screaming hysterics. It had taken her ladies an hour to calm her, and the fit had returned on and off all day until she was so exhausted her breathing had appeared to fail and she had nearly choked. That had frightened her even more, not that she feared to die but that she feared to leave Arthur without any protection. She began to struggle to control herself, concentrating on drawing one breath and then another.

The next messenger was brought into the quiet garden supported in the guardsmen's arms. He was dirty and bloodied, his arms and armour cast away.

'The battle is lost,' he sobbed, 'lost. The king is fled. Save yourself, madam. Take your son and fly to sanctuary.'

Margaret cried out, but Elizabeth sat still as death. She drew another careful breath. 'What did you say – about the king, not about the battle?'

'The king is fled to save his life. All is lost.'

'Take this man and put him in prison,' Elizabeth said quietly to the frightened guardsmen. 'Hold him full straitly, chained,

302

and with a man to guard him also. He lies. To lie on such a matter is high treason, and the king will desire to know who set him to speak treason.'

The guardsmen were less tender as they dragged the messenger out, and also more grim and less alarmed.

'Well done, Elizabeth,' Margaret whispered shakily. 'Oh, well done. Now what shall we do? The world is overturned. Even the Bible is reversed. Now the mother-in-law says to her husband's wife "Whither thou goest, I shall go." Where shall we go, Elizabeth?'

'Go?' Elizabeth asked, breathing carefully. 'We will bide still here until word comes from Harry. The man did lie.'

'Such things happen.' Margaret had lived through news of lost battles that seemed just as incredible as this.

'Not to Henry.' Elizabeth looked into her mother-in-law's frightened eyes. 'I have not lost my wits. A lost battle could happen to Henry, but he would not have fled the field. If I were told that the battle was lost and the king was dead – that I would believe, but Henry would not run. He has had sufficient of that in the past. He would rather die.'

Margaret covered her face with her hands. 'Pray God you are right. In faith, I think you know my son better than I know him myself.'

Night fell, candles were lighted in the queen's chamber. Very quietly some of her clothing and jewels were packed. Charles Brandon, Buckingham, and Arthur were put to sleep in her bedchamber. To disbelieve was reasonable; but it was also necessary to be ready if the news was bad. The hours crawled. Midnight, one of the clock, two of the clock – nearly three it was before the women tensed at the sound of spurs clinking in the passageway.

'Lord Willoughby de Broke,' the guard announced.

He entered smiling, but his expression changed to astonishment when Margaret and Elizabeth burst into loud weeping at the sight of him. 'Madam! Your Grace! The news is good! It could not be better. We have destroyed their entire army. Lincoln and the Irishman are dead. The false Warwick is taken. The king is safe. I pray you, do not weep.'

And to his greater astonishment, the queen whom he had always believed disliked him, flew out of her chair and kissed him all over his sweaty face.

'Your Grace,' he cried, recoiling.

But retreat was impossible. He was grasped by the hand and pushed into a chair by a glowing Elizabeth who laughed and wept at once. The king's mother herself poured wine and pressed it upon him. The queen took his hat and gloves from his nerveless fingers. Together they would have knelt to unfasten his spurs and pull off his boots with their own hands except that his horror of such an act restrained them.

'Tell us, tell us,' they cried in chorus, and drew up chairs themselves, too impatient to wait for the servants to help them, so that they could sit almost knee to knee with him.

'Madam. Your Grace,' de Broke stammered, 'I am no teller of tales. It was a hard-fought battle, that I say. Harder than we thought it would be. And it was the king in his own person who won it. He was like a lion. Oxford was stalled. The Germans and the Irish fought bravely. They were our enemies, but no man can deny their courage. It was the king who broke the battle. When our troops could not win forward, His Grace charged himself. Then they tried to trick us. One dressed like unto His Grace fled and many cried out of that, but Surrey cried out that the king was still fighting, and I knew it for I was with him the whole time, and then – we won.'

Margaret and Elizabeth laughed and cried again. Lord de Broke certainly was no teller of tales, but he had greater comfort for them. Henry expected to be home by the next day or the day after that at the latest, and they knew they would have a clearer recounting from him.

The battle of Stoke – the last full-scale battle of the Wars of the Roses – was over. Henry was regarded with even greater admiration by his friends while his enemies drew in their horns, accepting the fact that the king was temporarily invincible. All expected his customary leniency; they were mistaken. Every man who had been on the field at Stoke and was caught was slaughtered. Then Henry came home and tried to wash the blood from his body and his memory. But he was not finished. He had determined to teach his people a lesson. After a few days' rest at Kenilworth, the king travelled north and like an avenging angel turned his attention to those who had not responded to his summons. All men who could not show proof that they had contributed in some way to his struggle were

304

pulled from their houses, sometimes from their beds, and questioned. Henry was still squeamish. Little blood flowed, but money from fines poured into his treasury. He would not wait until the customs and other revenues had replenished his capital. He would make more than political profit out of this rebellion. When he was through, he would be rich and the rebellious would be too poor to rebel again. To friend and foe alike he said the same thing.

'Once I forgave and I gave warning. I will never forgive – not even simple disobedience – again. Never again.'

Only to the false Warwick, whose name they now knew to be Lambert Simnel, the son of an Oxford tradesman, was Henry softer. And even that had its purpose. He listened to the young man's story, to the tale of the bad priest Symonds who had seen in him a resemblance to the Yorkist rulers and had therefore taught him manners and speech above his station, who had convinced him he would be gloriously rewarded by the real Warwick, who had forced him between flattery and threats into the imposture.

'The masters of Ireland,' Henry had laughed, 'they will crown apes at last.'

He made sure that many heard him, and when the masters of Ireland came to wait on him humbly, two years later, he summoned Lambert Simnel from the kitchen and bade him serve them wine, and repeated his remark to their faces.

Simnel was pardoned; he was taken into the king's service – to become a turnspit in the kitchen, a laughable object for display to others who considered rebellion. Symonds, his evil genius, was handed over to Canterbury – for only the Church had jurisdiction over a priest. In this case Henry had no fault to find with the system. When John Morton was through with Symonds, he would have wished for the king's justice to have had him many times over – the king was a good deal more squeamish, at his worst, than John Morton.

It was a long, hard summer and autumn, but when the writs summoning parliament went out on September 1st the men who received them came quickly. They came humbly with bowed heads, knowing that on November 9th whatever the king asked, suggested, or even hinted would be given without a single dissenting voice. Henry was the absolute master of his kingdom. Whatever of the Yorkist nobility and squirearchy he had not previously won to his side by his energy and clemency, he had now cowed by cold severity.

The treatment that Henry used was particularly effective. No hot passions were aroused by the cruelty of executions. No sympathy was drawn to a victim stripped naked of his lands, exiled, or left starving. Whoever had flouted Henry's orders became pitiful, yes, but a pitiful laughingstock for his property was left to him, as were the means of redeeming his position in the future. The fines were carefully adjusted so that a man, mortgaging what he had up to the hilt, could pay without being destroyed. Such a man could be accounted a fool by his more loyal neighbours, could arouse a rich sense of caution in them, without creating sensations of horror.

'And I cannot tell,' Henry laughed – the day after he had entered London with the usual triumph and was sitting in council with his financial advisers – 'why any king has ever been stupid enough to lop off his subjects' heads. What profit can be made from a dead man? And do not tell me I would then have the lands as my own. Would it not cost me to run the property – for overseers, labourers, repairs? Would I not have to support the widow and children? Here I am with a fine, clear profit' – Henry glanced fondly at the fat tally sheets which lay on the table – 'while the victim of my pruning will be kept so busy saving his property from the moneylenders that he will not have time to hate me or to trouble about politics.'

'Very true, sire. Now, about the use of this gold. Some should be kept in reserve; but the remainder might well be invested in shipping, in which Your Grace seems interested and which is a great good to the realm. Now I have here—'

Henry sighed, rested his head on his hand, and let his mind wander. Usually he was keenly interested in anything to do with money, but just now he was in a holiday mood. He was thinking of his reception by the Londoners, which had been loud and joyous, and of his reception by Elizabeth, which had been quieter but equally joyous. Arthur, too, had greeted him; Henry laughed involuntarily and had to excuse himself to Dynham who looked surprised and a trifle affronted. Arthur had thrown a block of wood at his fond father's head, shrieking with joy, and when Henry had lifted him to kiss, had wet his somewhat less fond father all down his doublet and hose.

Margaret had been there, too, but in a more serious mood

306

than the others. First she had told him she was retiring to Richmond again.

'But why, mother?'

'For your purposes, because I wish to. My other reasons are my own affair,' she replied tartly. 'But before I go, I wish to speak to you about Elizabeth.'

'What about Bess?' Henry asked, his voice a trace cooler.

Margaret had stared at her son, startled, and then laughed in his face. 'It is time for you to eat some words, Henry. I have heard it rumoured that you said Elizabeth would never be crowned. I thought until this moment that you still mistrusted her, but if you are willing to snap at me in her defence, you are merely being stubborn. It is not just to wound Elizabeth's pride to salve your own.'

'I had not thought of it that way. I suppose I did not think much about the question. Elizabeth has never asked to be crowned.'

'Well, you had better think about it. Do you think it would be to a proud woman's taste to ask for what she is certain would be refused?'

So while Dynham suggested the building of ships of his own and Henry agreed, giving enough of his mind to the subject now to appoint Reginald Bray and Guildford to be responsible for the construction, the other part of his mind considered crowning Elizabeth. He found a strange reluctance in himself to do it, and he worried away at the feeling on and off throughout the day. Did he distrust her any longer? Nonsense. Her love for him was unquestionable, and the few times he had offered her the exercise of a shred of political power she had fled the suggestion. In fact, the only duties Elizabeth ever tried to shirk were political ones, and the only times she ever seemed to be bored by Henry were the occasions when he was so absorbed in an affair of state that he tried to talk to her about it.

That might be partly policy, in that she could have grown interested if he had urged her to apply herself. She could speak with intelligence about music, art, literature, and even philosophy. Henry assumed correctly that Elizabeth understood his jealousy of his power and had closed her mind to state affairs. He tried to think objectively about the subject, and decided that he preferred things the way they were. After dealing with statesmen all day long, to have to go to bed with one would be too much. No, Elizabeth would never contest his power. She had made that plain by her voluntary mental withdrawal. Why then should she not be queen if she desired it?

Was it because the people loved her too much and he was jealous? Perhaps. The thought of the people made Henry more uncomfortable. In fact, it was during a discussion with Morton of the public celebrations over the victory at Stoke that Henry found the answer. Public celebrations were beginning to bore him, and he rather resented having to exhibit himself like a trained bear. He did it without protest and always would do it because the king's person was a public property to some extent. That was it! The queen, too, would belong partly to the people, and Henry discovered that he did not wish to share his wife with the dirty, yelling crowds.

But if Elizabeth wished it? At that point Morton reproved the king gently for not paying attention, and Henry apologized to him, also, thinking irritably that if he did not soon settle the matter he would end by offending every minister he had. Having agreed rather hastily to everything Morton proposed, Henry rid himself of Morton's company and retired to his closet. It was here that he was forced to acknowledge humbly that what Elizabeth desired had never been very important to him. Other things always came first – his needs, his country's needs. The crowning was basically of no real significance. Could he not please her in this when in so many other things he could not even consider her? Well, he could!

Greatly relieved, Henry turned his attention to the piles of bills being drafted for the session of parliament which would meet in four days. He read thoroughly, making notes of amendments and comment in the margin in his careful handwriting until the dinner hour. Elizabeth sat beside him in high beauty and good humour, but somehow it was not the right time or place to introduce the subject. Henry gave himself with pleasure to listening to her domestic anecdotes, laughing heartily at the exploits of the obstreperous Charles Brandon and the so-far ineffectual efforts of his own son who seemed to be trying to emulate that outrageous young man's behaviour.

'I wish this accursed parliament were over,' Elizabeth said suddenly.

'Why?' Henry asked in surprise.

308

'Because you look so tired, and you work harder than ever during the session. How you can read all those, dull endless arguments and bills, I do not know.'

'They may be endless, but I do not find them dull.'

'You say you do not because you are determined to have your finger in every pie. Will you at least come and listen to some music this evening, Harry? I have come across a child that plays the recorder like an angel.'

About to agree, Henry thought of Dynham and Lovell and Edgecombe and Morton and all the others who had proposed bills and expected to have their work commented upon so that they could draft final measures.

'I cannot, Bess. After the session opens, perhaps I will have more freedom.'

'You sound like a prisoner instead of a king.'

'A king is a kind of prisoner – if he is a good king. But do not waste your sympathy upon me, Bess. I love my confinement.' He kissed her cheek and rose. 'I will come tonight, as always.'

After dinner Henry saw the French ambassador, who gave him indigestion, and then Maximillian's envoy, who made him bilious. By the time he returned to his closet, he was more than ready to agree to increase the appropriations requested for renewing and adding to the defences of Calais and Berwick. The warm feeling of satisfaction he had felt at setting aside his own preferences to please Elizabeth had evaporated. He had made up his mind to have her crowned, and he would stick to the decision; but he resented it.

When Henry had twice read through a bill, submitted by Dynham concerning stabilization of the currency, without understanding one word, he cursed his faithful treasurer for an idiot. But when he had done the same with a letter from Foxe, who was in Scotland conducting a delicate and complicated negotiation, and could not make sense of it, he began to suspect that he and not his ministers was at fault. Henry considered joining his gentlemen. He knew he would merely make them uncomfortable in this humour, but that would not have stopped him if he thought snapping at them would make him feel any better. It was both too late and too early to join Elizabeth, so he changed into his bedrobe and slippers and sat down to while away the time with something that would require no thought.

A glance around the table solved the problem at once. He could check through Elizabeth's privy purse accounts.

Twenty minutes later Henry erupted suddenly into his wife's bedchamber where she was having her hair brushed before retiring. 'Elizabeth, what the devil is this?' he asked, thrusting a page of the account book under her nose.

She withdrew her head to where her eyes would focus. 'My account book,' she replied mischievously.

'Get out,' Henry snarled, and the ladies fled. He shook the book in Elizabeth's face. 'These items. What do they mean?'

The lines he pointed to read: 'Item, for mending Her Grace's gown, 5d. Item, for turning Her Grace's blue gown anew, 2s.'

Plainly Henry was spoiling for a fight and equally plainly he could find no serious cause to be cross with her. Elizabeth considered whether it would be better to calm him or provoke him, found herself in too gay a mood for soothing, and decided for provocation.

'Would you have me wear a gown with holes – or one frayed at the sleeves and seams?' she asked.

Henry threw the book violently on the floor. 'If your privy purse is not sufficient to provide you with a new gown, why do you not say so? I do not condone extravagance, but the queen of England must be decently garbed.'

Because Henry was so careful in administering his moneys and so eager in collecting more, he was getting the reputation of a miser. Although he knew that what he did was necessary for the security of the throne and reason forbade him to change his ways, he was growing sensitive about the allegation. Elizabeth knew the reputation was false. Henry was as lavish in expenditure as he was assiduous in collection, and he had always been most generous to her. Still, he demanded an accounting for every penny, which Elizabeth found annoying, so she could not forbear teasing him when she found a weak chink in his self-possession.

'But Harry,' she said gravely, 'you know how confused the management of money makes me. If you give me more, I will but grow more confused.'

'What do you want me to do, hand you a few pence a day from my purse as I do for Charles? You do not attend properly. You tell this one to buy a thing and that one to give a beggar a coin, and you never make a note of it or remember to tell your clerk. What have you an almoner and a chamberlain for?'

To hide the fact that she was laughing, Elizabeth bent her head. Henry saw her shoulders shaking. He bit his lip and spoke in a much softer voice.

'This is all nothing to the point. Do you need money now, my dear?'

It was too bad of her to tease him when he was so tired and so kind. 'Nay, I have sufficient. Those items are a mere chance, my love. I trod a hole in a new gown when we danced one night. Do you not remember? And the blue gown is a favourite – I cannot part with it. I wear it only to play with the children and suchlike. Dear Harry, I am sorry I made you cross. I will try to pay more mind to my accounts.'

Henry came up behind her and put his hand under her hair on her throat. 'You keep one thing at a time in your mind, do you not, Bess? Did you hear what I called you?'

'Called me?' she asked vaguely. He was naked under the bedgown and ready. He had not really come to quarrel, she thought.

'I called you queen of England. When would you like to have the coronation, Bess?'

Elizabeth jumped to her feet with wide eyes. 'But Henry—' She did not want to be crowned queen!

Thinking he was forestalling a long explanation of his past fears that could only hurt her, Henry said quickly, 'I desire it greatly. It is right for a crowned king to have a crowned queen.'

It was a symbol Elizabeth could not refuse. Henry was trying to give her all he had to give. She had long had his body and his heart. Now he was yielding her his trust and his faith. Elizabeth curtsied to the ground and kissed her husband's hand.

Author's Notes

Henry VII's life falls into three distinct sections that might be called the dangerous years, the bright years, and the dark years. This novel covers only the dangerous years when Henry fought to stay alive and to establish himself on the throne of England. In matters of known fact, the novel is as accurate as possible. Although the conversations and the emotions accredited to the characters are mostly fictional, the personalities are as close to the truth as the author can come by estimation of their acts as recorded in history, comments upon them by their contemporaries, and, where available, their biographies.

The treatment of Richard III is an exception; he has been sadly maligned, but the opinions stated about him are those of the characters, who were his enemies, not those of the author. In fact, Henry VII revised his own opinion of Richard when, in later years, he was driven into one similar cruelty by the pressure of circumstances. He displayed his mute apology to his predecessor on the throne by raising a magnificent tomb over Richard's hitherto neglected grave.

This brings the author to the objections that knowledgeable readers may make to the favourable light in which Henry VII is portrayed. Usually he is considered a dour, avaricious, heartless monarch of gloomy, suspicious disposition who mistreated his wife, loved no one, and was himself unloved. Indeed, this is the light in which he was considered by Francis Bacon, and most authors have merely repeated that great biographer's viewpoint. Any serious investigation of the original sources gives the lie immediately to this interpretation of Henry VII's character. The letters that have been preserved from and to his wife and mother make clear the tender affection both these ladies had for him, and that he returned their love in full measure. His eldest daughter, Margaret, after she had been married to James IV of Scotland, wrote to her father that though she was well treated she wished she was 'with him now and many times more'.

It is true that Henry VII's character darkened with the years.

His early experience with enmity and poverty made him both avaricious and suspicious, and these qualities increased with age. He was, however, neither a miser nor a murderer. He spent lavishly, and his reign was stained only by the political murder of the earl of Warwick – a peccadillo compared with the bloodletting (however necessary) of Richard III and that (however unnecessary) of his own son Henry VIII. (In fact, Henry VIII used the headsman's axe with a frequency that must have made his father turn, shuddering, in his grave.)

There is much to excuse Henry VII's increasing coldness in his later years. His warmth had always been reserved for those close to him and, one by one, they dropped away. His beloved uncle, Jasper, duke of Bedford, died in 1495, and in 1502 and 1503 two tragedies, major because they were unexpected, marked him permanently. Arthur, his eldest son, died suddenly only five months after his marriage to Catherine of Aragon, and Elizabeth, Henry's white rose, died in childbirth when she tried to make the succession secure by giving him another son to replace Arthur. The infant, a daughter, followed her mother to the grave after only five days. Perhaps Henry felt he had murdered Elizabeth; perhaps he felt the deaths of his dear ones were retribution – he was both religious and superstitious – for the execution of Warwick, who was certainly blameless of any crime but the political crime of being born. In any case, 1503 marks the end of the bright years and a decided change for the worse in Henry's personality.

In addition, the last years of Henry VII's life were made miserable by ill health. Whether he had, as some authors have suggested, tuberculosis of the bone, or whether he was merely arthritic, cannot now be determined. What is sure is that Henry VII suffered continuous and excruciating physical pain for many years in a period when analgesics were unknown. In spite of this, he remained a tender father – as witnessed by reports from various foreign envoys. Unlike Henry VIII, who turned on his friends and even on his own children when they failed to grant his desires, Henry VII was invariably loyal. He did not punish his ministers when his diplomacy went awry nor his commanding officers for land or naval battle losses. He became financially tighter and lost control of his temper, but the number of executions did not increase and those who served him well were rewarded adequately, if not with the foolish

314

lavishness that nearly bankrupted the crown under Henry VIII.

In essentials Henry VII did not change in spite of personal grief and physical agony. Gladys Temperly says:

The old picture of the harsh and sinister despot gives way to that of a king who was both kindly and considerate. He admitted his subjects to intimate personal relations and gave ear to their petitions. To take at random from a month of his life: he dealt with the woes of a disappointed lover, deceived by the 'nygromancer' who had promised to help him to the woman he desired, he gave his protection to the wife of a lunatic, and interfered to protect a nun who had suffered ill-usage. He did not forget his schoolmaster or the son of his old nurse. We find him giving £1 'to one that was hurt with a gunne' and so forth.

He was not difficult to approach, and as he journied through his kingdom came into contact with many of his poorer subjects. Thus we hear of him drinking ale in a farmer's house, stopping to watch the reapers in a field and giving them a tip of 2s....

Henry was an ardent sportsman, and took every opportunity of getting away from the cares of state for a few weeks hunting. . . . He jousted, shot at the butts, played tennis, dice, cards, and 'chequer board', was interested in bull-baiting, bear-baiting, and cock-fighting. Besides splendid tournaments, banquets, and 'goodly disguisings', we hear of 'plays in the White Hall'. . . .

In other words, Henry VII, a remarkable king, was truly a man of his own time. He continued to love music, although he could no longer dance, and sports, although he could no longer participate. Last and not least, he struggled unremittingly to keep his nation prosperous and free of war – a most enlightened attitude.

Henry VII well deserves to be remembered in a kindlier personal light than that Bacon has cast upon him, although Bacon does full justice to his genius as a king. J. D. Mackie points out, 'True it is that there were flaws in Henry's character.' But he adds, as the conclusion to his chapters on Henry VII, 'He has some claim to be regarded as the greatest of the Tudors.'

Select Genealogy of Lancaster and York

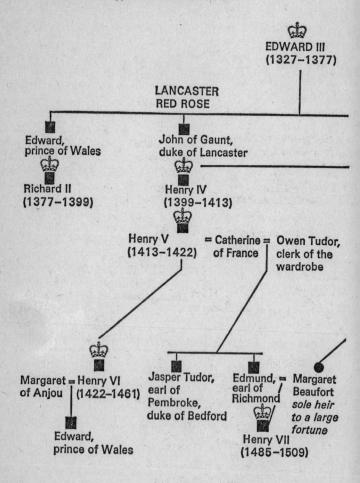

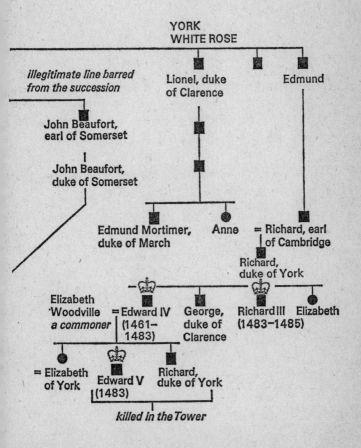

YORK
WHITE ROSE

illegitimate line barred
from the succession

Lionel, duke
of Clarence

Edmund

John Beaufort,
earl of Somerset

John Beaufort,
duke of Somerset

Edmund Mortimer,
duke of March

Anne

= Richard, earl
of Cambridge

Richard,
duke of York

Elizabeth
Woodville
a commoner

= Edward IV
(1461–
1483)

George,
duke of
Clarence

Richard III
(1483–1485)

Elizabeth

= Elizabeth
of York

Edward V
(1483)

Richard,
duke of York

killed in the Tower

OUTSTANDING WOMEN'S FICTION IN MAYFLOWER BOOKS

Mary E Pearce

Apple Tree Lean Down	75p	☐
Jack Mercybright	75p	☐
The Sorrowing Wind	75p	☐

Paula Allardyce

The Gentle Sex	60p	☐
The Respectable Miss Parkington-Smith	60p	☐
Miss Jonas's Boy	60p	☐

Kathleen Winsor

Wanderers Eastward, Wanderers West (*Volume 1*)	95p	☐
Wanderers Eastward, Wanderers West (*Volume 2*)	95p	☐

Anne Rundle

Amberwood	85p	☐
Heronbrook	80p	☐
Judith Lammeter	65p	☐

Charlotte Paul

Phoenix Island	75p	☐

Anne Worboys

The Lion of Delos	75p	☐
Every Man a King	75p	☐

Emma Woodhouse

A Rainbow Summer	40p	☐
A Well-Painted Passion	40p	☐
Romany Magic	50p	☐

HEALTH AND FITNESS BOOKS
AVAILABLE FROM MAYFLOWER

Laurence Morehouse & Leonard Gross
Total Fitness   85p ☐

Constance Mellor
Natural Remedies for Common Ailments   95p ☐
Constance Mellor's Guide to Natural Health   75p ☐

Desmonde Dunne
Yoga Made Easy   60p ☐

Sonya Richmond
Yoga and Your Health (illustrated)   50p ☐

Clare Maxwell-Hudson
The Natural Beauty Book   £1.00 ☐

Bruce Tegner
Karate (illustrated)   75p ☐

Bee Nilson
Bee Nilson's Slimming Cookbook   95p ☐

*All these books are available at your local bookshop or newsagent, or can
be ordered direct from the publisher. Just tick the titles you want and fill
in the form below.*

Name..

Address...

....

Write to Mayflower Cash Sales, PO Box 11, Falmouth, Cornwall
TR10 9EN.
Please enclose remittance to the value of the cover price plus:
UK: 22p for the first book plus 10p per copy for each additional book
ordered to a maximum charge of 82p.
BFPO and EIRE: 22p for the first book plus 10p per copy for the next
6 books, thereafter 3p per book.
OVERSEAS: 30p for the first book and 10p for each additional book.
*Granada Publishing reserve the right to show new retail prices on covers,
which may differ from those previously advertised in the text or elsewhere.*